Daisy's War

Shayne Parkinson

Introduction

Daisy's War is the fifth book in the series that began with *Sentence of Marriage*.

We first met Amy as a twelve-year-old in 1881. Now we're coming to the years of the Great War, 1914 to 1918, and Amy is a grandmother.

Amy's two grandchildren, one from each of her sons, made their first appearance in *A Second Chance*. Eddie is the child of Amy's late son Malcolm. Since his mother's death, Amy has raised him while living in Auckland with her daughter Sarah.

Daisy is the daughter of Amy's son David and Lizzie's daughter Beth, so she is the grandchild of Amy and Charlie as well as Lizzie and Frank. She lives in the valley where we met Amy all those years ago.

Prologue

December 1912

It was early December, but already warm enough for the height of summer. Daisy's teacher, Miss Cameron, was finding her pupils restive. The older children sitting at the back of the room were gazing out the windows to where the sun was beating down on a knot of trees beside the horse paddock, the cool pool of shade beneath the branches making more than one child think longingly of the creek that wound along the Waituhi Valley.

The little ones in the front row were the most restless of all. Daisy wriggled on the long bench, trying to find a way of sitting that was more comfortable, but no matter how she moved the bench felt as hard as ever against her bottom. She looked at the row of letters she was supposed to be copying. There seemed an awful lot of them, and it was hard to get the curly bits just right. She clutched her pencil more firmly and let out a sigh.

The sigh came out louder than she had meant it to. Miss Cameron looked up from her desk at Daisy, then cast a glance at the clock on the wall. Daisy followed the teacher's gaze; the little hand still looked a long way from three o'clock and home time.

Miss Cameron got to her feet. 'Standard Five and Six, have you all finished your grammar exercises?' she asked. Daisy peeped around and saw lowered eyes and guilty expressions along the back row. 'Come along, you need to work more quickly than that. The Inspector will be here for the examinations next week, remember. I think you'd better do the next page as well this afternoon.' There was a muffled chorus of groans, and the sound of pages rustling.

She walked between the desks, checking that the children in the middle row were making progress on their sums, then returned to the front of the room. 'That's enough writing for now,' she told the youngest children.

Daisy placed her pencil neatly by her slate and stretched out her cramped fingers, then sat up straight, arms folded, and watched as Miss Cameron carried her chair over to sit in front of the little ones. She quite liked watching Miss Cameron. The teacher had glossy black hair swept up from her face like two wings, pink cheeks, and small, bright eyes. She was the only person Daisy knew who wore spectacles; Daisy's mother had told her that meant Miss Cameron was especially clever, and had read even more books than Daisy's Granny had.

'Now,' Miss Cameron said, 'who can tell me what's the important thing that happens at the end of the month?'

Daisy's hand was up and waving at once. 'Miss, Miss! I know!'

Miss Cameron looked at her over the top of her spectacles. 'Daisy, what have I told you about calling out? You know you're supposed to wait to be asked.'

'Sorry, Miss Cameron.' Daisy's arm felt heavy, waving pointlessly in the air; she let it drop and knotted her hands in her lap, all too aware of the giggles of the other children.

Daisy was the youngest pupil. She had only been at school since April, and while she did her best to be a good girl, in the excitement of having so many new things to learn she sometimes forgot one of the rules.

But Miss Cameron was a nice lady; Daisy's parents often told her how lucky she was to have a teacher like that instead of the crabby one they had had. She hardly ever used the strap on the youngest children. Daisy had only been whacked with the ruler a few times, usually for daydreaming. 'All right, Daisy, you can tell us,' Miss Cameron said.

Daisy sat up even straighter and beamed at the teacher. 'Eddie's coming!'

There was an eruption of laughter, and not just from the front row. Daisy felt her face grow hot. 'He is coming!' she said, twisting on the bench to glare around the room. 'He's coming the week after school finishes.'

Miss Cameron was not laughing, though her mouth had a funny little twist to it, as if a smile was trying to get out. 'And who is Eddie?'

It was startling to realise that someone might not know who Eddie was. 'He's Eddie,' Daisy said simply. 'He's my cousin,' she added when Miss Cameron looked none the wiser. 'He's ten, and he lives in Auckland, but he always comes in the holidays.'

'That's very nice, Daisy, but something else happens in December, doesn't it?' Miss Cameron prompted.

'Well, Granny's coming, too,' said Daisy. There was more laughter, quickly silenced when Miss Cameron sent a warning glance over the heads of the smallest children. She looked back at Daisy; the smile had almost escaped now.

'But perhaps there's something even more important than that, Daisy?'

Daisy thought hard for something that might impress Miss Cameron, then she had it. It was certainly a piece of news that had caused a flurry at home, with Daisy's mother announcing that every room in the house would need a special seeing-to before the visitors arrived. 'Aunt Sarah's coming with them, and she hardly ever comes. She's got a big house, and she does important things.' It was almost a year since Daisy had last seen her Aunt Sarah; she had a dim memory of a tall, rather grand lady who had been kind in a serious sort of way, but who had not seemed someone with whom liberties could be taken.

'Goodness, what a lot of visitors you're going to have,' Miss Cameron said, but Daisy could see that even the news of Aunt Sarah's arrival had left her unmoved. 'Can anyone else tell me what happens in December?'

Benjy, Daisy's neighbour on the bench, raised his hand. Benjy was a year and a half older than her, and was her best friend at school. People usually assumed they were cousins, but Benjy was in fact her uncle, something they both found confusing.

'Yes, Benjy?' said Miss Cameron. Benjy grinned at Daisy, then turned a glowing smile on Miss Cameron. The teacher smiled back, as people generally did with Benjy.

'It's going to be Christmas, Miss Cameron,' he said.

'Yes, that's right. That's the big thing that's going to happen. And you're all going to make some nice cards for your mothers and fathers, and perhaps for your grandparents. Even your cousins, if you like,' Miss Cameron added, with a smiling glance at Daisy.

Daisy felt her lower lip beginning to stick out to make the sort of expression that her mother always warned her she would be stuck with if the wind changed. She lowered her head to hide it.

The teacher wrote 'Mother' and 'Father', and what Daisy sounded out to be 'Christmas', in large, clear letters on the blackboard. She set the little ones practising the words on their slates, and handed out sheets of card that they would be allowed to use when she judged that their printing was neat enough. When she came to Daisy, she crouched down beside her.

'I'm sure you're looking forward to having all those visitors, Daisy, but it's not so very important to other people,' Miss Cameron said quietly. 'You see that, don't you?'

Daisy bit her lip, then nodded. 'Yes, Miss Cameron,' she said, keeping the rest of her thoughts to herself. It seemed very silly to her. Of course it was going to be Christmas! What was the sense telling the teacher that when she already knew? And Christmas was all very well, but it wasn't the most important thing that was going to happen. A warm feeling crept over her, and when it reached her mouth it curved the corners into a smile. Christmas belonged to everyone. Eddie was just for her.

Chapter One

Summer was the best time of all. Eddie and Granny came to the farm whenever school was out, though the winter visits seemed over almost before they had begun. But every December, when school finished for the year, the summer holidays stretched out ahead of Daisy, long and seemingly endless, and bursting with the promise that Eddie would be there for all those weeks.

In December 1913 Daisy's second year at school ended. She rode home as swiftly as the old horse could be persuaded to go, and set to work getting ready for the visitors.

Daisy helped with all the extra cleaning and dusting, but what she enjoyed most was the baking. She knew Eddie's favourite biscuits and cakes, and insisted on making them all. Only when the tins were full to overflowing could she be persuaded to stop. She gave her father a stern warning that he was not to take any of 'Eddie's biscuits' before the visitors arrived.

The beds were made up with clean sheets, and the small room that had been made long before by building in part of the verandah was given a thorough airing. That room stood empty most of the year, but it was always called 'Eddie's room'.

When Eddie and Granny came on their own, Daisy shared her room with her grandmother, the two of them snuggled into Daisy's bed. But Aunt Sarah was to spend Christmas and New Year on the farm, where she and Granny would have Daisy's room to themselves. A little bed for Daisy, not much bigger than a baby's cot, was squeezed into her parents' bedroom during Aunt Sarah's visits.

Their gig was too small to carry everyone, and Aunt Sarah could certainly not be asked to ride in a cart, so they borrowed a buggy from one of the neighbouring farms when it came time to meet the boat. Daisy's mother stayed home doing some last-minute household tasks, leaving Daisy and her father to go into the nearby town of Ruatane on their own.

The buggy seemed to rattle along with painful slowness, but they got to the wharf in time to see the boat appear, with Eddie leaning over the rail waving to them.

Eddie was the first passenger off the boat, rushing to greet Daisy and her father, then darting back and forth to help unload the mountain of luggage that arrived with them. There were trunks and suitcases, along with some fascinating looking packages that Daisy was told might just contain something for her.

'I don't know if we can fit everything in the buggy. You might have to run along behind, Daisy,' her father said, pretending to be worried. He said the same thing every year, but it never failed to put Daisy in fits of giggles. She scrambled onto the back seat beside Eddie, and the two of them began the mammoth task of catching up on months spent apart.

Those mysterious packages always proved to have wonderful contents. Daisy opened a box on Christmas morning to find the most beautiful doll she had ever seen, even nicer than the one her mother had been given as a little girl. Eddie, she was told, had dragged their granny around half of Auckland in a fruitless attempt to find a doll with red hair. They had eventually agreed that black hair would have to do. But the doll was perfect in Daisy's eyes; even more so when Eddie proudly pointed out that the flowers on its dress were tiny daisies.

There were new summer clothes for Daisy; lovely, frilly dresses for Sunday best, and simpler ones of sprigged cotton for everyday. And a wonderful book of fairy tales, with thick board covers and pages of illustrations, some of them in colour.

As far as Daisy was concerned, these gifts all came from Eddie. She thanked her aunt and grandmother with due politeness, and now that she had a better understanding of financial matters she had come to realise that it was probably Aunt Sarah who paid for it all. But it was Eddie who chose the books, and Eddie whose opinion was sought on what dresses she would like best.

Daisy's mother always said there was no need for her to help around the house while Eddie was staying, so when the weather allowed it the two of them spent the days outside from dawn till dusk, only coming indoors for meals. Eddie helped with the afternoon milking, much to Daisy's father's amusement.

'You weren't so keen on anything to do with farm work when you lived here,' he pointed out.

Eddie grinned back. 'I don't mind doing a bit of it when I'm on holiday. It's not like I have to go milking cows the rest of the year.'

Eddie had lived on the farm for some months when Daisy was a baby, a period everyone remembered except Daisy herself. The grown-ups often talked of how she and Eddie had always been such friends. 'Eddie used to carry you around all the time,' someone would remark, and Eddie would take that as a cue to show that he could still lift her and swing her around, precarious though that was if done indoors.

Daisy had no real memories of her babyhood, but that hardly

mattered. Not when she had Eddie for the whole summer.

Soon after Christmas the haymaking began. Girls generally stayed at home during haymaking, but Daisy was allowed to ride out every day with her father and Eddie, going up and down the valley to each farm as the grass was cut, turned, and gathered into haystacks.

By the middle of January, with the hay safely in and the days still long, they had more time to wander around Daisy's farm. On days when the horses could be spared from their work, the children went riding around the farm; side by side if they had the use of two horses, or Daisy clinging on around Eddie's waist when they had to make do with one. If they could not use the horses they ran around the paddocks, climbed trees, and played on rope swings. When the sun grew fierce, they went for walks in the bush or slithered down the banks of the creek and into the cool brown water. They knew without bothering to ask that they would be forbidden from going swimming together, so they made do with wading as deeply as they could manage, Eddie with his trouser legs rolled up and Daisy with her dress tucked into her drawers. There was always a good deal of splashing, and occasionally one or both of them would fall over amidst fits of laughter. The sun dried their clothes enough to avoid awkward questions back at the house.

Sitting on the creek bank, or backs pressed against a tree in one of the bush clearings, they talked and talked. Daisy never tired of having Eddie tell her about what she thought of as his other life; the one he spent in Auckland between visits to the farm. She tried to picture in her mind his tales of circuses and plays and pantomimes; of garden parties, concerts, and rides in the park. The sheer numbers of people that he so casually spoke of moving amongst were difficult for her to comprehend; there were twice as many children in his class as there were in Daisy's whole school. When Eddie described the horseless carriages and trams that rushed up and down the streets of Auckland, she could not decide if it sounded exciting or terrifying.

There were fewer things for Daisy to tell Eddie in her turn, though he seemed happy to listen to her accounts of looking after the animals on the farm, and what she had been learning at school. Sometimes they briefly ran out of things to say; at such times they sat in companionable silence, content just to know the other was there.

Even in summer there were occasional rainy days that kept them inside. They sprawled on the parlour floor with their new books, taking turns at reading passages aloud. This required a certain amount of patience from Eddie, waiting while Daisy stumbled through the more difficult words and helping her when she had to admit defeat.

Endless though the summer holidays seemed in December, they had a way of drawing to a close with startling suddenness. On an evening late in January, Daisy's mother tucked her into bed, then stood looking down at her.

'Eddie and Granny are going back to Auckland this week,' she said. 'You won't get upset when we go and see them off, will you?'

Daisy shook her head. 'No, I won't.' She was guiltily aware that she had a history of getting into a state at these farewells. On one dreadful occasion two years before, she remembered howling loudly as the boat pulled away; unfortunately for her, Grandma Kelly had decided to come into town with them that day. She had smacked Daisy's bottom right there on the wharf in front of what had felt like the whole of Ruatane, and scolded her for making such a fuss. Daisy's face felt hot at the memory of it.

That had been bad enough, but even worse was the memory of how worried her parents always looked on such occasions, and the knowledge that it was her fault. This year Daisy had resolved that there would be no more making a fuss.

She did her best when the day came. There was no sobbing or wailing as the farewells were made on the wharf, and she even managed a smile when Eddie kissed her on the cheek. She wound her arms around his neck, but only for a moment.

There was a last hug from Granny, an assurance that it would hardly be any time at all before she and Eddie were back, and then the boat was dwindling into the distance while Daisy stood on the wharf with her parents. A single tear escaped to trickle down her cheek; Daisy wiped it away with the back of her hand.

Her mother slipped an arm around Daisy and drew her close. 'That's a good girl,' she murmured.

'We might as well pick up a couple of things at the store,' her father said, taking hold of Daisy's hand as he spoke. 'You want some lollies, love?'

The lump in Daisy's throat would not allow any words past it. She nodded, and the three of them set out for the general store.

The storekeeper, Mr Craig, came out from behind the counter to present Daisy with the large bag of sweets her father asked for. She thanked him politely, trying not to think too hard of how nice it would have been to share them with Eddie.

Daisy wandered around the store, keeping a careful hold of her sweets, while she waited for Mr Craig to wrap the other items. At the far end of the long counter she noticed a pile of papers. She looked more closely, then went back and tugged at her father's sleeve.

'Papa, could I have one of those calendars?'

He glanced down the counter to where she was pointing. 'We've already got one, Daisy. It's on the wall in the kitchen.'

'I know, but could I have one for in my room?'

She had spoken quietly, but Mr Craig overheard. 'Of course little Missy can have a calendar. Those ones are left over—we've given them to all our good customers already.' He rolled one up and handed it across the counter to Daisy.

On the way home Daisy perched in the middle of the cart's driving board, occasionally passing sweets to her mother and father, though most of them disappeared into her own mouth. She unrolled the calendar and admired the picture of a snow-capped mountain with trees at its base.

'Why were you so keen on getting a calendar, Daisy?' her mother asked.

'I can write things on it, like when my birthday is.'

'Oh, that'll be handy,' Papa said. Daisy could hear the smile in his voice. 'We wouldn't want to go forgetting that.' His hand darted out and tickled Daisy, making her squeal.

'And I can do a big mark to show when the holidays start,' she said when she had recovered from her fit of giggles. 'Then I can tell how many weeks till Eddie's coming back.'

Her mother gave her an odd sort of smile that seemed halfway to being a frown. 'Oh, Daisy,' she said, shaking her head. Then the smile won, the frown disappeared, and she kissed Daisy on the top of her head before helping herself to one of the sweets.

School started again, and Daisy's days were full. Her parents considered her too young to help with the morning milking on school days, but she got herself up and dressed while they were down at the cowshed, and then busied herself in the kitchen, where it was her job to get the range going and the table set for breakfast.

She rode down the track to school, let her horse out into the paddock and joined the other children in the schoolroom. All the reading she had done with Eddie over the summer, doing her best to keep up with him, made her schoolbooks seem easy by comparison, and it was not long before Miss Cameron, preoccupied with two small boys who had just started school, allowed Daisy to start sharing Benjy's books.

After school there was farm work to help with, then dinner to prepare, eat, and clean up after. When her mother had set the bread dough near the range to rise overnight, the three of them would snuggle up together on the sofa for the short time that remained until Daisy's bedtime, Mama stitching at something, and Daisy doing her best with her own modest attempts at needlework. Then after a kiss from her father it would be off to bed, tucked in by her mother after saying her prayers. Daisy generally slept soundly.

Daisy turned seven near the end of March. Two days later she tore the March page from her calendar and looked at it in satisfaction. April meant it was little over a month till the school holidays and Eddie's return.

The month was half over when she came home from school one day to find her parents sitting at the kitchen table with cups of tea. An open letter lay beside her mother's saucer; Daisy only knew of one person who regularly wrote to them.

'Is that from Granny?' she asked, peering at the pages. 'Did Eddie send a message for me?'

Her mother's hand hovered over the letter, almost as if she wanted to hide its contents. 'Yes, it's from Granny. And she's got some good news about Eddie—she says he's ever so excited.'

'Are they coming early?' Daisy asked, though she hardly dared hope that might be the case. School terms were immutable things, not subject to the longings of children.

'No, they're not,' her mother said, shaking her head slowly. 'Eddie's been chosen to be in a rugby team for a special match—there's lots of schools all playing against each other.'

Daisy's chest swelled with pride. 'I bet he'll win—Eddie's good at *everything*. I wish I could see it. When's he playing?'

She felt her father's arm slide around her waist, while Mama watched her anxiously. 'It's in the holidays, Daisy. Eddie won't be coming down this time.'

Chapter Two

It had taken Eddie some time to consider school as anything other than a necessary evil; and he had been prepared to argue the 'necessary' part.

He was not sent to school until he was seven years old. Up till then he had lessons with his grandmother in her little schoolroom; pleasant sessions that were arranged around Eddie's own particular interests and attention span, and that had a way of spilling over into the garden or the park on fine days. Towards the end of that time his grandmother began telling him how much he would enjoy going to an ordinary school, where he would have other boys to play with.

He had been ready enough to believe her, especially since he was by then sharing the schoolroom with two little girls whom he found most unsatisfactory as playmates. They were both a mass of white lace and ribbons, and when Granny took them all outside for nature study they screamed in an absurd way if Eddie tried to show them any interesting beetles or worms. Not a bit like Daisy, who was always fascinated when he showed her such creatures, although she was inclined to try eating them. That was easily forgiven, as she was not yet three years old by the time Eddie turned seven.

But his first day at school was a bitter disappointment. He had walked the short distance with his granny, a tin box containing his lunch clutched firmly under one arm. They went up a few steps into a long corridor that stretched off into the distance, each side lined with closed doors. Granny left him in the corridor for a few moments while she went off to ask where Eddie's classroom was. She returned, took him by the hand, and led him to the first door on the left.

Eddie had found himself in a room full of children, all sitting in rows facing the front of the room where a grey-haired lady stood before a blackboard.

'And here's our new pupil,' the lady said brightly, advancing on Eddie and his granny. 'How do you do, Mrs Stewart? I'm Mrs Rankin. Children, this is Mrs Stewart and Eddie,' she said, turning to face the class. 'Say good morning to them.'

'Good mor-ning Mis-sus Stew-art. Good mor-ning Ed-die,' the children chanted. Eddie gazed around the room, but when he glanced back at his granny he saw a worried look on her face.

'I'm sorry, but isn't this Primer One?' Granny asked. 'Eddie's seven, you see. I thought he'd be in one of the older classes.'

'Yes, it's a shame he's late starting school,' said Mrs Rankin. 'He's a big boy for Primer One! But I'm sure he'll soon be learning things.'

'But... but I've been teaching him since he was four,' Granny said in her quiet way. 'I did explain that when I came in to see the headmaster last week. Eddie's very good at his lessons.'

'Well, we'll just see how he gets on,' Mrs Rankin said, ushering Granny towards the door. 'If he knows his alphabet and a bit of counting, that will be quite a help.'

Eddie watched the door being closed on Granny's anxious face. He looked about for the promised playmates, but the nearest boy was a pudding-faced child who stared at Eddie with his mouth open. When Mrs Rankin had Eddie sit on the bench beside him, the boy looked at Eddie towering over him and his face crumpled with threatened tears, much to Eddie's disgust.

He ignored the small boy and turned his attention to the front of the room, wondering what activity might be on offer. Perhaps there would be books he had not seen before, or perhaps they might be about to go outside and explore the grounds.

'And now we're going to recite the alphabet,' Mrs Rankin announced. 'Ready, children? Off we go!'

Eddie looked around the room in disbelief as the children began chanting their ABC. 'Come along, Eddie, see if you can join in,' the teacher said. When she got nothing more from Eddie than an indignant glare, she came to stand closer to him. 'Don't you know any of your letters, Eddie? Well, you just pay attention and we'll do them again. It's very important—once you've learned your letters you can start learning to read.'

So many words had tumbled into Eddie's mouth that it took him some time to form a sentence. 'I can read already!' he said at last. 'I can read just about anything.'

'Now, Eddie, it's wicked to tell lies. There's no need to be shy about not knowing your letters, I'm sure you'll soon get the way of it.'

Outrage robbed Eddie of speech. He stared grimly back at the teacher, and when she had the children repeat the alphabet he joined in the droning recitation.

Matters did not improve when Mrs Rankin set them to copying letters on their slates. Eddie scribbled a few half-heartedly, then looked over to where Mrs Rankin sat at her desk.

'When can I do some other stuff?' he asked.

'Eddie, you don't just call out in class. You put your hand up and wait to be told you may speak.'

Eddie blinked in surprise. 'Why?'

Mrs Rankin could move with surprising speed. Within moments of speaking, Eddie's arm was pulled out in front of him and a ruler landed on his palm. It stung a little. 'What did I just tell you about not speaking until you're asked to?' Mrs Rankin said. 'You just keep working at your letters till I say you can stop.'

'But this is boring,' Eddie complained. 'I'm sick of this stuff.'

The teacher hauled him from his chair and dragged him across the room, whacking his legs with the ruler as she went. 'You are a very naughty little boy. You can stand in the corner until you've learned some manners.'

She had wielded the ruler rather more energetically this time, and Eddie chose to brood over his wrongs in silence. He stood in the corner as ordered, idly picking at an interesting scab he found on the back of his hand and thinking about the ride he and his pony would take that afternoon.

When the teacher released him from the corner, the round-faced boy cried at the mere suggestion that Eddie should sit beside him again, so Mrs Rankin sent Eddie to sit by a very prim-looking little girl, who made a great show of sweeping her frilly skirt to one side so it would not be sullied by the least contact with him. Eddie scowled at her, scowled at the teacher, and scowled at the world in general before taking up his slate and scratching away at a row of letters.

After what felt like hours, a bell rang and the children were released into a small, paved area for their playtime. The girls started a skipping game, while the boys gathered into a huddle, but Eddie had had enough. He opened his lunch tin, took out a sandwich for the journey, and headed for home.

Eddie was surprised at the reaction his return provoked. His granny, who hardly ever got annoyed, made quite a fuss; she seemed particularly worried that he had crossed a busy road on his own, though he assured her he had run across much too quickly to have been at any risk of getting knocked down.

She got changed and took him straight back to the school, in spite of his protests.

'You just have to, Eddie,' she said. 'It's a shame if the work's too easy for you, but the law says you've got to go to school now you're seven, I can't teach you at home any more. And you mustn't ever go running off like that again! I'm going to tell Mrs Jenson there'll be no pudding for you tonight.'

As the cook had privately told Eddie she would be making one of his favourites in honour of his first day at school, Eddie found this particularly galling. But his grandmother was immune to all complaints. The one mercy, he thought to himself as he trudged gloomily at her side, was that Aunt Sarah had not been at home.

There was more fussing when they got to the school, where it seemed people had been searching the grounds for him. Granny found it necessary to tell the teacher several times how sorry she was that Eddie had caused so much bother.

'He might settle in better if he didn't have to be with the little ones,' Granny added, looking hopeful.

'All in good time, Mrs Stewart.' Mrs Rankin took Eddie back to the classroom, where he learned that as well as a ruler she had a heavy leather strap.

The day did not improve. The children were sent outside at lunchtime, and Eddie found he had eaten most of his lunch on the way home. He had a brief spark of excitement when he saw some bigger boys kicking a ball around on the far side of a fence. He searched in vain for a way through, and was at the point of climbing the fence when a teacher who was prowling around the grounds sternly informed him that the Primer children had to stay in their own playground.

In the afternoon Mrs Rankin gave them some reading practice, which consisted of insultingly easy words written up on the blackboard that they were supposed to chant as she pointed to them. Eddie, now beyond caring about the consequences, shouted them out the moment she wrote them, was told he was showing off, and was given physical evidence of Mrs Rankin's displeasure. Her attempts to have the class practise counting had similar results. Eddie's one crumb of comfort in the whole wretched affair was how thoroughly worn-out the teacher looked by the end of the day, when he was at last allowed to escape.

His grandmother was waiting by the school gate. She listened patiently to his diatribe all the way back to the house, looking concerned and making sympathetic noises, but offering no chance of escape. To crown all, Eddie got home to find that Aunt Sarah had been told about his unauthorised return at playtime, and she showed her disapproval by forbidding him to take his pony out that afternoon.

Eddie made one last attempt at protest the following morning, announcing over breakfast that he would not go back to the school, but he knew even as he said it that there was no real hope. Aunt Sarah lowered the sheaf of papers she was reading and gave him a hard stare. Aunt Sarah had a way of putting a whole sentence into a look, without uttering a single word. A little later, Eddie was once more heading off for school at his grandmother's side, dragging his feet and scuffing his shoes, but arriving all too quickly. His life stretched out before him in a nightmarish vision of mind-numbing boredom, leavened only by regular battles with the teacher. He went into the classroom utterly dejected.

That turned out to be the lowest point of Eddie's schooling, and matters looked up rapidly.

'I think perhaps you can manage in Primer Two,' Mrs Rankin said. She had him hurried through to the next room and handed over to another teacher almost before Eddie knew what was happening.

Eddie spent only a brief time in the new classroom and in the one beyond that. Before the month was out he found himself in Standard One, with children his own age and with work at least as challenging as he had been used to with his grandmother. And there were grassy fields to make use of, for impromptu races or for ball games with only the sketchiest of rules. School, Eddie decided, had possibilities after all.

His grandmother and aunt always wanted to hear what he had done at school, and Eddie found that if he expressed particular interest in a subject it would not be long before a new book appeared in his room. Aunt Sarah was equally helpful whenever he wanted to try a new sport, supplying any necessary equipment without murmur; the more energetic the activity, the more pleased she seemed.

When winter came, and with it the rugby season, Eddie found himself especially popular. His fearless nature and boundless energy were recommendations in themselves, but he had the height and strength of boys two or three years his senior, making his name always among the first called when teams were being formed. This was gratifying enough in the somewhat disorganised games played within the school, but right from his first season Eddie was told, often in hushed tones, of the matches every winter against other Auckland schools. Only the biggest boys, generally those in their final year at primary school, were picked for those.

At the age of seven, Eddie had determined that one day he would be among those boys chosen; in 1914 at the age of eleven he achieved just that.

The day he was selected, Eddie thought he might burst with happiness. After school he ran all the way home to tell everyone in the house, from his grandmother to a rather bewildered kitchen maid, basking in the glow of their admiration. The cook even produced a cake at short notice to add to the celebratory atmosphere.

'I'm going to write and tell Daisy,' Eddie said over dinner.

His grandmother paused in the act of picking up her knife and fork, her smile replaced by a look of concern. 'Oh, it's in the May holidays! You won't be able to go to the farm, dear.'

The glory of the day was dimmed, and for the briefest of instants Eddie was torn over what he should do. But a moment's reflection made it clear to him that of course he could not miss the match. Daisy would understand. He was quite sure she would be almost as excited over it as he was himself.

Eddie was not coming. Daisy could feel a fuss building up inside her chest and doing its best to burst out. Her father's arm was warm around her. She pressed more closely against him and slipped under his jacket until her head was hidden inside. It was a game they had played when she was very small, when he would say, 'Where's Daisy?' and pretend to be unable to see her while she shook with giggles. Now she was shaking with suppressed sobs.

It was dim and stuffy under the jacket, but oddly comforting. It smelt of cows and grass and sweat; it smelt of her father. She pressed her face against the rough cotton of his shirt. She could feel her mother's hand, much smaller than her father's, rubbing her back in slow circles, soothing away the fuss.

The edge of the jacket was peeled back, and Daisy looked up to see two faces watching her.

'You got any air in there?' her father asked. He lifted her onto his lap, and Mama placed a mug of milk before her. 'Granny's still coming,' he said. 'She'll come after the holidays instead. But there isn't time after Eddie's match for him to get down and back before school starts again, not with the way the boats run.'

Daisy loved her granny, but this seemed poor compensation for Eddie's absence. She took a gulp of milk and said nothing.

'Eddie's getting to be a big boy now, Daisy,' said her mother. 'He's got school and sports and everything, and he'll be starting high school in a couple of years. We can't expect him to keep coming here every holidays.'

Daisy felt the fuss threatening again. 'Won't he like me any more?'

'Of course he will! It's just that he's got things he wants to do in Auckland as well.'

'He's sure to come in September,' her father put in. 'That'll be good, we'll have the new calves by then for you to show him.'

September seemed a long time away. Daisy heaved a deep sigh, and accepted her father's magnanimous offer of the last biscuit on the plate.

She went off to her room, changed out of her school clothes and ran down to get the cows into the yard, where she was soon joined by her parents.

Daisy was quiet during the milking, lost as she was in her thoughts. When the last cow had been turned out into the paddock, she watched her father getting the milk ready for the next morning, swinging the heavy cans with practised ease. He filled a smaller one for their own use and carried it as the three of them walked back to the house.

Thoughts were tumbling over each other in Daisy's head; she tried to unravel them enough to put into words. 'If Eddie was my brother,' she said slowly, 'he'd live here all the time.'

'I suppose he would,' Mama said.

'Why isn't he my brother?' No, that wasn't quite how she had meant it to come out; two questions had got muddled into one.

'Well, because he had a different ma and pa,' her father said, sounding puzzled.

'I know, but... I wish he was my brother.' That was half the thought spoken.

Her mother took her hand and squeezed it. Daisy looked up at her, and the thought suddenly came clear. 'Why haven't I got any brothers or sisters?' she asked.

Both parents' steps faltered, and Daisy was aware of looks being exchanged over her head.

'We decided we didn't need any more kids once you came along,' Papa said. 'You were enough for us.'

Something in his voice told Daisy she was not being given the whole story. 'But everyone else has got brothers and sisters—everyone at school has except me.'

'I was quite sick when you were little,' said her mother. 'Uncle Richard helped me get better, but we decided I'd get too worn out if there were any more babies.'

'But Papa and I could look after you,' Daisy said, growing increasingly excited. 'We'd look after you and the baby, and we'd do all the work. You wouldn't get worn out then, not with us doing all that.'

They had reached the house by now; her father put the milk can down in the porch. 'What do you think about telling her?' he asked her mother.

'She's a bit young.' Mama studied Daisy's upturned face. 'Still, if she's old enough to ask questions...'

Her father nodded. 'I'll get the potatoes,' he announced.

Daisy and her mother took off their boots and went inside. Mama put on a clean apron, but instead of going to the bench and starting the preparations for dinner she led Daisy over to the table, sat down and drew her onto her lap. There was less room than on Papa's, and Daisy had to perch carefully. Her mother's apron was white and starched, and when Daisy rubbed a bit of it between her fingers it felt crackly. She looked up expectantly; this was clearly an important talk.

'It wasn't looking after you that made me get sick,' her mother said. 'It was when we knew there was going to be a baby. I wasn't feeling very well, and Uncle Richard came to see if he could find out what was wrong with me. He did find something to do with my blood, and he said I'd have to stay in bed until you arrived. But then he listened to my chest, and he could hear something wasn't quite right with my heart.'

Daisy reached out a hand and placed it over where she thought her mother's heart must be. 'Did it hurt?'

'No, not a bit. I didn't know anything was wrong till he said. But it meant…' She fell silent for a few moments. 'It's hard to explain, Daisy. There's bits that are too hard for you to understand just yet. But because I'd been sick, and my heart wasn't as strong as it should be, it meant everyone was worried when it came time for you to be born. Of course it turned out all right,' she said, smiling down at Daisy. 'But Uncle Richard said it'd been too much work for my heart, and there'd better not be any more babies.' She drew her arms closer around Daisy and squeezed. 'We didn't mind, not when we had our Daisy. And you don't mind so very much about not having any brothers or sisters, do you?'

Her eyes looked especially bright just now. They were lovely, soft eyes, and Daisy could never quite decide if they were green or brown. She shook her head solemnly. 'No, I don't mind. I don't want your heart to hurt.' She brushed her fingers against her mother's cheek. 'Were you really sick, Mama? Did they think you were going to die?'

Her mother hesitated before answering. 'Yes, they did. And I think I might have if it wasn't for Uncle Richard. He saved me, Daisy—and maybe saved you as well.'

Daisy sat quietly, taking in this momentous revelation. 'Was Uncle Richard here when I was born?'

She heard Mama catch her breath. 'Yes, he was.' Daisy wondered why she sounded so reluctant to say it.

'Is it like calves?' she asked.

Her mother made an odd sort of noise, like a laugh that thought it might want to be a sob. 'More or less, I suppose. But that's not for little girls to talk about.'

Daisy pressed her head against her mother's chest and sat very still, listening hard. She thought she could feel an occasional tiny flutter, as if every now and again the heart danced for a moment. But when it was not dancing, the heartbeat was slow and steady and infinitely reassuring. It seemed as if it was a sound she had always known; it was unthinkable that it should ever stop.

Chapter Three

The week before the May holidays were to begin, Daisy came home from school to find her parents looking pleased with themselves.

'We went to see Aunt Maudie when we were in town today,' her mother said. 'How would you like to go and stay with Lucy and Flora next week?'

Daisy was used to seeing her cousins on Sundays, when her family occasionally went to her Uncle Richard's for lunch after church, but this would be the first time she had ever stayed with them. It would also be the first time she had ever spent a night away from home.

A week, the three of them agreed, would be too long for Daisy to be away. So it was decided to have her stay from Wednesday afternoon, when she could go into Ruatane with her parents on their weekly shopping trip, till Sunday.

'It's only four nights, that'll go quite fast,' her mother said as they drove into town. 'Now I know you'll be a good girl for Aunt Maudie and Uncle Richard, but you don't have to do what Lucy tells you. Just because she's a little bit older, that doesn't mean she's in charge of you. But she might get a bit bossy.'

'Gee, I don't know where Lucy would get that from,' Daisy's father remarked. Her mother smiled, but said nothing more on the subject.

Lucy was nine years old, two years older than Daisy, while her sister Flora was six. Flora was a placid child whose chief virtue as a playmate was her acceptance of whatever role Lucy assigned her. They had two little brothers, both too young for Lucy to see any use in them, though Daisy could tell she was fond of them in an offhand sort of way.

Lucy liked to decide what the three girls would do, but she had a way of darting about from one activity to another that Daisy found dizzying. She would announce that they were going to play with dolls, then five minutes later insist that they go outside and play in the garden. Then she might be possessed by the urge to do some drawing; Flora and Daisy, who did not share this interest of hers, found themselves left to their own devices when this happened.

Daisy barely saw Uncle Richard on her first day there. Lucy said he was out on his rounds; Daisy gathered from her sketchy explanation that this meant visiting people who were ill. He was home briefly in the late afternoon, when he spoke kindly to Daisy before going out again, this time to see someone on a distant farm who had broken his leg. He did not return till after the children were in bed. Lucy argued vehemently to be allowed to wait up till her father was back; when after some heated words her mother's will prevailed, Lucy claimed that she would still be awake no matter how late he came home.

As it happened, Lucy was asleep long before then. At first there was much whispering and giggling, which Daisy, used as she was to sleeping on her own, quite enjoyed. When the talking subsided, Lucy tossed and turned for some time, making it impossible for Daisy, who was sharing with her, to find a comfortable position of her own. Lucy eventually nodded off, sprawled across a good deal more than half of the little bed.

Daisy lay awake for a long time, the strangeness of being in a house other than her own making it difficult to settle. She heard the crunch of gig wheels on gravel, soon followed by muffled voices, and knew her uncle must be home at last. Soon after that, she drifted off to sleep.

Daisy woke earlier than Lucy and Flora. While the dim greyness that marked the windows gradually became lighter, she lay in bed thinking about her mother and father, who were no doubt already up and about. She imagined them moving around the kitchen, getting ready to go out and see to the animals, and perhaps wondering what Daisy was doing. She was glad when Aunt Maudie came in to tell them it was time to get up.

With seven at the table, breakfast was a far noisier affair than Daisy was used to. She enjoyed being surrounded by cheerful voices, but had no urge to make her own heard above the general hubbub. Lucy claimed the lion's share of her father's attention, telling him in some detail what the girls had done the previous day. Flora was diligently applying herself to her breakfast; seeing Aunt Maudie busy with getting three-year-old Nicky to eat his, Daisy finished off her own bowlful and shyly asked if she could help with baby Timmy. Her aunt thanked her, and Daisy soon found herself coaxing Timmy to take mouthfuls of milky porridge. He was a lovely baby, plump and giggly and far too lazy to be walking yet, although he was quite old enough. At least as much of the porridge went down his front as in his mouth, but he seemed to enjoy the process.

'Lucy, get on and eat your breakfast,' Aunt Maudie said when Lucy paused for breath. 'That porridge will be stone cold if you leave it much longer.' Lucy gulped down a spoonful, then opened her mouth to speak again.

'Lucy, do as your mother says,' her father said mildly. 'And did you have a nice day, Daisy?' he asked, taking advantage of the relative silence.

Daisy looked up from feeding Timmy. 'Yes, thank you. It was very nice.' She tried to think of something more to say, but she was finding herself tongue-tied around Uncle Richard, awed as she was by the knowledge that he had saved her mother. But he looked more down-to-earth at breakfast time, eating porridge like an ordinary person, and with his jacket undone. He had a kind face, and a nice voice. He spoke differently from most of the people she knew; unlike Aunt Maudie, who was Daisy's mother's big sister, Uncle Richard did not come from Ruatane but from England. Lucy, who was good at finding things out whether other people wanted her to or not, had told Daisy that Uncle Richard was forty, which sounded quite old; much older than Daisy's own father, who had turned twenty-six at his last birthday. Daisy had heard the bigger children at school having a lesson on what the teacher called 'Great Men'; Uncle Richard, she felt, was an especially great man to have saved her mother's life.

'Papa, you should get out the croquet set,' Lucy put in. 'Daisy doesn't have croquet at home, and she said she'd like to try it.' Daisy perked up at the suggestion; Eddie played croquet at Aunt Sarah's. He had talked of trying to rig up some sort of croquet game at the farm, but the lack of an area of smooth ground, not to mention anything that could truly be called a lawn, had ruled out the idea.

'I'm not sure that it's the most suitable time of year for croquet,' said Uncle Richard. 'But I don't see why we shouldn't, as long as it doesn't look like rain. We don't want to disappoint Daisy,' he added, smiling at her.

The morning held fine, and Uncle Richard duly set up a croquet game for the girls. He even played it with them for a time, while Aunt Maudie watched from the verandah, Timmy on her lap and Nicky beside her amusing himself with some wooden blocks.

Uncle Richard went off to his consulting room, which was attached to one side of the house, and the girls carried on with their croquet.

Aunt Maudie joined in the game while Timmy had a nap, then later in the morning she took the children on a shopping expedition. The little boys both rode in a large pram, while the girls took turns pushing a much daintier pram loaded with dolls. Daisy thought the dolls' pram quite lovely, though she knew its small wheels and flimsy build would make it unusable on the farm. It was made of dark brown cane twisted into intricate shapes, and lined with lace-edged white cotton. Lucy generously allowed Daisy to have the longest turn with it.

The afternoon was largely devoted to baking. Flora was given the job of cutting circles of pastry for jam tarts, which suited her ability to do the same simple task over and over without growing bored. Lucy sat at one end of the table with a sheet of pastry, creating elaborate decorations for the pies her mother was making. Daisy was impressed by the realistic-looking flowers and leaves Lucy produced, though it was a slow process, and the pies could not go in the range until Lucy was satisfied with her work.

As well as the pies, Daisy helped her aunt make several batches of the same sorts of biscuits she was used to having at home. When all the trays were laden, the three girls sat around the table scraping leftover mixture from the bowls.

'When do you make the bread, Aunt Maudie?' Daisy asked, realising that she had seen no sign of breadmaking the day before.

'I don't,' said her aunt. 'We get it from the baker's—a boy brings it around in the morning.'

'Oh. I didn't know you could buy bread.'

'It's one of the nice things about living in town. None of that having to pound away at bread dough every night.' Aunt Maudie gave Daisy a conspiratorial grin. 'Don't tell Grandma, though—she thinks it's a terrible thing to buy bread.'

Daisy checked for any last trace of cake mixture on the wooden spoon she was holding, but it was quite bare. 'My papa's good at kneading the dough,' she said, dropping the spoon into the bowl.

Lucy gave a snort. 'Fathers don't do cooking! That's just silly.'

'My papa does,' Daisy said, bridling. 'And Mama says he kneads it better than anyone else she's ever seen, because he's got such big, strong hands.'

'But—'

'Now, Lucy, don't pass remarks,' Aunt Maudie interrupted. 'It's very nice that Uncle Dave helps Aunt Beth with things.' But she smiled as she said it, as if she, too, thought it was funny. Daisy looked down at the table rather than risk a response that might be cheeky. Her mother said people should do the things they were best at, and that seemed perfectly sensible to Daisy.

On Friday afternoon, after she had settled Nicky in for his nap, Aunt Maudie went out to visit a lady who was unwell, taking baby Timmy with her. The girls played a board game in their room, and Daisy managed to win the second round, largely by ignoring Lucy's stream of instructions. Halfway through a third game Lucy tired of it, despite being ahead.

'Let's play dress-ups,' she said, running over to a chest in the corner of the room. She flung it open and began hauling out armloads of fabric in a variety of colours. 'It's Mama's old clothes. We can dress up and be ladies.'

Dressing up was a game Daisy had never played before; and never before had she seen so many fancy clothes all at the same time. There were dresses, jackets, skirts and blouses; scarves and gloves, and even a lacy chemise. Closer inspection showed that most of the garments had signs of wear: a torn seam, or fraying around the edges. But some appeared to have been discarded for no other reason than being 'not in the fashion', as Lucy said. Daisy sat on the floor and ran her fingers over the fabrics: slippery satin, soft cotton, heavy brocade, all with their own distinctive feel.

Lucy put on a pink gown, with a scarf around her middle to shorten the fabric. She thrust another pink dress at Flora and a blue one at Daisy, but Daisy's eyes were drawn to a pale green silk jacket. She wrapped a flimsy cream shawl around her waist as a skirt and slipped into the jacket. It was far too big for her, even over her pinafore, and it looked odd to see her own small hands peeping out from the overlong sleeves, but she felt like a princess as she stroked the lustrous silk.

They were in the parlour having a tea party with the girls' miniature tea-set when Lucy dropped her cup noisily onto its saucer. 'We've forgotten the jewellery! We can't be ladies without jewellery.' She ran into her room, and came back with two necklaces of coral beads, one each for Daisy and Flora, and a brooch with several missing stones, which she fastened to the front of the dress she was wearing. She studied the effect of the beads against Daisy's green silk with a critical eye.

'No, that's no good, the colour's wrong.' Her face lit up. 'I know what you should wear!' And she was off again at a run.

When Lucy returned and showed Daisy what was in her hands, Daisy knew at once that these necklaces had not come from the girls' room. One was a rope of pearls similar to the one Grandma Kelly sometimes wore on special occasions, and the other was a gold chain with a dark green stone at its centre.

'I'm going to wear the pearls,' Lucy said. 'And this green one will be just right on you, Daisy. It's called an emerald.'

'Are we allowed to play with those?' Daisy asked doubtfully.

'It'll be all right. Anyway, we *need* these ones, or the dresses won't look right. Turn around, I'll put it on you.'

Lucy dropped the pearls onto a small table and approached Daisy, holding out the emerald pendant.

'I don't want to,' Daisy said, backing away as she spoke. 'I might break it. And Aunt Maudie didn't say we could play with them.'

'You *have* to,' Lucy insisted, but Daisy shook her head.

'I don't have to do what you say. And I don't want to play any more.'

She took off the dress-up clothes, folded them carefully and placed them on a chair, then retreated to the far corner of the room. Flora had left a book lying there; it was one Daisy had already read, and was a good deal too simple for her, but she picked it up and pretended to be engrossed, while darting covert glances at Lucy.

Lucy tossed her head. 'Well, *I'm* going to wear these.' She dropped the pendant and snatched up the pearls. Daisy could see her struggling unsuccessfully with the catch; she gave up the attempt and held the pearls around her neck as she sauntered back and forth.

The sound of the back door opening took them all by surprise. 'I'm home,' Aunt Maudie called. A moment later she was in the parlour, Timmy balanced on one hip. She looked around the room, smiling at the girls, until her eyes lighted on Lucy, who was still holding the pearls in place.

'What are you doing with my pearls?' She saw the emerald pendant lying discarded on the floor; she scooped it up and advanced on Lucy, Timmy still perched on her hip. 'Give me those.'

Lucy's grip on the pearls wavered for a moment, then she took a tighter hold. 'No. I want to play with them.'

'Lucy, you're being very naughty. Give me those at once.' Aunt Maudie reached out and grabbed at the pearls; at the same moment Lucy, still clutching them, took a step backwards. As Daisy watched, the string gave way with an audible snap.

The pearls scattered in a wide arc, the small sound of each one striking the floor unnaturally loud in the sudden silence. Lucy and her mother stared at each other, shocked into stillness.

Aunt Maudie was the first to move. 'Look what you've done! You wicked girl!' She grabbed Lucy by the sleeve, pulled her closer and gave her a slap on the bottom.

Lucy let out a shriek so loud that Daisy thought she heard the windows rattling. 'You're horrible!' she shouted. 'I hate you! I hate you!' She ran crying from the parlour and into her bedroom, slamming its door behind her.

It seemed a huge fuss to be making over a smack Daisy was sure could not have hurt as much as getting the strap at school. She made herself very small in the corner and wondered what she should do.

Lucy's scream had upset even the placid Timmy. His face screwed up; he let out a whimpering cry, and seemed on the point of working up to greater volume. Aunt Maudie, who had not moved since Lucy had run off, jiggled him up and down in an unsuccessful attempt at settling him, then carried him off in the direction of the front bedroom.

Flora was sitting on a sofa, crying quietly. Daisy sat down by her and put an arm around the younger girl. 'Do you want to help me pick up the beads?' she asked. Flora nodded, Daisy fetched a bowl from the kitchen, and Flora's tears soon disappeared as she scrabbled about on the floor with Daisy, seeking the scattered pearls and placing each one in the bowl as they found it.

It took some time before Daisy felt they must have retrieved almost all of them. To attract her attention she tapped Flora's plump little bottom, just visible under the edge of the sofa where she had squeezed in to get one last bead, and helped her out when she realised Flora was wedged in place.

Flora settled herself on the sofa, while Daisy took the bowl of pearls through to her aunt's room. Timmy was in his cradle, gurgling away contentedly to himself, and Aunt Maudie sat on the edge of the bed near him; she looked sad, and it made Daisy feel shy.

'We picked them up,' she said, holding the bowl out to Aunt Maudie. 'Are they still any good?'

Her aunt, who had been staring into an unseen distance, seemed to notice Daisy for the first time. 'Thank you, Daisy, that was very thoughtful of you.' She took the bowl, and carefully stirred the pearls with one finger until the clasp appeared. 'Yes, I expect I can get them restrung—I'll take them to the jeweller's and see what he says.' Her face softened into a smile. 'Your Uncle Richard gave me these when Nicky was born.'

'Oh,' Daisy said, unable to think of anything more profound.

'I don't know what to do with Lucy sometimes,' Aunt Maudie said, looking sad again. 'I'm sure I wasn't like that at her age, wanting my own way all the time. And it's not as if I'm hard on her, not like—' She stopped abruptly; Daisy had the feeling that her aunt had for a moment forgotten who she was talking to. Aunt Maudie fingered the pearls again, while Daisy stood awkwardly, wondering if she should slip out of the room.

A small tornado entered in the form of Lucy. She flung herself against her mother. 'I'm sorry, Mama,' she sobbed. 'I didn't mean it—I don't hate you—I'm sorry.' She pressed her face into her mother's lap, muffling the sobs still racking her.

Aunt Maudie stroked Lucy's hair, her own eyes bright. 'Shh,' she soothed. 'There's no need to get in such a state.'

Lucy sat up and climbed onto the bed, pressed close to her mother's side. Her blonde curls, pulled loose from their ribbons, stood out around her head; her mother undid the ribbons and tied them again. 'You won't go helping yourself to my jewel box again, will you, Lucy?'

'No,' Lucy said, though her manner did not strike Daisy as particularly convincing. She bounced up and down on the bed and clutched at her mother's arm. 'Mama, you should show Daisy your special dress!'

Aunt Maudie smiled. 'Would you like to see my wedding dress, Daisy?'

'Yes, please,' Daisy said politely, though she rather felt she had had enough of dresses for one day.

Her aunt went to a large wardrobe that stood against one wall. It looked full to bursting with clothes; she had to slide a whole row of hangers along before she could reach the dress.

She pulled out a confection in white shot through with silver. She held the dress up against herself and twirled slowly. 'Isn't it beautiful?'

Daisy realised her mouth was hanging open. 'I didn't know there were dresses like that.' She reached out a hand and cautiously stroked the dress. It frothed with lace, the silver thread sparkling as it caught the light.

'We sent away to Auckland to have it made. You couldn't get dresses like this in Ruatane, and it had to be a special dress for my special day.'

'I've never seen Mama's wedding dress,' Daisy said, frowning in thought.

Aunt Maudie's smile faltered. 'Your mother decided to wear Grandma's dress instead of bothering with a new one. And she looked very pretty in it, too.' She carefully replaced the dress in the wardrobe. Lucy was hovering near; Aunt Maudie placed a hand on her shoulder. 'I expect Lucy and Flora will want to wear mine one day.'

Lucy's attention had wandered, and she was currently engaged in staring out the window, but she beamed up at her mother. It was nice to see them being friends again, though it did seem a wearing sort of way to go about things.

Daisy followed Lucy, who was already bounding off to chase whatever new thought had struck her, out of the room, looking about as she did so. It was a pleasant room; larger than the bedrooms in Daisy's home, but cosy and inviting. The jewel box, still open on the dressing table, looked to have other necklaces in it, as well as rings and bracelets and things that Daisy could not identify. The room had two large windows along the front, with lacy curtains that let the light through and heavy velvet drapes drawn back at either side.

All the window coverings in Daisy's house were of plain calico. Her parents had a lacy bedspread that, while pretty, was worn right through in several places. It was very old; Daisy had been told that her granny had helped her own grandmother to make it when she was a small girl. That bedspread was nothing like the embroidered satin affair, stuffed with down, that covered her uncle and aunt's bed.

Daisy had never thought of her family as poor; but until these last few days she had never spent a large amount of time in a household where there were so many visible signs of prosperity. It was not a matter of food; in fact Daisy was used to larger portions at home, though the roast beef Aunt Maudie sometimes served was an interesting change from mutton. And Daisy's own clothes, thanks to all those packages from Auckland, were just as nice as Lucy's and Flora's. But her mother's dresses were simple affairs, even the grey wool one she wore for best, and the only jewellery she owned was her wedding ring and a brooch Granny had given her before Daisy was born. Their house was quite new; slightly newer than Daisy herself, as they had moved into it when she was a baby; but it was small, and the furniture was plain and sturdy.

But there were only the three of them, so they did not need a great big house that would take a lot of work to keep clean. Her parents must know that Uncle Richard and Aunt Maudie had more things than they did, though Daisy had never heard them speak of it. Perhaps that meant it did not really matter, although she could not help wondering what it was like for her mother to have a big sister with all those lovely things.

Saturday offered a thin, grey sunlight that was enough to have Lucy once again demand croquet. The girls played for much of the morning, but by lunchtime a chilly wind and drizzly rain had driven them indoors. In the afternoon Lucy devoted herself to making a pastel drawing of a bowl of fruit, while Daisy played board games with Flora. Flora always lost the games, but she never seemed to mind.

Lucy studied her work and pulled a face. 'I can't get the shape of the pears just right. I'll have a go in pencil first.' She glanced at the pile of crumpled paper that had built up around the base of her chair. 'I need more paper—and a better pencil. Come and help me look, Daisy.'

The attraction of winning every game had begun to pall on Daisy, and she followed Lucy willingly enough, leaving Flora undressing one of the dolls.

Lucy led her to a part of the house Daisy had not visited before. 'This is Papa's office,' Lucy said as she pushed open a door. 'He sees patients in here sometimes, but he hasn't got anyone coming today.'

Daisy did not bother asking if they were allowed to be in the office, since she had doubts as to the likely frankness of the answer. She followed Lucy in, hoping for the best. Lucy rummaged in the large, leather-topped desk, while Daisy gazed at the shelves that lined the room. They were crammed with books, most of which looked well-thumbed. Daisy did not dare disturb the arrangement of the shelves, but one book had been left on top of the desk. She slid the heavy volume closer and carefully opened it.

The print was small, and many of the words were unintelligible, but the pictures were fascinating. Daisy soon realised that they showed the human body, but in a very unfamiliar form. The skin, and much of the flesh, had been peeled away to show what lay beneath. There were illustrations of bones and muscles, and things that Daisy could not have given a name to. She turned page after page, so engrossed that she did not hear her uncle come into the room.

'What are you up to, Goosey Lucy?' Daisy jumped at the sound of his voice, and moved the book a little to one side just in case she was not meant to be touching it. But her uncle had not noticed; he was smiling at Lucy, who had spread out half a dozen pencils on the desk and was examining them with a critical eye.

'I need a pencil, but none of these are sharp enough. I need some more paper, too,' Lucy told him.

Uncle Richard took a penknife from his pocket. He sat on the edge of the desk and worked on one of the pencils until it met Lucy's exacting standards.

'That's good, Papa,' she pronounced. 'Do me another one in case I break the lead.'

'Ah, you're a true artist, thinking of every detail,' Uncle Richard said, and Lucy giggled.

'Papa's really good at painting,' she told Daisy. 'He did that one.' She pointed to a small water-colour on the wall behind Daisy; it showed a woman with a child in her lap. 'That's Mama and me, when I was little. He hardly ever does it now, though. Papa, you should paint Daisy,' she said, her eyes bright at the notion.

Uncle Richard laughed softly. 'I'm afraid you overrate my skill, my dear. And I'm dreadfully out of practice.' He turned his smile on Daisy. 'It would be quite the challenge to capture your Titian hair.'

'What's ti-shun?' Daisy asked. It sounded like a sneeze; that did not seem a nice thing to have her hair compared to. It was bad enough that the older boys at school sometimes called her 'Carrots'.

'It was the name of an artist from a long time ago who particularly liked painting lovely red hair like yours,' Uncle Richard said, and Daisy felt rather better. He peered more closely at the book beside her. 'Whatever are you reading, Daisy?'

There was no point in denying it. 'It was just on the desk, and I was looking at the pictures. My hands are quite clean, though.'

'I've no concerns over the state of your hands, dear. But those drawings aren't really suitable for girls—I hope they don't give you bad dreams.'

'No, they were very interesting,' Daisy said, puzzled that he could think the pictures might upset her. 'It was a bit like when Papa kills a sheep, and you can see their insides and how it all fits together. I never really thought about people looking like that on the inside.'

Her uncle looked startled, then amused. 'My apologies, Daisy, I should know better. Farmers' daughters are made of sterner stuff than to be troubled by such matters.'

'Can I look at the book some more?' Daisy asked, her courage rising.

'Another time, perhaps, after I've looked through it myself. I'd like to refresh my memory of its contents, in case there's anything that even a brave girl like you shouldn't see.' He picked up the book and replaced it on a shelf. Daisy looked thoughtfully around the room, wondering what other treasures might be hidden on those shelves.

She went to bed that evening warm and sleepy from the bath. Aunt Maudie tucked her in; she was almost as good at it as Daisy's own mother. Daisy noticed how soft her aunt's hands were. That must be because a lady came in to do the scrubbing for her, and another lady collected the washing each week and brought it back ironed.

Daisy thought of her mother's hands, the skin roughened from work but their touch always gentle, and hugged to herself the knowledge that she would see her parents again the next day.

As well as the light gig that he used to visit patients, Uncle Richard had a buggy big enough to take the whole family. But Sunday morning was fine enough for them to walk the modest distance to church. The little boys were loaded into the pram, and Daisy was allowed to push it some of the way, although Uncle Richard had to take over when they crossed the rough, stony roads.

As soon as the church came into sight, Daisy looked around for her parents. She saw her Uncle Bill and Aunt Lily, who lived further up the valley from Daisy's family. Their daughter Emma stood off to one side, talking to a young man of about her own age whom Daisy thought she might have seen in the Post Office. Daisy looked beyond her uncle's family and saw her father, a head taller than most of the other men in sight.

Running at church was not to be thought of, but Daisy managed a scamper that came close to it. Her father picked her up, and Daisy kissed both parents soundly before allowing him to lower her to the ground.

'Did you say thank you to Aunt Maudie for having you?' her mother asked; Daisy, with a rush of guilt, admitted that she had not. She took her mother and father by a hand each and led them over to her aunt and uncle's little group.

'Thank you for having me to stay, Aunt Maudie. Thank you, Uncle Richard.'

'You're most welcome, Daisy,' said her uncle.

'She was no trouble at all,' Aunt Maudie said. 'We'd be happy to have her again any time.'

'And I believe I've all but promised her the use of my library, so she must come again,' Uncle Richard added, his eyes twinkling.

'Did you enjoy yourself at Aunt Maudie's?' Daisy's mother asked on the way home from church.

'Yes, it was nice,' Daisy said. 'We went to the shops, and I helped a bit with the baby. And they've got some games you can play when there's more than one of you—and they've got croquet like Eddie has in Auckland.'

'Oh, it must be good if Eddie's got it,' her mother said, a smile in her voice.

Her father held the reins in one hand so he could slip an arm around Daisy. 'It was pretty quiet at home without you.'

Daisy pressed against him, and took her mother's hand in both her own. Through the glove she felt its familiar roughness. 'I think I like things a bit quiet,' she said.

Chapter Four

Daisy's grandmother arrived from Auckland a few days later. It made Daisy all the more conscious of Eddie's first-ever May absence, but it was nice to see Granny again.

Granny was little and gentle; she looked small even against Daisy's mother. It was strange to think that Granny was Papa's mother, when he was so big and tall. She had a lovely soft voice, and she usually seemed to be smiling. Daisy loved her other grandmother too; when she left her stays off, which she sometimes did at home, Grandma Kelly had the softest lap of anyone Daisy knew, as well as a bosom like a big, soft pillow. But although Grandma only smacked if someone was silly enough not to do what she told them, Daisy always felt she had to pay particular attention around her. When something caught Daisy's interest, she was inclined to concentrate on it with an intensity that others might mistake for daydreaming, and which sometimes meant she did not hear what was said to her. This could be risky around Grandma.

It was not so with Granny, who was endlessly patient. One of her first tasks on her arrival was to share with Daisy all the details she could manage about Eddie's rugby match. His team had not won, but he had done something called a 'try', which in spite of sounding like a mere attempt was, Granny told Daisy, an important thing that had scored some points.

The boys at school sometimes kicked a ball around at lunchtime, in the process often losing it in the surrounding scrub, but Daisy had never seen a rugby match, or indeed any kind of serious sports match. 'I wish I'd been there,' she said.

'I wish you had, too, sweetheart.' Granny leaned closer to Daisy across the seat of the gig and lowered her voice; not that anyone was there to hear them except Daisy's father. 'I think I might've got a bit bored watching if Eddie hadn't been playing. Nothing's ever boring when Eddie's around, though, is it?'

During previous visits Daisy had been only vaguely aware of what Granny did during the daytime, absorbed as she was with Eddie's company. Now she realised that her grandmother called on the family members scattered up and down the valley, and this time Daisy went with her on the weekend and after school. Granny was a great walker, unlike Grandma, and for all but the furthest outings they went on foot. It was never boring going for walks with Granny, who would tell Daisy stories about when she had been a little girl going to the valley school, or when Daisy's father was a boy, or answer Daisy's stream of questions about Eddie's life in Auckland.

They went first to see Granny's two brothers, Daisy's Uncle John and Uncle Harry, and their families, who lived on the next farm up the valley. It meant a walk across the paddocks, scrambling over stiles and doing their best to avoid muddy patches. Daisy was fussed over by the girls of the family, who took her off to plait her hair and try different coloured ribbons in it. Her scalp was tender by the time they left, but the green satin ribbons she was given more than made up for that.

On the next fine afternoon they went to the furthest house in the valley, where Uncle Bill and Aunt Lily lived. This was too far to walk, so they took the gig. The ride up the valley was an adventure in itself, as Granny was out of practice at driving, something the horse was clearly aware of. But they arrived safely, and to a warm welcome.

Three generations lived here: Uncle Bill and Aunt Lily with their three children, Uncle Bill's brothers Alf and Ernie, and Daisy's elderly great-grandmother. Great-grandma sat in the parlour beaming at them all, only fitfully contributing to the conversation and never to the purpose. Once or twice she asked where 'Arthur' was; this did not, Daisy knew, mean Uncle Bill and Aunt Lily's son of that name, but Great-grandpa, who had died a few years before. 'He's asleep,' someone would tell Great-grandma, and that seemed to content her for a time.

Aunt Lily played the piano, and her daughter Emma, who had a pretty voice, sang for them. Daisy would have liked to hear more, but Great-grandma dozed off in her chair, and Granny said it was time they left. The drive back, with the horse aware it was on the way home, was rather brisker than they would have chosen, but they survived it with nothing worse than a shaking.

Their final visit was to Grandpa's farm, which shared a boundary with Daisy's father's but was separated from it by steep land that had never been cleared of bush, so that the only way to get there was by the road that ran up the valley. It was a fine day with a brisk wind, and they both had pink cheeks by the time they had walked down the track, along the road, and up a further track to Grandpa's.

Apart from Aunt Maudie and Daisy's mother, all Grandma and Grandpa's children still lived on the farm, so the house was always full of people. There was Aunt Maisie, who wasn't really related to anyone, but who had been in the family since before Daisy was born. The three big boys, Joe, Mickey and Danny, were around the same age as Daisy's mother and all much older than Benjy. After the big boys came Rosie, who was going on seventeen, and was engaged to Mr Reynolds, who owned a saddlery in the town. She had announced that Daisy was to call her *Aunt* Rosie from now on, as she was a grown-up lady about to be married. The youngest girl in the family was thirteen, and said she was quite happy to go on being called just Kate.

Granny sat and drank tea with Grandma and Grandpa and the others, but Daisy and Benjy soon took their biscuits out to the verandah, where they could talk without having to wait for gaps in the grown-ups' conversation.

Even in that short time Grandma had managed to say much on the subject of how well Benjy was doing at school, how worried she had been by a cough he had had the previous month, and how astonished Granny must be at the amount he had grown since her last visit. Daisy could not understand how Benjy could listen to such things without squirming with embarrassment, but Benjy somehow managed to accept it calmly and with no trace of arrogance. He smiled at his mother, and Grandma beamed at him with her face as close to foolishness as Daisy ever saw it.

Out on the verandah Benjy sat with his knees gathered up close to his chest against the coolness of the day. He was still smiling, but it was a look of general contentment with the world, not the glowing one that had been turned on his mother a few minutes earlier.

Daisy sometimes felt that Benjy was able to show a different self depending on who he was with; not in a deceitful way, but rather like changing a suit of clothes to fit the occasion and the company. When he was with those he loved, the face he showed them was the one that would make them happiest. With others, like some of the bigger boys at school, Daisy suspected it was more a matter of surviving unscathed; or at least without the humiliation of having his mother arrive at the school to take vengeance on his behalf. Benjy would kick a ball around the schoolyard with the other boys, or engage in the casual wrestling matches that erupted most days, with every sign of enjoyment, but Daisy had noticed that he withdrew himself from such play as soon as he safely could. Daisy was good at noticing things; she was becoming just as good at knowing when to keep her opinions to herself.

Whatever face he showed, it was still Benjy inside, and he was good company. They had abstracted several iced biscuits before coming outside; they ate them with great care, nibbling away at the cakey base till just the shell of icing was left, white and brittle, to be hurried into the mouth in one gulp before it collapsed. This was not considered an appropriate way of eating biscuits at the dining table, but out here there was no one to see. Daisy showed Benjy the embroidered edge of her new petticoat, and Benjy showed her the blackened fingernail he had got from getting a hand twisted in the reins; both were equally admired.

'I like your Granny,' Benjy remarked, brushing biscuit crumbs from his knees. Daisy smiled, feeling no need to reply; who could help liking Granny? 'She makes it sound good, all those things she goes to in Auckland. She's keen on plays, eh?'

'Mmm. They go to them a lot, I think—her and Eddie and Aunt Sarah.'

Benjy was staring through the verandah rails; Daisy followed his gaze and saw the valley stretching out before them, the view divided into stripes by the rails like a row of narrow pictures that shifted and changed when she tilted her head to one side then the other. 'What do you reckon it would be like to be in a play?' he asked.

Daisy frowned, not sure she had understood him. 'You mean go and see one?'

'No, be *in* one. You know, acting. Dressing up like a king or something, and saying the lines.'

'In front of all those people?' Daisy shuddered at the thought. 'I don't think I could do that, not with everyone looking at me. What say you forgot the words? You'd just have to stand there looking stupid.'

'But you don't forget things when you have to say poems at school,' Benjy pointed out. They were both good at reciting poems from memory, and Benjy had a way of breathing life into the words that Daisy admired, especially when contrasted with the at best dully plodding, at worst painfully faltering, efforts of many of their schoolmates.

'That's different. That's all people we know. And if you forget, Miss Cameron just reminds you, except you might get the strap if she thinks you haven't tried properly.' She studied Benjy, who had a wistful expression that was quite unfamiliar. 'Wouldn't you be scared of all those people looking at you if you were in a play?'

'I don't think so. I think it'd be good.' Benjy gave himself a small shake, and his gaze returned from whatever distant object it had been directed on. There was no more talk of plays, and a little later they went indoors in search of more biscuits.

Granny went back to Auckland the following week, entrusted with a special hug from Daisy to Eddie. Daisy missed her, but school was soon keeping her busy. She learned a whole poem off by heart, quite a long one, and earned her teacher's approval and Benjy's praise.

The winter wore on. July came, and calving was due. One afternoon Daisy came home from school to find her parents in a shed near the house, where they had put one of the young Jersey cows into a wooden pen.

'I think she'll have hers tomorrow,' Mama said, but instead of looking happy at the news Daisy could see that she was worried. 'I want to keep an eye on her, that's why we've got her in here.'

If her mother was worried, it must be for good reason. Her father and grandfather both said Daisy's mother had a special way with animals; she always knew when a cow was unwell before anyone else noticed anything, and she usually knew how to nurse them back to health. Grandpa said she had been like that right from a little girl, and that the cows had always given more milk for her than for anyone else. 'They just about talk to her,' Daisy had heard Grandpa say. She rubbed the bony crest between the horns, and felt a trembling under her hand.

The cow was a two-year-old, having her first calf, and small for her age. Every spring Daisy taught that year's batch of calves to drink from a bucket, and she knew them all. This one had been smaller than the rest of the heifers, but with lines that her mother said showed the best of her breeding. They had named her 'Petal', for her dainty size and prettiness.

'She'll all right,' Papa said. 'She's sure to be, with you looking after her.' Daisy's mother smiled in response, but it was a tight, anxious smile.

Daisy lay in bed staring into the darkness, wondering what had roused her from sleep. Then she heard it again: her parents' voices, muffled through the wall, and the sound of them moving about. She was sure it must be very late; she had the sense of having been asleep for hours, but she was wide-awake now.

A faint strip of light appeared under her bedroom door. She slipped out of bed and through to the kitchen. Her parents were there with their daytime clothes on. Her mother held a lantern that her father was lighting from a stub of candle.

'What are you doing out here?' Daisy asked.

Her mother looked up from the lantern. 'We're going out to see to Petal—I think it's started. Go back to bed, Daisy, you'll get cold standing there.'

Through the open back door Daisy heard the lowing of a cow, and she thought she could hear distress in it. 'Is that Petal crying? Can I help? Please? I could... I could fetch things or something. And I won't get to sleep till you come back, I know I won't.'

Her parents exchanged a look. 'All right, then, but hurry,' her mother said. 'Just put your dressing-gown on, there isn't time to get you dressed.'

Daisy ran back to her room to snatch up her heavy woollen dressing-gown and wrap it round herself. The three of them sat on the porch steps and hauled their boots on, then walked over to the shed, Daisy hurrying to keep up. As well as the lantern, her father was carrying a bucket of water, while her mother had several old towels.

The shed was full of looming shadows that twisted and shifted with the swinging of the lantern. Her father placed it on a post at one end of the pen, and the shadows shrank away into the corners, leaving them in a pool of light. Petal moved about restlessly, white showing around the edges of her huge brown eyes. She tossed her head and let out a low moan.

Daisy stood by the corner of the pen, doing her best to keep out of the way, and watched her parents checking Petal over. Her mother put a hand on the cow's flank; Petal flinched, then stood still, shuddering slightly. Daisy's father shifted Petal's tail to one side so that they could see what was under it.

'Looks like she's going to need a hand getting it out,' her father said. 'Nothing much happening there.'

Mama leaned closer to explore the area with her fingers. 'It's not sitting right,' she said, frowning. 'I think one of the legs is bent back under. We'll have to move that before there's any hope of pulling the calf out.'

Daisy had seen calves born before, when they had been considerate enough to arrive in the daytime and when she was not at school. They slid into the world all wet and shiny, head resting neatly on the two front legs. But there was no sign of tiny hooves emerging from the red, distended area under Petal's tail.

'Keep her still,' her mother said. Daisy's father put one long arm across Petal's chest, holding the tail out of the way with his other hand. The cow's hooves moved in an awkward little dance, but Papa's arm held her in place.

Mama washed her hands in the bucket and inserted one, still wet and soapy. She tilted her head from side to side, trying to get a clear view. 'It's no good, I keep getting in my own light. Daisy, can you hold the lantern?'

Daisy picked it up by the metal handle and held it at the height her mother indicated, putting her other hand underneath to hold it steady. She watched Mama slide her hand in further, then the other hand. One little hoof was teased out; the other seemed to be stubbornly wedged. A

39

hand was pushed in even further; Daisy saw the strain on her mother's face as she worked away at the unseen leg. 'I've got it,' she muttered. 'The elbow's caught—if I push the body back the leg should—that's it.' She went from pushing to gently pulling, and the tip of another hoof appeared. 'That'll have to do,' she said, withdrawing her hands and straightening from an awkward crouch.

'You ready for me to start pulling yet?' Daisy's father asked; Mama nodded, and he moved to take her place, leaving her to hold the tail. Mama leaned her face against Petal's flank; Daisy heard her murmur soothing noises.

Her father took hold of the little hooves and pulled, slowly and carefully. The head appeared, then the shoulders. He turned the calf a little, still pulling, and the last part seemed to happen in a rush. The calf was a soft, damp bundle on the straw of the pen, her father was gathering it up in his hands, and her mother was telling Petal what a good girl she was, how brave, how clever.

'It's a heifer,' Papa said. He carried the calf around closer to Petal's head; she stared at the tiny creature in what looked like astonishment, nosed it cautiously, then began licking. Her eyes closed contentedly.

Daisy's father took the lantern from her, and she realised her arms were aching from having held it rigidly still for so long. The three of them stood watching mother and child. Daisy felt warm right through.

'They'll be all right,' Mama said when they had seen the calf make its first attempt at suckling. She picked up a towel and wiped the worst of the muck from her hands, then slipped an arm around Daisy's shoulders and squeezed. 'Let's give them a bit of peace and quiet.'

Back in the kitchen, Daisy's father coaxed the smouldering embers of the range into life while her mother got the tea things out. Daisy perched on a chair, so wide-awake that it was almost as if she were watching her mother and father move about the room in slow motion. At the same time, she was so tired that it was beyond her to speak, let alone stir from her place. The world was glassy and brittle around her, every sound clear in the dim room.

Her father lifted her onto his lap, and her mother pulled a chair nearer, so that the three of them were huddled close in the light of a single candle placed on the table. The tea was poured; even Daisy was given a little in a cup, diluted with hot water and with generous amounts of milk and sugar added. It was warm and sweet and comforting, the bitter edge only just noticeable.

Daisy snuggled against her father and listened to her parents talking quietly to each other. As she watched her mother's face in the shifting candlelight, vague images gradually took shape into thoughts. They had been worried about Petal tonight, and back when Daisy was born everyone had been worried about her mother. They had thought she might die. And Uncle Richard had been there; he had saved her mother's life. She frowned, trying to get the thoughts to make sense. Her mother had put her hands right up inside Petal to help the calf out, and then her father had had to pull and pull on it. She looked down at her mother's lap; surely Uncle Richard hadn't put his hands up *there?* There wouldn't be room, even if... No, she was sure she couldn't have it quite right, but it must have been awful for her mother to have a man looking down there, even a nice man like Uncle Richard, especially when she was so ill that they thought she might die. Poor Mama.

Her mother caught the intent gaze turned on her and smiled at Daisy. 'You were a big help tonight, holding the lantern. Would you like to think of a name for the calf?'

Daisy gazed at her, images of hands and calves and red, swollen flesh swimming before her eyes. The world was beginning to waver at the edges. She opened her mouth to speak, but all that emerged was a huge yawn.

'Look at her, she's just about asleep,' her mother said, stroking Daisy's face.

'I'll carry her through in a minute.' He must have, as Daisy woke next morning in her own bed, but with no memory of how she had got there.

Chapter Five

After their long parting, Daisy looked forward to Eddie's next visit even more than usual. She particularly wanted to tell him about helping with Petal's calving. But when he and their grandmother arrived in September, Daisy had difficulty getting him to pay attention to anything beyond what had been filling the newspapers for weeks: war had been declared.

It was the first time Eddie had ever wanted to talk at such length about a subject that held so little interest for Daisy. She had heard about the war, of course, at home as well as at school. There was a big map along one wall of the schoolroom; Miss Cameron had pointed out Germany, which unlike the countries of the Empire was not marked in red, and had explained that the German King, who sounded very like a wicked king from a story, wanted to be the King of all the other countries around him. The German soldiers had already taken over a little country called Belgium, which Daisy could only just see on the map, and Miss Cameron said they had done terrible things to the people there.

It all sounded horrible, but it seemed a long way away, and Daisy could not quite understand why everyone should think that people from New Zealand needed to go all that way to fight over it.

'My dad was in the other war, you know,' Eddie said. 'That was in South Africa. He took his horse, too—they called it cavalry, his sort of soldier, the ones on horses.'

'I know.' Daisy had grown up on tales of her father's big brother, her Uncle Mal, who had been Eddie's father and who had died in South Africa before either Eddie or Daisy had been born. 'Papa says Uncle Mal was the best rider he ever saw.' It did not seem right to question just why her uncle should have chosen to go so far from home to fight in a war that was even more of a mystery than the current one. Daisy did not think the bad people in South Africa could have done anything to the people in Belgium.

She knew that some men from Ruatane had already gone off to the war, and Eddie claimed that 'hundreds and hundreds' had done so from Auckland.

'Walter was all set to join up,' he told her. Walter helped with looking after the gardens and the horses at Aunt Sarah's, where his mother was cook and his father was gardener and coachman. 'His dad said he could, too, but his mother said he wasn't to, because he'd only go and get his head shot off. So then his dad said he'd better not.' Daisy found herself in sympathy with Walter's mother.

After the first day or so, when Eddie had exhausted all that could be said on the subject without raising a satisfactory response, he began paying attention to other matters. He admired the new calves; Petal's calf, which Daisy had named Sunny because of the particularly rich colour of her coat, received special fussing over. Eddie described his recent rugby games in a level of detail that strained even Daisy's loyal interest. He told her about school; he would be in Standard Six the next year, his last before starting high school. They read aloud to each other from a book of adventure stories that Eddie had brought down with him, and one wet day they did their best to act out one of them in a barn. It involved the daring capture of a gang of robbers who looked remarkably like bags of grain, but who nevertheless put up quite a fight.

But Eddie could not be kept off the subject of the war for long. Talk of school led to a description of the drill he would be doing with the other boys once he turned twelve, marching and using dummy guns made of wood. He was going to learn to shoot a real one when he started at high school, he told Daisy. The imaginary robbers came close to being turned into German soldiers, until Daisy announced that she would not play if the story departed so radically from what was in the book. It brought them as close as they had ever been to an argument. Daisy prevailed on that occasion, but she watched Eddie's fervour with mounting concern.

She was still awake when her grandmother slipped into bed beside her one evening. 'Granny?' she whispered.

'I'm sorry, darling, did I wake you up?'

'No, I can't get to sleep. Granny, do they let boys fight in wars?'

She felt rather than heard the sigh that came from her grandmother. 'Yes, they do. Some of them are just boys.'

For a moment Daisy could not speak for the panic that gripped her. 'Would they... would they let Eddie go?' she managed at last.

'Eddie?' Her grandmother sounded startled. 'Oh, no, Daisy, I didn't mean boys as young as Eddie. He's not even twelve yet. No, I think they're allowed to join up when they're eighteen.'

The panic slipped away as relief flooded through Daisy. 'Eighteen's years and years away. And everyone says it'll be over by Christmas.'

Her grandmother was silent for a time. 'Yes, they do say that, don't they?' she murmured.

The year of 1914 wore on towards its close, and people were no longer talking of a rapid end to the war.

No one from the valley or the nearby farms had as yet signed up; while their fathers all voiced a proper patriotic support for Britain, and an acknowledgement that New Zealand should do its part, they all felt there were plenty of boys in the towns who could easily be spared, while they had farms to run, and needed a full quota of sons to do so. That did not stop the boys at Daisy's school from claiming that their older brothers were sure to go off to fight the Germans soon, and proclaiming their own readiness to go if only they were old enough.

In the meantime, they made do with their lunchtime games. Battles were not possible, given the universal refusal to play the part of a German, but the boys regularly disappeared into the bush to hunt imaginary spies. At first they used branches snapped from manuka trees to beat the bush, but when one boy came back to class with his head bleeding profusely after getting too close to an over-enthusiastic spy hunter, Miss Cameron outlawed such weapons.

A large part of the girls' needlework classes were now turned over to knitting the socks for which the soldiers apparently had an insatiable need. Daisy had yet to get the knack of turning the heel, but one of the bigger girls was always ready to help with that. Apart from the mystifying heels, and the challenge of casting on and off, it was not a task that demanded great concentration, and Daisy's mind was free to wander. While the girls were busy knitting, the boys had extra lessons in arithmetic. Daisy studied the sums written up on the blackboard and did her best to calculate the answers in her head. She found herself getting quite good at this mental arithmetic as the months passed.

The war still seemed a distant thing, with little relevance to Daisy's life. Other than the endless knitting of socks, which she and her mother were also doing in the evenings, the only real change was that the name of one of her favourite sorts of baking, German biscuits, was no longer considered appropriate. But as they were quickly renamed Belgian biscuits, Daisy was not deprived of the dark, spicy biscuits with their jam filling and layer of icing.

Eddie, Granny and Aunt Sarah arrived just after school finished for the year. It was Christmas, and the war was not over.

But Eddie was only twelve, so it would be a long time before Daisy needed to worry about him. She might have managed to forget all about the war had Eddie not been bursting with the latest news.

'Walter went to a sermon just for men,' he told Daisy the morning after his arrival. 'No girls or women or anything. He told me some of the stuff the minister said, about what the Huns do. Really awful things.'

Daisy had by now heard many sermons delivered in ringing tones on the subject of the war, and had done her best to make sense of the talk of 'sacred duty' and 'fighting rampant militarism', but Eddie was clearly speaking of something more ominous. She could see how eager he was to share the forbidden knowledge, so almost despite herself she asked, 'What things?'

'I shouldn't really tell you, with it just being for men,' Eddie said, affecting a superior air. Daisy glared at him, and he grinned back. 'Walter wouldn't tell me much, anyway,' he admitted. 'He said it might give me bad dreams, and then his mum might find out and his life wouldn't be worth living. But it was about what those Germans did in Belgium.'

'I heard about that at school,' said Daisy. 'About them killing people. So our soldiers have to go there and kill their soldiers till they stop doing it.'

'Yes, but Walter said they did awful things to women. And babies, too—especially baby boys.'

He was waiting for her to prompt him, Daisy knew. 'What do they do?' she asked after a suitable pause.

'Well, he didn't say much about the women, just that they like hurting them. But the boys—they don't want them to grow up to be soldiers, so they... they cut bits off them.' Eddie's eyes widened with the enormity of it.

Daisy frowned, trying to puzzle it out. 'You mean... you mean like we do with the ram lambs so they won't taste funny?'

'Yes,' said Eddie. 'Just like that.'

'But that's stupid! They wouldn't do that to boys, they'd just kill them.'

'It must be true. It was in a *sermon*. Walter *said*.'

'Well... well, I'm sure the minister thought it was true—a minister wouldn't tell a lie—but someone probably made it up.'

Eddie looked doubtful, but he allowed himself to be drawn onto other, more cheerful topics as they wandered around the farm. He had been taken to a play not long before school got out, set in the time of Napoleon, and Daisy had him tell her all about what sounded a grand spectacle, with dozens of actors, although she heard more about its portrayal of the Battle of Waterloo than she might have wished. That afternoon they went for a walk in the bush and found what Eddie claimed was a new sort of beetle. They studied it closely as it crawled around the leaf litter, then took it back to the house, where Eddie made notes on it and a drawing that Daisy considered very fine. The beetle was then released to an uncertain fate in the garden.

Haymaking started after Christmas, and Eddie was now big enough to be considered quite useful when he took a turn at tossing hay onto the stacks. On a fiercely hot day spent at Daisy's grandfather's farm, Daisy, Eddie and Benjy took their share of the afternoon tea and ate it on the creek bank, in the shade of some scrubby trees. Daisy could feel bits of hay scattered over her face and neck, stiffening in place as a welcome breeze dried the film of sweat. She brushed them off as well as she could, and the boys helped disentangle hay and twigs from her hair.

'Tell Benjy about the play you went to, Eddie,' said Daisy, and Eddie obliged readily enough. Daisy had been satisfied with being told something of the story and the characters, along with a rather cursory description of the costumes, but Benjy wanted more. He pressed Eddie for details of how the stage had been decorated, and how the changes of scene were managed.

Eddie did his best, describing pieces of scenery that were slid back and forth on what he thought had been rails. 'They make it look different with the lights, too,' he added. 'They switch them on and off so the shadows move around.'

'It must be so good, that electric light,' Benjy said, sounding almost yearning. Daisy, too, was fascinated by the idea of a light that came on at the pull of a cord and was, according to Eddie, far brighter than their lamps on the farm. 'It'd be much easier than trying to do a play just with candles or lamps,' he added. 'We'd have to do it in the daytime if we had one here.'

Benjy's imagination had carried him off into a world of his own. Daisy and Eddie talked quietly to each other, careful not to disturb him.

With the distraction of running around outside, and with Benjy showing as little interest in the war as Daisy did, the subject of fighting had not come up all day. Daisy felt pleasantly tired that evening in the parlour, the grown-ups talking among themselves while the children sat on the floor with their books. Eddie was reading one that had been among his Christmas presents, full of thrilling tales of boys doing heroic deeds. Daisy glanced across at it and saw a picture of what appeared to be a small army of dark-skinned men, all armed with spears, being watched from behind a convenient clump of bushes by two boys.

Eddie noticed where she was looking, and pointed to the spears. 'They look pretty bad, eh? Hey, do you know what a bayonet charge is?'

'Eddie!' came the outraged voices of four grown-ups at the same time.

'Not in front of Daisy, Eddie,' said Granny. 'She'll have bad dreams.'

'And that's hardly a fit topic of discussion for the parlour,' Aunt Sarah added. 'I'm not sure it's a fit topic for a boy your age at all, come to that.'

'But we learned about it at drill,' Eddie said, unabashed. 'Our drill teacher told us all about how they do it.' Daisy could see in his eyes that he was debating with himself whether or not to press the point, but he subsided after a glance at the row of stern expressions turned on him.

'Well, at any rate, your teacher wasn't in a parlour at the time,' said Aunt Sarah. 'I imagine he moderates his speech when he is.'

Daisy was aware that she was the only person present still in ignorance of what a bayonet charge was, but given the response of the grown-ups it did not seem a good idea to ask. In any case, she was quite sure Eddie would tell her when they were next alone.

Eddie and Daisy read quietly for a little while, then Eddie moved his book so Daisy could see another picture, this time showing a group of pyramids. A camel stood in front of the largest one, looking out of the page with a supercilious expression. Beside the animal was a man with what seemed to be a striped towel around his head. He had a shifty look, and was being confronted by a boy with wavy fair hair. 'That's in Egypt,' said Eddie. 'That's where our soldiers have gone, you know. I saw a thing in the paper about the guns they use—great big ones that can blow up—'

'Hey, Eddie, that's enough, eh,' Daisy's father interrupted. 'Talk about something else.'

'But it's not bayonets. I stopped talking about bayonets.'

'It's still fighting. We've had enough of hearing about that lately.' Her father was frowning, but he looked more unhappy than annoyed.

'Eddie, we don't want to hear about the war all the time,' Granny said. 'It's a sad thing, with boys going off to fight.'

Daisy saw her gaze go to the photograph on the mantelpiece. Her father was looking at it too, she realised. It had been taken right here on the farm, outside the old house. It showed Granny, looking even younger than Daisy's mother did, holding a pretty baby with a mop of dark curls who would grow up to become Daisy's father. Closer to the camera a stern-looking man, the grandfather Daisy had never known, held the reins of a horse. Perched on the horse, stiff with pride, was a small boy who looked very like Eddie, though much younger. That was her Uncle Mal, Eddie's father, dead and buried somewhere in South Africa. Daisy thought she saw her grandmother brush away a tear, and even her father's eyes looked suspiciously bright.

Daisy got up and went over to perch on the edge of her grandmother's chair. She put her arms around Granny's neck and gave her a hug. On the other side of the fireplace she saw her mother place a hand on Papa's. The room felt full of solemn thoughts until Eddie broke the silence by asking if there were any more biscuits.

Daisy resigned herself to another long parting as she farewelled Eddie late in January. He had every hope of being picked for the rugby team again, and of playing in the May tournament. She kept up a brave face at the wharf, and afterwards hugged to herself the memory of Eddie sitting beside her on the way into town, his trouser legs riding up to reveal the socks he was wearing: Daisy's most successful knitting effort so far, and her Christmas present to him. Eddie had declared them the best socks he had ever owned.

Early one February afternoon, Daisy saw her father in the shed where they kept the harness, lifting down the heavy side-saddle. The saddle belonged in theory to Grandma, and had only been loaned to Daisy's mother, but it had lived here on the farm for as far back as Daisy could remember. It had been many years since Grandma had ridden a horse.

The side-saddle was rarely disturbed from its place high on the wall, as Daisy's mother disliked using it. If she wanted to ride over to visit one of the other valley families, she rode astride, trusting in the fact that it was unlikely she would encounter anyone outside her family on these short trips. Daisy remembered being taken to visit Grandma when she was too small to ride on her own, perched in front of an ordinary saddle with her mother holding her snugly in place. Once, Grandma had come outside and scolded Daisy's mother for riding 'like a boy'.

'But the other saddle's so heavy, and Davie was busy, so I didn't want to bother him getting it down for me,' her mother had said. And somehow it always was too much of a bother, and the saddle was never moved to a place where she could have lifted it down for herself.

Mama came up to the shed, leading one of the horses. 'I'm going out to Gaskells' place,' she explained, as Daisy's father hoisted the saddle onto the horse. 'It'll be faster riding than taking the gig, and I'd better look respectable.'

The Gaskell farm was not far from the mouth of the valley, a little further down the coast. The two youngest Gaskell boys went to the valley school, though they were too many years Daisy's senior for her to know them well. 'Why are you going there?' she asked. Visits outside the family were a rare thing.

Her mother tightened the girth, then Papa gave her a leg-up to the horse's back. 'I feel stupid sitting like this,' she grumbled as she arranged herself in the side-saddle, skirts bunching awkwardly around her. 'We saw Mr Gaskell at the store yesterday. He asked me if I'd come and have a look at one of his cows.'

'Word's got out that your ma knows more about doctoring animals than anyone else in Ruatane,' Daisy's father said.

'Oh, I don't know about that.' Her mother laughed, but she looked pleased at the same time. 'I think he would've rather asked your grandpa—it's one he bought off Grandpa a couple of years ago. He said he didn't want to trouble Grandpa, with him being busy with the dairy factory and everything, but he'd take it as a kindness if I could spare the time. I don't know that I *can* spare the time, mind you, but I don't like to think of a cow not well.' Daisy's father passed up a brown glass bottle, which she stowed in one of the saddlebags. 'I'll give it some of my tonic, that always does our cows good.'

In spite of the grumbles, Daisy thought her mother looked very grand perched in the side-saddle, just like ladies she had seen in photographs. Mama was wearing an ordinary dress, not a fancy riding outfit like those ladies, but Daisy was sure the ladies in the photographs would not be asked specially to come and look at a sick cow.

'I'll try not to be too long,' her mother said, turning the horse towards the track. 'You have your afternoon tea if I'm not back in time, though.'

She had not returned by afternoon tea time, although Daisy and her father managed to wait a full quarter of an hour later than usual. By milking time there was still no sign of her, so the two of them set off to the cowshed on their own. They had the first cows in the bails when they heard her calling; Daisy looked up to see her mother hurrying down the hill towards them.

'It took so long!' she exclaimed, taking a milking stool by one of the cows as she spoke. The steady *swish, swish* of milk going into the buckets soon made a soft accompaniment to her voice. 'It wasn't just the cow he'd told me about—I ended up going right around the herd. They none of them had much condition, you could tell just by looking at them. I felt like telling him off—what's the point of having good cows if you're not going to look after them properly?'

'Any of them really crook?' Daisy's father asked.

'Most of them just need better pasture. He's leaving them on it too long, and they all looked a bit wormy. The worst one's got quite a cough, and her coat's rough as anything. I left the tonic with him so he can give it to her every day, and I said he was to keep a good eye on her. I'll get you to take some of my worm medicine to the factory, he can pick it up there. He'd bought some of that rubbish they advertise in the paper—I told him he might as well pour that in the creek, for all the good it does.'

Daisy stared at her, impressed. Mr Gaskell was a large man, and it was difficult to picture her softly spoken mother giving him such a scolding. But poor treatment of animals was guaranteed to rouse her ire.

When they got back to the house after milking, Daisy saw a sack lying in a corner of the porch. She gave it a cautious prod with one foot, and it made a rattly noise.

'It's a load of bottles,' her mother said. 'Mr Gaskell said he'd like to buy more tonic, and worm medicine, too. I told him I haven't got the bottles, and he had a lot of them lying around, so he put them in that sack for me. They'll need a good cleaning, but we can boil them up in the copper.'

'Is he going to pay money for your medicines?' Daisy asked, more impressed than ever.

'He said he would. And he gave me one and sixpence for coming out today.' Her mother smiled at Daisy's awed expression. 'He gave me something else you might like. Come and see.'

Daisy followed her into the kitchen, then stopped in her tracks. On the table was a watermelon, green and glossy and mouthwatering. For the moment, it overshadowed even the one and sixpence her mother had earned.

The melon was moved to the bench to be out of the way while they ate dinner. Daisy was so captivated by the sight of it that she had to be reminded several times to concentrate on the food before her.

'Let's take it out to the verandah, then we won't have to worry about making a mess,' her mother said when their plates were empty.

Daisy carried the melon, a task that required both hands. They sat on the top step of the verandah and her father cut a large chunk of watermelon for each of them. Daisy sank her teeth into the sweet red flesh and felt cool juice running down her chin.

They ate slice after slice, spitting out the pips as they went, and competing to see who could get their pips furthest. Daisy's father was much the best at this, though he claimed that one of Daisy's efforts had narrowly missed a cow on the far side of a paddock.

Daisy added her latest piece of picked-clean rind to the growing pile. 'What are you going to do with the money Mr Gaskell gave you, Mama?'

'I hadn't really thought about it. What do you think I should do, Daisy-May?'

Daisy gave a small wriggle of pleasure at her mother's pet name for her. Her name was, in fact, Margaret Amy, as she had discovered to her amazement the day she started school, but that was the first and last time she had ever heard herself called Margaret. She thought hard. 'Buy more watermelons?'

Her mother laughed. 'Save some of the pips and we can have a go at growing our own next summer. The big black ones, not these little ones.' She reached out and removed a small white pip from Daisy's chin. 'I might put the money towards some new sheets. We could all do with them.'

Daisy had put her foot through her own lower sheet just the previous week, although it had been neatly patched since. 'You could get a new dress,' she suggested, remembering the rows of gowns in her Aunt Maudie's wardrobe.

'One and six wouldn't buy much material. If Mr Gaskell buys more of my tonic and things I should get enough for new sheets, though.'

'Do you want a new dress, love?' Daisy's father asked. 'We could run to a bit of material.'

Mama shook her head. 'No, I don't need any more. My good dress has still got plenty of wear in it.'

Her good summer dress was a plain blue cotton that seemed to have been around for years. 'You should get something just for you,' Daisy pressed. 'Something pretty.'

Her mother reached over Daisy to run her hand along Papa's collar. She twirled a lock of his hair, just at the base of his neck where it formed into curls, around her finger, then bent down to kiss Daisy on the top of her head. 'I've got all the pretty things I need,' she said.

Mr Gaskell did indeed buy several bottles of Daisy's mother's remedies; he also sang her praises to his near neighbours and acquaintances. It became a not uncommon thing for Daisy to come home from school to find her mother just back from attending to animals on one of the farms beyond the valley. She would always return with a few coins, and often with some fruit that they did not grow on their own farm, or a different sort of jam than they usually had.

'It's because the farm prices are good just now,' her mother said when Daisy asked why so many of the farmers were calling on her help.

'That's the one good thing that's come out of the war,' her father put in. 'With the government buying up a lot of butter and things to send to England, it's pushed the prices up.'

'So everyone wants to get the most they can out of their animals, and they don't mind spending a bit on it.'

'And they've got the sense to ask the best person around,' her father said, as if that settled matters.

Those coins must be mounting up, Daisy reflected. New sheets soon made their appearance, quickly followed by fluffy new towels, and even new underwear for everyone. And of course the higher prices for farm produce must mean their own milk was also bringing in more money. Their farm was much the smallest in the valley, and with only the three of them to work the land their herd was smaller than anyone else's, but, as Daisy's father said when she asked about the prices, every little helped.

Her mother had set a jar on the kitchen shelf, and after each of her visits to ailing stock she would put a little of her earnings into it; usually a penny or two, and occasionally a whole threepenny bit. At first Daisy assumed this money was being spent on the new items that were appearing in the house; it was only when she noticed that the jar was steadily getting fuller that she thought to ask her mother just what it was for.

'You'll find out all in good time,' her mother said mysteriously; then she added, 'Someone might need a bit of pocket money in the May holidays.'

This remark was accompanied by knowing smiles and significant looks exchanged over Daisy's head. Her mother and father must be planning to send her to Lucy's again, Daisy decided. She had spent an occasional weekend with her cousins since the previous May; Lucy had grown used to the fact that Daisy would not blindly follow her lead, and had become better company as a result. Daisy was happy enough at the idea of staying at Lucy's, but she wondered why her parents seemed to consider it such a weighty matter. Perhaps they had forgotten about her holiday there the previous May. She had better try to appear surprised and excited when they finally told her.

One afternoon towards the end of April, Daisy came out of school with the rest of the children and was startled to see her mother there, sitting on a rough wooden bench near the porch.

'I'm just going to have a talk with Miss Cameron,' Daisy was told. 'You go and catch Brownie, I shouldn't be long.'

The horse, perhaps with the sweeter grass of home on his mind as he grazed half-heartedly in the school's paddock, was easily caught. Daisy had the reins and blanket on him well before her mother emerged from the schoolroom, Miss Cameron farewelling her from the porch.

Her mother gave Daisy a leg-up, then walked along beside the horse, her hand resting on the halter. Daisy was bursting to know why she should have wanted to visit the school, but under the teacher's eyes she felt shy. She waited until they had gone a short way up the road and were out of sight before asking.

Mama looked around to check that no one was watching them. 'Shove up a bit nearer Brownie's head,' she said, leading the horse close to a fence. She climbed onto a rail, and from there to the horse's back, where she sat with her arms around Daisy's waist. 'I was checking up on you, just to see if you're behaving at school.'

Daisy could hear the smile in her mother's voice, and knew she was being teased. 'Why did you really come down, Mama?'

'It's a surprise. But you'll have to wait till we get home—Papa wants to help me tell you.'

She was proof against any further attempts to get the secret out of her, and Daisy thought Brownie had never gone so slowly. It felt as if an hour had passed by the time they had him turned out into his paddock and the two of them were walking up the path to the house.

Daisy's father was just outside the back door, chopping kindling. Usually she liked to watch him at the task, every stroke of the axe landing just where he meant it to, and a slab of wood transformed into a pile of neat sticks as if by magic and with little visible effort. But today she was more interested in finding out whatever secret her parents were keeping. She was relieved when her father put down the axe and followed them into the kitchen.

Afternoon tea was set out on the table. Daisy sat between her mother and father, and looked expectantly from one face to the other. They were exchanging smiles, clearly pleased with themselves.

Her mother made a great show of sipping slowly at her tea and even more slowly replacing the cup on its saucer. 'I was telling Miss Cameron about Granny having a little school in Auckland,' she said at last. 'And Aunt Sarah used to be a teacher, too, years ago.'

'I know.' Daisy felt a squirming of embarrassment that her mother should have thought Miss Cameron might be interested in such small matters of family history.

'She said you're doing very well at school. So she says it'll be all right for you to miss a week.'

Daisy frowned. 'Why am I going to miss school?'

'Well, with Eddie not coming down in May any more, we knew you were a bit disappointed, so we thought we'd see if…' Her mother trailed off, and smiled across at her father. 'You can tell her.'

'Because,' Papa announced, 'you're going to Auckland for the holidays.'

Chapter Six

After a few moments of being unable to manage more than an incoherent squeak, all Daisy's questions began tumbling out in a rush. When was she to go? How long would she be away? Would she have to go on her own? In the euphoria of the moment, she almost thought she might be brave enough for that, but she was soon reassured that it would not be necessary.

It seemed there had been letters back and forth between Ruatane and Auckland for many weeks, deciding how it could be done, and now it was all organised. She was to go up with Grandpa, who had been invited to a special meeting in Auckland to do with dairy co-operatives, since he was the chairman of Ruatane's. That meant going a week before the school holidays started, but Miss Cameron's approval had removed the last obstacle.

'It won't be such a rush, with you having a bit longer,' her mother said. 'It seems a shame to go all that way just for a week.'

'And then you can come back with Granny at the end of the holidays,' said her father. 'So you'll be all right both ways.'

Daisy found it astonishing that such a thing had been planned with her having no inkling of it. But far more astonishing was the knowledge that she was to go to the city; to have two whole weeks staying with Eddie; to see at last the places she had been hearing stories about all her life.

The time till she was to leave dragged by at a painful pace, but somehow the final week disappeared in a rush. The last day was carefully marked off on Daisy's calendar, her mother made a last check of the clothes packed in the small suitcase they had borrowed, adding a few more clean handkerchiefs, and they set off for town.

'You're not a bit scared of going all that way,' her mother said, smiling at Daisy's eagerness to catch the first sight of the wharf. 'You're braver than I am, Daisy-girl.'

Daisy's mother had never been out of Ruatane, and had never expressed any desire to do so. But Daisy did not feel she was being brave. There was no room for anything as dull as worrying, when she was so very full of excitement.

Grandma and Benjy had come along to see Daisy and her grandfather off, Benjy making a heroic effort not to show any jealousy of Daisy's adventure. There were hugs all round, and an admonition from Grandma, who did not quite approve of boats, to stay well away from the edge. Grandpa led her on board, Daisy's hand held firmly in his, the lines were cast off, and they stood on the deck waving the others out of sight.

Grandpa was one of Daisy's favourite people in the whole world, and having him all to herself was a rare treat. As soon as Ruatane had been left behind, every bit of coast was new and unfamiliar. Her grandfather had made the journey many times; he answered Daisy's stream of questions about the places they were passing, and her frequent requests to know how far they still had to go. He knew the names of all the small settlements along the coast, and had even sold pedigree Jersey cows to farmers at some of them over the years.

Daisy never felt herself shy around Grandpa. She told him about the cows her mother had been called out to see to; after some time she realised that he had almost certainly heard all the details before, from Daisy's mother herself, but he showed no sign of being anything but engrossed by Daisy's account. They walked about the deck, Daisy too eager to see every inch of the coast to be content with sitting inside.

The day was fine but cold. When a chill breeze began biting at their faces, Grandpa found a corner out of the worst of the wind where there was just room to sit on a fairly flat hatch cover. Daisy snuggled against him, his jacket around both of them. She recited for him the poems she had been learning at school; she sang all the songs she could remember. Grandpa praised it all. He even seemed impressed by her times tables, although she needed prompting with the seven times. She told him that Eddie could do his all the way up to twelve times, and Grandpa said he was not sure he could manage that himself. They occasionally left their sheltered spot to stroll once more around the deck, in deference to Grandpa's stiff legs as well as Daisy's curiosity over what could be seen from the bow.

In the late afternoon they caught the first sight of Tauranga Harbour. With the sun low in the sky the boat docked, and Daisy found herself on solid land again, the ground seeming to move under her feet after their hours spent at sea. The town's main street was lined with shops, all of which were closed, to Daisy's regret. Through their windows she caught glimpses of pretty dresses, fancy toys, and piles of books. Grandpa said there were more, and larger, shops in Auckland, and Daisy did her best to imagine such a thing.

They dined in a hotel restaurant, where a lady in a black dress and a lacy white apron brought the food to their table and called Daisy 'Miss'. The table was spread with a white damask cloth, and there were so many knives and forks that Daisy was at a loss to know which ones to use until

Grandpa helped her. They had roast chicken; a treat for Daisy, whose previous experience of poultry had mostly been hens too old to lay, rendered edible only by long boiling. The apple pie that followed was almost as good as her mother's, although the cream that accompanied it did not seem as rich or fresh as she was used to at home. Grandpa ordered a special drink for her, sweet and pink and so fizzy it made her nose tickle.

It was quite dark by the time the boat sailed. Daisy watched the lights of Tauranga, rows and rows of them, fading from sight as the boat pulled away. She had to part from her grandfather to spend the night in the ladies' cabin, though he said he would be close by in the saloon if she happened to need him. The stewardess told Grandpa she would put Daisy at the back of the cabin; Daisy would have preferred to be by the door, but her grandfather agreed with the stewardess that it would be better for her to be tucked away well inside.

Daisy slept soundly, rocked by the boat's motion. She woke in the dim pre-dawn light, but stayed curled up in her warm nest of blankets until she heard the ladies begin moving about the cabin. She was dressed before the stewardess had the chance to ask if she needed any help, and was soon having breakfast with her grandfather, after which they went out on the deck for Daisy to once again study the coastline and wish the miles away.

'It'll be lunchtime before we get there,' Grandpa said. Fortunately he always seemed to have sweets about his person, so there was no risk of going hungry.

The final part of the voyage was spent threading through islands. Grandpa told her their names, but Daisy did not pay much heed; she was too busy trying to catch a glimpse of Auckland. Every time she saw a small jetty jutting out into the water, she would ask, 'Is that Auckland?' And every time Grandpa would shake his head and say it was a bit further yet.

'There it is,' Grandpa said at last. Buildings spread out beyond a row of wharves, straggling along the edge of Auckland's harbour and scattered upon the hills behind.

The boat slowed as it entered shallower waters, and it felt an age before the wharves grew larger. The blobs on them gradually resolved into a mass of people; more people, it seemed to Daisy, than the entire population of Ruatane. She clutched her grandfather's hand more tightly.

She felt the boat turning towards the wharf that seemed to be their destination; a sudden shaft of sunlight darted through the clouds and caught a flash of colour within the mass of soberly dressed people.

'Eddie!' Daisy cried. 'It's Eddie!'

Eddie stood out from the crowd not just because of his bright shock of hair, but also because he was moving down the wharf at some speed, pushing his way through with no apparent awareness of any disruption he might be causing. He reached the end of the wharf, saw Daisy waving, and waved vigorously back.

With a wanton disregard for all Grandma's warnings, Grandpa lifted Daisy onto the boat's railing so that she could see Eddie more easily. He kept a careful hold around her middle, leaving Daisy free to wave both arms. She and Eddie called back and forth to each other, their voices mutually unintelligible over the noise and distance, as the boat made its way to the head of the wharf, Eddie keeping pace with it.

The mooring lines were thrown out, and Daisy became aware that people were moving along the deck, several of them smiling at the sight of her fruitless attempts at communication. Her grandfather lifted her down from the rail and led her towards the gangplank, which they reached just in time to meet Eddie surging aboard. The children found themselves face to face. Torn between the urge to fling her arms around Eddie and her awareness of the strangers surrounding them, Daisy stood irresolute until Eddie took hold of her free hand. He tugged her along the gangplank, talking away the whole time.

Granny was on the wharf, having wisely left it up to Eddie to force a way onto the boat against the flow of passengers, laughing at the vigour with which he herded their guests toward her. 'Daisy, I'm so happy to have you here,' she said, enfolding Daisy in a hug. 'Eddie's been counting down the days ever since we knew you were coming. And Frank, it's lovely to see you.' She greeted Daisy's grandfather with a kiss on the cheek. 'You'll come home with us, won't you? Sarah's expecting you for lunch.'

'Come and meet Walter,' Eddie said. In a very short time Daisy had been introduced to Eddie's friend, as well as the horses he was in charge of, then helped into the carriage and seated next to Eddie, while Granny and Grandpa took the seat facing them.

Daisy had had no time for more than a quick, somewhat confused glance at her surroundings before being bundled into the carriage. As they rattled along the street Eddie occasionally pointed out places of interest, but they spent most of the ride doing their best to catch up with each other's news in the shortest possible time.

'I don't know how they manage to hear each other when they're both talking at the same time,' Daisy heard her grandfather remark during a brief pause in their conversation.

'It's a knack they've got between them,' Granny answered, a smile in her voice. 'They're always like this when they first get back together.'

The carriage came to a halt in front of the house. Daisy found it exactly as she had pictured: two stories high, with white-painted walls that gleamed in the winter sunlight. A verandah ran the length of the house, a large, curved entrance porch at its centre. Standing at the head of the verandah steps was the tall, imposing figure of Aunt Sarah, smiling in welcome.

Daisy only managed a step or two in her aunt's direction before Eddie took hold of her hand. 'Come around to the stables and I'll show you Baron.'

'Eddie, Daisy's just got off the boat,' their grandmother protested. 'She'll want to have a wash and get changed before she goes rushing off to see your horse.'

Daisy was quite happy to rush off, crumpled and unwashed as she was, but Granny and Aunt Sarah united in insisting that the horse could wait.

'Take your coat off, at least,' said Granny.

'And you must meet the staff,' Aunt Sarah said. 'Eddie's been talking of your arrival so much, they've been looking forward to making your acquaintance.'

On hearing this suggestion, Eddie at once wanted nothing more than to introduce Daisy to everyone in the house. He ushered her into the entrance hall, where two ladies in smart black uniforms were waiting.

'This is Alice, and this is Ivy,' Eddie said, while Granny helped Daisy out of her coat and the older of the two maids took it to be hung up. It was something of a relief to shed the coat; it had become rather tight since the previous winter, and the weather was warm for May. 'Ivy's only been here a year—it used to be Nellie, but she got married.'

Daisy smiled shyly at the maids; it was all she had time for before Eddie took her through to the kitchen, a room he was clearly at home in, and which was larger than the parlour on the farm. A table, its wood scrubbed to a pale cream colour, ran for much of the room's length, neat stacks of sliced vegetables showing that meal preparation was in progress. There was a large range, cupboards and bins in abundance, and a fancy sink that looked to be made of a heavy white china was set into a wooden bench. Saucepans of all sizes hung from a rack above the table, and a variety of utensils, many of them quite mysterious in shape and possible use, were on the table and the bench. A delicious smell of baking filled the room.

Eddie introduced Daisy to Mrs Jenson and the kitchen maid, Polly.

Mrs Jenson, who as well as being Aunt Sarah's cook was Walter's mother, was a cheerful-looking woman who beamed at Daisy.

'Fancy you having such a pretty little cousin, Master Eddie,' she remarked. 'Who'd have thought it?'

When Daisy worked this out in her head it did not seem a very complimentary thing to have said to Eddie, but he grinned at the cook, quite happy to be teased a little. 'I told you she was,' he said.

Granny had followed them into the kitchen. 'Do you want to come and see your room now, Daisy?' she asked.

'No, she wants to see my horse,' Eddie said, tugging on Daisy's hand. She went willingly enough, out through the far door of the kitchen, down a few steps to the back garden, and across to a large, smart-looking shed. Eddie led her through the tall doors that almost filled one end of the shed, past the carriage and over to a row of stalls. 'Here he is,' Eddie said, stopping in front of the nearest stall. 'Here's Baron.'

Daisy stared at the tall bay gelding, impressed. The horses she was familiar with on the farm were sturdy beasts of placid disposition, as likely to be used for hauling a cart as for riding, and very different from the fine-boned creature before her, bright-eyed and groomed to glossiness.

Baron had let out a whinny of greeting at Eddie's approach, but he tossed his head and showed a little white around the eyes at the sight of Daisy. She stood her ground and held out her hand, making small noises of encouragement. Baron's ears came forward, and he stretched out to nuzzle softly at her palm, the whiskers around his mouth tickling her. Eddie moved away for a moment and returned with an apple, snatched up from a bag near the doorway. He passed it to Daisy and she held it out for Baron, who took it eagerly from her.

Eddie's friend Walter appeared, carrying a piece of harness which he hung upon a hook on the stable wall. He offered to lift Daisy onto Baron's back, and she had got as far as scrambling partway up the wooden rails of the horse's stall when she heard her grandmother's voice.

'Eddie,' Granny called from the direction of the house. 'Bring Daisy inside—it's time to get ready for lunch.'

Eddie was not someone who took the prospect of his next meal lightly. He helped Daisy down from the rail and the two of them hurried to the back door of the house, where their grandmother was waiting for them.

Granny took Daisy up the magnificent staircase that led from the entrance hall to the upper floor of the house. Daisy rested a hand on the banister railing, her fingers sliding along the satin-smooth wood that was the colour of dark honey and smelled faintly of beeswax polish. A strip of dark red carpet ran down the centre of the stairs, held in place by a brass rod at the base of each step. At the head of the staircase a passage stretched out to either side, lined with a wider variety of the same carpet.

'I've given you the room next to mine,' said Granny.

'It's my old room,' Eddie said, immediately rendering the room perfect in Daisy's eyes. 'I had that one when I was little. Come and see the one I've got now.'

Eddie's room was spacious by Daisy's standards, plainly but comfortably furnished, with a coverlet and drapes in a matching dark blue. She was surprised by its tidiness; every available surface in his room on the farm tended within a day or so of his arrival to have acquired an assortment of clothes, books, and various objects that caught his eye on their wanderings. Daisy's mother always wisely closed the door on the chaos, moving only what was in the way of making his bed, and knowing it would all disappear along with Eddie at the end of his visit. Perhaps the maids picked up after him here.

On a low table against the far wall Daisy saw what she knew was one of Eddie's chief treasures: an army of toy soldiers arrayed for battle. He had described these soldiers for her in such detail that she felt she could have named most of them. Eddie saw where she was looking, and was on the point of urging her over to examine the soldiers more closely when Granny, too, noticed.

'Not the soldiers, not just now, Eddie,' she said. 'We'll be waiting lunch half the afternoon if you get telling Daisy all about them.'

'I'll show you later, then,' Eddie said, following Daisy and Granny from the room. 'I used to have them down in the drawing room, but Aunt Sarah said to bring them up here,' he told Daisy as they walked along the passage. 'She said there was enough about war and soldiers and all in the papers without having to have them in the drawing room.'

The door of what Daisy was informed was Aunt Sarah's room was ajar, and she took the opportunity to peep inside as they passed. She caught a glimpse of creams and golds, elaborate lampshades and elegant wooden furniture, and then Granny led her into her own room.

Granny's bedroom had dainty furniture and a good deal of lace. An odd sort of sofa, which Granny told her was called a *chaise longue*, was covered in the same pale blue silk the drapes were made of. There was a dressing table between two tall windows, with small boxes of inlaid wood and a row of glass bottles with silver tops. Granny had a brass bedstead with a frilly white coverlet, and a large wardrobe dominated one corner of the room.

'It's lovely,' Daisy said, twirling on the spot to see every part of the bedroom.

Granny smiled. 'Yes, isn't it? I'm very lucky. Now, your room's just through here,' she said, leading Daisy toward another door. 'It's only little, but I wanted to keep you close by in case you wake up in the night.'

The room had a bed about the same size as Daisy's at home, but its headboard had a pattern of leaves and flowers carved around the edge, unlike the plain wood of the one her father had made for her on the farm. Against one wall was a small chest of drawers, and next to that a tiny dressing table.

'It's very nice, thank you,' Daisy said. She walked into the centre of the room, turned to see the corner that had been hidden from view behind the door, and stood stock still. '*Oh*,' she breathed at the sight of a dolls' pram, complete with two porcelain dolls.

'It was Aunt Sarah's when she was a little girl,' Granny said, smiling at Daisy's expression. 'She thought you might like to play with it while you're here.'

'It's *beautiful*.' Two steps took Daisy to it; she rested her fingers on the handle and moved the pram gently back and forth.

'We can take it out tomorrow if you like, if the weather's nice,' said Granny.

Eddie had been hovering in the doorway, unable to find a way to claim any responsibility for the idea of the dolls' pram, but unwilling to be left out. 'I got you something, too,' he said, darting over to the dressing table. He picked up a small package Daisy had not noticed earlier; she opened it, and exclaimed in delight when she found two pretty hair clips, each with a tiny enameled daisy.

Granny helped her slide them into place while Eddie looked on. She glanced down at a silver watch pinned to her bodice. 'We'd better get a move on. Let's get you along to the bathroom, Daisy, so you can wash your hands before lunch.'

'I'll show you how the taps work,' Eddie said, leading the way back into the passage.

The bathroom was an expanse of porcelain and shining brass; surfaces that Daisy thought must demand a good deal of work to keep clean. The floor was covered in hard white tiles that went partway up the walls and ended in a dark green border. There was a basin against one wall, but what chiefly caught Daisy's eye was the bath. It was magnificent; a deep vessel of white porcelain perched on brass feet in the shape of lions' paws.

'You can have a bath tonight,' Granny said, noticing where Daisy's gaze was directed. 'I'll get Alice to run you one after dinner.'

'Look at this, Daisy,' Eddie said, calling Daisy's attention back to the basin. 'This is how you turn on the tap.' It was Daisy's first experience of running water, although Eddie had described it for her several times over the years, including once drawing her a picture of a tap.

'Wash your hands, Eddie, then you can go downstairs,' Granny said. 'Tell Aunt Sarah we'll be down soon.'

Eddie obliged, in the process giving Daisy a careful demonstration of the use of taps and basin. The moment he was safely out of sight, Granny took Daisy into a much smaller room beside the bathroom and showed her how a flush toilet worked, then left her alone to make use of it. Her own hands and face washed, Daisy went downstairs with her grandmother, to the dining room where the others were already at the table.

With all the excitement since her arrival she had almost forgotten about her grandfather, but he seemed happy enough talking to Aunt Sarah. Daisy caught snatches about committees and meetings as she took her seat between Eddie and their grandmother. Eddie was not joining in the conversation; he was instead studying the place set before him as if hoping food might materialise there of its own accord.

The long dining table had a crisp, white tablecloth set with silver candlesticks and gleaming cutlery, and the food was served on china patterned in blue and white. Other than between courses Eddie was not much disposed for speech, but Daisy was content to look around the room and listen to the grown-ups. Granny was asking after everyone at home, and by the time Grandpa had given her the news of all his eight children and their own families, from Aunt Maudie down to Benjy, the soup course was finished and the roast beef that succeeded it had largely disappeared.

As well as family news, Granny wanted to hear about the meeting Grandpa had come to Auckland for. Daisy heard discussion about dairy production and how more butter could be sent to England; this was to do with the war, she knew. Fortunately there was no shortage of such things at Aunt Sarah's table, where there was ample butter for the potatoes and a huge jug of cream for the pudding that ended the meal.

It was a substantial lunch, and afterwards the five of them walked about the garden; the grown-ups at a leisurely pace, while Eddie led Daisy on a more energetic inspection of the grounds, with their fine trees and garden beds. Not a weed was to be seen; not so much as a twig was out of place to spoil the symmetry of the ornamental shrubs.

The sky had clouded over, and a feeble drizzle began, driving them indoors. Grandpa, who had arranged to stay in another part of Auckland closer to where his meeting was being held, said it was time he went, and Aunt Sarah, in spite of his assurance that he would be quite happy to catch the tram, insisted she would have her carriage take him.

'And if there's any difficulty with your accommodation, you're most welcome to stay here,' she said.

Grandpa would be returning to Ruatane a few days later, catching a sailing that was too early in the day for him to visit them on his way to the wharves. Daisy kissed him goodbye at the door of the carriage, and gave him an extra hug for her mother, which he promised to deliver as soon as he got home.

What was left of the afternoon passed in pleasant idleness. The weather kept them indoors, but that was no hardship. Daisy found that her suitcase had been unpacked and her clothes all put away while she had been otherwise occupied. She changed into another frock, gladly discarding the much-crumpled one in which she had travelled to Auckland, and joined Eddie, who was waiting more or less patiently outside her door.

Eddie showed Daisy his toy soldiers, spending some time explaining in detail what each uniform meant and how their weapons were deployed. They then staged a short battle; hostilities were well advanced before Eddie admitted that playing with the soldiers was not an approved activity for a Sunday. 'But I had to show you how they work,' he said, quite unabashed. 'We'd better not make too much noise with them, though.'

They were left to complete the action undisturbed; Eddie declared it a draw, which Daisy suspected was overly generous. He then led her on a fuller exploration of the downstairs rooms. Granny and Aunt Sarah were sitting in the drawing room; rather than join them for afternoon tea, Eddie took her on another visit to the kitchen, where they sampled a selection of biscuits.

The room that impressed Daisy most was not the largest, nor the most sumptuously decorated; it was Aunt Sarah's study, which was also the house's library. Never before had Daisy seen so many books in the one place; books of all sizes, on every subject imaginable. Many were beautifully bound in a soft leather that felt smooth under her fingers, and the room itself seemed scented by them with a faint musky aroma.

As well as a bookshelf in his bedroom, where he kept special favourites and whatever he was currently reading, Eddie was allowed free use of the library.

'There's a few up there that Granny said to leave alone,' he said, indicating a high shelf behind the desk. 'I had a look at them once, but they were all about kissing and stuff. There's plenty of good things to read, though—I'll find you some.'

Aunt Sarah's own childhood books were in the library, as were several that Eddie had grown out of. He piled several on the desk for Daisy to choose from; she selected a few more or less at random, Eddie's recommendation enough to convince her that she would enjoy any of them.

Eddie carried Daisy's books, plus two or three for himself, through to join the adults in the drawing room. They sat in two remarkably comfortable armchairs reading by the light of an electric lamp until dinner time, Eddie helping Daisy with any passages that puzzled her.

It was not long after dinner before Daisy found herself yawning, the day's excitement on top of a long journey catching up with her. When Granny asked if she still wanted a bath that evening Daisy, who had no intention of missing such a treat, assured her that she did, doing her best to muffle the yawns until the maid returned to announce that the bathroom was ready. Daisy said her goodnights to Eddie and Aunt Sarah, exchanging a kiss with each of them, and went upstairs with Granny.

Daisy had begun to think she might have exaggerated the bath in her mind after her brief sight of it earlier, but if anything it looked even larger now, with steaming water partway up the sides. Granny helped her out of her clothes, and kept a hand on her arm as Daisy stepped carefully over the edge and lowered herself into the wonderfully warm water. It was much hotter than they had their baths at home, and so deep! She felt almost dizzy at the thought of how much wood would have to be chopped, and how many kerosene tins full of water hauled inside and onto the range, to heat such a vast quantity.

Even with her legs stretched out it still seemed a long way to the far end of the bath. She slid down a little to see how much further her feet could go; the bath was smooth to the point of being slippery, and for a moment Daisy thought she was going to slide right under the water. But Granny caught hold of her in time and tugged her back upright, laughing softly at Daisy's startled squeak.

Scrubbed clean, she lay in the warm water, so comfortable that she felt she could go to sleep right there. The skin on her fingers was water-shriveled by the time Granny said she had better get out before the bath got cold. While Granny wrapped her in a big, fluffy towel and rubbed her dry, Daisy watched the water disappearing down the plug hole in a miniature whirlpool.

Her nightdress and dressing-gown had been set out ready for her by the maid. She snuggled into them, then went through to her grandmother's bedroom to have her hair brushed. Granny had clever fingers that managed to tease out the knots without pulling. She ran the brush through Daisy's hair with slow, soothing strokes, then plaited it loosely for sleeping.

'All finished,' Granny said, smoothing down the plaits. She put her arms around Daisy and drew her into a warm embrace. 'I'm so glad you've come, Daisy. It's lovely to have a little girl to fuss over.'

She took Daisy through to the next room and tucked her into bed.

'I'll just be downstairs—I'll try not to wake you up when I come to bed. You won't be frightened sleeping in a strange house, will you?'

'No, I won't be a bit frightened,' Daisy said.

'That's a good girl.' Granny patted down the covers. 'I thought you might find it a lot to get used to after the farm. It took me a little while, even though everyone's so nice.'

It was hard to explain, especially when she was feeling so deliciously sleepy, but the house did not seem strange at all; not when she had heard so much about it. She was under the same roof as Eddie; she had Granny looking after her; and Daisy had never yet met anyone who would dare take liberties with Aunt Sarah. She could not have felt any safer in her own bed at home, with her mother and father just through the wall.

She snuggled further under the covers and let her heavy eyelids fall, murmuring an answer to Granny's goodnight.

'Is Daisy still awake?' That was Eddie's voice, in what he seemed to think was a whisper, coming from just through the doorway into Granny's room. 'I forgot to tell her about what we're going to do while she's here.'

Even for Eddie, Daisy was unable to summon the energy to call out. 'It can wait till tomorrow, Eddie, she's asleep,' Granny said softly. And a few moments later, she was.

Daisy woke from what she thought had been a pleasant dream, to find an even pleasanter reality: she really was in the big house in Auckland. She drew back the curtains to reveal a garden touched with wintry sunlight; she rested her elbows on the windowsill and stared out at the trees, then got herself dressed. By the time Granny came through Daisy was ready to go downstairs for breakfast.

Eddie was already at the table, and Aunt Sarah came in a few minutes later. As soon as he saw their grandmother, Eddie began claiming that he should stay home from school to keep Daisy company, though something in his expression told Daisy that he knew he had little chance of success.

'No, Eddie, we've already talked about that,' said Granny. 'You know you have to go to school. It's only a week till the holidays, you can wait that long. Anyway, Daisy and I will be busy ourselves—Daisy's going to have lessons with me all week.'

Eddie muttered what sounded like half-hearted grumbling under his breath, shoved in a mouthful of porridge, and abruptly looked brighter. 'Hey, Daisy, we're going to take you to a play!' he said as soon as the porridge had gone down.

'Well, we haven't quite decided about that,' Granny said. 'Sarah, there's still only the one on while Daisy's here, isn't there?'

Aunt Sarah had a newspaper beside her plate, so neatly folded that it almost looked as if it had been ironed. She opened it and turned to the entertainments. 'Yes, only that French play. I must say it seems to be getting good reviews.'

'Yes, I know, but… well, it sounds a bit grown-up for Daisy. For Eddie, too, come to that. Do you really think you'd like to go to a play, Daisy?'

'Of course she would,' Eddie said.

Daisy did indeed want it very much, and not just because Benjy had all but begged her to make sure she saw one while she was in Auckland. She did her best to look grown-up and thoughtful as she answered. 'Yes, please, Granny. I think I'd like it a lot.'

Granny smiled at her serious expression. 'Well, we'll see.'

'That means we're going,' Eddie told Daisy, full of confidence.

'But we might decide not to take *you*, Eddie,' Aunt Sarah said, her eyes twinkling. Eddie's answering grin made it clear that he knew he was in no real danger of being left at home.

After breakfast Eddie went off to school, and Daisy went with Granny upstairs to the little schoolroom. She had had only a brief glimpse of this room the previous day; on closer inspection it was revealed to be light and airy, with walls painted a cheerful shade of pale yellow. A vase with branches of flowering daphne stood on a shelf near one of the windows, and the room smelled pleasantly fresh. It was all quite unlike the schoolroom in the valley, which was dark and dusty and inclined to smell of boys.

The two small girls who were Granny's current pupils were, she told Daisy, a child of almost five and her little sister, who was barely three. Granny did not usually take children quite as young as three, but the little girl had apparently made such a fuss at being deprived of her big sister that she had been permitted to come with her, on condition that she behaved herself.

While they waited for the little girls, Daisy settled in at the low table in a chair much more comfortable than the bench she shared with Benjy at school. She had wondered if Granny might suddenly become strict when she was being a teacher, but there was no such uncomfortable transformation. Not a strap was to be seen in the schoolroom, and the ruler seemed intended only for ruling lines.

Daisy had brought to Auckland the reader she was currently using at school. Granny studied the first few pages, then checked the cover more closely.

'This is the reader for Standard Three, Daisy. Are you up to this already?'

'It's just because I'm the only one in Standard Two,' Daisy said. 'And I did some of the Standard Two work last year, so Miss Cameron said I could be on the same reader as Benjy.'

'I'm glad you're so keen on reading. Would you like to use this, or would you rather have a change while you're here?'

Daisy admitted that the reader, with its stories that were all much the same in their stuffy correctness, was somewhat boring, and leapt at Granny's suggestion that she instead bring to class one of the books Eddie had lent her. She fetched one she had made a start on the previous evening; it was about a boy called Peter Pan, and was much more fun than her school reader.

'Yes, that's just the thing,' Granny said. Daisy's reading lesson was to read a chapter, then show her comprehension of it by summing up its events; Granny also made a spelling list for her from some of the more challenging words.

Daisy read aloud from the chapter until the little girls arrived and for a time took up all her grandmother's attention. The three-year-old was settled on a rug with some wooden blocks, while her older sister was set to practising her alphabet and other simple lessons. A little later, with both small girls busy drawing pictures, Granny could spend more time with Daisy, going over some arithmetic rules then setting her problems to work out.

Daisy's writing lesson consisted of a letter to her parents, and she found no difficulty filling a whole page of notepaper with an account of all that she had seen and done already. They would post the letter that very day, Granny said; the little girls only came for lessons in the mornings, and mornings would be sufficient for Daisy's work, too. 'We'll just enjoy ourselves in the afternoons.'

Late in the morning the small girls were collected by their nursemaid. Daisy finished off her grammar exercises, then Granny said they had time for a walk before lunch. The glorious dolls' pram could now be tried out. They put on their warm coats, but did not bother getting changed, since they were going no further than the park a short distance from Aunt Sarah's house.

Albert Park had often been part of Eddie's accounts of his life in Auckland. Daisy recognised the impressive fountain near the gates and the statue of Queen Victoria, but she was more interested in the other statue that Granny led her to.

'It's Eddie's father,' Daisy said, gazing up at the image of a young soldier of the Boer War. One foot rested on a broken gun, and he held a sword in his hand.

'Well, not really. But Eddie's father would have had a uniform just like that. I never saw him in it, that was after he went away, but I remember how excited he was about it all. So young he was.'

Daisy took one hand off the pram and slipped it into Granny's. They stood before the statue in silence for a few moments, then Granny smiled down at Daisy and gave her hand a squeeze.

They walked around the paths that snaked through the park, Daisy comfortably certain that anyone they saw must be admiring the dolls' pram. Then they sat on a bench near the fountain, making the most of the thin sunlight. A knot of men in uniform walked past; flesh-and-blood soldiers this time. Daisy saw Granny's eyes following them. 'Far too young,' Granny murmured. She shivered a little, as if the sun had lost its power to warm her, and soon afterwards she and Daisy went back to the house to have lunch with Aunt Sarah.

'We must get your letter posted,' Granny said after the meal. 'And Sarah, I think I'll take Daisy shopping. Do you want to come?'

Aunt Sarah had papers to go over in her study, so excused herself from the outing. Granny and Daisy went upstairs to get changed. Daisy put on her Sunday best frock, as it seemed the only one she had that was smart enough for the streets of Auckland. She came back into her grandmother's room to find Granny doing up the buttons of a walking costume in dark blue wool.

The wardrobe door was open, and Daisy saw a swirl of fabrics, some in jewel-like colours and others in darker tones. Granny noticed her intent gaze.

'Aren't they lovely? I'm very spoiled, Aunt Sarah's always wanting me to have new dresses. Go on, have a look at them if you like.'

Daisy carefully pushed several of the dresses along the wardrobe rail, admiring each garment in turn, until she came to something so soft and inviting to her questing fingers that she could not resist pressing her face against it.

'That's fur,' Granny told her. 'Aunt Sarah gave me that coat for my birthday one year. I sometimes wear it when we go out in the evening— only to quite grand things, though.'

Many of the dresses, Daisy thought, must also be kept for grand things. Only the simplest of them had ever made an appearance during her grandmother's visits to Ruatane; the fur had never even been spoken of.

The dolls' pram was left safely at home when they set off; the dainty thing might be damaged in the busy main street, Granny said.

Unlike the little town of Ruatane, which was built on a river flat, Auckland seemed all hills. They walked down a fairly steep path towards Queen Street; when they came to a red pillar box, Daisy dropped her letter into its slot, and imagined the letter retracing her own journey all the way to the farm.

They turned a corner, and suddenly the broad street was before them. The footpath was crowded with people, some bustling about on errands and others ambling along as if with no particular destination. Daisy saw more soldiers, generally in groups of three or four, all of them cheerful-looking young men.

The road was as busy as the footpath, and a good deal noisier, with buggies and carts of all sizes as well as a few motor cars.

'See the tracks down the middle of the road?' Granny said, guiding Daisy's notice. 'That's for the trams. Look, there's one coming along now.' She pointed out an enormous carriage sidling up Queen Street.

She promised to take Daisy for a tram ride one afternoon. 'Not today, though. We'd better get on—we'll want to be back before Eddie's home from school.'

As Grandpa had said, Auckland truly did have more shops than Tauranga. Some were disappointingly commonplace affairs like barbers and tobacconists, but many rewarded a second glance. The first one they entered was a bookshop, a place that held even more books than Aunt Sarah's library. Daisy sat at a low table and looked through a picture book while Granny discussed a new book with the man behind the counter; so new that it was not yet in the shop, though the man told Granny he had it on order.

They walked further along the street, Granny patiently waiting whenever something in a window caught Daisy's attention, and taking her right inside a jeweller's shop so that she could peep at trays of rings and bracelets, necklaces and watches.

'We don't need to try and see all the shops today,' Granny said when they were back on the street. 'Is there anything you'd specially like to look at?'

Daisy's mother had stressed to her that she must be sure to thank Aunt Sarah for having her to stay, but just saying thank you did not seem quite enough.

'I'd like to buy a present for Aunt Sarah,' she said. 'I've got some money—Mama gave me some out of what she got for fixing people's cows and things.' The money was in a small leather purse tucked safely in Daisy's pocket; the princely sum of three shillings and eightpence, though she privately hoped she would not have to spend the whole amount on this gift. 'She said I could spend it on anything I want. I don't know what I could get Aunt Sarah, though.'

'That's a lovely idea, Daisy. And I know just the thing.'

Granny led Daisy along the road, then held her hand tightly as they crossed the street. A few more steps and they were in a store that seemed as enormous as a dozen barns joined together. Daisy looked around in awe.

'This is Milne and Choyce,' Granny said. 'They have everything here. Stay close to me, darling, it can be a bit confusing at first.'

Daisy did not need the warning. She felt that if she lost her way in this cavernous space she might never be seen again. Her grandmother guided her deftly through what seemed a maze of counters and displays, seeming quite at home as they made their way towards the back of the store.

'Aunt Sarah could do with a nice handkerchief,' Granny said. 'A pretty one with lace. And you can stitch her initials on it, so it'll be special for her. That can be your needlework lesson while we're doing school in the mornings.'

They were shown a range of crisp white handkerchiefs, and Daisy chose one with lace set into one corner. It only cost sixpence, and Granny said she had plenty of embroidery silks at home, so there was no need for Daisy to buy any.

'Now, let's see what else we can find to look at,' Granny said when the wrapped handkerchief had been stowed in a bag she carried. She led

Daisy to another part of the store.

Daisy saw clothes on display all around her. And not just any sort of clothes. 'Are all these for girls?'

'Yes, they are. I'd like to buy you a few things while you're here to try them on. You're growing so fast these days, it's hard to know if I'm getting the right size. Anyway,' Granny added, smiling at Daisy, 'it's nice to able to take you shopping.'

The first thing they looked for was a new coat for Daisy, in place of the one she had all but outgrown. There were all manner of warm coats, but Granny picked out one in a dark green wool that Daisy loved at once. A hat went with it, a cosy Tam o'Shanter bonnet that covered the tops of her ears. The finishing touch was a sealskin muff; a thing of wonder to Daisy, who had never encountered sealskin before. She tilted it this way and that in the light; a pattern flowed through the short fur like waves running up a beach. She rubbed it against her cheek, and found it was smooth and slippery in one direction, a little tickly when stroked against the grain.

Granny persuaded her to lay aside the muff and look at the dress chosen for her, one to be worn for best: blue velvet, soft to the touch when Daisy stroked it, with a smocked bodice and full skirt. Daisy twirled in front of the long mirror, the shyness she had at first felt in front of the lady shop assistant now completely evaporated.

Daisy's sturdy shoes, bought new for her in Ruatane just a few weeks before, would see her through the winter, but Granny felt she needed something rather different. She took Daisy through to a part of the store that had nothing but shoes, and chose for her a dainty pair so light and soft that they felt more like slippers. The soles were of leather, but the uppers were black satin, with decorative stitching done in a silvery thread. Daisy thought she would hardly dare wear the shoes for fear of ruining them, but Granny told her that such shoes were not meant to be worn outside.

'Only for going a few steps to and from the carriage, anyway. They'll go nicely with your new dress.'

Their purchases were tied into neat parcels, and the helpful lady asked if they wanted them delivered, to arrive at Aunt Sarah's the following morning. Granny seemed about to say yes, then she saw Daisy's expression.

'Perhaps we could take one or two things with us, so my granddaughter can have them right away. Which ones, Daisy?'

It was an easy decision. Daisy pointed to the parcels containing the muff and the shoes. Granny offered to carry one, but Daisy said she could manage both.

'Goodness, we've been a long time here,' Granny said, checking her watch as they made their way towards the front of the store. 'Let's go straight home now.'

Aunt Sarah admired Daisy's new shoes and the sealskin muff, and when Eddie erupted into the house on his return from school they were admired again, though more briefly.

As soon as he had fortified himself with milk and biscuits, Eddie was eager to take Daisy for a ride in the park. The two of them went out to the stable, and Daisy helped Eddie and Walter saddle up Baron. Walter's father, Mr Jenson, was there, leaning on a walking stick and smiling benignly on the scene as he issued instructions to his son. He had lumbago, Eddie had told Daisy the previous evening, and while he was still in charge of seeing that the horses, carriage and garden were kept in good order, it was Walter who now did all of the heavy work. They both seemed quite happy with this arrangement.

Albert Park was not large enough to take the horse beyond a walking pace, and with the short daylight hours of May there was no question of going further afield, but Daisy was content just to be tucked behind Eddie, her arms around his waist, talking over the events of the day while he guided Baron around the paths that wound between the trees. She told him all about the wonderful day she had had; even her school lessons had been more like playing than working.

'You're lucky, having them with Granny,' Eddie grumbled. 'Miss Hudson keeps doing just about the same stuff every day. She reckoned I was showing off when I said I'd finished the reader already. And last week she said spiders are insects,' he said, outrage in his voice. 'I told her they aren't—insects have six legs—and she said they are, and when I kept saying they aren't she said I was a know-all. I got the strap for it. But I was right,' he finished grimly.

Daisy stored away the information regarding insect legs for future use, and expressed sympathy at the injustice Eddie had suffered. But Eddie's was not a brooding nature, and he soon moved on to the more cheerful topic of his upcoming rugby match. There was one more practice, he told Daisy, and then the game itself on the following Saturday.

'The other team's supposed to be really good,' he said. 'Especially their winger—people reckon he's as fast as a high school boy. I hope I can keep up with him.'

Eddie made it sound like a joke, but Daisy heard a trace of doubt in his voice. She pressed her cheek against his back. 'You'll be the best of them all,' she told him. It was not flattery; just her quiet conviction that no one could be better than Eddie. It was simply how the world worked. Eddie made no answer, but she felt him sit up a little straighter.

Chapter Seven

Sunday had been free of any needlework, but Daisy's second evening brought familiar tasks. After dinner she took her knitting bag and joined the others in the drawing room, where Granny and Aunt Sarah sat with nondescript grey tubes of wool dangling from clacking needles.

The only one free of any obligation to knit was Eddie, who was ensconced with the day's newspaper, occasionally reading snippets to the others. While Daisy settled herself on the sofa, Eddie read aloud an article about a boat called the *Lusitania*. Just a few weeks earlier, the huge boat had been sunk by a German submarine, and more than a thousand people had died. With her own recent sea-going experience, Daisy thought she could imagine a little of what it must have felt like to be trapped on a ship that was slowly sinking into cold, dark water.

The story of the *Lusitania* told, with Eddie faithfully reproducing all the outrage of the text, he flicked through the rest of the paper. There were other articles he considered worth reading aloud, all of which said things like 'The German offensive has reached a desperate phase', 'The British Line is stronger than ever', or 'The Enemy Sustains a Reverse'. In August the war would have been going a whole year, but it did sound as if it would not last much longer. Daisy wondered if all the soldiers she had seen in Auckland would even need to go overseas.

But in the meantime, there were socks to be knitted. Daisy worked away, the task more pleasant when Eddie, at Granny's suggestion, laid aside the newspaper and began reading to them from a book called *Treasure Island*, full of pirates and sea voyages and, of course, hunting for treasure. Eddie read well, his voice clear and with a wide range of expression; he even made a fair attempt at using different voices for the various characters. The sock dangling from Daisy's needles grew at a satisfying rate.

She reached the stage of turning the heel, and touched Granny's elbow to get her attention. 'Please can you do this part for me?' Daisy asked, keeping her voice low so as not to distract Eddie from his reading.

'In a moment, darling,' her grandmother answered as quietly. 'I'm just helping Aunt Sarah with hers.'

Daisy stared in astonishment, and saw that it was true: Aunt Sarah was as unskilled at the increasing and decreasing of stitches as Daisy was herself. It was the first intimation Daisy had ever had of there being anything beyond Aunt Sarah's capabilities.

Belatedly she remembered her manners and looked away, but her aunt did not appear embarrassed by her lack of skill. Although she certainly did not seem to enjoy the task overmuch. Covert glances at Aunt Sarah when Granny had returned the knitting showed occasional grimaces, and an irritable tugging at the yarn coupled with a hasty looping of stitches. In the most recent rows the tension was so uneven that Daisy would have been scolded for it at school.

After a time Aunt Sarah's knitting slowed, then came to a halt. 'I suppose...' she said, choosing a moment when Eddie had paused for breath after a particularly exciting section in his reading, 'I suppose it matters if a stitch has been dropped. But what does one do about it?' She held up her knitting; the dropped stitch was several rows down, and threatening to travel further still.

'Yes, it'll turn into a big hole if it's left like that,' said Granny. 'It's easily fixed, though—here, I'll take it.'

'Oh, that's a relief,' Aunt Sarah said. 'It would be dreadful to think I'd made some poor fellow in the trenches fall ill for want of a stitch on my part.'

Granny knew the trick of using a crochet hook to pick up a dropped stitch that Daisy had seen her mother use, and the stitch was quickly recaptured. Aunt Sarah, however, did not seem eager to take her knitting back.

'Eddie, I'm sure you'd like a rest from reading to us,' she said, rising from her seat and crossing to the piano. 'I'll give you all the dubious pleasure of hearing me play.'

Aunt Sarah chose pretty, lively pieces that seemed to help the wool dance under Daisy's fingers. Some of them were familiar; Daisy often heard Benjy or his sister Kate play the piano at Grandpa's.

'That's lovely, Sarah,' Granny said when Aunt Sarah paused between pieces. 'I always like hearing you play.'

'I'll accept that my playing is better than my knitting, but that's hardly high praise. I rather think my skills may lie in encouraging others—and in buying the wool.' She took up another piece of music, and as soon as she was safely engrossed in it Daisy saw her grandmother pick up Aunt Sarah's knitting and begin unravelling the last few rows.

The days fell into a pleasant routine of lessons in the mornings and outings in the afternoons. Much of each evening continued to be devoted to knitting, although Aunt Sarah did not touch hers again for the remainder of Daisy's visit.

'My conscience is quite at ease while you're here, Daisy,' Aunt Sarah said on Tuesday evening. 'As long as there are two ladies at work on those never-ending socks, I feel perfectly at liberty to spend my time in other ways.'

Aunt Sarah had a way of saying things with serious words that were funny underneath. She was, in fact, a good deal more fun than Daisy had ever quite realised. Daisy had always been somewhat in awe of her aunt, with her imposing demeanour and the steady gaze that always made Daisy wonder if she had misbehaved in some way. Now she had grown more aware of the twinkle that was often to be found in those piercing blue eyes.

Her aunt played a few pieces on the piano for them every evening, but she spent much of the time after dinner sitting at a little table in the drawing room writing letters. It was something to do with the war; 'Fund-raising for the war effort,' Daisy was told when she asked her grandmother.

'My knitting might be considered more of a hindrance to the cause,' Aunt Sarah remarked. 'I hope I can make myself more useful this way.'

Daisy spent part of each morning on the gift for her aunt. Granny helped her work out just how she should place Aunt Sarah's initials on the handkerchief, and supervised her first few stitches. Daisy's sewing had greatly improved over recent months; her early attempts had resulted in many pricked fingers and occasionally in a ruined piece of cloth. But Granny praised her neat stitching, and every day saw a satisfactory amount of progress. Daisy had been taken aback to learn that Aunt Sarah had four initials, but her grandmother had reassured her that she would do a share herself if it looked as if Daisy might run out of time.

Every afternoon Daisy and her grandmother went for a walk together; at the very least to the park, and farther afield if the weather was pleasant. Wednesday afternoon was particularly sunny, and they made the most of it by taking a long walk, setting off in a different direction from the path that led to the downtown area.

They took a meandering route, first going uphill almost as far as the large windmill atop a ridge on the outskirts of town, then circling back towards home. After wandering past so many houses, some as grand as Aunt Sarah's, others far more modest, that Daisy was beginning to feel she had seen enough of them for one day, they came to a long, low building with a tower at its centre.

'This is the Grammar School,' Granny said. 'It's a high school for boys. I was so pleased when we decided we'd send Eddie here when he finishes primary school—we were tossing up between this one and

King's College, everyone says they're both very good, but this one's close enough for Eddie to walk. But now the school's moving away.'

'The whole school?' Daisy asked, wondering how many wagons would be needed to carry all those classrooms. 'It looks very heavy.'

Granny saw her expression and smiled. 'Not the rooms, darling, they'll leave those here. They're going to use them for the university. No, they're building a new school up near Mount Eden.' She pointed towards the tallest hill Daisy had seen in Auckland. 'It'll be very nice, I'm sure—all smart new buildings, and big grounds for sports, not cramped like it is here. Eddie'll have to go on the tram, though.' Daisy was glad to have been on a tram ride the length of Queen Street with her grandmother the day before, so that she could picture Eddie travelling the same way.

They had been out walking so long that it was almost time for Eddie to get out of school for the day, and they were close enough to his primary school that Granny said they might as well go to meet him.

The primary school was several times the size of Daisy's, although small by Auckland standards. 'I wish the new Grammar School was a bit closer,' Granny said as they stood waiting by the school gates, 'but I'm glad he'll be starting high school next year. He's been getting a bit sick of school these last few months—he's outgrown it, really. I think he'll enjoy it more at the big school, with all the new things to learn.'

A bell rang, and soon afterwards children emerged from several doors. Eddie was easily spotted, not only because of his bright hair but also because he was the tallest child in sight. He walked along looking down at the ground, frowning a little and appearing lost in thought. He looked up and saw Daisy and their grandmother, and his face broke into a broad grin. He crossed to the gate at a loping run, then the three of them set off for home, Eddie reducing his pace to theirs and demanding the details of what they had done that day.

Aunt Sarah was often busy during the daytime, working at papers in her study or out at meetings, and it was Thursday before she joined Daisy and Granny on an outing. Daisy had a second letter to her parents ready for posting. Granny took her into the study to get a stamp; her aunt opened the drawer where she kept them, and found only three were left.

'And I've a mountain of my own letters to be sent,' she said, indicating the pile on one side of her desk. 'I could do with some fresh air—shall we make an expedition to the Post Office?'

The Post Office was a grand building down at the bottom of Queen

Street, near the waterfront. Daisy gazed at the row of arches along the front of the building, and at the tall windows edged with columns on the level above. Each end of the building had a squat domed tower.

With her grandmother and aunt, she climbed a flight of steps that led through the central arches into the building. Daisy tilted her head to study the large glass dome in the ceiling, with its white and coloured panes.

They went over to a long counter with a row of tellers behind it. Aunt Sarah bought a whole sheet of stamps, and Daisy helped put them on all the letters they had brought, including her own.

With the letters safely despatched, the three of them headed back up the street. Daisy was aware of several people turning to look as they passed, and occasionally she heard someone murmur, 'That's Sarah Millish.' She felt just a little important herself in being out and about with her aunt.

They were in no particular hurry; Eddie had rugby practice after school, so would not be home till close to dinner time. They ambled along, glancing in a few shop windows, and when they passed a tearoom Aunt Sarah suggested they go there for afternoon tea.

It was a very smart tearoom, with dark wood panelling and deep red velvet seats. Daisy sipped her hot cocoa, trying to hold her cup as daintily as the grown-ups did their cups of tea. The tearoom was cosy; the fancy biscuits they shared were delicious. And just as Daisy was thinking the afternoon could not possibly be any nicer, Granny made it so.

'It's Friday tomorrow,' she said. 'That's the last day of school—Eddie'll be home every day after that.'

On Friday afternoon, Eddie arrived home from school so breathless that it was clear he had run most of the way. The holidays had begun.

The next afternoon was to bring his much-anticipated rugby match. It rained on Friday evening, and Eddie cast many an anxious glance through the drapes, but Saturday dawned clear and calm.

Lunch was served earlier than usual, and soon afterwards they set off in the carriage, giving themselves ample time before the game to take a detour past the new site of the Grammar School. Eddie pointed out to Daisy the buildings in various stages of construction, and where he guessed the sports fields would be. The site was fifteen acres, he told her. The school had a magnificent setting, with a view over the city and a large swathe of the harbour. It was easy to see why Eddie so looked forward to going there.

They left the Grammar School behind, and travelled on to the school where the rugby match was to be held. Daisy ran through in her head all she could recall of Eddie's descriptions of how rugby worked, hoping she could keep it all straight; she could hardly bear to think she might miss anything important that Eddie did in the game.

Eddie went off to join his team, the family's well-wishes called after him. Walter retrieved three canvas stools from the carriage and set them up for Granny, Aunt Sarah and Daisy; he made do with an oilskin spread on the ground for his own seating.

Daisy was soon glad of Walter's presence. Aunt Sarah and Granny did their best to explain what was happening in the game, but Walter's explanations made a good deal more sense. She was also glad the teams were wearing jerseys of different colours, so that she could tell who was on each side, although it grew increasingly difficult to identify particular players as the game went on. The previous evening's rain had left the ground soft, and the boys were churning it into a sticky mud that adhered to every part of them. Even Eddie's red hair was less conspicuous than usual.

There were bursts of running back and forth, accompanied by much pushing and shoving, interspersed with periods of standing about. Daisy was sure Eddie was a faster runner than any of the others, and he seemed able to find a way through knots of other boys that left at least one of his opponents sprawled on the ground. Every time she saw him with the ball Daisy squealed in delight; the first time it happened she felt a flush of embarrassment, but as the game wore on other people were shouting just as enthusiastically. Even Granny called out her encouragement, although her soft voice would not have been heard by anyone more than a foot or two away.

The teams seemed well-matched, and the score stayed close through much of the game. Daisy sensed the growing excitement of the people around her as the match entered its final minutes. Eddie's team was behind, but only by a few points, and when she saw him emerge with the ball from a scrum, as Walter told her it was called, Daisy rose to her feet and screamed his name.

The ball firmly tucked under one arm, Eddie pounded down the field, seemingly impervious to attack. He flung himself onto the ground at the goal line, arms outstretched as he planted the ball.

'Eddie, Eddie!' Daisy screamed more loudly than ever, and perhaps he heard her, even through the cheers from all around; he certainly turned in her direction, grinning through the mud that coated his face.

The final, and winning, points of the match were scored soon afterwards by a boy from Eddie's team who kicked the ball between the two tall goalposts. The spectators cheered, but for Daisy it was almost an anticlimax after watching Eddie's triumph. She clapped and cheered with the others as a man gave a silver cup to Eddie's team, which the boys passed among themselves for a few minutes before their coach claimed it for safe-keeping, then at last Eddie ran over to them.

Daisy had never seen anyone so thick with mud. Even Eddie's hair was caked with it, reduced to red-brown spikes poking through grey slop. His broad grin was a split in the mud covering his face, but his eyes glowed.

'We won! Did you see that try I scored?'

'You were so good!' Daisy's voice was hoarse from all the shouting she had done. 'You were the best one of all.' Only her shyness of the crowd, mingled with a realisation of just how thick the mud was on his face, prevented her from kissing him.

Aunt Sarah and Granny added their congratulations, and Walter pumped Eddie's hand vigorously.

'We'd better go home before it gets any colder,' Granny said, glancing at the sky, which was now steel-grey. 'Eddie, make sure you have a good wash,' she called as Eddie headed off towards the changing sheds.

Eddie returned a few minutes later in his ordinary clothes and with his rugby clothes spilling from a canvas bag; he claimed that he had indeed had a good wash, but he was deemed unfit for the interior of the carriage. His spirits were not dampened when he was banished to the driving-box. He spent much of the ride home twisting round to talk to Daisy, then back again to go over details of the game with Walter.

Alice, the older of the two maids, was in the hall to greet them, and to hear the news of Eddie's game; when Granny could get a word in, she asked Alice to run a bath for Eddie, and he was soon sent upstairs to make use of it.

'You can have yours after dinner,' Granny told Daisy. It would be her third since she had arrived in Auckland, and she had only been there a week!

Dinner had something of a celebratory feel about it, with two kinds of pudding and a chocolate cake to follow. The children were told they could sit up later than usual in honour of the occasion, as they could all sleep in the next morning. There was no school, of course, and they were to go to Evensong rather than a morning service.

Eddie could talk of nothing but the game all through dinner; fortunately he had a tolerant audience. One of his team mates had told him the coach of a Grammar School team had been there. Another had claimed he saw an All Black, although Eddie admitted that was unlikely, as most of them had joined the army by now. But the day had been a triumph; of that he was sure, and no one showed any desire to contradict him.

Daisy had her promised bath soon after dinner, and afterwards Granny brought her downstairs in her nightdress and dressing-gown. She sat on one of the sofas between Eddie and Granny, Granny brushing then plaiting her hair while Eddie read to them. The room was warm, the sofa was deep and soft, and Eddie smelt of the same soap as Daisy herself did. This, she thought, had been the best day yet.

Daisy woke next morning to a silent house, and knew at once that it was too early to get up. She was quite certain Eddie was not yet awake; no matter how distant a part of the house he was in, Eddie always contrived to make his presence known.

She tried lying very still and keeping her eyes shut, hoping to fall asleep again, but it was no use; she was wide awake. She sat up as quietly as she could and looked through the curtains to see a glimpse of pale sky, still with a hint of pink dawn, then lay down again. The bed creaked a little.

'Daisy?' She looked up and saw her grandmother standing in the doorway. 'Are you awake already, darling? It's very early.'

'Sorry, Granny, I didn't mean to wake you up.'

'Don't worry, I wasn't asleep. Come on,' Granny said, holding out her arms in invitation. 'Come and have a cuddle with me.'

They both climbed into the big bed. Her grandmother's nightdress had a faint scent of lavender about it, and her hair was twisted into a thick rope that hung over one shoulder, tickling Daisy's cheek. 'Do you know, I've lived in Auckland for seven years now, but I still wake up too early as often as not,' Granny said. 'I can't seem to get out of the way of it, not after all those years on the farm.'

Once while Granny had been staying with them, Daisy had asked her why she had left the farm and come to live in Auckland, taking Eddie with her. Granny had explained that Aunt Sarah had been living in her big house all by herself and needed someone to keep her company. Daisy had always had a secret hope that Granny might decide to come back to the farm with Eddie; now that she had seen things for herself, she knew there was no chance of it. Especially not with the smart new school Eddie would be going to.

If only there was a way for her mother and father to come and live here, too, it would all be perfect. But then there would be no one to look after the farm; in any case, Daisy was quite sure that her parents would not want to leave the valley. Things could never be perfect; not when there could never be a place where Eddie and her parents could all be equally happy.

'What a big sigh,' Granny said, breaking into her reverie. 'Are you all right, Daisy?'

'Yes,' Daisy said, and sighed again. It did not seem worth worrying Granny by trying to explain it all.

Granny squeezed her more closely. 'We've got a surprise for you today,' she whispered in Daisy's ear.

Daisy's pensive mood was gone in a moment. 'What? What is it?'

'You'll find out soon enough. After breakfast, anyway.'

'Eddie didn't say anything about a surprise,' Daisy said, on the verge of indignation.

'That's because he doesn't know about it. We wanted it to *stay* a surprise.' Daisy heard the smile in her grandmother's voice.

A few minutes after breakfast, Daisy stood staring open-mouthed at the surprise, which took the form of a chestnut pony, specially hired for her and at her disposal for the remainder of her stay.

'She's *lovely*,' Daisy breathed, stroking the pony's neck. The pony, Granny had told her, was called Star, in honour of the white blaze on its forehead.

Eddie had quickly moved from outrage at being left out of the plot to admiration of the pony. 'Can we take her and Baron down to Albert Park?' he asked.

'We thought we might go a little further and make an expedition of it,' said Aunt Sarah. 'Mrs Jenson's made up a picnic basket, and we're all going to the Domain.'

The carriage was loaded with rugs and warm coats, while a huge picnic hamper took up most of one seat. Mr Jenson drove Granny and Aunt Sarah, Mrs Jenson having claimed Walter's attendance with her at church that morning, while the two children walked their mounts just behind.

The Domain was a substantial park, far bigger than Albert Park, with tree-lined avenues and broad areas of open grass. Daisy and Eddie dismounted to help unload the carriage and to spread rugs for Granny and Aunt Sarah in a sheltered grove of trees. Mr Jenson found a quiet spot where the carriage horses could graze and he could settle in comfortably with his pipe and a newspaper.

They mounted again, and Daisy had the chance to try out Star's paces.

The pony was a delight to ride, with a smooth gait and a soft mouth, responsive to the slightest suggestion from her rider. Daisy trotted her up and down an open area, then nudged her into a canter that was as comfortable as sitting in a rocking-chair.

Eddie kept Baron's pace to Star's, the long-legged horse moving effortlessly. They cantered right around the grassy clearing, up and down its slopes. Daisy felt the wind in her face, making her hair fly out behind her head. She looked over at Eddie, who grinned back at her, and without a word being spoken she was sure that he was thinking exactly the same thing as she was: *this* was the best day yet.

Daisy and Eddie rode in the Domain every fine morning after that, Walter escorting them to and fro riding one of the carriage horses. In the afternoons they read or played with the soldiers, or walked in the garden when one or both of them felt unable to sit still any longer. And on Tuesday evening came a visit to the theatre.

Wearing her blue velvet dress, her hair neatly brushed and held in check by a matching blue ribbon and the hair clips Eddie had given her, Daisy gazed in admiration at Aunt Sarah and Granny when they met on the landing. Granny was wearing blue, too; a darker shade than Daisy's, and in a heavy silk that caught the light as she moved. She had a necklace of blue stones that she said were called sapphires; they were just the colour of her eyes.

Aunt Sarah wore a dress that was a dark brownish-red; the same colour as old rusty tools, Daisy thought but did not say aloud, and was then startled when her aunt herself described the colour as 'rust'. But it looked pretty against Aunt Sarah's pale skin and dark hair, and her eyes that were the same colour as Granny's. Her necklace had green stones, and she wore a small gold brooch in the shape of a letter 'A' on her bodice. She admired Daisy's outfit, then disappeared to her room for a few moments.

She returned with a chain made of delicately twisted links of gold. 'I'll lend you this for tonight, Daisy, I think it'll set your outfit off nicely. I used to wear it when I was about your age, but it's rather too short for me now.'

Granny fastened the gold chain for Daisy. They descended the staircase, and Daisy saw her reflection in the hall mirror, her aunt and grandmother on either side. The three of them looked grand.

They joined Eddie, who had already gone out to the carriage. Daisy sat next to him, looking out at the darkened garden and occasionally slipping a hand out of the sealskin muff just for the pleasure of stroking it. It seemed an adventure just to be out so late; the play did not begin till eight o'clock at night, close to her bedtime at home.

The theatre was only a short ride away. She was soon being helped out of the carriage and led inside, careful to keep her new shoes out of any puddles.

Daisy stared around the crowded foyer. It was like looking at a room full of flowers, the ladies' dresses in all the colours she had ever seen, set off to best advantage by the dark suits the men wore. But when she looked back at *her* ladies, she was quite sure that Granny and Aunt Sarah were the finest looking of all. And of course Eddie, resplendent in his Sunday best suit, was the finest of the males.

Imitating the people she saw around her, Daisy slipped her arm through Eddie's as they walked up the stairs, and did her best to move in a graceful glide. She was aware that people were smiling at them; she smiled back, too excited to feel shy.

They had a small room to themselves, open towards the stage. Daisy peered over the edge and saw that most people were sitting in rows, looking far more squashed than her group. The room, Granny told her, was called a 'box'; that seemed too plain a name for something so comfortable.

The lights grew dim, the buzz of talking died away, and the curtains were drawn back. Daisy leaned forward eagerly, anxious not to miss a single word.

It was a confusing sort of story. People kept getting mistaken for each other, and there was a complicated part where a man pretended a very pretty lady was his wife, but then another man wanted her to go away with him. There was hiding in wardrobes, and in one scene the pretty lady was wearing what looked like a nightdress, although Daisy was sure it couldn't be. She laughed when everyone else did, though she was not always sure just why they were. It was easy enough to laugh when she was so very happy.

At one point, when there was a lot of standing about talking, Daisy remembered Benjy's plea for all she could find out about plays, and for the rest of the performance she took careful note of the painted scenery, the furniture that was moved about from scene to scene, and where the lights seemed to be shining from.

When the play ended, all the actors lined up at the front of the stage, bowing and smiling while the audience applauded. The tall red curtains drew closed, hiding the actors from view, the lights were turned up, and the theatre became once again a bright, noisy room in the middle of Auckland, far from the make-believe setting of France.

Granny took Daisy's hand and kept a firm hold as they made their way through the crowd and out onto the street. The night air was cold and bracing; it stung Daisy's cheeks, making her aware of how deliciously warm the rest of her was. She was bundled into the carriage, once again at Eddie's side.

'You've done very well, Daisy, staying awake so late,' Granny said. 'It must be eleven o'clock.' Eleven o'clock! Daisy had never sat up to such an hour before. She stared out of the carriage to see what eleven o'clock might look like; dark, she found, lit only by gleams from some of the houses. 'Did you enjoy the play, darling?'

'Yes, it was lovely,' said Daisy. 'Especially the dresses the pretty lady wore. And the bit when she had to keep hiding, that was good. Why were those men wearing big sashes, though? It looked funny.' She had, in fact, come close to laughing out loud at the first appearance of a rather rotund man with a wide sash diagonally across his chest.

'They do that in France, I think,' said Granny. 'I've seen pictures of their president dressed up like that.' By the faint gleam of the carriage lights, Daisy saw her grandmother lean forward. 'And what did you think it was about, Daisy?'

The light was too dim to see her grandmother's expression, but Daisy thought she sounded a little anxious. 'Um... it was to do with all those men liking the same lady, and one of them pretended they were married, but that important man thought she might like him anyway, and he got her and the other man to come and live at his place. I didn't really understand that bit,' she admitted.

She had been worried that this confession might make her grandmother think Daisy had, after all, been too young for the play, and should not have been taken to it, but Granny laughed softly.

'It *was* a bit confusing, wasn't it? Well, as long as you enjoyed it.'

'I liked it, too,' Eddie put in. 'That stuff about who the lady was married to didn't make any sense, though.'

'Quite right, Eddie,' said Aunt Sarah. 'None whatsoever. Fortunately plays don't have to make sense.'

Daisy felt so wide awake that she wondered if she would be able to sleep at all that night, but even in the short time it took to get back to the house drowsiness began creeping over her. The cold air that rushed at her face when she climbed down from the carriage revived her only briefly; the stairs to the upper floor seemed steeper than usual, and she was glad of Granny's arm around her waist and Eddie's hand holding her free one.

*

She woke the next morning unable to remember having been put to bed, and looked out her window to see a leaden curtain of rain. There would be no riding that morning.

Eddie gazed at the dining room window while he waited for the arrival of the toast. 'Still raining,' he said gloomily.

'Yes, it's really set in,' said Granny. She poured more coffee from the silver pot on the table. Daisy had never encountered this drink before coming to Auckland; she found the smell of it delicious, but when Granny gave her a sip one day she thought it bitter and nasty. Granny had told her she had taken a long time to get a taste for coffee after coming to live with Aunt Sarah; Daisy found it hard to imagine ever developing a liking for the drink herself. 'Daisy, why don't you write a letter home this morning? We can run out with it to catch the post if the rain goes off later, and Mama and Papa should get it by Friday. It won't be worth writing again after today—you and I will be in Ruatane with the next mail.'

Only three days till she was to leave. How could almost two whole weeks have slipped away so quickly? The thought of seeing her mother and father again was a warm glow inside Daisy; the knowledge that she would so soon be saying goodbye to Eddie and all the excitements of Auckland was like being splashed with cold water.

She wrote her letter after breakfast; it might have taken all the morning, she had so much to tell her parents, but she would see them again so soon that it did not seem worth writing pages and pages. She included a special message for Benjy about going to see a play; she knew that when she got home he would be eager for all the details she could give.

By the middle of the afternoon the rain had dwindled to a sullen drizzle, and Eddie was sent to run down to the post box, bundled up in his oilskin. Daisy handed over her letter and watched Eddie from the doorway. Sending that final letter home felt like the first step to leaving Auckland herself.

But it would be silly to spoil what time was left by moping. There was no going outside that day, but the next two mornings were fine enough to go riding again, although the soft ground meant the children and their mounts returned to the house thoroughly splashed with mud. Daisy helped groom the horses afterwards; it was the closest she had come to anything like work all week, but there was nothing remotely burdensome about restoring Star's coat to glossiness, aware as she wielded the brushes that Eddie was close by doing just the same with Baron. Walter was off doing something that involved horse dung and the compost heap, so she and Eddie shared the stable only with the horses. Their low murmurs and the horses' nickering mingled, and made it sound as if they were all talking much the same language.

'We can leave your packing till tonight, Daisy, there's not a lot of it,' Granny said over lunch on Friday. 'I asked Alice to check there's nothing of yours just ironed, she said if she found anything she'd put it in your room.'

Packing would mean leaving this place was another step closer, and Daisy was glad to have it put off for as long as possible.

After lunch she and Eddie played an ancient-looking board game that Aunt Sarah had produced, winning a game each. They were about to settle down to a deciding match when Granny remarked that she did not think Daisy was dressed warmly enough, and sent her upstairs to put a cardigan on.

Daisy found a neatly folded pile of clean clothes on her bed, with the dress she had worn riding that morning draped over the bed end. The maids had done wonders with the dress, brushing away all traces of mud and horse hairs.

Her purse was on the dressing table; Daisy opened it and saw a jumble of coins, copper pennies sprinkled with silver threepences and one or two sixpenny bits. She realised that she had not spent so much as a halfpenny since buying the handkerchief for her aunt; anything she might have bought for herself from her little hoard had been provided almost before she had had the chance to think she might want it. Well, after seeing all those ladies dressed in their finery at the theatre, she knew just how she wanted to use the money.

She replaced the purse, put on her cardigan and went back downstairs. Granny and Aunt Sarah were discussing something; Daisy waited for a pause in their conversation.

'Granny, could we go to the shops again?' she asked.

'This afternoon? Oh, I don't think so, Daisy.'

Daisy felt her mouth trembling, but she nodded and tried to smile.

Granny studied her expression. 'Well, I suppose I could…'

'But Amy, we're visiting Emily this afternoon,' Aunt Sarah put in. 'She's expecting us both, you know, and she's invited one or two other people as well.'

'Yes, you're right, Sarah, and I won't be able to see her again till I'm back from Ruatane. I'm sorry, Daisy, I'm going out with Aunt Sarah this afternoon.'

'That's all right, Granny, it doesn't matter.' If only she had thought of it earlier in the week!

'I'll take her,' said Eddie. 'I can take Daisy shopping.'

Daisy turned a beaming smile on him. Everything would be all right now that Eddie had taken charge.

'How very gallant of you, Eddie,' Aunt Sarah said. 'That should serve everyone's purposes nicely.'

Granny praised Eddie for being so thoughtful, and when he and Daisy were ready to set out she gave him sixpence to spend as he wished.

'But do be careful crossing the road, Eddie. It can be so busy of an afternoon.'

'I know how to cross the road!'

'Yes, but Daisy's not used to all the motor cars and everything. Keep hold of her hand—and don't let her out of your sight in the shops.'

Eddie assured Granny that he would do no such thing. The sixpence safely stowed in his pocket, he led Daisy out of the house.

'Where do you want to go shopping?' he asked as they walked down the hill towards Queen Street.

'That big shop that has everything—Milne and something? I want to get a present for Mama.'

'Milne and Choyce. Come on, then.'

Daisy quickened her stride, Eddie shortened his, and they were soon opposite the large store. Before they stepped off the footpath Eddie took her hand as he had been instructed; his was large and knuckly, and Daisy enjoyed the feeling of having her own engulfed in it.

'So which part of the shop are we going to?' Eddie asked when they were standing before the large doors. His face fell abruptly. 'You don't want to look at… you know… ladies' things for under their clothes, do you?' The last few words came out in a mumble.

'No, it's not an under sort of thing, it's like a scarf. But I don't know where they'd have them in here. I suppose they might be with ladies' underclothes.'

Eddie's jaw set in determined lines. 'All right, we'll ask.'

Just inside the store stood a man dressed in a smart uniform, whose job seemed to be sending people in the right direction. He had white hair and a rather grand manner.

'We want to get a scarf,' Eddie said with a boldness Daisy admired.

The man gave the impression that he might have liked to look down his nose at them, had Eddie not been very nearly as tall as he was. 'Boys' scarves?' he asked distantly.

'No, ladies' ones.'

'Fourth aisle on the left,' the man said, then turned away to greet other customers.

They made their way down the indicated aisle, and found themselves before a counter presided over by a lady in a black dress.

'What a good boy, to be taking your little sister shopping,' she said, beaming at Eddie. 'And how may I assist you two?'

'She's not my sister, she's my cousin,' said Eddie. 'We want a scarf for her mother.'

To Daisy's dismay, the lady lifted an armful of scarves down from a shelf and onto the counter. They were heavy woollen affairs; thoroughly sensible-looking and not at all what Daisy had in mind. She tugged at Eddie's sleeve and whispered urgently, 'Tell her I want a different sort. Fancy ones—you know, like some of the ladies were wearing at the play.'

She had not whispered quite as softly as she had thought. The lady paused in her task of spreading out the scarves. 'What's the matter, dear?'

'Sorry, Daisy, I didn't take any notice of that stuff. You tell her what you want. Go on, you can,' Eddie urged.

Daisy clutched more tightly at his sleeve, and took a deep breath. She was unused to speaking to strangers, but the lady had a kind smile. And this was her last chance to get something special for her mother. 'Sort of like a scarf, only lacy, and ladies wear them like this.' Daisy let go of Eddie's sleeve and drew her hands over her shoulders and down her chest to shape a triangle. 'They wear them with fancy clothes—I saw them at a play.'

'Oh, you mean a fichu. Certainly, dear.' The lady pushed the scarves to one side, ducked behind the counter and emerged with a bundle of soft white cloth. She spread it out carefully for inspection.

Daisy saw deep frills of frothy lace gathered onto a shiny fabric that she knew must be silk. Her fingers crept out to stroke the lovely thing.

'This one's seven and sixpence,' the lady said, and Daisy pulled back her fingers as if they had been burned.

'I haven't got that much,' she confessed, her heart sinking. She had thought three and twopence a fine amount; now her face grew hot at the thought that she was probably making a fool of herself and, even worse, of Eddie. She felt tears pricking at her eyes.

'Well, I'm sure I have one or two more moderately priced pieces,' the lady said. 'Would your mother like one in cotton, do you think?'

Daisy did not trust her voice, but she nodded, at the same time glancing around to determine the fastest way to escape. The new fichu presented for her notice had narrower bands of lace, and was of a fine cotton lawn with a pattern of pintucks; a good deal less grand than the silk one, it was still very pretty, and a garment that Daisy could more easily picture her mother wearing.

'I like this one,' she managed to murmur.

'And it's the most reasonably priced of all our fichus,' the lady announced brightly. 'Only five and sixpence.'

'How much have you got, Daisy?' Eddie asked.

Daisy stood on tiptoe to whisper the shameful truth in his ear. 'Three and twopence. Can we go now?'

Eddie frowned, and for a dreadful moment Daisy thought he was annoyed with her. But she soon realised that his brows were drawn together in thought rather than irritation. He pulled out the sixpence that their grandmother had given him, and placed it on the counter. His hand went deeper into his pocket; Daisy could see the movement of his fingers through the heavy serge fabric. His excavation produced a handkerchief that looked as if it had avoided washday for a while, as well as a handful of coins. The handkerchief disappeared back into his pocket, while the coins were piled alongside the sixpence.

Daisy added the contents of her purse and watched Eddie counting the total, murmuring the numbers under his breath.

'Four and ninepence… five shillings… two, three…'

He looked up from the task and met the lady's eyes. 'We've got five and fourpence, so we're twopence short. But I can pay you the rest next week when I get my pocket money. I'll give you an IOU for now.'

Eddie looked resolute; the lady looked startled, then Daisy saw her mouth twitch. 'Well, perhaps I could give you a small reduction, since this is last season's stock. Five and fourpence it is, then.'

Again Daisy had to fight back tears; this time from sheer relief. She rested her head against Eddie's arm for a moment, then watched as the fichu was folded, wrapped in tissue paper, and placed in a flat box tied with ribbon, producing a package that was to Daisy's eyes a work of art.

Safely across the busy road on their way back to the house, when Eddie made to let go of her hand Daisy grabbed at his and squeezed. 'Thanks for giving me your money, Eddie.'

Eddie grinned at her. 'Tell Aunt Beth it's from me as well. It's mostly from you, though.'

'It was a lot you gave me—nearly two shillings! Fancy having all that just in your pocket.'

'I wanted to have it handy. I've been keeping an eye out for an air rifle—Granny's not keen on me having one, but I've been saving up in case someone's got one cheap. A boy at school reckoned his brother might, but that was a load of rot.'

'And you even spent Granny's sixpence on it instead of getting lollies or something.'

'It doesn't matter,' said Eddie. 'There'll be plenty of biscuits at home.' Driven to new efforts by this cheerful thought, they quickened their steps.

Daisy showed her beautiful parcel to Granny and Aunt Sarah, and described the fichu as best she could.

'But I don't want to spoil the wrapping, so is it all right if I don't open it?' she asked.

They admired the parcel, but left it undisturbed. Aunt Sarah also told Daisy how fichu was spelled; quite differently from the way she had imagined.

After an excellent dinner of roast beef and vegetables, a chocolate pudding was served; rich and dark, and just a little gooey inside. They had had the same kind of pudding one evening during the first week of Daisy's stay, and she had found it so delicious that she ate two helpings and secretly hoped to be offered a third. It was being served tonight, Granny told her, specially in Daisy's honour.

'Because I told Mrs Jenson you like this one the best,' Eddie said, pausing from the task of doing justice to his own large bowlful.

It would be Daisy's last dinner in Auckland. The evening felt full of last things, and she did her best to store away all the details of her surroundings, to be brought forth from memory bright and fresh when she was back at home. The last sight of the dining table adorned with candlesticks and vases of flowers, and with the fine china and silverware that would be quietly whisked away by a maid as soon as they left the room. The last time watching Granny in the drawing room pouring tea for herself and Aunt Sarah from a beautiful silver teapot. The last time listening to Aunt Sarah playing the piano, occasionally muttering under her breath when a passage did not go well.

Daisy's knitting remained untouched; Granny had suggested she have a rest from it on this final evening. She sat in front of the fire with Eddie, curled up on the thick rug and tracing its pattern with a fingertip, unable to give full attention to the book in front of her. The rug was in rich shades of red and gold; another picture to be stored away, along with the memory of pressing her fingers deep into the pile.

She wished this evening could be longer than an ordinary one, but their sailing was to be early in the morning, which meant there was no chance of being allowed to sit up late. An hour after dinner Granny took her upstairs for a bath; this bathroom, Daisy reflected as she lay back in the tub watching the wisps of steam, would be one of the things she would miss most.

Granny helped her pack her little bag and set out the clothes she would wear in the morning. Still warm from the bath and cosy in her nightdress and dressing-gown, Daisy went downstairs with the gift for her aunt.

'Thank you for having me to stay, Aunt Sarah,' she said, holding out the handkerchief.

Her aunt praised Daisy's stitching, and said she would save the handkerchief for best.

'And it's been a pleasure having you, Daisy. I do hope you'll come again, if your parents can spare you.'

Daisy got goodnight kisses from Aunt Sarah and from Eddie, and was soon being tucked into bed by her grandmother. When she was alone in the room she looked around at the shadows on the walls, cast by the glow of the fire in Granny's room just through the doorway. The shadows changed shape with the flaring and dying of the fire, growing then shrinking. She would remember the comfortable dimness of this room; the way it never quite got dark, and the small noises that were always to be heard if she listened hard enough: an occasional carriage rumbling past; wind tugging at the bare stems of a climbing rose outside the window; Eddie thumping up the stairs, grumbling half-heartedly about being sent to bed so early.

It was well before sunrise when Daisy's grandmother woke her next morning. While she dressed, Granny packed away the last few things and set Daisy's case beside her own larger one.

The dining room was chilly when they went downstairs; the freshly lit fire in the grate had not yet done much to warm the room. They had toast and boiled eggs for breakfast; Granny had told Mrs Jenson there was no need to cook fish or anything heavier for them so early in the day. Eddie arrived at the table in time to help himself from the toast rack; Aunt Sarah appeared a little later, yawning behind her hand and insisting that she wanted nothing but tea.

The suitcases had been carried down and were in the hall near the front door when Daisy came out of the dining room. She went upstairs to get her hat and gloves, and came back down the staircase slowly; counting as she went so that she would be able to retrace the stairs in memory; feeling the smooth wood of the railing slide beneath her fingers.

Eddie was to come in the carriage with Daisy and their grandmother to see them off at the wharf; Aunt Sarah declared herself not fit for public display at such an hour. The maids and the cook assembled in the hallway. Daisy thanked them for looking after her, and found herself engulfed in a hug from Mrs Jenson. The maids all wanted to kiss her goodbye, and Mrs Jenson presented her with a squishy package wrapped in brown paper.

'In case you get hungry on the way. Just a few sandwiches and biscuits. And there's no need for you to go interfering with it, Master Eddie.' Mrs Jenson fixed Eddie with a narrow stare; his mouth was too occupied with the last of the toast for him to protest his innocence. 'Your breakfast will be ready and waiting for you when you get back. I've got a nice bit of smoked fish for you this morning,' she added, her face softening into its usual cheerful lines.

Granny stowed the package away in her bag, Walter emerged from the kitchen to carry their cases out to the carriage, and Daisy asked to be allowed to visit the stables to make the last of her farewells.

'Just for a minute, Daisy,' her grandmother said. 'We need to get on. Yes, Eddie, you can go with her.'

Daisy hurried through the grey pre-dawn gloom at Eddie's side, guided to the open stable doors by a hint of yellow light that proved to be a lantern hanging from a hook. Mr Jenson was there, leaning on the rail of Baron's stall. Daisy took the opportunity to thank him and say goodbye; Mr Jenson gave her a nod, and a smile that came out twisted around the stem of his pipe.

She and Eddie took two apples from the bag on the wall, and while Eddie took his to Baron, Daisy went over to Star's stall. For the last time she felt that soft mouth nuzzling at her hand; for the last time she gazed into those bright eyes. Star devoured the apple, then gave a questioning flick of her ears.

'No, no riding today,' Daisy murmured. 'Bye bye, Star. I hope you get hired again soon and go somewhere else nice.' She stroked the pony's neck one last time, then walked with Eddie back to the house.

Aunt Sarah waved to them from the verandah as the carriage pulled away. The wheels crunched over the gravel of the driveway, gaining the road with a bump.

The streets near Aunt Sarah's house were quiet at this hour of the day, but the wharves were already busy. Walter carried their cases down to the boat, then loped off back to the carriage, leaving Eddie to say his goodbyes.

Daisy could feel tears brimming, but she was determined not to embarrass Eddie by crying in front of strangers. She looked away for a moment and dashed her sleeve over her eyes, then was struck by a sudden inspiration. 'I could write you a letter when I get home.'

'All right,' said Eddie. 'I'll write to you as well.'

He gave her a quick peck of a kiss and allowed Granny to kiss him. The boat's hooter sounded; Granny took Daisy by the hand and led her on board.

Daisy stood by the rail, Granny's hand still firmly around hers, and watched Eddie growing smaller and smaller as the boat pulled away. They rounded a larger vessel that hid him from sight, and Daisy turned to face the open sea.

Chapter Eight

When the boat docked at Ruatane's wharf and the gangplank was run out, Daisy's father came on board, gathered her up as if she was a baby and carried her to shore, her grandmother walking ahead. Her mother was waiting, laughing at the sight of them and at the same time brushing away tears. Daisy's father lowered her to the ground, and she was enfolded in her mother's arms.

There was so much to tell them. Daisy sat on her father's lap, the three grown-ups squashed onto the seat of the gig, and they had passed right through the town and were bumping their way along the beach before she paused in her account of all she had seen and done in Auckland; paused because her voice was getting tired, not because she had run out of things to say.

Her mother stroked Daisy's hair. 'You've had quite an adventure, haven't you? I hope you're not going to miss all those plays and trams and things too much.' She smiled as she said it, as if not quite believing anyone could prefer the city to the farm. 'Didn't you get homesick?'

'I missed you and Papa.' Daisy took hold of her mother's hand and squeezed it. 'It was nice at Aunt Sarah's. But it's nice at home, too.'

Mama held out her arms, and Daisy wriggled across to her lap. It was a less comfortable fit than her father's, but that did not matter.

As soon as they were home, Daisy fetched the ribbon-tied package from her case and brought it out to the kitchen. 'I got you a present, Mama.'

Her mother opened the package and lifted out the fichu. 'Oh, it's beautiful! I didn't expect you to get me anything, Daisy—especially not a fancy thing like this. Did you really have enough money to buy this?'

'Eddie helped me. He had some he'd been saving up, and he gave it all to me. *And* he got the lady to take a little bit off the price so we had enough. But it was mostly from the money you gave me.'

Granny placed the fichu around Mama's shoulders, teasing out the frill to lie smoothly. 'Daisy thought of it all on her own—she didn't say a word to me about why she wanted to go to the shops. I had to go out that afternoon, but Eddie took her and she came back with this. She chose it herself.'

Her mother twisted her head this way and that to see the effect of the fichu. 'That was very nice of you and Eddie. I meant you to have that bit of money for yourself, though, Daisy. You helped wash the bottles for the tonic and things.'

'There wasn't anything to spend it on—I didn't need to buy lollies or anything. And Granny got me some lovely new clothes.'

So then of course the new clothes had to be brought out and admired, and Granny thanked several times over. Daisy almost thought her mother was more excited about Daisy's new things than her own. But Mama wore the fichu all that evening, and to church the following Sunday, where she told everyone who complimented her on the fichu that it was a gift from Daisy and Eddie; every time she said it, she would give Daisy an especially warm smile.

It was wonderful to see her mother and father again, but for a while after Daisy's return home everything seemed small and just a little shabby. She was careful not to speak of this to her parents; it would be dreadful to make them feel bad about not having such a nice house as Aunt Sarah's. She felt dull and out of sorts for a day or two; feelings she did her best to hide. Her mood was not helped by the weather, which had collapsed into winter. The skies were leaden; sheets of rain came down most days, driven by a biting wind; and the cows quickly churned each fresh paddock into mud.

Her mother said she must be tired after all the excitement of her trip, and seemed ready to put any unusual quietness down to that. And Daisy was soon too busy for moping. School started the day after she got home; for the first composition lesson, Daisy was allowed to write about her trip, and Miss Cameron put her report up on the wall; a rare honour. Benjy took up much of the first lunchtime pressing for details of the play; Daisy was only too glad to share everything she could remember of that wonderful evening.

The cows had been dried off for the winter, so there was only the house cow to be milked, which Daisy sometimes did before school if her mother was busy. On the weekends she helped with feeding out hay to the cattle, or moving them from one paddock to another, and there was always work to be done in the kitchen after school.

She wrote her first letter to Eddie a few days after getting back home. She told him about school and the farm and the animals, and how pleased her mother was with the fichu. Her letter was tucked in with one Granny was sending to Aunt Sarah, and when a reply came from her aunt it included a letter from Eddie.

After that, they exchanged letters most weeks. Eddie proved to be a good correspondent, giving news of his own doings at school, what outings he had been on, the health of Baron and the other members of the household; all in a lively style that helped Daisy picture the scenes he described.

Her grandmother went back to Auckland, and the days slipped back into their usual courses. Daisy had not seen her Aunt Rosie for some time; her mother said Aunt Rosie was poorly, but she did not seem especially worried about her sister. In June Daisy was told a baby boy had arrived, and she realised that must have been what all the mysterious whisperings of the last few days had been about. She was taken to Uncle Bernard's one Sunday after church to see Aunt Rosie and the new baby, whom she thought rather funny-looking with his red, scrunched-up face. She was allowed to hold the baby, while Aunt Rosie watched her like a hawk.

Daisy's family went to her Uncle Bill's farm at the head of the valley more than usual that winter, so that they could see Daisy's great-grandmother. Great-grandma was not very well, though it was certainly nothing to do with babies. Just a cough, Aunt Lily said, but she was not to go out, not even to church on Sundays, until she was better. So instead of sitting in the parlour most of the day, Great-grandma sat up in bed. She seemed as cheerful as ever, and Uncle Richard said she was doing well, but he agreed with Aunt Lily that she should stay inside.

If they were at Uncle Bill's for Sunday lunch, Emma's young man was usually there. They were now engaged to be married.

'And you can be a bridesmaid, Daisy,' Emma said. 'You and Lucy and Flora.'

The wedding would not be for a long time; not until at least the next year. Emma's fiancé boarded in Ruatane, where he worked at the Post Office, and he had to save up for a house of his own before he would be allowed to marry Emma. Daisy liked Mr Barton, who told her she could call him Uncle Doug. He had a face that seemed made for smiling, and a nice voice even when he was just talking; then one day he sang for them while Aunt Lily played the piano, and his voice was so lovely that Daisy wanted to cry and smile at the same time.

August that year was more like the first month of spring than a stubbornly lingering winter. Great-grandma's cough went away, and she returned to her usual chair in the parlour. Aunt Rosie's baby started looking like a person instead of an angry tomato; he smiled at Daisy one day, and she could truthfully tell Aunt Rosie she thought him a very nice baby. Best of all, August gave way to September, the school holidays arrived, and with them Eddie and Granny.

The holidays flew by in the mysterious manner of especially pleasant times. Daisy showed off the new calves to Eddie, and he helped her with feeding them. The calves would push their faces greedily into the buckets, then raise them with long, sticky trails of milky saliva dangling from their mouths. They were more inclined to take the milk if it was Daisy holding the bucket, but both children came back from calf feeding with their clothes smeared with the sticky stuff.

They went riding together, one day going all the way to Uncle Bill's farm on their own. Great-grandma always called Eddie 'Mal', which had been his father's name, but she seemed pleased to see them. Sometimes they walked beside the creek; sometimes they sat on the verandah and talked. Then Eddie went back to Auckland, and the world became a little less bright.

The war had gone on for more than a year now. The newspapers seemed to say much the same thing every day, making it sound as if the Germans were about to give up, but somehow it never happened. When Daisy had been staying in Auckland, once or twice Eddie had read aloud from the newspaper a section called the Roll of Honour, which was a fancy name for a list of the men who had been killed. Daisy occasionally saw the newspaper at home open to that page; some days there were so many names on the list that she thought even Eddie would grow tired of reading them out.

But the war still seemed a distant thing; a matter of maps on the classroom wall and lists of strangers' names. As long as it was over before Eddie was old enough to be allowed to go, there seemed nothing for Daisy to worry about. Until one dreadful evening in November.

The dishes had been done and the kitchen tidied, and Daisy's father sat at the table with pen and inkwell. Daisy had thought he was writing a letter to Granny, but when she looked more closely she saw that the sheet of paper before him was not notepaper but a printed form.

'What's that, Papa?' she asked.

'Just a thing I've got to fill in about the army. It has to be in by next Tuesday, so I'd better take it to the Post Office when we go in tomorrow.'

'Why? What's the army got to do with you?'

'There was a notice about it. I have to fill this thing out and say whether I'd sign up and go off to the war.'

A jolt went through Daisy. She felt her mouth making a big 'O' of surprise, but her throat was too tightly clenched to allow any sound to escape.

Her father glanced up and saw her expression. 'Hey, I'm telling them I'm not going anywhere, Daisy! Don't worry about it, love.'

Daisy swallowed hard, and managed to speak. 'But why do you have to write on that paper? Are they going to make you go to the war? They mustn't!' She took hold of her father's sleeve, tugging at it so he could no longer write.

Her mother came over from the bench, where she had been getting the yeast ready for breadmaking. She placed a hand on Daisy's shoulder and rubbed it gently. 'They're not going to make Papa go, Daisy. There's been lots of men joining up, ever since the war started. That form's just a silly thing they're making all the men fill out—even Grandpa has to do it.'

'Grandpa? They're taking Grandpa as well?' Daisy felt tears filling her eyes.

'Of course they're not! They'd never take a man his age—Grandpa's over fifty now.'

'So they *would* take Papa, then! Papa's not even thirty.' The tears were overflowing now.

'No, I didn't mean that...' Daisy watched her mother exchange a helpless glance with her father, then sink into the chair on Daisy's other side.

'Come and have a look at it,' her father said, disentangling Daisy's fingers from his sleeve and lifting her onto his lap. 'See? "Register of Intent to Volunteer",' he read aloud. 'That means all the men between... where does it say... seventeen and sixty, that's right—have to say yes or no about going in the army. I just have to fill my name in, and how old I am,' he pointed to different columns on the form as he spoke, 'whether I'm married, and how many kids I've got.' Daisy saw a large 'One' in that column. 'And see, I've put "No" in the bit about going off to fight. So that'll be the end of it.'

Daisy studied the form carefully, looking for any traps that might be concealed in the words. 'So they'll only take the men who say yes?'

'I suppose so,' her father said. 'They're taking anyone who'll go, far as I can see.'

'I think they have to be twenty, though,' her mother put in. 'And forty-five's the oldest they'll take. So they wouldn't take Grandpa or Uncle Bill, even if they wanted to go.'

'But if men the right age can just join up like you said, and they're not allowed to if they're too old or too young even if they want to, what's this paper for?' Daisy asked.

Her father shrugged. 'I don't know, Daisy. It's the government. They do things like that.'

Daisy remained unsatisfied. She stared suspiciously at the form, which was put to one side of the table for the ink to dry. When it was safe to touch, her father folded it and put it into a special envelope that had an address on it done in typewriting. Daisy wished she could snatch up that envelope and throw it into the fire.

She found it difficult to settle to anything that evening. After having to pick up several dropped stitches for her, Daisy's mother suggested she leave her knitting for another time, and read one of her story books. But the book also failed to hold her attention. When it was time to kiss her father goodnight she wound her arms around his neck and pressed her head against his chest, only reluctantly releasing him and going off to her bedroom.

Daisy woke to the sound of her own voice, what had been a scream within her nightmare muffled to a feeble whimper in the waking world. Her arms were pinned against her sides by the sheet that she had tossed and turned into a crumpled, sweat-dampened muddle. She untangled herself from the clinging sheet, flung back the covers and lay trembling, the film of perspiration across her upper body gradually cooling to clamminess while her breathing slowed.

She remembered the dream vividly. She and her mother had clutched at her father's arms, only to be pushed to the ground by a mob of soldiers who dragged him away while Daisy screamed helplessly. These soldiers were not like the uniformed men she had seen in Auckland, laughing and smiling as they wandered along Queen Street. They were huge, menacing creatures who loomed over Daisy's father, himself the tallest man she knew, grinning malevolently. Behind them was another figure, in the old-fashioned uniform she had seen on the statue in Albert Park; a man she recognised although she had never seen him. It was Eddie's father, her Uncle Mal. But the face that should have been an older version of Eddie's was instead a grinning skull, yellowing bone with strips of rotting flesh clinging to it, looking more like the dead sheep Daisy had once encountered in a back paddock than anything she had ever seen on a human body.

Try as she might to think of something cheerful, to picture the new calves chasing each other around the paddocks, or herself riding Star at Eddie's side, the image of those men dragging her father away kept returning. She knew that if she let herself fall asleep, the nightmare would take hold of her again.

She got out of bed and padded through the silent house. The door-handle of her parents' bedroom was cold under her hand when she turned it and pushed the door open.

A sliver of moonlight came in through the gap where the curtains did not quite meet. By its light Daisy saw a mound in the bed; two bodies pressed together in sleep. The nearer part of the mound moved, pushed itself up against the pillows and turned into Daisy's mother.

'Daisy? What's wrong?' She sounded wide-awake despite having been asleep moments before. 'Don't you feel well?' The rest of the mound moved more sluggishly, and a grunting noise that might have been a question came from that direction.

Daisy came right into the room and stood beside the bed. She opened her mouth to explain, but all that came out were great, heaving sobs.

Her mother reached out and pulled Daisy over to sit on the bed, an arm firmly around her. 'Where does it hurt? Have you got a tummy ache?'

Daisy shook her head. 'They were t-taking P-Papa away,' she choked out between sobs. 'Soldiers c-came and took him away.' Talking about it made the pictures from her dream come creeping back.

'Shh, shh,' her mother soothed, holding Daisy close. 'It was just a bad dream. Come in with us for a bit, till you feel sleepy,' she said, folding back the covers.

'Hang on,' said her father. 'I'll just get sorted out…' He moved under the covers; probably straightening his nightshirt, Daisy thought. Her nightdress often rode up if she was restless in the night, and something similar might happen to him.

Daisy settled in between them. 'Are you still worrying about that silly form?' her father asked.

'Yes,' she admitted. 'In the dream they were going to make you go and fight in the war.'

'Well, they're not going to. I've got too much work to do here.'

'If they need to start making men go, there's plenty of them without wives and families just doing things in shops and suchlike,' her mother said. 'They've no need to be taking married men.'

Her father made no reply. He was so quiet that Daisy wondered if he was a little grumpy over being disturbed, though she was not sure she had ever known her father to be grumpy. She listened harder, and decided he was only asleep.

Daisy lay very still, a warm body on either side, her father such a solid presence that she could not imagine anyone dragging him away. Her mother talked quietly for a little longer, and Daisy answered her until speaking became too much of an effort.

Daisy was guiltily aware that it was her fault her parents were so yawny over breakfast, although nothing was said about the broken night she had given them. The envelope containing her father's form was on the table, propped against the teapot. By the time she got home from school it had been taken into town and posted off.

Her bad dream was not nearly so frightening when it returned that night. Before the dream-soldiers had done more than take a few steps towards her father, Daisy woke to find herself in the silent house, her face wet with tears and her sheet once again tangled around her legs. She retrieved a handkerchief from under the pillow and blew her nose, then did her best to put the dream out of her mind. It was not fair to keep waking her parents up because of a silly dream. And they must know more about the war than she did; it must be true that the government would not take married men away.

The dream returned several more times, never again as frightening as on that first night, and by the time a fortnight had passed it had disappeared. Daisy tore the November page from her calendar and worked out how many days it was till the Christmas holidays.

School finished for the year of 1915, and Eddie arrived with Granny and Aunt Sarah. There was a huge Christmas dinner at Grandpa's farm, and Boxing Day was fine enough for the annual haymaking to begin.

Once haymaking was over, Daisy and Eddie had more time to roam about as they pleased. One of Eddie's Christmas presents from Granny and Aunt Sarah had been a magnificent book called 'Explorers of the Empire', with coloured illustrations of men trudging through the jungle, being paddled along rivers, or climbing mountains. Daisy and Eddie had pored over every page, and it inspired them to spend much of one afternoon searching for the source of a small stream that flowed into the Waituhi Creek. They clambered through scrub and bush, battling with cutty grass that sliced at incautious fingers, sharp twigs that scratched arms and faces, and impenetrable tangles of supple-jack, finally emerging dirty, disheveled and triumphant into a small clearing that contained a muddy patch from which spilled a tiny trickle of water.

'We should claim it for the Empire,' Eddie said, gazing proudly at their discovery.

'But it's already in the Empire, isn't it? Because New Zealand is. And I suppose it belongs to the farm, really.'

'We can still claim it, though. Uncle Dave won't mind.' Eddie had a smart pocket-knife, another of his Christmas gifts and still sharp. He used it to cut a stick from one of the manuka bushes that edged the clearing, then pushed the stick into the soft ground. Daisy, who had more nimble fingers, took a ripped handkerchief that Eddie produced from the depths of a pocket and tied it to the stick as a makeshift flag. They saluted the flag before turning to painfully retrace their steps and share the news of their discovery with the grown-ups.

The subject of the Grammar School, where Eddie would be enrolling when the new term began, came up more than once in the evenings. Daisy was pleased to have seen for herself the grand site with its views over the city. She could tell that her parents were making an effort to sound more impressed than they were by Eddie's talk of playing fields and dozens of classrooms. They were probably imagining a place much like Ruatane's little District High School, with its handful of modest wooden buildings set in a paddock close to the edge of town. Children from five years old went there; it had just enough older children to scrape together a secondary department, and there was constant talk that it might lose its status and become an ordinary primary school again if the secondary roll dropped by a few pupils.

'And of course Daisy will be going to high school in a few years,' Aunt Sarah remarked one evening, making Daisy start in surprise.

'But there isn't a high school in the valley, only the one in town.' She did not want to contradict her aunt, but Aunt Sarah seemed to have missed this vital point.

'That's not so very far. I'm sure ways could be found.' Aunt Sarah turned to Daisy's father, smiling but with something about her eyes that told Daisy she might be getting ready for an argument. 'I do hope there won't be any nonsense about girls not needing an education, David.'

No one ever called Daisy's father David. Even Aunt Sarah usually called him Dave, although it sounded a more serious sort of name when she said it than when other people did. Most of the time he seemed quite at ease with Aunt Sarah, but just occasionally he would look a little nervous. This appeared to be one of those times.

'It's not to do with her being a girl, it's just... it'd take a bit of doing, and...' He glanced from Aunt Sarah to Daisy and back again. 'Well, I don't know how we'd get her there every day, anyway.' He turned to Daisy's mother with an expression that looked like a plea for help.

Mama would not, of course, be able to state outright that it was a silly idea, but Daisy expected her to find a polite way of saying much the same thing. Instead, what she said had Daisy staring at her in disbelief. 'You're quite right, Sarah, we might want to send her to high school. She's doing very well at school—you never know, she might even want to be a teacher.' She smiled down at Daisy, who realised her mouth was wide open. 'That's a long way off, anyway. We'll think about it when the time comes.'

The grown-ups' conversation had shifted to other, less interesting, subjects before Daisy had found her voice, and Eddie was engrossed in his book of explorers. Daisy sat on the floor close to him, looking from face to face and trying to take in the astonishing idea that she might one day go to high school. She might be a teacher, just like Granny. It had never occurred to her that she might want any such thing. But to go to high school, just like Eddie?

She picked up her new book of fairy stories and leaned back against the convenient support of her father's long legs. The notion seemed about as unlikely as anything in the book before her.

Chapter Nine

Eddie was somewhat mystified by his grandmother's decision that they should return to Auckland earlier than they usually did, over a week before school enrolment. She said she needed the extra time to get his clothes organised for his new school, and she certainly seemed busy in the days after they got back. Granny bought new vests, socks and drawers for him, and took him down to the shops to buy a school uniform of blue shirt and shorts and a round cap with the school's crest of a rampant lion. He got a pair of sturdy black shoes to wear with his uniform, a smart new pair of tennis shoes, and the promise of new rugby boots in time for winter. Granny also gave him a haircut; 'So you'll look nice and tidy for school,' she said, though being tidy was not something that came naturally to Eddie's hair, inclined as it was to stick out in random directions within minutes of having been combed.

He went with Granny to buy exercise books, pencils and drawing things; textbooks could wait, Aunt Sarah had been told when she contacted the school, till it was decided what class Eddie would be in. A few days before school was to start, Aunt Sarah made him a gift of a fine fountain pen, engraved with his initials. He sat at the desk in her study, filled the pen from a silver inkwell, and carefully wrote his name on the first page of his new exercise books.

On the Saturday before enrolment Aunt Sarah's friends Mr and Mrs Wells came for the afternoon, bringing their daughters. All four of the girls had been in Granny's school when they were little, and she always seemed pleased to see them. They were all younger than Eddie, and not the least interested in rugby or horses, or anything else of significance as far as he could tell, and beyond what politeness demanded he did his best to ignore them.

But Mrs Wells was nice, and Eddie liked Mr Wells a lot. He talked about interesting things, and always seemed to know what was going on to do with the war, even before it had been in the newspapers. His work was something important at the Customs Department, and Aunt Sarah said he knew everyone in Auckland and half the people in Wellington.

Mr Wells had gone to Grammar when he was a boy, and he was delighted that Eddie would be following in his footsteps. They talked a little about what subjects Eddie might take, but they were both rather more interested in the sports on offer. Rugby, of course; the Grammar School was well-known in Auckland for the quality of its teams. And Mr Wells was keen that Eddie try out for a cricket eleven, cricket being one of his own great interests. He had taken Eddie to a cricket match the previous summer, an outing Eddie had mixed feelings about. The parts of the game where players actually ran from one wicket to the other, trying to get there without being caught or run out, were quite exciting, but there seemed to be an awful lot of standing about in between such moments. They had spent an afternoon at the game, and Eddie had been astonished to learn that a match could go on for days.

But it had been fun to go out with Mr Wells, who talked to Eddie as if he were another man, and he was able to explain cricket so that it made quite a lot of sense. And Eddie liked the idea of being in a team for a summer sport as well as a winter one.

'Let's see how thoroughly you can thrash me on the court today, Ed,' Mr Wells said when he had changed into his tennis clothes after lunch. In the last few months he had taken to calling Eddie 'Ed'; he was the only person who did. 'You should go easy on an old chap like me, you know.'

Eddie grinned back at him. Aunt Sarah had taught Eddie to play tennis when he was quite small; at first it had been confined to friendly hits around the court, then for a time they had been fairly evenly matched. Eddie's strength and reach had increased to the point where they were now back to friendly hits, with Aunt Sarah reluctant to allow a score to be kept. Mr Wells, despite his protestations of age, was a good player, and his visits were the only times Eddie had a real challenge to his own skill. There were tennis courts at the Grammar School, and Eddie was glad of the chance to brush up his game before school began.

The others strolled around the garden, then the ladies sat in the shade while the little girls played complicated skipping games and picked flowers to weave into one another's hair. Mr Wells had won three games to Eddie's two, and they were at thirty all in the sixth game. Eddie could feel sweat running down his back, and Mr Wells' face was bright red.

'Perhaps you should concede the game now, dear,' Mrs Wells remarked from the sideline while Eddie was retrieving a ball that had bounced out of the court. 'There's no shame in letting the better man win.'

'Better man indeed!' Mr Wells put on a stern voice, but it was spoiled by the smile he directed at his wife.

Eddie carried the ball back to his baseline, and stood waiting for his opponent to give the sign that he was ready. Mr Wells was leaning forward with his hands on his thighs, and appeared to be breathing heavily. He caught Eddie's eye, gave him a rueful grin, then straightened himself and looked over at Mrs Wells again.

'Care for a wager, Emily?' he asked. 'If I can take one more game off this fellow, how about you and Sarah join us for a set of mixed doubles? Very mixed in your case, my dear,' he teased.

'Oh, but it's so hot,' Mrs Wells protested. 'And I haven't brought anything to wear for playing.'

'But you seem to think you're in no danger of having to make good on the bet, so where's the risk?' Mr Wells was making a rapid recovery from his shortness of breath, to Eddie's relief.

'I'm sure I could find you something if necessary, Emily,' Aunt Sarah put in. 'And I'll be happy to do my share in preserving the honour of the household if Martin somehow manages to overpower Eddie. Do your best, Eddie, but don't over-exert yourself,' she said, turning in his direction. 'I'd rather enjoy a game or two.'

Eddie did do his best, but Mr Wells had got over his apparent exhaustion surprisingly quickly. He also had a hoard of tricky shots, some of which he appeared to have saved till now. Eddie found himself running back and forth across the court, straining to get to a ball placed neatly in the far corner from where he had been a moment before. He was getting somewhat short of breath himself when the ball flew just beyond the tip of his racquet and Mr Wells shouted, 'Game!'

Eddie went to shake hands with him across the net. 'Good game, Mr Wells.'

'Thank you—well-played yourself.' He gripped Eddie's hand. 'Let that be a lesson, Ed—never take your opponent for granted, no matter how old he is. And don't be deceived by appearances,' he added, grinning broadly.

They joined the ladies and the little girls in their shady spot under tall trees, afternoon tea spread before them. Lemonade slid down Eddie's throat, deliciously cold, and soon followed by sandwiches and small cakes. Mr Wells pretended to be offended at Mrs Wells' lack of faith in him, and she pretended to feel guilty about it. The little girls went back to their skipping, Granny moved closer to watch them, and Aunt Sarah took Mrs Wells off to find some tennis clothes to wear.

Eddie generally took little interest in ladies' clothes, but he could see that Mrs Wells' borrowed garments were not a comfortable fit. Aunt Sarah was a good deal taller than she was, as well as somewhat slimmer. The cuffs of the blouse were folded back; the skirt was turned over several times at the waistband, and when Eddie saw Mrs Wells from behind he noticed that it was held closed by a safety pin.

Mr Wells snorted with laughter at the sight of her. 'Good Lord, Emily, how do you expect us to win with you in that state? Will you even be able to run?' He pointed towards Mrs Wells' feet; the skirt was just high enough to reveal a pair of shoes that were clearly too large for her, even with the thick socks she was wearing over her stockings.

'It was your idea, Martin, you've only yourself to blame if I disgrace you,' Mrs Wells said, smiling sweetly.

Mr Wells raised his eyes heavenwards. 'Let's get it over with, then. Best of three?'

Eddie was sure Mrs Wells put at least as much energy into laughing as she did into running after the ball. Every time she missed a shot she laughed all the more merrily, and when one of her over-large borrowed shoes came off, she was almost convulsed with mirth.

Aunt Sarah, on the other hand, took the game quite seriously. She and Eddie worked well as a team, moving nimbly around the court without getting in each other's way. Mr Wells had to take the lion's share of the game on his side of the net, and with two opponents he was soon red-faced again. Their 'best of three' match turned out to be two games, both won comfortably by Eddie and Aunt Sarah.

Mr Wells did not seem to mind overmuch. They left the court, had a little more afternoon tea, and after washing and getting changed the Wellses gathered their daughters and took their leave.

'Best of luck with settling in at school, Ed,' Mr Wells said as they were shaking hands in the hallway. 'I'll look forward to hearing how you get on. And I'll expect an invitation to all your sports matches.'

'So that he can call advice from the sidelines,' said Mrs Wells. 'Terribly valuable advice, of course.'

On enrolment day, Eddie put on his smart new uniform and with his grandmother caught a tram from Queen Street. They walked the short distance from the tram stop to his school, passed through the arched gateway, and found their way into an assembly hall full of boys and their parents.

Granny spoke to a man near the door, and after a time Eddie heard his name being called. He tucked his cap into his belt, as he saw other boys doing, and he and Granny went to the front of the hall where a burly man with a white moustache sat behind a table. This turned out to be the headmaster, Mr Tibbs, a name that sounded so much like what a cat might be called that Eddie had to make an effort not to laugh.

Granny handed Mr Tibbs the piece of paper with Eddie's marks from the Proficiency examination he had sat two months earlier.

'Edmund Stewart? Good marks you have here,' Mr Tibbs said, scanning the paper. 'Yes, you'll be going straight into Three A.' He nodded at Granny. 'We'll expect great things from your son, Mrs Stewart.'

'He's my grandson,' Granny said, smiling over at Eddie.

It was not the first time someone had thought Granny was his mother. He had occasionally met other boys' grandmothers at birthday parties or outings; they were generally solid, grey-haired ladies who did not stir from the most comfortable chair in the room. Granny was little (Eddie had been taller than her for years), and her hair was black and shiny, with only a few strands of grey. She said being around young ones all the time kept her young.

Eddie did remember his mother. He even knew what she had looked like, though only because he had a photograph of her, with a much smaller version of himself perched on her lap. That was the only way he could picture her face: flat and dull in sepia tints.

His memories were a hazy muddle of senses: his mother singing a nursery rhyme; a spoonful of jam slipped into his mouth; wind whistling through cracks in the walls of the bedroom they shared, and her body a warm buttress against it. She had always lain between him and the draughts.

'Your grandson? I do beg your pardon,' Mr Tibbs said. 'Though I must say it's an understandable error, Mrs Stewart.' He turned his attention back to Eddie. 'You look like a rugby player, my boy.'

'I want to be in the First Fifteen,' Eddie blurted out.

Mr Tibbs laughed, setting the ends of his moustache quivering. 'That's the story, lad. Always aim for the heights. "Per Angusta ad Augusta". To the hallowed heights, eh?'

Eddie recognised the odd-sounding words from the archway at the school's entrance. He would have liked to ask what they meant, but Mr Tibbs was looking down at a list of names for the next pupil to call, and it was clearly time for them to leave. Eddie said the words under his breath, committing them to memory.

'Three A, Eddie! That's good—that's the top class,' Granny said outside the school gates on their way back to the tram stop.

Aunt Sarah seemed just as pleased by the news when they got home. She also made an attempt at translating the motto for him.

'Something about through struggle to greatness, I think. But you'll be able to make it out yourself soon enough—you'll be studying Latin, of course.'

The following week term began. Eddie caught the tram again, on his own this time. Mr Wells had warned him that new boys sometimes suffered the indignity of having their caps snatched by older lads, so

Eddie kept his eyes about him as he walked towards the school gates.

'Though they might think better of it when they've sized you up,' Mr Wells had added, and that seemed to be the case. One or two boys glanced speculatively at Eddie, then looked away, attention apparently caught by some distant object.

The assembly hall was a roiling mass of boys, efficiently shoaled by masters. Eddie soon found himself in a group following the billowing black gown of their form master, Mr Watkins, out of the hall and up to a second floor classroom.

'This will be your form room for the year,' Mr Watkins told them. 'Most of you will proceed through Four A, Five A and Six A, then on to the university.'

Granny and Aunt Sarah sometimes talked about the university, saying they hoped Eddie would go there one day. It seemed an unimaginable distance in the future. For now, Eddie was more interested in the list of subjects Mr Watkins had written on the board. He copied them out carefully on the first page of an exercise book: English, History, Chemistry and Physics, Mathematics, French, Latin and Drawing.

The rooms for the different subjects were scattered around the school. Over the next few days Eddie had the chance to explore most of the buildings in the process of getting to all his classes.

Drawing was fun from the first lesson; Eddie had always enjoyed drawing, and the teacher had lots of useful tips for getting what he put on the page closer to what he saw in his head. His English master had a fine voice, quite different from the nasal bray of Eddie's last teacher at primary school, and he brought to life the poems or passages of Shakespeare he declaimed for them. The history master spoke of kings and battles, though Eddie's attention tended to rove to the two rusty swords that stood in one corner. They were never mentioned, let alone wielded, other than in Eddie's imagination.

Science lessons held their own delights in the guise of chemical experiments that might produce coloured fumes or pungent smells. In contrast, mathematics was a dull matter of copying down sums from the board and plodding through them, watched over by a sharp-eyed master who reminded Eddie of the hawks he sometimes saw on the farm.

It seemed an odd notion that he should learn even one new language, let alone two. But Latin had unexpected attractions. Mr Watkins, who as well as being 3A's form master took them for Latin, was as inclined to tell them about Roman generals as to coach them through the mysteries of conjugation. He also remarked during one lesson that the scientific names of all plants and animals were in Latin. Eddie at once resolved to find out the official names of all the plants and bugs in the garden.

French did not have Latin's advantages to recommend it, but it did have particular encouragement at home. Aunt Sarah, it transpired, had learned French herself when she was at school. On an evening soon after Eddie's first lesson, she produced an ancient notebook filled with French phrases in her careful handwriting, and suggested that they practise together.

Reciting his homework aloud did not strike Eddie as fun, but life generally went more smoothly if one went along with Aunt Sarah's suggestions. She made something of a game of their French practice, correcting Eddie's pronunciation by comparing the sounds of the French words to English ones. *Je m'appelle*, she told him, was nothing to do with apples.

Granny gave a little laugh. 'I wish I knew what you two were talking about. What's all this about apples?'

'Amy, you must learn, too,' Aunt Sarah said, turning her attention from Eddie.

Granny protested that she couldn't; that it would be too hard for her. But Aunt Sarah insisted she must try, and Aunt Sarah got her way. She had Eddie say a phrase, repeated it herself with what she said was a better pronunciation, then had Granny recite it. They practised introducing themselves, silly though that seemed, and asking after each other's health. Aunt Sarah hunted out words in her notebook and had the others guess their meaning.

Sometimes there was a clue in the word, which might sound more or less the same as it did in English, but much of the time it was a matter of increasingly wild guesses. When Granny suggested that *Je sais* might mean Jersey, and said Aunt Sarah was claiming there was a cow in the room, Eddie gave a snort, Granny and Aunt Sarah both laughed, and next moment the three of them were giggling helplessly.

Aunt Sarah was the first to recover. 'Yes, we'll do this every evening,' she said. 'It'll be just the thing for Eddie's pronunciation. But it must be the three of us, so we can have proper conversations.'

'Well, if it'll help Eddie, I'll try my best,' Granny said. She had an odd sort of look on her face, as if she could not quite decide if she were happy or sad. 'It seems funny to have you teaching me how to talk, Sarah.'

Aunt Sarah put her hand over Granny's, and for a moment she, too, had a strange expression. She squeezed Granny's little hand. 'We'll all get quite proficient at it, and then when this wretched war's over perhaps we'll all go to France.'

She made it sound more than half a joke, and Granny smiled. 'All that way? Well, you never know, I suppose. I'm sure it would be lovely, dear.'

'And we'll take Daisy,' Eddie put in.

'Of course,' said Aunt Sarah. 'Daisy must come, too.'

The first week had passed almost before Eddie knew it, in a blur of new lessons and new friends. At lunchtime he sat outside with a group of boys from his class, and found that the lunches Mrs Jenson packed for him, particularly the small cakes she included in generous quantities, made for highly desirable swaps. Someone generally produced a ball, which they kicked around the playground until the bell summoned them back to class. There was even better to look forward to, as sports were to start the following week.

It was all very different from his last months at primary school, when he had grown increasingly bored with lessons that seemed mainly to consist of preparations for the Proficiency Certificate, the same work being drilled over and over even when Eddie and one or two others had it off by heart. In the final few weeks of term, Eddie had resorted to feigning illness once or twice. But while his grandmother was prepared to give him the benefit of the doubt, Aunt Sarah had pointed out that if Eddie was too ill to go to school, he was clearly too ill to exercise his horse. She said that perhaps Walter should take over the care of Baron till the end of the year if school was making Eddie too tired. Eddie had at once declared himself feeling much better.

Granny remarked on his new-found ability to get himself washed and dressed well in time for school these days. While she and Aunt Sarah had told him he would enjoy the work at his new school, Eddie had not given a great deal of thought to what classes would be like; his main interest had been in the sports on offer and in escaping from Miss Hudson. But even mathematics wasn't too bad, and in the other subjects with the most inspiring of his teachers it was as though a light had gone on in his head.

He had an endlessly interested audience at home with Granny and Aunt Sarah, but something more was needed to make it complete. He had to tell Daisy all about school.

Eddie's science master had taken them though an experiment with coloured glass and a prism, showing that it took all the colours and something called wavelengths to get proper bright light, and how thin and lacking light was when it was missing any of its parts. It was like that with Daisy. No matter how exciting a thing might be, somehow it was never quite complete until he had shared it with her. It needed to be reflected back from her; made brighter in responding to her response. The best thing would be to see the glow in her eyes, but for now he could make do with a letter in her familiar handwriting, one that would let him hear her voice as he read.

Eddie set out notepaper, pen and ink on a writing table in the drawing room. His fine new fountain pen poised above the page, he carefully wrote,

Dear Daisy,

Chapter Ten

When Daisy got home from school that Friday, a satisfyingly thick envelope was waiting for her on the kitchen table. She had never before had such a long letter from Eddie. Three pages were covered, telling her about his subjects, what the rooms were like, the names of his masters and the classmates he liked best; and describing assembly each morning, when the boys all sat in the hall alphabetically within their classes. The masters wore gowns, he told her, which sounded funny until it struck Daisy that perhaps they dressed a little like the minister did at church.

The letter darted back and forth between one idea and the next, just as Eddie did when he was talking about something and a new thought struck him. He described the buildings and the grounds; Daisy closed her eyes and did her best to picture the school. In her imagination she replaced the mud and muddle of the unfinished site with the grandest of the buildings she had seen elsewhere in Auckland, and placed Eddie at the centre of the picture, surveying the whole like a proud owner. Then the letter went back to tell her more about the classrooms, and about his first game of cricket, where he had found he particularly enjoyed bowling.

Daisy turned to the last page, and was startled to be presented with what looked like nonsense. She knew Eddie's handwriting almost as well as her own; why should she suddenly find herself unable to read anything apart from his name?

The mystery was explained a few lines later. This was French, Eddie told her. They were words he had been learning at school and practising at home with Granny and Aunt Sarah. It said, 'My name is Eddie. I am thirteen. How old are you?'

Daisy studied the lines again, fascinated. She made an attempt at saying the words aloud, but despite trying several different ways of pronouncing them they felt strange in her mouth.

Her parents were as much at a loss as Daisy over how the strange words should be said.

'Miss Cameron might know,' her father said. 'She must've gone to high school, so she probably learned French, too.'

'But I want to say it *properly*, and school's not till Monday.' That was an entire weekend away. Daisy gave a deep sigh.

'I think Aunt Lily might know French,' her mother said. 'We can go and see them on Sunday if you like.'

Aunt Lily had been the teacher at the valley's school before she married Uncle Bill. The visit was something to look forward to, though it still meant waiting two days. In the meantime, Daisy read the whole letter aloud to her parents, once in the kitchen and then later in the parlour, before putting it in her chest of drawers along with Eddie's other letters. That night she drifted off to sleep while murmuring the names of his school subjects.

As well as the uncles and aunts and cousins, Emma's fiancé was at Uncle Bill's farm that Sunday afternoon. They were all on the verandah, making the most of its shade, when Daisy and her parents arrived. Uncle Doug did not seem his usual cheerful self, and Daisy noticed that Emma's eyes were red.

Everyone at Uncle Bill's seemed a little quieter than usual, though in Great-grandma's case that was because she was inclined to drop off to sleep from time to time. Daisy sat on a small stool, clutching a glass of lemonade and listening to the voices around her. She was bursting with the need to ask Aunt Lily about Eddie's letter, but it would not be polite to butt into the grown-ups' conversation.

'Sorry about your bit of trouble, Doug,' she heard her father say.

Uncle Doug gave a shrug, and turned the corners of his mouth up into what seemed meant to be a smile. 'Can't be helped,' he said. Emma brushed her hand against his sleeve, and he managed a real smile. Daisy stored away the snatch of conversation as a puzzle to be solved later; for now the letter was her chief concern.

Emma's brothers, Arfie and Will, announced that they were going for a swim in the creek, and Emma and Uncle Doug took themselves off for a stroll around the garden.

The verandah was quieter now. Daisy waited for a lull in the conversation, then went to stand beside her aunt's chair.

'Excuse me, Aunt Lily, Mama said you might know about French,' she said.

'French?' her aunt echoed. 'Well, yes, I did learn it, a long time ago. Why ever are you interested in French, dear?'

Daisy took the letter from her mother's bag and placed it on Aunt Lily's lap. 'Eddie sent me this with French in it, but I don't know how to say it.' She met her aunt's eyes, hoping that she had managed to convey the seriousness of the matter.

Aunt Lily's eyebrows drew together as she studied the letter. 'Now, let me see,' she murmured. Her lips moved, silently shaping the words, then she read aloud:

' "Je m'appelle Eddie. J'ai treize ans. Quel âge as-tu?" '

The sounds she made bore only a passing resemblance to Daisy's attempts. But Aunt Lily had been a teacher, so she must be right. Daisy had her aunt repeat the words, then said them back to her until Aunt Lily declared that she was saying them very well.

'And can you tell me how to write something back to Eddie?' Daisy asked. 'Because he sent a question, so I should send an answer, shouldn't I?'

'Of course you must, dear,' her aunt said, smiling.

Daisy's mother produced a scrap of paper and a pencil from her bag, and Aunt Lily wrote on the side that had not been used as a shopping list. 'This says that you're called Daisy, and you're eight years old.' She sounded out the words for Daisy. 'And here's how to say you're well, and to ask how Eddie is,' she added, much to Daisy's delight.

'And can I say about the farm, and the calves, and when Miss Cameron put my story up on the wall?'

Her aunt shook her head. 'I'm afraid that's well beyond my abilities, Daisy. I'm almost surprised I remember any, after all these years.'

Daisy was only briefly downcast. Thanks to Aunt Lily, she would be able to send a proper reply to Eddie's French, and she could write the more interesting news in ordinary language.

Great-grandma had nodded off to sleep again. She let out a snorty sort of breath, and slumped a little in her chair. Aunt Lily propped her up, rearranged the cushions behind her, and settled her again, all without waking her, though Great-grandma smiled and murmured something.

Not long afterwards Daisy's parents said it was time to go; perhaps they had had enough of having to talk in whispers so as not to wake Great-grandma. They were soon back in the gig, rattling along the track down the valley.

Daisy sat in the middle of the gig's seat, head bent over the paper in her lap, practising the phrases Aunt Lily had taught her. She was aware of her parents talking over her head, but was too engrossed in her study to take any notice of what they were saying; so engrossed that she did not hear the approaching rider until her father called out a greeting.

She looked up to see Uncle Doug coming alongside the gig. Daisy waved to him, while keeping a firm grip on her piece of paper. He waved back, but did not slow his pace.

'It's such a shame about him and Emma,' Daisy's mother said when Uncle Doug was out of earshot.

'What's wrong with them?' Daisy asked.

Her mother gave a sigh. 'Well, they don't know when they'll be able to get married now. Doug's been saving up for a house—he's got to have

116

somewhere for them to live before Uncle Bill will let them get married, he only boards with old Mrs Finch now. He was up for a promotion at work, so he'd get paid a bit more, and he thought he might be able to put some money down on a house by the end of the year.'

'That's good, isn't it?'

'But now they're saying they won't give him the promotion after all,' her father said. 'It's a bit rough, he's due for one—he's been with the Post and Telegraph right from school, and he was meant to get a good one after that many years.'

'So why won't they give it to him?' Daisy asked, indignant on his behalf.

He pulled a face. 'It's because they want young fellows like him to sign up for the army.'

'Not boys as young as Eddie,' her mother said, forestalling Daisy's next question. 'And not married men, either.' She reached across the seat of the gig and squeezed Papa's hand where it rested on the reins.

'But they're calling men like Doug shirkers for not going to the war,' her father said. 'And they reckon they shouldn't be allowed to move up at work.'

'Shirker' sounded an awful word. 'It's not fair,' said Daisy. No wonder Emma had looked unhappy.

Daisy was outside the schoolroom a few mornings later when she saw Benjy running towards her from the horse paddock, clearly bursting with news. Before he got close enough to speak, Miss Cameron came out and rang the bell, which meant it was time to line up in front of the steps ready to go inside. Benjy just made it into line before the bell stopped ringing.

Once or twice during the morning Daisy thought he might actually risk talking in class, but Miss Cameron stayed at the front of the room, her strap clearly in view. Playtime had never seemed so long in coming.

When they were at last given permission to go outside, Benjy was barely down the steps before the words began tumbling out.

'Doug's going off to the war! He's signed up, and he'll be off next month.'

Daisy was briefly lost for words. By the time she had mustered her thoughts sufficiently for speech, the other children had gathered around, attracted by Benjy's news. They all looked impressed, especially the boys.

'He'll be the first one from the valley,' a big boy called Aitken said.

'He's not really from the valley,' said Benjy.

'Near enough,' the Aitken boy, who himself lived a good two miles away, said. ''Cause he's getting married to your cousin, and she's from the valley.'

Miss Cameron called them back inside before the boys had exhausted the subject. Daisy just had time to ask Benjy, 'Do you know how long he has to go away for?'

'I'm not sure—I think it might be a year.'

There no longer seemed to be any talk of the war's being over by Christmas, or by any time at all. A whole year for Uncle Doug to be away; maybe even longer. Poor Emma wouldn't have her wedding for an awfully long time.

The air had the sticky heat that only a February afternoon following a morning of rain could bring. Bill Leith's newspaper was limp in his hands. He wiped his fingers against a blank edge, removing as much as he could of the inky smears the type had left, then let the paper slide to the floor.

He slumped back in the armchair and closed his eyes, giving his full attention to Lily's piano playing. In deference to the Sabbath, she had chosen sedate pieces that had a soothing, almost cooling feel about them. But there was no denying that it was too hot a day to be inside. Lily had even said earlier that it was 'almost too hot to play'; he was not sure he had ever heard such a remark from her before.

Their sons had gone off to the creek with Bill's brothers, and Lily had persuaded Bill's mother to have a lie-down in her room rather than nodding off in a chair, so they had the parlour to themselves. It was probably much pleasanter out on the verandah, where Emma and Doug were, but Bill had no wish to intrude on what privacy that offered. The two of them would have little enough time together before Doug was due to leave for the army camp.

After the morning's downpour, the ground was too muddy for the young couple to go any distance from the house dressed in their Sunday best; otherwise they would, no doubt, have gone for one of their strolls. Bill did not find it necessary to ask where they went on such walks; still less to insist that they be chaperoned. His own father would not have been so easy going. But his father had not been faced with a young fellow going off to this war that showed no sign of ending. Lily said she trusted Emma, and Bill did not begrudge Doug the pleasure of Emma's company.

He heard steps in the passage, and looked up to see Emma enter the parlour, Doug just behind her. Coming in for Doug to say goodbye before heading back to town, Bill assumed. Lily ceased playing and

118

turned around on the stool.

Emma and Doug stood side-by-side on the rug. Something in their stance, as well as their set expressions, suggested they had weighty matters to discuss.

Doug cleared his throat. 'Mr Leith, I've something to ask—'

'*We've* something to ask,' Emma interrupted. She slipped her arm through Doug's; he patted her hand, and his mouth eased into a smile.

'We'd like to get married,' he said.

Bill frowned, wondering if he had missed some vital piece of information. 'Well, yes. I think we sorted that out a while back.'

'No, I know, but I—' Doug shot a glance at Emma, who looked on the point of cutting in again, 'we'd like to do it a bit sooner.'

'Now,' Emma said. 'Well, as soon as we can, anyway—I know there's banns and suchlike.'

'Before I go away. We want to get married before then.' Doug plunged on before Bill had a chance to respond. 'I know we can't set up house properly yet—'

'I'd have to stay on here, just till Doug comes home again,' Emma said.

'I couldn't have her at Mrs Finch's, she only takes single men.'

'But at least we'd be able to see a bit more of each other. And… and maybe Doug could stay here on the weekends.' Emma turned aside a little. Bill saw a flush mount her neck and spread over her face.

'I'd like to have things properly settled for Emma, not go away with us only being engaged. This way I'd get a married man's allowance, and I'll see that it all goes to Emma.'

Bill would not insult Doug's earnestness by saying that there was no need for any such arrangement; that he was more than happy to provide for his own daughter for as long as might be needed. He thought all the more of Doug for having Emma so clearly in the forefront of his thoughts.

Doug appeared to have exhausted his eloquence for the moment. He and Emma were both watching Bill expectantly. Bill glanced over at Lily; he could see she was as taken aback by all this as he was, though a slight smile was playing on her lips.

He gathered his thoughts as best he could, but all he managed to say was, 'Well, I'll have a think about it.' Bill half expected arguments, especially since Emma wore an expression that reminded him of his sister Lizzie at her most determined, but she kept her lips pursed and gave a quick nod. Doug dipped his head in a similar motion.

The farewells made, Emma went out with Doug to see him off. Bill turned to Lily.

'Well, what do you think?'

'I think we should let them,' Lily said, her voice as mild as usual, but with a quiet firmness to it.

Bill raised his eyebrows. 'It's not much of a start for them, is it? Not even able to live under the same roof.'

'It's better than nothing at all. And it seems a shame to make them wait, when we don't know how long Doug might be away, or even...' Lily lapsed into silence, but Bill could trace her thoughts clearly enough: Doug might not come back at all.

Lily rose from the piano stool, moving with the gracefulness he particularly associated with her; 'deportment', she had once told him it was called. She lowered herself into the chair beside his. 'Bill, dear, they've only these few weeks till Doug has to leave. Let them make the most of it.'

'I suppose you're right.' Bill made an attempt at a grin. 'I thought we'd be able to hang onto her a bit longer yet.'

Lily laughed softly. 'If it were a little later in the year, they wouldn't have had to ask permission at all—Emma will come of age in September. Though I rather think Doug would have done you the courtesy of asking even so.'

It seemed only a year or two since Emma had been a little girl running around with her brothers, and now she was on the verge of turning twenty-one. 'The years go quick, eh?'

'They do when one's happy.' Lily reached out and placed her hand on his. 'I want Emma to have whatever happiness the world offers. I'm sure you do, too.'

Daisy had only ever been to one wedding: her Aunt Rosie's, two years before. It had been at Grandpa's, and almost everyone in Ruatane had come. Kate and Emma had been bridesmaids; Benjy told Daisy that Maisie had refused to be one.

'She says she's had enough of it, after Maudie and then your mother,' Benjy had reported. 'And she says she's too old to wear pink satin, anyway.'

The bridesmaids had indeed worn matching dresses of pink satin, while Aunt Rosie had almost disappeared in folds of embroidered white silk and a veil all the way to her feet.

Then there was a good deal of standing around while photographs were taken of the bride and groom and various assortments of family members; Daisy had been in several of them. When the photographs were finally finished, plate after plate of especially nice food had appeared from the kitchen; Daisy and Benjy had agreed that was the high point of the day, in spite of having the eating interrupted by one speech after another.

It all seemed to go on for hours; Daisy's mother had called it 'a lot of fuss'. Daisy had fallen asleep before the reception was over, and had woken to find herself being lifted into the gig.

There was no fuss at Emma's wedding early in March 1916; there were not even new dresses for it. Just before the end of an ordinary Sunday service, the minister called Emma and Uncle Doug up to the altar rail, and they said the words from the marriage section of the Prayer Book. Emma just wore her usual Sunday best frock, but Daisy thought she looked very pretty, with Grandma's tortoiseshell comb in her hair and Aunt Lily's cameo brooch pinned to her bodice, and with her cheeks especially bright.

Emma had Daisy, Lucy and Flora come up to the front with her, and she gave Daisy her posy to hold while Uncle Doug slipped a ring onto Emma's finger. When the service was over, the little bridal group walked down the aisle ahead of the rest of the congregation. Lucy took Daisy and Flora by the hand and attempted a slow, elegant walk, but as Uncle Doug and Emma set off at their usual pace the three girls soon had to hurry to catch up.

Afterwards they all went across to the church hall for morning tea. It was a small affair compared to the feast at Aunt Rosie's wedding, but everyone had brought plates of cakes and sandwiches to share. All the men were keen to shake Uncle Doug's hand, and the ladies fussed over Emma.

Uncle Doug's landlady, Mrs Finch, was there, wearing a hat that looked as if someone might have sat on it. She was a short, heavyset woman, with a squashed appearance that matched her hat. People were making something of a fuss over her, too, as she had told Uncle Doug he was allowed to bring Emma to come and live with him in town until he went away to the war.

'I've just had single chaps as lodgers in the past, but I'm only too pleased to help the young people out, with Mr Barton going off to do his duty like he is,' Mrs Finch announced to anyone within hearing. 'It's not as if it'll be for long, anyway.'

After Emma had moved into town, Daisy still saw her with Uncle Doug every week at church. And one shopping day two weeks after the wedding, while her father went off to see about a new piece of harness

Daisy and her mother walked the short distance to Mrs Finch's house to visit Emma.

Mrs Finch opened the front door to their knock and showed them inside. A moment later Emma appeared in the passage from a side door and greeted them with delight.

They were ushered into a parlour so dim after the brightness of outdoors that for a few moments Daisy could only make the furniture out as vague shapes in the gloom. Heavy curtains of dark green velvet were drawn across the windows, open only an inch or so to admit a chink of light.

Mrs Finch twitched one curtain, widening the gap by perhaps half an inch. 'I don't like to get sunlight on the good furniture. It *fades*, you see.' Her tone made it clear that *fading* was a dreadful thing, to be avoided at all costs. She peered into the nearest corner of the room, as if searching for any sunbeams that might have slipped in while her back was turned, then went off to fetch the tea things.

Emma and Daisy's mother sat side-by-side on a hard-looking settee, while Daisy perched on a footstool nearby. 'It's very nice here,' Daisy's mother said, looking around the parlour.

Her mother always said it was important to be polite, and Daisy could tell that she was doing just that. The parlour was not actually horrible, but with its dark walls, dim light and (despite Mrs Finch's vigilance) faded furniture, it seemed a room that demanded hushed voices.

'Yes, we're so lucky to live here,' Emma said. 'And Mrs Finch has been very kind. I help her around the house a little bit, just to keep busy.'

'You're nice and handy to town,' Daisy's mother said.

Emma nodded. 'Doug comes home for lunch every day, it's so close to his work. And him and I go for a walk of an evening when the weather's nice. We're really very lucky,' she repeated, as if someone was arguing with her, but Daisy's mother smiled and said of course they were.

Mrs Finch came back into the parlour with a tray. There was tea for the grown-ups, a glass of milk for Daisy, and a biscuit each. The milk was a thin, watery affair compared to the Jerseys' milk Daisy was used to at home, and after a few chews the biscuit formed a gluey lump in the roof of her mouth.

She worked away at the lump with her tongue, doing her best not to let anyone see her struggles, and had just managed to loosen it when her mother said it was time they were going. Daisy gulped down the remains of the biscuit and thanked Mrs Finch before following her mother and Emma out of the parlour.

A door on the other side of the passage stood ajar; Emma pushed it open a little wider. 'This is our room.'

Daisy peered past her mother and caught a glimpse of a small room with a narrow bed along one wall, a chest of drawers taking up much of what space remained. Various items of male clothing were folded on the bed or draped over a chair, and reels of cotton stood in a row on the chest of drawers.

'I've been getting Doug's things sorted out,' Emma said. 'For when he goes away.' The last words came out on a sort of hiccup, and for the first time since their arrival Emma's smile slipped. But only for a moment; by the time she was waving goodbye to them from the front gate, she looked her usual bright self.

'Poor Emma,' Daisy's mother sighed as they walked along the road.

Chapter Eleven

Doug sailed from Ruatane at the end of March, not quite a month after the wedding. Emma's father brought her back home to the farm straight from seeing Doug off at the wharf.

He was not going overseas straight away; first he had to learn about being a soldier. There was a camp that the men were sent to; Daisy's parents were vague about exactly where it was, but her father thought it might be near Wellington. Now as Daisy knitted away at the latest socks, she told herself they were for Uncle Doug, and was especially careful with her stitches.

Letters soon began arriving for Emma, two or three a week, and she shared them around the family, reserving only an occasional page that she considered too private. Every day was much the same in the camp, Uncle Doug said, and Daisy was sure he must miss Emma. But he managed to sound cheerful, and he sent his best to everyone, sometimes mentioning even Daisy by name.

Emma sent him a tin of baking every week; Daisy and her mother often added some biscuits of their own. Daisy finished a pair of socks, and Emma slipped them into that week's parcel.

May came in, bringing sullen skies with it. Doug was due to sail any day now, and Emma did not smile so often.

Winter looked to be arriving early this year, the grown-ups all said. Chilblains had certainly started earlier than usual, pinching Daisy's toes when she squeezed into her boots each morning. The schoolroom was full of the snorty sound of noses being blown, with Miss Cameron having to remind many of the children to use a handkerchief rather than a sleeve. Daisy caught a cold that made her voice go husky, and gave her a constantly streaming nose. Her mother ripped an old sheet into rags when Daisy had exhausted her supply of clean handkerchiefs. A bitter wind whistled up the valley, leaving chapped lips and red cheeks in its wake. Every day down at the cowshed Daisy's parents discussed how many days it might be till they could dry the herd off for the season.

The month before, Great-grandma had had a nasty cough that went to her chest, and although she was almost well again everyone thought it would be better if Daisy stayed away from Uncle Bill's till her nose stopped being so runny.

'Great-grandma takes a long time to come right when she gets sick,' Daisy's mother said. 'It's like that with old people. Emma needs to be careful just now, too,' she added in a quieter voice, puzzling Daisy, as

Emma was not at all old.

The calendar on Daisy's wall showed that the May school holidays were rapidly approaching. Nothing had been said at home about any trips to Auckland. Granny would come to the farm as usual, but Eddie was far too busy, with sports and with studying for exams. He would definitely come in September, he said in his letters.

September seemed a long way off, but Daisy did not say anything to her parents, who clearly had a lot on their minds. She knew her mother was worried about Great-grandma, and just lately the news in the paper was often greeted by both parents with frowns or clicking of tongues, and mutterings about the war and the government.

Daisy's cold dried up at last, and they went to visit everyone at Uncle Bill's. Great-grandma was asleep when they arrived. She stirred a little, and smiled at them, but by the time Aunt Lily brought the tea things through she had nodded off again. 'Granny's sleepier than usual lately,' Emma said; that meant very sleepy indeed.

Emma looked quite well, so she must have been as careful as Daisy's mother had said she should be. She had a letter from Doug that had arrived the day before, and she read some of it aloud to them. Uncle Doug said that he was wearing Daisy's socks, and they were the best ones he'd ever had.

'"I don't like to let the other chaps see them, though, because they might pinch them."' Emma put on a voice that sounded a little like Uncle Doug's much deeper one to read that part out, making everyone laugh.

'His feet'll be warm, anyway, even if there's snow and stuff over there,' Emma's brother Arfie remarked.

Emma's smile faltered. 'He'll be on his way by now,' she said, clutching the letter more tightly. 'He must've posted this just before he left.'

The room went quiet for a few moments, then Uncle Bill broke the silence.

'He'll be back before you know it,' he said. 'The war's going well, it won't last much longer.'

Several of the other grown-ups murmured in agreement, and the corners of Emma's mouth turned up again. It was nice to see her smiling, but this cheerful talk about the war did not match what Daisy had been hearing at home. She could see that they were all doing their best to keep Emma's spirits up.

'Especially once Doug's there to sort those Germans out,' Uncle Ernie said. There was loud agreement, and laughing that sounded just a bit too hearty. They made so much noise that Great-grandma woke up and looked around the room smiling at everyone, though Daisy was sure she had no idea what they were all laughing about.

Daisy's great-grandmother, Edith Leith, spent most of the hours of daylight drifting somewhere between sleep and wakefulness. So her daughter-in-law Lily was not especially concerned on the afternoon later in May when she came into the parlour and found Edith apparently sound asleep in her armchair. Lily slipped quietly out of the room, and did not return until afternoon tea was ready.

Only when she was close enough to stroke her mother-in-law's hand where it lay limp in her lap did Lily realise that there would be no waking Edith this time.

Daisy had often watched her father kill a sheep, and once she had found a cow lying dead in a paddock, legs pointing stiffly in the air, but she had never seen a dead person before. So she was not sure what to expect when her parents took her to see her great-grandmother.

Great-grandma was lying on her own bed in the big front bedroom of Uncle Bill's house. Her hands were folded across her chest, and she wore a slight smile. She looked as if she were asleep, perhaps enjoying a nice dream; but when Daisy, encouraged by her mother, bent to kiss Great-grandma, her lips brushed against a cheek so cold that it sent a little shiver through her.

Aunt Lily's and Emma's eyes were red and puffy, and Uncle Bill seemed to have to clear his throat whenever he said anything. Daisy waited quietly as the grown-ups talked, her attention caught from time to time by the peaceful figure on the bed. Great-grandma had often called people by the wrong names, and at times she had not quite seemed to know who Daisy was, but she had always been cheerful. It was odd to see her lying so still and silent.

When Daisy's father said they had better be leaving, it was something of a relief. They were soon back in the gig and heading for home.

'I should be able to get into town before the Post Office closes,' her father said. 'I want to get a telegram off today.'

'It's a good thing the weather's so cold, or they'd have to have the funeral tomorrow.' Her mother's voice had a thickness to it that crying had left behind. 'I hope Aunt Amy can get down in time, though—it's only a couple of days away.'

'Aunt Amy' was what her mother called Granny. A rush of excitement went through Daisy; if Granny was coming down from Auckland for the funeral, perhaps Eddie would come, too.

The excitement was soon replaced by a surge of guilt, mixed with relief that she had not said anything out loud. She should be thinking about Great-grandma, and how sad everyone was. In any case, a few moments' reflection told her Eddie would almost certainly not be coming. Great-grandma wasn't actually *his* great-grandmother, and he would not be allowed to take time off from an important school like that just for a great-great-aunt.

Granny arrived on the very day of the funeral; and, as Daisy had resigned herself to expecting, she came on her own. There was time only for a hurried visit to Aunt Rosie's for Granny to freshen up from her travels before they all went off to church.

Daisy joined in the hymns and prayers while casting occasional glances at the wooden box resting on trestles near the front of the church. It was strange to think of Great-grandma lying in there, probably still smiling just as Daisy had last seen her.

After the service several of Daisy's uncles and cousins carried the box outside and onto the carpenter's wagon, which had been swept clean of its usual sawdust and wood scraps before being draped in black cloth. The wagon set off at the head of a procession of gigs and buggies that made its dragging way along Ruatane's main street, the horses held to a slow walk.

People came out of shops as they passed, men removing their hats to show respect. Daisy sat between her parents in their gig, glancing around the procession while keeping as still as such a solemn occasion required. She caught a glimpse of Granny a little ahead of them, sitting amongst some of the cousins in Uncle John's buggy.

The lowering clouds that had threatened rain all day were oozing a fine drizzle when they reached the cemetery gates. Daisy's father retrieved an umbrella from under the gig's seat, and did his best to shelter Daisy and her mother with it as they walked to the graveside.

A deep hole had been carved out alongside the place where Great-grandpa was buried, the raw earth a pale scar in the well-tended cemetery lawns. The drizzle gathered itself into fat drops that plopped onto the umbrella and slithered off to splash at Daisy's feet. The minister stood at one end of the grave and said prayers for Great-grandma, raising his voice to be heard above the rain pelting the umbrella someone was holding over his head.

Water ran down the sides of the grave, making the earth slick. It flung itself against the wooden box with a dull, drumming noise. Daisy saw that Grandma was crying in a quiet sort of way, tears sliding down her face. Grandpa had her arm through his, and he was patting at her hand.

Great-grandma had been Grandma's mother, and she couldn't always have been sleepy all the time and forgetting who people were. No wonder Grandma was so sad. Daisy put her arms around her own mother's waist and pressed against her.

The rain had shrunk to drizzle again by the time they drove back to the valley, Daisy's father picking a careful way along the track to avoid the worst of the puddles. They went up to Uncle Bill's house, where the parlour was already crowded.

Granny's brothers, Uncle John and Uncle Harry, were there with their families. Grandpa and Grandma arrived soon afterwards, with Benjy, Aunt Maisie and Kate in the buggy; their big boys rode up separately. There were cakes and sandwiches and cups of tea, and everyone seemed a little more cheerful now that the funeral was over.

Daisy perched on the arm of her mother's chair, listening to the grown-ups' stories of their own childhood days in the valley, and wondering how long it would be before her parents said it was time to go home. Then Benjy beckoned her, and the two of them went out to the verandah. They shared some particularly nice biscuits Benjy had managed to help himself to, and watched fantails swooping around the verandah posts in search of insects. Benjy was good company, though of course it was not like being with Eddie.

Granny stayed with them for the rest of the week. When Daisy was not in school she spent much of her time with her grandmother, sitting on the verandah watching the rain, or going for walks when the weather allowed. Granny's capacity for talking about Eddie was as boundless as Daisy could have wished.

To Daisy's delight, Granny taught her some French phrases; though when Daisy asked about Latin, her grandmother said Aunt Sarah felt French was quite enough to dredge up from her own schooldays. Granny wrote out the French for her, and Daisy made sure to go over the words every day while she was there to help, sometimes whispering them over last thing at night if she was still awake when her grandmother slipped into their shared room.

On the way home from seeing Granny off at the wharf, Daisy practised her precious few phrases under her breath. That very afternoon she wrote a letter to Eddie, carefully copying some of the French words where they more or less fitted with what she wanted to say.

The May school holidays began the following week, and Daisy was told what she had already guessed from snatches of overheard conversations: there would be no other travelling to and from Auckland that month. Grandpa, she learned, did not want to be far from home these days.

'It's the war, you see,' her mother said. 'They've brought in a law about—now, Daisy, you're not to get upset, but they're going to start taking men with this conscription thing.'

'Like Uncle Doug had to go because of them being mean to him at his work?' Daisy asked.

She saw her parents exchange a glance. 'Well, they're not going to give the fellows much say about it,' her father said. 'The conscription says the Government can make them go in the army.'

'They're not taking married men,' her mother put in quickly. 'Or boys Eddie's age,' she added before Daisy could ask. 'Only men over twenty. But it means they might take Uncle Joey, or one of Grandpa's other big boys, and Grandpa has to think out how he'll manage.'

'They're not going to start taking men straight away, but it'll probably be some time this year,' her father said. 'So your Grandpa's thinking he wants to get the jobs done early if he can.'

And that meant Grandpa could not afford the time for trips away; certainly not for so small a reason as Daisy's longing to visit Auckland again. Uncle Doug had had to go away and leave Emma, and now there was no chance of seeing Eddie for months. She could tell that her mother was worried about Grandpa's big boys, who were her brothers. Everyone seemed just a little distracted these days. That horrible war made everything go wrong.

Auckland was out of reach, but Daisy went to Lucy's again for the May holidays. Her aunt and uncle made her very welcome, and Lucy was clearly delighted at having her come to stay. For the first day she barely let Daisy out of her sight, insisting that they walk arm in arm whenever they left the house, and almost unable to get the words out quickly enough to keep up with whatever new idea struck her. She showed Daisy her new winter dresses, the beads she had been given for her eleventh birthday earlier that month, and all the drawings she had recently done.

Lucy eventually settled down into something approaching calm, but Lucy's quieter moods could not be relied on to last. On the third day of Daisy's visit, tension over a painting that refused to turn out to Lucy's satisfaction ended in a drama of spilled paints, raised voices, and an exasperated Aunt Maudie sending Lucy to her room, with a threat of no pudding that evening.

Lucy slammed the bedroom door hard enough to make the floor shake, and although the resulting peace was an improvement, Daisy found herself with a solid wall between her and any books or toys she might have wished to look at.

She wondered if she should ask Aunt Maudie if there were any jobs she could help with, but on further consideration decided it might be wiser to let her aunt recover from Lucy's outburst before bothering her.

A better idea suggested itself. Daisy made her way through the house to Uncle Richard's office. The door stood ajar; Daisy knocked, and a moment later heard her uncle say, 'Come in.' She slipped inside and went to stand in front of the large desk where he sat.

Uncle Richard saw patients in this room, which as well as the passage door Daisy had just used also had its own private entrance from the outside, but he sometimes stayed in the office even when no one had come to see him; especially, Daisy had noticed, when things got particularly noisy. He had a tall book open in front of him that looked like the accounts book Daisy's parents used on the farm.

Her uncle looked surprised to see her, but he smiled at Daisy. 'What can I do for you, dear?'

'Could I please have a read of that book about people's insides?' Daisy asked. 'The one I looked at when I stayed here before,' she added, seeing his puzzled expression. 'You said perhaps it'd be all right for me to look at it again.'

'An anatomy book? Oh, yes, I do remember that occasion.' Her uncle's smile returned. He rose from his chair, and ran his finger along the books on one of the nearer shelves. 'Let me see, I think it must have been… yes, this is the one.'

He opened the book and glanced at the list of chapters. 'I don't believe there's anything unsuitable, though I must say it's an odd choice of reading material for a girl your age, Daisy. But you're welcome to look at it.'

'Thank you.' Daisy picked up the heavy book and took a step towards the door.

'Oh, I'd rather you kept it in here,' Uncle Richard said, stopping her in her tracks. 'I'm sure you'd be careful with it, but Nicky and Timmy have an unfortunate habit of destroying anything that falls into their hands.'

Daisy's notion of curling up in one of the parlour's comfortable armchairs with the fascinating book evaporated, but she could not think of a way to say she had changed her mind that would not sound ill-mannered. Her uncle carried a chair over to the side of his desk, cleared a space for Daisy to open the book, and went back to his work.

She felt a little awkward at first, as if she should sit up especially straight, but Uncle Richard seemed too busy with whatever he was doing to take much notice of her.

The book was as fascinating as she had remembered. There were drawings of muscles and how they worked together; illustrations of bones all the way from an entire skeleton to the small joints of the fingers. Daisy flexed her own hand, studying the way the fingers moved, and imagined the bones and muscles under the skin.

She turned a few more pages, and found the section of the book devoted to various organs. Daisy was familiar with several of these, though from the bodies of sheep rather than people. Lungs, she knew, were for breathing, but she had never considered how they might change shape as air came in and out. She recognised the liver, but could not recall ever having been told what it was for, other than as something her mother occasionally cooked for breakfast.

Daisy abruptly realised that she had not heard the click of her uncle's pen against his inkwell for some time. She looked up from the book to see him smiling at her.

'My goodness, how engrossed you are, Daisy.' He placed the pen in its holder, slid his chair a little closer and glanced at the page. 'Ah, studying the liver, I see. Yes, a most useful organ.'

Uncle Richard was so nice that Daisy found it strange to think she had once been shy of talking to him. 'What does it do?' she asked.

'It plays an important part in digestion—it produces bile, for one thing. You wouldn't be able to digest your food without a healthy liver.'

He named the various parts of the liver for Daisy, and she peered closely at the tiny writing as he indicated each section. 'What's he-pa-tic mean?' she asked, sounding the unfamiliar word carefully.

'Relating to the liver. It's Latin, though originally from the Greek if memory serves me.'

For a brief moment Daisy forgot the book entirely. 'Do you know Latin, Uncle Richard?'

'Of course,' he said, as if it were the most obvious of facts.

'Eddie does, too,' she said, feeling a tiny glow of reflected glory. 'He's learning it at school.'

'Yes, I believe he's attending quite a good school, so no doubt he'll be given a grounding in all the important subjects. Your Aunt Sarah has rather firm ideas regarding education.'

Aunt Sarah had firm ideas on most things, as far as Daisy could tell. 'Thank you for telling me about livers.'

'It's a pleasure, dear, with such an attentive audience.' Uncle Richard glanced at the clock that stood on his mantel shelf. 'It's nearly afternoon tea time. Have you had enough of anatomy for now?'

Daisy knew this might be her only opportunity that week. 'Could I just look at one more page first?' When her uncle nodded, she carefully turned the leaf.

'Oh, it's a heart,' she said, studying the new series of drawings. 'What a lot of bits it's got in it.'

'Mm, hearts are a complicated business. See, here are the different chambers, and the veins and arteries leading in and out.'

Hearts were indeed complicated. Blood came in and out on both sides, with valves to keep everything going in the right direction. Each side seemed to have its own particular tasks. Her uncle traced his finger along the lines drawn around the heart, and showed Daisy where they led off towards the lungs, for air to be put into the blood.

'I hope I haven't thoroughly confused you with all that,' he said, glancing up from the book.

'I *think* I understand how it works,' Daisy said, frowning in concentration. 'A little bit, anyway.'

'Well, I wouldn't claim to know everything about hearts myself. I do know enough to treat the subject with great respect, though—there's a good deal that can go wrong in that area.'

The room seemed to grow very quiet. It was Daisy who broke the silence. 'Like with Mama?'

Her uncle regarded her thoughtfully. 'Has your mother spoken to you about that?'

'She told me she had a thing wrong with her heart. She said she found out when...' Daisy trailed off. *When I was born*, she had been on the point of saying, but she was sure her mother would not want her to speak of such things; not when it meant talking about Uncle Richard helping get Daisy out from down *there*. 'When I was really little,' she made do with. She hesitated, then the words came out in a rush. 'And Mama said you saved her life.'

'Well, that might be claiming a little too much for myself,' her uncle said. 'One can never know how things might have turned out. But I'm glad I was able to help you into the world, my dear—not to mention having the honour of being your godfather.'

'It must be good to be able to save people's lives.' Especially when the life in question was her mother's. It was hard to imagine a greater achievement.

Uncle Richard's expression changed to a more solemn one. 'It's inexpressibly wonderful, Daisy, and I give thanks every time I receive that great blessing.' He closed the book and slid it away, smiling once more. 'Now, let's go and see about this afternoon tea before your Aunt Maudie has to come and fetch us.'

On Sunday afternoons when it was not too wet, Daisy and her parents often went up the valley to Uncle Bill's. She found it strange to go into the parlour and see an empty chair in Great-grandma's old corner, instead of her great-grandmother smiling around at everyone.

Uncle Bill and Aunt Lily had moved into the big front bedroom that had been Great-grandma's, and Emma now had their old room. Uncle Bill's house had never had quite enough rooms to go around, so for years Emma had slept in an alcove off the kitchen where jams and preserves were kept. On one visit she took Daisy into her new bedroom, and opened the chest of drawers to reveal the table linen and doilies she was accumulating.

'I've still got quite a few more to make,' she said. 'I want to have it all ready for when Doug comes home, and we can set up house properly.' Daisy was careful not to ask how far off that might be.

Emma often had letters from Doug to read out from. Occasionally one of his letters might be in a green envelope; these were rather special, Emma explained. The rules said that an officer had to read letters written by ordinary soldiers like Doug before they could be sent on to New Zealand, just in case there were any war secrets written in them. The officers were trusted not to write war secrets, and they wrote home using these envelopes. But sometimes a kind-hearted officer would give a married man like Doug one of his green envelopes, so that he could write what he liked without having to worry about someone reading his and Emma's private business. Daisy noticed that Emma never read aloud from those particular letters.

Doug's letters no longer arrived as reliably as they had when he was still in the training camp. Now a week or more might go by without any, to be followed by several all at once. Doug was writing as regularly as ever, Emma said, but it all depended on when he could get letters away. And the mail took such a long time that letters might be two months old when she finally received them.

Towards the end of July, Daisy noticed that Emma had stopped going out, even to church. Her mother told her that Emma was poorly, though she looked well to Daisy. When they went up to Uncle Bill's one Sunday in August, Daisy noticed that Emma was really getting quite plump; she was almost as round as Grandma now.

Daisy recalled much the same sort of talk about Aunt Rosie the year before, when she had supposedly been poorly. It must mean there was a baby on the way for Emma.

Emma was in a particularly cheerful mood that day. She had three new letters from Doug, including one in a green envelope, as well as a pretty card with flowers embroidered on it. She set the card on a small table by her chair, moving aside some knitting to make room for it. The knitting was white and lacy; more complicated than anything Daisy had yet mastered, and certainly not socks for a man. Doug probably had enough socks for now.

While they had their afternoon tea, Emma read to them from the letter that had been sent most recently. Doug did not say exactly where he was, just 'somewhere in France'; that was as much as he was allowed to tell them, she explained.

When Daisy's family were about to leave, Emma called Daisy over and held out the embroidered card.

'You can have this if you like, Daisy—I've got a few of them more or less the same.' She opened the card to reveal the single line of writing inside. 'See, it says, "Love to all at home", and that means you as well.'

Daisy thanked her, and carefully took hold of the precious card that had come all the way from France. When she got back home she put the card on her chest of drawers with her other treasures, propped against her books and close to the hair clips from Eddie.

Next day at school, rather than going straight outside at playtime Daisy asked Miss Cameron if she could look at the map. France was a big country, but Daisy knew from the newspapers that the fighting was in the part near Belgium. She studied the map, wondering just where Uncle Doug might be and what he might be doing.

She had looked forward to sharing the latest news of Uncle Doug with Benjy, but he was not at school that day. Daisy was not greatly surprised; on Sunday at church she had noticed that Benjy had a slight cough, and Grandma always made him stay home from school if he seemed the least bit unwell.

The day went more slowly without Benjy for company, but by the middle of the afternoon Daisy was concentrating too hard on a set of sums to take much notice of the time. One particularly difficult piece of long division claimed all her attention; only when she had carefully checked the final result did she become aware of murmuring from the bench immediately behind her, where the oldest pupils sat.

Miss Cameron had also noticed the restlessness. 'No talking in class.' She cast a meaningful look at the strap that lay on the edge of her desk.

'Yes, Elsie, what is it?'

Daisy looked over her shoulder to see one of the three pupils in the back row lower her hand. 'Please, Miss, Daisy's pa's out there,' the girl said, pointing towards the window.

A startled Daisy followed the direction of the pointing finger to see her father by the school's horse paddock. He had already caught her horse; now he stood holding both sets of reins in one hand and his hat in the other, pressed against his chest. Daisy made to rise from her bench, then remembered herself and looked to the teacher for permission.

'Have you finished your arithmetic, Daisy?' Miss Cameron asked.

'I've still got two sums to go,' Daisy admitted.

The teacher glanced up at the clock. 'It's almost home time, anyway. Yes, you may leave now—I'm sure your father has a good reason for fetching you.'

Daisy hastily packed up her books and rushed outside. One look at her father's face told her that something terrible had happened.

'We're going up to Uncle Bill's,' he said. 'There's been a telegram— Uncle Ernie came down to tell us. Doug's been killed.'

Chapter Twelve

Emma sat hunched on the sofa, staring off into some invisible distance with red, swollen eyes. She seemed unaware of anyone else in the room; even of Aunt Lily close beside her, one arm around Emma's waist. Daisy had never seen anyone so wretchedly unhappy.

The men stood about talking in low voices, Emma's brothers among them, while the women clustered near Emma, each taking a turn sitting by her on the sofa across from Aunt Lily. Daisy's mother kissed Emma, and murmured something in her ear, but Emma was beyond even Mama's special way of making everything all right.

Daisy found an inconspicuous spot behind a chair. She sat on a footstool there, and did her best not to attract any attention to herself. She was shy in the face of Emma's grief, and frightened of somehow making it even worse by anything she might say or do.

When they had been there so long that she was sure it must be time to go home, her mother sought her out.

'Talk to Emma before we leave,' she said quietly. 'You don't have to say much,' she added, seeing Daisy's expression. 'Just tell her you're sorry about Doug.'

Uncle Bill's parlour was not large, but it seemed a long walk across it to where Emma was sitting. Daisy stood in front of the sofa, biting at her lip. She felt her mother's hand on her shoulder, giving it an encouraging squeeze. 'I'm sorry about Uncle Doug,' she said, although her voice came out so small that she was not quite sure she had managed to speak aloud. She hesitated, then drew out of her pocket the card Emma had given her the previous day.

Was it really only one day ago? Yesterday Emma had been bright with confidence, talking gaily about what they would do when Doug came home. Now it was hard to imagine that she might ever smile again.

The card had caught Daisy's eye when she was changing out of her school clothes before coming over to Uncle Bill's, and without quite thinking why she did so she had slipped it into her pocket. *I thought you might want it back. Because it was the last thing from Uncle Doug.* That was what she had meant to say, but she found herself unable to speak. She placed the card on Emma's lap, and saw her hand reach out to cover it.

Over the next few days Daisy caught snatches of conversation between her parents about how ill Emma was. 'I hope everything's all right,' her mother said one day, which puzzled Daisy, because how could things be all right for Emma?

The minister devoted part of his sermon to Doug on the following Sunday, but Emma was not there to hear it. Even if she had not stopped going out because of the baby, she would have been in no state to face the world.

There would be no funeral in Ruatane for Doug. It was too far to send bodies all the way from France, not when the boats took so long. They had to get on and bury them.

Daisy remembered Great-grandma lying on the bed, looking as if she were enjoying a pleasant dream, only the coldness of her cheek revealing the truth. At the funeral, everyone had talked about the long and contented life she had had, and such a peaceful passing to be with Great-grandpa again. It was her time, everyone said.

The minister used words like 'noble' and 'sacrifice' when he spoke of Doug. He talked of the glory of laying down one's life in an honourable cause.

But Daisy had seen animals slaughtered. She knew what death could look like. It was hard to avoid the images of blood and splintered bone; harder still to think of it as glorious.

At school, the boys still had their mock battles, naming various parts of the muddy ground around the school building after sites currently in the news. The horse paddock was declared to be the Somme, which was where the fateful telegram had revealed Doug's 'somewhere in France' to be; no longer a secret now that it had claimed his life. The other boys had stopped asking Benjy to join in these games, and occasionally one of them would, after glancing over at Daisy and Benjy, suggest kicking a ball around instead.

By October of 1916 there was much playground talk of conscription, especially among the boys with older brothers. The first of the ballots to call up soldiers was going to be next month, everyone said.

Daisy did her best to ignore such talk. Perhaps no one in her family would be called up; perhaps the war would not take anyone else from them. She almost believed it. Until she heard the news.

Bill Leith had not thought much of it when his brother went into town that afternoon. Ernie might be the youngest in the family, but he was thirty-six years old; too old for Bill to feel the need to question him on his comings and goings.

Over lunch Ernie had said he would be back in time for the afternoon milking, which was all that really mattered. He had a rather knowing, self-important manner as he said it, which made Bill wonder if the reason for Ernie's outing was not fit for the women to hear.

But that was nothing Bill wanted to pry into. His brothers seemed well and truly confirmed bachelors by now; Bill did not grudge them whatever pleasure they might find in a drink at the hotel, or a visit to the women upstairs

Ernie did get back just in time for milking. Bill and Alf were already down at the cowshed, leaning against a railing and discussing the weather while Bill's two sons herded the cows into the yard. Ernie ambled up to them, looking pleased with himself.

'I've been in to see the Army fellow at the Post Office,' he announced. 'I've joined up.'

Bill and Alf gazed at him, both open-mouthed with astonishment. 'What the hell have you done that for?' Bill asked when he regained the power of speech.

'Well, it's a chance to see a bit of the world, eh? Might as well have a holiday and have the government pay for it.'

'Didn't turn out too well for Doug, did it?' Bill said. It had been two months since the news of Doug's death; perhaps that was long enough for his brothers to have got over the shock of it. Neither of them had a daughter carrying a child who would never know its father.

'The young fellows like Doug don't know how to look out for themselves the same as blokes my age. I'll just keep my head down when things get lively, and see the sights of Paris and all that in between times.'

Ernie had never shown much sign of wanderlust. And he had never been a particularly good liar. Bill gave him a hard stare, and Ernie's mouth twisted into something closer to grimace than grin.

'Look, they're going to start calling chaps up any time now. I'd just as soon get on with it—better than waiting around to see if my name comes up in the ballot.'

He glanced over his shoulder towards Bill's sons; Arfie and Will were engrossed in a conversation of their own as they waited for the last of the cows to file past the gate. 'Anyway, I've been thinking about it—if someone from the farm's already signed up, they mightn't take your young fellows when the conscription starts.'

Relief and guilt warred within Bill. The thought that his boys might be called up had been weighing heavily on his mind. Will was only eighteen, and safe from conscription for now; although who knew how much longer this war might drag on? But Arfie was twenty-four, and subject to the ballot.

Hardly an evening had gone by since conscription was announced when Bill and Lily had not turned the subject over in fruitless discussion. With five men working the farm, there would be little chance of gaining an exemption for Arfie. Their fears for him were made all the worse by how difficult it was to imagine Arfie taking much notice of orders, even those that might keep him safe.

Ernie was holding out an unlooked-for hope; but did Bill have any right to take it? As the oldest in the family, it had always been up to him to look after the others. 'Keep an eye on the young fellows,' his father would say if the boys were heading off to the creek, or anywhere near the horses and farm machinery. Bill had accepted his role as a fact of nature even with Alf, who was five years his junior, but especially with Ernie.

Bill had been fifteen when Ernie was born. He had dragged his little brother out of the path of horses' hooves; rescued him from tangles of blackberry; hauled him wriggling and protesting from swimming holes too deep for him. He was the oldest. It was his job.

'I don't like to think of you going over there,' conscience made him say.

Ernie gave a crooked-mouthed grin that brought before Bill's eyes a sharp vision of that cheeky-faced little boy. 'Too late for that now, it's all signed and sealed. Don't worry about me, I can look after myself.'

Alf cleared his throat. 'We can look out for each other,' he said; the first words he had uttered since Ernie's announcement. 'I'll go in tomorrow and sign up.'

Conscience was no longer pricking at Bill; it was twisting like a knife. 'You can't do that, Alf!'

'I don't think they'd take a bloke your age,' Ernie said. 'Forty-five's the oldest they want, and you're forty-six.'

'I'll say I'm a couple of years younger, then. You're not going off on your own.'

Bill looked helplessly from one to the other. Both his brothers going off to the war while he sat comfortably at home. Not a damned thing he could do to stop them, and a guilty awareness that he might not want to even if he could. Not when it meant keeping Arfie and Will safe. 'Thanks,' he said. The word had never seemed so feeble.

Alf and Ernie were on their way barely a fortnight later. Lily had busied herself with their clothes, doing any necessary mending and sewing new garments to replace threadbare ones. She had allowed Emma to help her with the lightest of the work, though only because, as she privately told Bill, she thought the distraction might be good for her.

The baby was due in a few weeks now, and was making Emma increasingly uncomfortable. She had managed to appear composed when told of her uncles' enlistment, but on the morning of their departure she fled straight from the breakfast table to her room, and could not be coaxed out to wave them off.

Bill drove his brothers to Ruatane in the spring cart, Alf sharing the plank seat with him while Ernie found room for himself in the back with their bags. The *Ngatiawa* was already tied up at the wharf, taking on a load of flax. Bill fiddled with his pipe as he and his brothers waited for the last of the cargo to be stowed, grateful for the distraction offered by the pipe's reluctance to be lit. Ernie joked that he would be glad of a holiday from milking cows; Bill pretended to grumble at being left two men short on the farm.

The *Ngatiawa*'s horn blew, signalling that it was ready to sail. The brothers shook hands, and Alf and Ernie hoisted their packs.

'Hooray, then,' Alf said.

'Drop us a line when you can,' Bill said. 'Let us know how you're getting on.'

He waited on the wharf until the *Ngatiawa* rounded a curve of the river and was hidden from sight.

The first balloting for conscription took place in November, just a month after Daisy's uncles left Ruatane. Daisy was alert for any hint that fathers might be taken after all, but when the list was published neither of the two chosen from the valley were married men.

One of Daisy's next-door cousins from Granny's family, Uncle Harry's oldest son Rob, was turned down by the medical examiner, who told him his eyesight was weak. Rob complained about this to anyone who would listen; not because of any disappointment at missing the call-up, but from old resentment dating back to his school days.

'Miss Metcalf was always giving me the strap for getting stuff wrong,' he grumbled. 'I reckon it's because I couldn't see the board properly.' None of the others around his age were very sympathetic; Miss Metcalf, they pointed out, had given everyone the strap for the slightest reason.

The other family member called up, Grandpa and Grandma's second son Mick, was passed fit for service, and told to report for duty.

Daisy's mother was quiet at the news, and Daisy could tell she was worried for her younger brother. But everyone tried to find cheerful things to say to Uncle Mick. He was sure to meet up with Uncle Alf and Uncle Ernie in the training camp near Wellington, although they might be sailing for Europe any time now. No one was sure just when, as the uncles were not good correspondents. Aunt Lily wrote to them faithfully every week, but they had only sent two postcards back so far, with no more than a sentence or so scrawled on each.

By early December Uncle Mick had left, loaded down with everyone's good wishes and with tins of cakes and biscuits.

Two weeks before Christmas, Emma had a baby boy. Daisy was taken up the valley to visit them a few days later. Emma lay propped against the pillows, baby Dougie in her arms, and for the first time in many months Daisy saw Emma smiling.

The Inspector came to the valley school for the annual examinations that month. Daisy found the questions for her Standard Three tests quite easy, as she was used to doing Standard Four work with Benjy much of the time.

Miss Cameron had announced that there would be a prize-giving on the last day of school, and when she happened to see Daisy's grandfather riding up the valley that afternoon she sent Benjy hurrying outside to ask him if he would mind giving out the prizes.

Grandpa did not mind at all. He handed out certificates for good attendance and careful work, making each award sound important as he read the pupil's name aloud. He shook hands with the older ones, and patted the little ones on the head.

When the certificates had all been given out, Miss Cameron handed Grandpa a small book. He opened it, and read out, ' "Waituhi Valley School 1916, Special Prize for Achievement, Margaret Stewart".'

Daisy did not often hear her proper name, and it took her a moment to realise just why Grandpa was smiling at her. She went up to the front of the room and took the book from his outstretched hand, almost forgetting to thank him in the excitement of the moment, and only belatedly realising when she got back to her seat that she had completely forgotten to thank Miss Cameron.

She had her chance to put that right when school finished, by which time Daisy had studied her new book whenever Miss Cameron's attention was elsewhere. It had poems; quite grown-up ones, with long words that Daisy looked forward to reading aloud. In between the poems were drawings of trees and flowers, and two or three pages had coloured paintings. It was just the right size of book to go in a pocket, to be taken out and read at some convenient moment.

Miss Cameron said the children could leave a little early, as it was the last day of term, but she asked Daisy to stay behind and help with clearing up.

Daisy filled a bucket of water from the rain barrel, and set to washing the blackboards while her teacher swept the floor. 'Thank you for the lovely book, Miss Cameron,' she said.

Miss Cameron smiled. 'You're most welcome—you've worked very well this year.' She paused in her sweeping. 'If it were up to me, I'd move you on to Standard Five next year with Benjy. But I'm afraid it's not quite approved of to let a child get too far ahead of their age—you're doing well to be starting Standard Four while you're still only nine.'

Daisy finished cleaning the blackboards and made to start on some shelves, but Miss Cameron took the cloth from her hand.

'You go off home, I'll finish up here. Enjoy the holidays, Daisy.'

Daisy's parents made much of her prize, inspecting it carefully, reading aloud the inscription from Miss Cameron, and then placing the book on the mantelpiece so that it could be admired as they sat in the parlour that evening.

'Looks like we'll be sending you to high school in a few years, all right.' Her father was smiling, but not as if it were just a joke.

'We'll need to, if you're going to be a teacher,' her mother said. 'I don't see why you couldn't be one, if Miss Cameron thinks you're doing so well.'

The thought of going to high school just as Eddie did was a warm feeling inside Daisy. There would be so many interesting things to learn, with sciences and languages and all the rest of those subjects; far more than there was room for at the little valley school.

Being a teacher was an important job, and it seemed that it was what girls who went to high school did. Learning all those new things was wonderful to look forward to; perhaps it did not matter that she did not feel nearly as excited at the idea of teaching.

Christmas was subdued that year, with the memory of Doug's death still fresh, Uncle Mick gone, and the two empty places at Uncle Bill's. There would be another conscription ballot soon; once in a while someone would mention it, then quickly change the subject. Even Eddie was no longer so keen to talk about the war.

Haymaking began soon after Christmas, the work harder than usual with three men missing. Eddie, now fourteen and big for his age, was much in demand, and threw himself into the work with great energy. By midday his face was bright pink, and his shirt plastered to his body with sweat. He and the other boys often slipped off for a quick splash in the creek while the women set out lunch.

Daisy made herself useful helping with the food, but her favourite part of the day was when she and Eddie rode home together. By then the sun would be skimming the hills that edged the valley, turning the light golden. Sometimes they walked along beside the horses for part of the way, paddling in the stony shallows of the creek.

The haymaking finished, and for a few short weeks Daisy and Eddie were free to roam the farm all day long. And then Eddie was gone, on his way back to Auckland with Granny, and the summer holidays were over.

On the hottest February afternoons, sun beating down on the iron roof of the schoolhouse until Daisy felt she must be like a dinner roasting in the oven, she would gaze out the window and dream of those days spent wandering in the cool of the bush and paddling in the creek, Eddie at her side. Then Miss Cameron's voice would recall her sharply to the present, and Daisy returned to her schoolwork.

While most of the country had regular conscription ballots to call up more and more men, over the next few months there were so many volunteers in the Bay of Plenty that no ballot was necessary there. The local newspaper often took the opportunity to mention this, as if the men of the Bay of Plenty were particularly brave and loyal. But Daisy wondered how many of these men might be like Uncle Doug, pushed into going off to the war because the people in charge made it too hard to stay home.

The cows were dried off in May, much to the relief of Benjy, who had to help with milking now that Uncle Mick had gone. Of course there would be no travelling to Auckland for the school holidays; Grandpa could not possibly leave the farm now, when they were one man short.

Once again, Daisy went to her uncle and aunt's for the holidays. Her first afternoon with them was bright and clear, although chilly, and Uncle Richard got out the croquet set; 'In honour of your visit, Daisy,' he said.

The whole family played. The youngest, four-year-old Timmy, was not much taller than the croquet mallet, so Uncle Richard placed his own hands over Timmy's chubby little fists and guided each stroke for him. Daisy noticed that Uncle Richard and Aunt Maudie often pretended to forget to score their own points, and when they adjusted the scores according to everyone's age, it somehow worked out that they all had exactly the same number of points.

That was the last they saw of the sun all week. Weather that varied from gloomy to downright stormy held them indoors most of the time.

Aunt Maudie kept a fire going even in the daytime against the chill.

In the evenings, the heavy velvet drapes were drawn across the windows and the fire built up to a cheery blaze. Before Aunt Maudie took Nicky and Timmy off to bed, Uncle Richard read to them all from a book called *Kidnapped*. Daisy already knew the story; Eddie had brought his own copy to the farm one year, and the two of them had read it aloud to each other. But Uncle Richard had a nice reading voice, and Daisy enjoyed watching the little boys listening wide-eyed, one of them occasionally letting out a squeak of excitement. The girls were allowed to sit up later than anyone did back home on the farm, and with everyone doing their own reading, drawing or sewing it made for a peaceful end to the day.

On Tuesday, Aunt Maudie took advantage of an afternoon that was simply grey and cold rather than actually raining, and went out to visit a lady friend, telling the girls to keep an eye on Nicky and Timmy.

The little boys played with a set of toy soldiers that Daisy privately considered not a patch on Eddie's, while Flora practised on the piano.

Lucy and Flora had both been sent to a lady on the other side of Ruatane for piano lessons, but after a few weeks Lucy had announced that she wasn't a bit interested in the piano. Aunt Maudie had said she was a silly girl not to want to learn, but it wasn't worth the fuss of trying to make her.

Flora practised quite diligently, including what seemed to Daisy like hours on her scales. Now she was trying out a new piece she had started just the week before.

Lucy looked up from her drawing. 'Do you have to play that same bit over and over?'

'Yes, I do,' Flora said. 'I have to practise till I've learned this line. Then I can do the next line.'

Plink, plink, plink, the piano went. *Plink,* plink, plink.

Lucy flung down her pencil and stalked around the room. She peered over Daisy's shoulder to see what she was reading; Daisy pretended not to notice. She wandered over to the piano and pressed a few keys at random, but that just meant Flora lost her place and went back to the beginning.

Plink, plink, plink.

Nicky waved one of the toy soldiers over his head, then plunged it amongst the army, knocking over half a dozen others. Timmy squealed and grabbed at his hand, sending more soldiers sprawling.

'Stop that at once!' Lucy scolded. 'Be quiet, you two.'

The boys ignored her. A few moments later the soldiers were

scattered over the floor, Nicky and Timmy rolling amongst them wrestling with each other, making more noise than ever.

Daisy lowered her book and studied Lucy. Her cousin sometimes seemed to feel that being twelve meant she should be ladylike. At the moment she looked uncertain whether to scream at the boys, fling herself onto the nearer one, or show with cold scorn that she was above such childish behaviour, but the glint in her eye suggested that she was likely to choose a noisy reaction.

The boys' wrestling match was clearly good-natured, but their high-pitched squeals were loud enough without the risk that Lucy might add her own voice to the mix. Daisy got up and slipped unnoticed from the room.

'Ah, Daisy, have you come to take refuge in my sanctuary?' her uncle said when Daisy knocked and then entered his office. 'I'm just taking stock of my supplies.'

Uncle Richard had had patients come to see him that morning, but Daisy had heard him say at lunchtime that he expected to have a quiet afternoon, so that he could get some paperwork done. The glass-fronted cabinet stood open, and it looked as though her uncle had been moving around the jars and bottles it held. Under the cabinet was a row of wooden drawers; these, too, were open, revealing small tins and paper packets. Several containers had been taken from the cabinet and drawers, and were spread out on the desk.

Daisy had closed the parlour door behind her, but Lucy's voice could be made out in the muffled noise coming from that direction, rising above the giggles of the little boys and Flora's dogged practising. 'Is it all right if I sit in here for a bit?' she asked.

'Of course, dear.' He glanced in the direction of the parlour. 'Sometimes a little peace and quiet is the best prescription of all. Was there anything you particularly wanted to look at? Were you planning on taking your anatomy studies further while you're here?'

Her uncle was holding one of the paper packets from the drawers; it looked as if he had been counting whatever was in it. He had a notebook open on his desk; each line had a few words, some with a number written alongside, but most with a blank space where the number should go. He seemed busy, and his desk was already quite full without her asking him for books to put on it.

'I don't think I need any books just now, thank you,' Daisy said. 'Do you have any jobs I could do?'

'You'd best ask your aunt—oh, Aunt Maudie's out at the moment, isn't she? What were you thinking of in particular, Daisy?'

Daisy had not been thinking of any particular jobs at all. 'Um… dusting or something?'

'Your aunt takes care of that sort of thing, but thank you, dear.' He looked down at the notebook, at the packets and tins spread around it, then back at Daisy. 'I don't suppose you'd like to help me with my stocktaking, would you?'

'Yes, I would,' Daisy said, quietly pleased not only at being asked to help, but also at having the chance to find out what was in some of those bottles, tins and papers.

Uncle Richard let her sit in his own chair, which was on castors and could swivel on the spot, and which Daisy had been secretly wanting to try ever since she first saw it, and stood alongside, looking over her shoulder.

'I need to make a note of how much I have of each item, so that I know what I should order,' he explained. 'If I call out the name, would you be able to find it on the list and write down the amount I tell you? Here, let me show you what I mean.'

He picked up one of the paper packets, read out, 'Dyspepsia tablets,' and pointed to the same words in the notebook. 'I go through rather a lot of these. There are…' Uncle Richard looked in the packet and counted under his breath. 'Two dozen tablets left. Write it as doz—d-o-z. That's right, very good. All right? Shall we go on?'

He read out each name and quantity, starting off slowly to make sure that Daisy could keep up, then gradually getting faster. Some of the medicines were measured in drachms, some in fluid ounces, and some just by the number of tablets. Daisy dipped the pen in and out of its inkwell and wiped it on the blotter, careful to write each line as neatly as she could.

'Tincture of benzoin, twelve ounces,' her uncle read.

Daisy looked over at the label to check the name. 'Tincture of benzoin,' she murmured as she wrote, trying out the sound of the unfamiliar words.

'Yes, that's the one,' Uncle Richard said, glancing down at the page. 'It's useful as an inhalant in bronchitis.'

As they worked, her uncle told Daisy about some of the different medicines. A fine powder called Flowers of Sulphur was used against scabies, he said. Oxymel of Squills was good for stubborn coughs, and he always made sure to have extra stocks of it in time for winter. Iodide of potassium was a most useful medicine for disorders of several different organs.

Uncle Richard moved each item to one side of the desk as he read it off. When they had all been checked, he gathered up the containers to put back in the drawers and cabinet. While she waited for the ink to dry, Daisy studied the list of medicines with their strange names, saying them over to herself.

'How do you remember what all the different ones are for?' she asked.

'Well, just between you and I, Daisy, I do occasionally have to look up the correct treatment in one of my reference books. But the more commonly used ones are easy enough to remember—you probably know some of them yourself. This, for instance,' he showed Daisy a bottle labelled 'Mag sulph', 'is simply Epsom salts by the correct Latin name. And I'm sure you're familiar with Oleum Palma Christi under the name of castor oil.'

Daisy was indeed familiar with the nasty-tasting oil that she risked being dosed with if she admitted to not having had a recent bowel movement. Grandma had firm opinions about 'keeping regular'.

Her uncle closed the cabinet, then reached down a large book from one of the shelves. 'This is one of the references I sometimes consult,' he said, opening the book and placing it before Daisy.

'Oh, it's a pharmacopoeia.' Daisy hoped she was saying the word properly. 'Mama's got one at home.' The battered old book lived on a shelf in the kitchen, and her mother was always careful to wipe her hands before lifting it down and handling its fragile pages. 'She looks things up in it sometimes when she's making medicines for the cows.' Daisy had never done more than glance at the book herself; her mother knew whatever the animals might need, and everyone else left her to it.

'I believe it's my old one, actually,' Uncle Richard said. 'I gave it to your grandfather years ago, but he always said it was your mother who made most use of it. Let's see what this one has to say about castor oil.'

Daisy felt inclined to dispute the book's description of castor oil as 'A valuable mild purgative', but she was in full agreement with its remark that 'It is nauseous to the taste'.

She looked over at the facing page, and saw a row of similar names. 'Does "oleum" mean oil?'

'That's right, it's Latin for oil. As you can see, there are a great many useful ones.'

'Clove oil,' Daisy read aloud; the entry was headed 'Oleum Caryophilli', but it seemed safer to choose the more familiar words that came just afterwards. 'We've got that one at home, too.'

'Yes, that's very useful for the relief of toothache.'

'And Mama uses it when a cow gets a sore udder. She mixes it up with lard and rubs it on.'

'Really? Now that's a use I've never had occasion to make of it.' Her uncle's eyes were twinkling. 'Unlike me, your mother is an expert in all things relating to farm animals—and that must take a good deal of skill when the patient can't explain just where it hurts!'

He closed the book and returned it to its shelf. 'Thank you, Daisy, you've been a big help. And such neat writing you have,' he added, looking down at the notebook. 'Rather tidier than mine, actually.' He smiled at her. 'I think you may have a knack for this sort of thing, dear.'

For the rest of Daisy's stay, she spent part of each day with her uncle in his office, making sure to choose a time when Lucy was engrossed in her drawing and painting.

One afternoon she cut and folded a roll of bandages into useful lengths; another day she wrote out labels for some medicines that Uncle Richard had sorted into smaller packets. She noticed that he checked what she had written to be sure there were no mistakes, and was relieved when he praised her work.

He told her more about the medicines and what they were for, sounding out the Latin names and saying what they meant. Uncle Richard was good at explaining things so they were easy to understand.

Daisy enjoyed these hours with her uncle so much that she would almost have been sorry when it came time to leave if she had not been eager to be back home with her parents, and to find out what had been happening on the farm.

Chapter Thirteen

When school started again, Daisy found that Benjy had spent much of the holidays waiting for the chance to share an idea with her.

'What do you think about us putting on a play?' he asked as soon as they were sitting outside on a bench sheltered from the wind. 'You and me and a couple of others.'

'A play?' Daisy repeated. 'What sort of play?'

'Well, we wouldn't be able to do one you need a lot of stuff for, or many people. I thought I might write one.'

He said it as if it were the simplest thing in the world to write a play. Daisy stared at him, impressed. 'I don't know if I could do acting.'

'Of course you could—I reckon you'd be really good at it.'

'*You'd* be good,' Daisy said. Benjy could hold people's attention even when reading from quite dull books.

'But you've seen a play—a real one—so you'll be able to tell me what it should look like.'

'I suppose so.' Daisy closed her eyes, and thought back to that magical evening in Auckland: the carriage ride, with Granny and Aunt Sarah in their lovely gowns; the dazzling lights of the theatre; the actors in their fancy costumes, gliding about the stage among scenery that changed every time the lights went down, and looked so real she had soon forgotten it was only painted wood. She remembered the brand-new sealskin muff nestled in her lap; her fingers brushed instead against the stiff calico of her pinafore, and she opened her eyes to meet Benjy's earnest gaze.

'Where would we have it, then?' she asked.

'In our parlour, I suppose. Do you think that'd do?'

Daisy dropped out of her daydream and back down to earth with a thump. 'But for real plays they have big curtains, and special lights and things.'

Benjy shrugged. 'We could rig something up for curtains. And we'll do it in the daytime, so we won't need lights.'

'But...' Daisy began, then decided to keep her doubts to herself. Benjy did have a way of making things happen when there was something he really wanted. 'I expect it'll be all right. What's the play going to be about?'

'I'm not sure yet. It needs to have some funny bits, though, and something about a prince and a princess. Sort of like a fairy tale.'

'That's a good idea—everyone likes fairy tales.'

'Mmm. I have to think the story out a bit more yet, though.'

There were fewer volunteers in the Bay of Plenty now, and conscription returned to the area. At the end of May, Benjy's brother Danny was called up.

'Pa says him and Joe can manage all right while the cows are dried off,' Benjy told Daisy. 'I might have to miss a bit of school come spring, though.'

But for now, Benjy's mind was on other matters. He talked about his play whenever he and Daisy had a quiet spot to themselves. Not long had passed before Daisy found herself caught up in his enthusiasm.

He soon had the outline of a story worked out. 'There's six parts,' he said. 'There's a king and queen, a prince and a princess, and two fairies—a good one and a bad one.'

'Can we get six people for it, though?' Daisy asked.

'Maybe. I'll see how it goes. I thought Lucy and Flora might like to be in it.'

'Lucy would, anyway. She'll want to be the Princess.'

Benjy grinned. 'Of course she will.'

While the grown-ups stood around talking after church the following Sunday, Benjy told Lucy and Flora about the play.

'And I want you to be the Princess,' he said before Lucy had the chance to demand the role for herself. Daisy hid a smile; Lucy of course at once said that she would be in the play.

Flora, however, looked horrified at the idea. 'I couldn't do that,' she said, her eyes wide. 'Not with everyone looking at me. I'd forget what to say, or say it at the wrong time or something.'

Benjy claimed that he was sure Flora would manage, but he did not press the point when she continued to shake her head.

'I'll talk her round,' he told Daisy later that day. Daisy and her parents had had Sunday lunch at Grandpa's; there were two empty places at the table now, where Uncle Mick and Uncle Danny should have been.

While the grown-ups sat in the parlour letting their enormous roast dinner settle, Benjy and Daisy had slipped off to Benjy's room; he had it to himself these days, with two of his brothers away. They were sprawled on a worn old rug, sheets of paper covered with Benjy's writing spread out around them. 'I'll give her a part with not much to say, anyway.'

Daisy looked up from a page of roughed-out ideas for scenery. 'Could she be one of the fairies?'

'No, they're too important—they have to explain things, otherwise everyone watching will just get muddled. I want you to do that, 'cause you'll say it all properly.'

Daisy frowned, puzzled. 'But there's two fairies. I can't be both of them.'

'I think you could—no, look at this,' Benjy said, cutting off her protest. He picked up a piece of paper that had lines and arrows drawn on it, connecting up various names and scribbled notes. 'See, we could have the good fairy go off before the other one comes on.' He pointed to different parts of the page as he spoke. 'We'll have to sort out something for you to get changed behind, but that'll be all right.'

Daisy admired the drawing, with its criss-crossing lines going in all directions and stick figures showing the actors. She was not entirely convinced that she could do two parts in the one play, but Benjy made it sound so simple that she found herself agreeing to try.

'You don't mind about not being the Princess, do you?' Benjy asked. 'I mean, I know she'll get to dress up and all, but the fairies will have a lot more to say.'

The Princess would have the fanciest clothes, and perhaps even some nice jewellery. 'No, I don't mind,' Daisy said, and it was very nearly true.

'I don't know who I'm going to have for the Prince, though,' Benjy said. 'Nicky and Timmy are too little, and none of the kids at Uncle John's or Uncle Harry's would be any good—anyway, I want to have it just yours and my family, or we'd never fit everyone in the parlour.'

It would be a squeeze even as it was. 'But don't you want to be the Prince yourself?'

Benjy shook his head. 'No, I'd sooner keep an eye on how everything's going, in case there's something I need to sort out. I wish I could get someone who *looked* like a prince, though—you know, tall and handsome and all that stuff.'

Daisy's thoughts at once turned to the most prince-like person she knew. 'What a shame Eddie can't be in it. He'd be so good.'

She expected Benjy to agree that it was a shame; instead he looked thoughtful.

'Maybe... maybe Eddie *could* be in it,' he said slowly. 'We could do it in the September holidays, then he'd be down here anyway. If I wrote out the lines and we sent it to him, do you think he'd be able to learn his part? I don't think the Prince will have to say a lot.'

'I'm *sure* he could,' Daisy said. Being in the play was suddenly far more worth looking forward to.

It was June now, so they had almost three months until the next school holidays. Daisy wrote to Eddie at once, and the next time she was at Benjy's for Sunday lunch she showed him Eddie's reply, telling them he would be happy to play the part of the Prince.

There was another conscription ballot late in the month. A few days later Benjy arrived at school one morning just as the bell was ringing. He slipped into line next to Daisy and whispered, 'Joe's been called up.'

When Daisy hurried home with the news that afternoon, she found that her mother had been to visit Grandma, and her parents already knew about Uncle Joe.

'That's all Grandpa's big boys,' her mother said. 'It's hard on him taking them all like that, he's not as young as he was.'

'He might have to let a few things slip, especially on the other place,' Papa said.

Daisy's grandfather owned a second farm closer to town. Most years he grew potatoes and maize on its flat paddocks, but there would be no chance of planting crops that spring.

Daisy's mother clicked her tongue in disapproval. 'They keep saying in the papers about how we should be growing lots of food, and making extra butter and all for the war effort, but then they go taking boys off the farms.'

There was talk of applying for an exemption to see if they could get Joe let off, though everyone agreed it would probably be a waste of effort. Grandpa did apply for one, as did Uncle John and Uncle Harry when they each had a son called up that month, but it turned out that everyone was right about it being no use. Whoever decided these things told Grandpa and the uncles that they still had enough labour on their farms, and would just have to manage. The war, they said, was more important than anything else.

Benjy had to spend more time helping on the farm, but he still worked steadily at his play, snatching moments during school breaks and then writing at the kitchen table as soon as evening meals were cleared away. Now he was ready to copy it out neatly, and Daisy offered to help.

She had expected that they would have to write out a copy for each actor, but when they went into his room Benjy triumphantly produced several sheets of paper with a waxy blue coating.

'It's called carbon paper,' he said. 'Ma was growling about me staying out there in the kitchen instead of sitting in the parlour with them. She said she had a good mind to go down to the school and tell Miss Cameron she was giving me too much homework. So I had to tell them about the play.'

'I didn't know it was supposed to be a secret,' Daisy said, guiltily aware that she had already told her own parents.

'Well, not really a secret. I just wasn't going to let on yet, not till a bit nearer the time. Anyway, Pa didn't say anything, but he went to one of his meetings at the dairy factory the other day, and he came back with this stuff—he got it from the office there. I'd said about us having to write out a copy for everyone, and he thought this might be good.'

He slipped a piece of carbon paper between two ordinary sheets of paper and showed Daisy how it worked, with the writing coming through to the bottom sheet as he used a pencil on the top one.

'It stops working properly after you've used it for a while, though, so we'd better not waste it,' Benjy said.

The two of them crouched either side of a low chest of drawers, the only surface in Benjy's room smooth enough for writing on. It would have been much easier to use the kitchen table, but they were not entirely sure that copying out a play would be allowed on a Sunday, and Benjy felt it was better not to ask. By afternoon tea time, Daisy had two copies to take home, one for herself and one to send off to Eddie.

Benjy's play was based on the story of Sleeping Beauty, but with some important changes. Lucy, as he told Daisy, would never agree to pretending to be asleep for much of the play, even if there had been room in the parlour to have her lying about getting in everyone's way. But he and Daisy both had their doubts as to whether Lucy could be trusted to learn a lot of lines; Benjy was particularly concerned that she might take it upon herself to 'improve' the words.

Instead of having the Princess be put under a spell that would send her to sleep, Benjy's clever idea was to have the bad fairy cast a spell that would make the Princess unable to talk.

'You'll have some talking at first,' he told Lucy. 'At the end, too. But this way you won't have to learn a lot of lines—I thought you might be too busy. And I need you for the costumes and all that.'

Once convinced that she would have her proper share of attention, Lucy was happy enough with her role. She showed rather more enthusiasm over the artistic side of things.

'Those are really good,' Benjy said, gazing at the large sheets of paper covered with bold strokes of paint that Lucy had spread across her bed and much of the bedroom floor. His family and Daisy's were all at Uncle Richard's for Sunday lunch, and Lucy had dragged Benjy and Daisy off to her room as soon as the meal was over.

Daisy was equally impressed by the sketches. Lofty stone walls and pointed turrets were set against a background of sheer mountain slopes dotted with forest. It made her think of the drawings in her favourite book of fairy tales. 'It looks just like the sort of place where they have castles.'

'I'll paint it up the proper size on some calico, and we can hang it against the walls in Benjy's parlour, then we'll do the acting in front of it,' Lucy said. 'That's what they do in real plays—have paintings of things. I'll get Papa to buy me a whole roll of it in case I have any bother getting the pictures right.'

As well as her drawings of the backdrop, Lucy had ideas for making crowns for the King and Queen out of stiff card that she would paint to look like gold. She had also thought of a clever way for Daisy to be both the fairies without everyone getting muddled.

'I'll make a mask for the bad fairy—I'll do it in papier maché, then paint it up to look like a face.'

When Daisy had tried making papier maché at school the results had never been very satisfactory, but Lucy had a deft hand with such things. And her drawings of the mask looked so very ugly that Daisy no longer worried about anyone getting confused in her two roles. No one could mistake that face for a good fairy.

Uncle Joe was gone by the time calving began late in July. Benjy now only managed to get to school one or two days a week, when Grandpa could spare him.

The herd was much smaller on Daisy's farm, and the calves were always born close together. 'I'll give your pa a hand with calving as soon as ours is finished,' her father said to her mother one morning. 'It's a lot for him and Benjy to manage on their own.'

That meant Papa would be working longer days than usual. Daisy's mother was busy, too, with farmers calling her in to look at ailing stock. From time to time she came home quite annoyed, having scolded some farmer for overworking his animals.

'Just because they're short of men, it doesn't mean they can make it up by pushing the horses and bullocks harder than ever,' Daisy heard her say more than once.

With everyone working so hard, Daisy decided it was time for her to do more on the farm. She told her parents that she wanted to start helping with the morning milking as well as the afternoon one.

'I'm ten now, that's old enough. I could easily do a few of the cows before school if I get up a bit earlier. Papa, you used to milk twice a day when you were ten, didn't you?'

'I suppose so—I was a bit younger than ten, come to that. But things were… well, harder in those days, Daisy.' She saw her parents exchange a glance.

'If you're as keen as all that, I don't see why you shouldn't,' her mother said. 'You're good with the cows. Just as long as it doesn't make you too tired at school.'

With three big brothers, all of them much older, and a mother inclined to think of him as even younger than he was, Benjy had never had a great deal to do with the farm work. But he was the only boy left at home, and his father needed him.

Grandpa had built up his herd to a size that took four grown men to milk; now it had to be done by one man and a boy. It became a common occurrence for Benjy to arrive late for school, clutching a note from his father. Miss Cameron didn't scold him, though she frowned in a worried sort of way.

'I think they'd like to take me out of school altogether,' Benjy said to Daisy one lunchtime. Daisy saw the red mark on his hand where Miss Cameron had strapped him for getting some of his spelling words wrong. She had only given him three whacks; Miss Cameron could always tell when people were doing their best. Benjy was usually good at spelling, but he seemed to be losing interest in his schoolwork lately. 'They're not supposed to till I've done Standard Six, though.'

That would not be till the next year, which still felt a long way off. Daisy took one of the jam-filled biscuits from her lunchbox and handed it to Benjy.

The smile he gave her was half-hearted, though he did take the offered biscuit. 'They might let me stay on till the end of the year, but I don't think I'll be allowed to any longer than that, even if it's the law. It's too much for Pa on his own.'

'Maybe Uncle Joe and the others will be back by then,' Daisy said, though more because she wanted to cheer Benjy up than because she really believed it.

Benjy shook his head. 'I shouldn't think so.' He managed to fit the whole biscuit into his mouth, and his next words came out muffled around it, but Daisy thought she heard, 'High school.'

'What did you say?'

He looked down at his feet. 'So I won't be able to go to high school. You need to pass Standard Six if you want to go there.'

'I didn't know you wanted to go to high school. You never said anything about that.'

'I thought I'd wait and see if your ma and pa were really going to let you—then maybe I could talk Ma into it.'

'So do you want to be a teacher?'

Benjy shrugged. 'I don't know. Maybe.' He met Daisy's eyes, and grinned ruefully. 'I'm not much good at milking cows and all that, but I can do stuff out of books all right.'

'You're the best in the whole school at reading out loud,' Daisy said. 'I really like the way you do different voices, and make things sound exciting.' Although she wasn't sure that had anything much to do with being a teacher.

Daisy and Benjy saw Lucy and Flora at church, and occasionally for Sunday lunch at Grandpa's or Uncle Richard's, but there was no chance for them to rehearse the play together.

Lucy airily claimed that she would remember her lines, and Benjy had been careful to give her very few of them. Benjy knew his by heart; but, as he told Daisy, it was easier for him since he had written them himself.

Daisy was sure that Eddie would arrive knowing all his lines perfectly, but she could not help being a little nervous about her own. Every day when she got home from school she read over her part while having afternoon tea with her parents, murmuring the words to herself in between gulps of milk and biscuits.

'That must be a long poem Miss Cameron's got you learning, you've been practising it for ages,' her mother remarked one afternoon while she stood at the bench buttering a second helping of scones.

'It's not a poem, it's Benjy's play,' Daisy said. 'I want to make sure I know all my words properly.'

Mama wiped her hands on her apron and came to look over Daisy's shoulder. 'I didn't know there was so much to it,' she said, gazing at the pages Daisy had spread out in front of her. 'Look at this, Davie.'

Daisy's father pulled his chair nearer. 'There's a lot to it, all right. And you have to learn it all by heart? I wouldn't be able to, that's for sure.'

'Fancy Benjy thinking up all that.' Her mother picked up a page to study it more closely. 'I'm looking forward to it—I just can't imagine what it must be like to see a real play. Not like you, Daisy-May,' she added, smiling. 'Do you think this'll be much like the one you went to in Auckland?'

'It might be a bit like it,' loyalty to Benjy made Daisy say.

The September holidays arrived, quickly followed by Granny and Eddie. Eddie brought with him the copy of the play that Daisy had sent, and on the buggy ride home from the wharf he delivered several lines from memory.

He made the words sound wonderful, just as Daisy had known he would. Even her father seemed impressed.

'That sounds pretty good, Eddie,' he said. 'Daisy's got all her words off by heart, too.'

So then of course Granny and Eddie said they wanted to hear Daisy. She recited a few of her lines, being careful to put the proper expression in her voice. Her father gave her a smile and a nod, and Granny said she was looking forward to the play even more now she'd heard Daisy.

'You're as good as the people in real plays in Auckland,' Eddie declared. Daisy was quite sure she wasn't *that* good, but just hearing Eddie say it filled her with a new-found confidence.

Benjy said there should be a dress rehearsal before the real performance, but their costumes were not a settled matter. What they wore on the day would depend on whatever they managed to borrow from various family members. It would also depend on whether Lucy finished the mask and crowns in time. Lucy was inclined to be snappish when questioned on this, so Benjy was leaving the matter alone and hoping for the best.

They made do with having a rehearsal in their ordinary clothes when Aunt Maudie brought Lucy, Flora and their brothers out to Grandpa's for a visit one day, meaning that the whole cast could be under one roof. After morning tea the ladies obligingly stayed in the kitchen and sent Nicky and Timmy outside with Grandpa, so that the actors could have the parlour to themselves.

Eddie and Benjy pushed some of the chairs back against the walls out of the way, and Benjy had Daisy and the others move around the room, telling them where they should be standing for different parts of the play. Although it was a much bigger room than the parlour in Daisy's house, it was still something of a challenge for them all to move around what Benjy called the stage without bumping into each other.

Then it was time to go through the whole play. Benjy took the scripts away from everyone; 'If you don't know your lines by now it's a bit late,' he said. 'I'll tell you what to say if anyone gets stuck.'

Daisy did manage to remember almost all of hers, only needing to be prompted once. Flora recited the few lines she had been given quite accurately, although the words might as well have been a shopping list for all the expression she put into them.

'You've learned those really well,' Benjy told Flora. 'Try and sound a bit excited when you say that first bit—don't worry, though,' he added quickly when a look of panic appeared on Flora's face. 'It's all right the way you're saying them.'

Daisy could tell that Benjy found it harder to be so calm and encouraging with Lucy. Lucy said her lines well enough when she paid attention, but that was rare. She would say a bit from the play, then suddenly start talking about where they would put the painted hangings, or what jewellery her mother might be persuaded to lend.

'Never mind that for now, we need to get on with practising,' Benjy said, with admirable patience. 'This is the only chance we'll have with all of us together.'

Eddie's part, which Daisy had been looking forward to hearing ever since they began rehearsing, came quite late in the play. He delivered his lines with great confidence; afterwards Benjy remarked that once or twice Eddie had said something different from what was written down, but he actually preferred it Eddie's way.

Benjy broke into the rehearsal just as Lucy and Eddie got to the point where the Prince was to free the Princess from the fairy's spell.

'We need to sort this next part out,' he said. He seemed to be avoiding Eddie's eyes as he spoke. 'It's an important bit, I want it to be just right.'

'But you can't go changing the words now, not when I've gone to all that trouble learning them,' Lucy protested.

'No, the words are all right.' Benjy shifted from foot to foot, shuffling his pages noisily. 'It's just… when Eddie breaks the spell, it should be like in the real Sleeping Beauty story.'

'How do you mean?' Eddie asked.

'Well… you should *kiss* her.'

Daisy did not quite manage to muffle her own startled protest, but the small sound was drowned out by Eddie's and Lucy's joint outrage.

Eddie was the first to manage understandable speech. 'I'm not kissing her!'

'As if I'd even let you—in front of everyone, too.'

'I don't care if you'd let me or not, I'm not going to.'

'But the Prince *always* kisses the Princess in stories,' Benjy said, a note of pleading in his voice. 'That's how you know she's a real princess, and she's going to marry the Prince and live happily ever after.'

Eddie's mouth set more firmly than ever, but Lucy looked thoughtful.

'I suppose I *might* let him kiss my hand,' she said.

Eddie shook his head. 'I'm not doing that, either.'

'But we have to make sure everyone knows I'm the Princess! Anyway, if the Princess tells you to kiss her you *have* to.'

'No, I don't.'

'Yes, you do!' Lucy's voice was becoming more shrill.

'I *don't!*' Eddie turned to face Benjy. 'And I don't see why she's the Princess, anyway. It should be Daisy—she's the best at acting.'

'Of course I have to be the Princess! I'm the oldest out of all the girls.'

'Well, Daisy's the prettiest,' Eddie flung at her.

Watching Lucy was like waiting for the storm to break on those days when dark clouds rolled over the hills and the air felt heavy with thunder. With a huge effort, Daisy managed to hold in the smile that wanted to break out, because that would be sure to make things worse. Lucy took a great gulp of air, but instead of letting out the scream Daisy was expecting, she turned a glare on Benjy.

'I don't want to be in your silly play, anyway.'

She stalked from the room, head held so high that she must have been staring at the ceiling. Daisy heard her wrench the front door open, and waited to hear it slammed behind Lucy.

But not even Lucy at her most outraged would dare slam a door in Grandma's house. The door was closed with nothing more than a firm click, and Daisy, Eddie and Benjy were left looking awkwardly at each other.

'Sorry, Benjy, I didn't mean to get her in a state like that,' Eddie said.

Benjy shrugged. 'It doesn't take much, you know what Lucy's like.'

'It was true what I said, anyway,' Eddie added. This time Daisy made no attempt to hide her smile. 'But I suppose we still need Lucy.'

'Yes, we do—I couldn't do her part as well,' Daisy said. 'Especially the bit when we're both on at the same time.'

'Yes, we need her, all right.' Benjy sighed. 'I suppose I'd better go and talk to her, see if I can settle her down.'

At any other time, Daisy might have offered to go out to Lucy herself. But given what had set Lucy off, it seemed more tactful to leave it to Benjy. She nodded in what she hoped was an encouraging sort of way.

'I wouldn't bother,' Flora spoke up from the corner where she had been amusing herself going through piano music; Daisy had almost forgotten she was there. 'Lucy'll be in it. She never wants to be left out of anything.'

Flora turned out to be quite right. After sitting on the verandah by herself for a few minutes, Lucy came back into the parlour and announced that she had decided to be in the play after all.

'I wouldn't want to spoil it for the younger ones,' she said. 'Daisy and Flora would be so disappointed—and you, of course, Benjy.'

Grandpa and Grandma's family was so spread-out that Benjy, although Lucy's uncle, was younger than she was. He usually ignored her when Lucy tried to make a point of the few months between them, but today he was all meek gratitude, stressing how much they needed her to make the play a success.

Lucy rewarded him with a glowing smile. Daisy was relieved when the same smile was turned on her, instead of the glare she had half-expected. But Lucy was not one to bear a grudge; not when she was getting her own way.

'That's really good you're going to be in it,' Eddie said. 'I... um... well, it's good.' That was as close as he could bring himself to saying sorry to Lucy, Daisy knew.

'Thank you,' Lucy said, her smile a little cooler. 'I'm still not going to let you kiss me, though.'

Lucy and Flora went home not long afterwards, by which time Daisy felt she had had quite enough of rehearsing.

She sat out on the verandah with Eddie and Benjy, the three of them enjoying the remains of Grandma's baking. The boys talked through mouthfuls of scone, but Daisy said little, content to listen to their voices.

The verandah post made a comfortable support. She leaned back, warmed by sunlight filtered through the branches of a karaka tree, and warmed far more by the memory of Eddie's words. He thought she was the best at acting, and he thought she was the prettiest. Daisy no longer felt the tiniest shred of regret at not being the Princess.

'It wasn't much of a rehearsal,' Benjy said. 'Not with Lucy playing up like that, saying she wouldn't be in it any more—and I don't even know if she's finished those things she's meant to be making.'

Eddie held out the plate to offer Daisy the last of the scones. When she shook her head, it quickly disappeared into his own mouth. 'No, it's good it turned out like that,' he said. 'I've heard Aunt Sarah say dress rehearsals are meant to go wrong—a bad dress rehearsal means a good play. That's what people in real theatres say.'

Benjy looked much happier, and Daisy squeezed Eddie's arm in silent thanks. Trust Eddie to say the right thing.

Chapter Fourteen

After all the weeks of waiting, the play took place the following Thursday afternoon. Daisy and Eddie rode down well ahead of time to help with setting up the parlour. They had the furniture moved and chairs carried through from the kitchen by the time Lucy and Flora arrived with their parents and brothers, shortly after Daisy's parents and Granny.

'Papa says he couldn't possibly miss such an important occasion,' Lucy said, her head just visible over the armloads of clothing she was carrying up the passage. 'He specially arranged all his appointments so he could come. Mind you don't drop that, Benjy.'

Daisy made a grab at the cardboard crown teetering on Benjy's pile, and added it to her own share.

It turned out that Lucy had everything ready after all, in spite of their earlier doubts. She had brought bundles of folded calico as well as dressing-up clothes, the crowns, and a wrapped package that Daisy was sure must be the mask. Eddie was carrying the heaviest load, but the others all had plenty to weigh them down.

In the parlour the bundles were opened to reveal Lucy's painted backdrops. Under Benjy's direction, Eddie tied rope to nails hammered into the walls and draped the lengths of calico over it.

One section of the backdrops showed the inside of a room, with two walls meeting at a corner. Yellow curtains were set against the pale blue walls, pulled closed as if they covered a window. Past the edge of the imaginary room was a section of castle wall, with a pointed turret at the far end. Beyond that were steep mountains with patches of trees; there was even a small waterfall just visible. Daisy had thought Lucy's sketches very clever; when she saw the completed hangings it was easy to praise them as highly as Lucy herself could have wished.

Daisy heard the noise of buggy wheels while they were all still admiring Lucy's work.

'It's probably Rosie,' Benjy said. 'She wouldn't tell Ma straight out whether she was coming or not. I thought she might turn up when we were halfway through it, that'd be just like her.'

He darted out to the kitchen, and was soon back with the news that Aunt Rosie had indeed arrived.

'So we'd better get started, or they'll all get fed up waiting. They haven't got enough chairs out there for everyone, with all the ones we've got in here.'

The girls got changed in the front bedroom, leaving the boys in the parlour. Lucy draped herself and Flora in skirts and sashes and the remnants of old bodices, making a dazzling mix of colours that was surprisingly pretty. Safety pins holding the skirts closed were quite invisible under the satin and lace covering them.

Daisy wore her Sunday best, a green velvet dress with a gathered skirt. Lucy offered a red silk scarf from her stores to brighten it, but Daisy instead chose an old lacy shawl of Aunt Maudie's, worn in places but with much of its silver fringing intact. Pinned around Daisy's waist, it made her outfit look more like something a fairy might wear.

Something a *good* fairy might wear, anyway. Daisy picked up the mask and held it against her face, then looked at herself in the mirror on Grandma's dressing-table. Staring back at her was a hideous creature with greenish-grey skin, a jutting forehead, and a hooked nose complete with a wart near its tip. The mask ended just above Daisy's mouth, so that it would not interfere with talking, and the abrupt change from grey, mottled mask to her own skin made it look even stranger.

Daisy tried out the hat elastic that held the mask in place, then took it off with some relief. She would just hold it until it was time to go on stage.

Her mother had made a cloak out of a worn old blanket for the wicked fairy to wear, with a loose hood that could be pulled forward over the face. Daisy slipped the cloak on over her good clothes so that nothing could be seen of them.

The play would begin with just Benjy and Flora, so when the girls went back to the parlour Daisy, Eddie and Lucy lurked behind the calico hangings, able to see what was going on through small holes in the cloth but hidden from the audience. Lucy sat on a cushion, while Daisy and Eddie shared a small footstool. Various props were squashed in with them ready for later in the play, including a dolls' bed; it had sharp edges that dug into Daisy's side if she was not careful.

Benjy called down the passage, and the grown-ups ambled in. Aunt Rosie made something of a fuss over wanting one of the best chairs; 'She's expecting again,' Lucy whispered in Daisy's ear. 'I heard Mama say.' She did manage to get one of the comfortable chairs, as well as an extra cushion, but Daisy noticed that Grandpa saved the nicest chair of all for Grandma.

Quite a crowd managed to squeeze into the parlour. As well as Grandpa and Grandma, Aunt Maisie and Kate, there were Daisy's parents and Granny, Uncle Richard and Aunt Maudie with Nicky and Timmy, and Aunt Rosie with her little boy Sammy. Daisy was quietly relieved that Aunt Rosie's husband had not come; Uncle Bernard, with his big, booming laugh, always seemed to take up more room than other people.

Kate went straight to the piano, carrying several sheets of music. Daisy had told Benjy that the play in Auckland had music in it, and he had easily persuaded his good-natured sister to help out.

Benjy was wearing a smart grey dressing-gown that belonged to Grandpa over his ordinary clothes, and he and Flora had the cardboard crowns Lucy had made for them, so that everyone would be able to tell they were King and Queen. Flora stood at his side, clutching a porcelain doll that belonged to Kate, and looking quite terrified.

'Thank you, ladies and gentlemen. The play will now begin,' Benjy said. There was some murmuring and scraping of chairs, a loud shushing from Grandma, and then the room went quiet. Even little Sammy was awed into silence for the moment.

Kate played a few lines from a lullaby. The music faded away, and Benjy took a step forward.

'Here we are at the christening of our little baby girl Marigold,' he said, waving an arm towards the doll in Flora's arms. 'Isn't she lovely?'

The last sentence was addressed to Flora, but got no response. After a few moments, Benjy went on. 'We hope she'll be as kind as she is beautiful. All the fairies came to the christening and cast good spells over Marigold.' The 'King' frowned suddenly. 'We did remember to invite *all* the fairies, didn't we?'

From her hiding place Daisy saw Flora's eyes widen. There was a pause that seemed very long, then Benjy said, 'Oh no! Did we forget Fairy Griselda's invitation?'

Flora stood quite unmoving, all the while looking just as frightened as the Queen herself was supposed to be. The older members of their audience were smiling; probably thinking it was all part of the acting, and how well Flora was doing. Perhaps they wondered why she did not seem to have a single line, or why Benjy gave her an encouraging nod and then waited some time before saying all the words himself.

'As you always say, dear, she's so bad-tempered and unpleasant. I hope she won't cause any trouble.' Benjy's last word was almost drowned out by some loud, clashing notes on the piano.

This was Daisy's cue. She fastened the mask over her ears, pulled up the hood of her cloak, and stepped out from behind the backdrop. With a dramatic gesture she flung back her hood, ready to speak her first line, but what cut through the room was the high-pitched wail of a small child.

Lucy had done rather too good a job with the ugliness of the mask. Little Sammy sat perched on his mother's lap, staring wide-eyed at Daisy and howling at the top of his voice. Daisy could see Aunt Rosie's lips moving, but whatever soothing words she was saying were thoroughly drowned out.

Daisy took the mask off and hid it behind her back while Aunt Rosie calmed Sammy. When his wails had quietened to small sobs, she held the mask out towards him.

'See, it's only pretend,' she said. 'It's really me underneath.'

Sammy wound his arms around Aunt Rosie's neck and hid his face against her chest, but was soon coaxed to peek out. By the time Kate had fetched him a biscuit, he was feeling brave enough to touch the mask, and when Daisy carefully put it back on he giggled at the sight.

It took some time, and more shushing from Grandma, to settle everyone down again to watch the play. When they were fairly quiet, Daisy went back behind the hangings to make a fresh entrance.

Lucy insisted on checking the mask for any damage from Sammy's having been allowed to touch it, but found nothing worse than some sticky finger-marks to tut-tut over.

'You did a good job of scaring them,' Eddie whispered, grinning. He had a long wait for his part, which was not till near the end of the play. He had brought along a book about nature study to help pass the time, and it was open on his lap to a picture of a large spider dangling from a twig.

Daisy grinned back, but did not stop to talk. After having the play so thoroughly interrupted, she worried that some of their audience might wander off if kept waiting too long. Once again she stepped out in front of everyone and pushed back her hood.

'What do you mean by leaving me out of the christening?' she demanded, making her voice as deep and threatening as she could. She cast a wary eye at Sammy, who was now sitting on the floor at Aunt Rosie's feet, but he was engrossed with a toy wagon someone had found for him. 'How dare you insult me thus?' Benjy had been quite proud of writing 'thus', and Daisy took care to hiss the s-sound.

Benjy was doing a good job of looking frightened. 'We're so very sorry, Fairy Griselda, the invitation must have got lost in the post. Of course my wife and I were terribly disappointed not to see you at Marigold's christening, weren't we, dear?'

Flora managed a nod in response to the pleading look Benjy sent her, though her mouth remained firmly closed.

'It was a wonderful occasion, except for everyone missing you,' Benjy said. 'All the fairies gave Marigold such fine gifts—they cast spells over her so she'll be good at singing and drawing, and all sorts of things.'

'Gifts, you say?' Daisy put a sly note into her voice. 'Would you like *me* to give the child a gift?'

'Well, only if it's no trouble.'

'Ha! Trouble, you say? Trouble it may be indeed, if she does not take care.'

Daisy walked slowly over to Flora, her cloak trailing on the floor. She turned down the top edge of the blanket wrapped around the doll, and peered at the porcelain face. Flora looked suitably frightened at having a bad-tempered fairy staring at her 'baby'.

'My gift is a warning against pride and selfishness.' Daisy waved her hands above the doll's face in what she hoped was a mysterious-looking pattern. 'And now the spell is cast. If this girl should ever turn away one in need, doom will come upon her. Doom! Doom!'

When they were writing out the play together, Benjy had said how good it would be if they could somehow arrange to have Daisy leave the stage in a puff of smoke, but as they would certainly not be allowed to do such a thing even if they knew how, she made do with leaving to the sound of more loud, jarring notes played by Kate.

Behind the calico backdrop, Eddie and Lucy helped her take off the mask and the drab cloak that hid her pretty dress.

'Oh, Good Fairy Mirabelle,' Benjy said when she returned to the stage, 'that wicked old Griselda cast a bad spell over Marigold. Can you take it off her?'

The world looked right again, now that Daisy could look around the parlour and see things properly rather than having to peer through the eyeholes of the mask. 'Alas, I cannot undo what has been done, but perhaps I can ease the doom.' Daisy placed a hand on the doll's head. 'Teach Marigold to be kind, and teach her that appearances can deceive. That may give her a measure of protection, and a way to put things to rights.'

This was Daisy's most complicated speech, and her favourite, since it meant she could use so many uncommon words. It was a relief to have it come out smoothly.

Benjy thanked her very politely, although his expression made it clear that the King was confused over just what he was thanking the fairy for.

'It's time for Marigold to have her sleep,' Benjy said, a line Daisy knew was supposed to be one of Flora's. It was Eddie's cue to push the dolls' bed out from behind the hangings. One corner of the bed emerged, but its base caught against the rug. Eddie must have given it a hard shove;

the bed made a rude noise against the floorboards before sliding onto the rug, and there was muffled laughter from the audience.

The Queen was supposed to put the baby in the bed, then the King and Queen were to talk quietly to each other, so that they would not hear what the good fairy said next. Benjy managed to tug the doll from Flora's grip; he placed it in the little bed and led Flora off to one side, where they pretended to be engrossed in their conversation; or rather Benjy did.

Daisy bent over the bed, waved her hands as if casting another spell, then stood and faced the audience. 'This is secret magic, and the King and Queen cannot be told of it,' she said. 'The doom that Griselda laid upon Marigold may be undone, but only by an act of true kindness to a stranger. That is her only chance to escape a dreadful curse.'

She turned and made her way off stage, careful to make her movements more graceful than Griselda's. 'Farewell, Your Majesties,' she called over her shoulder. 'Remember, remember, teach her kindness.'

Benjy was left on stage with the rigidly silent Flora. 'I expect it'll be all right,' Daisy heard him say. 'We'll bring her up to be good and kind to everyone, and as long as she takes notice of us the doom won't happen.' She was fairly sure that Flora was meant to have one last line here, but Benjy did not waste time on a hopeless cause. Through her peephole in the hangings, Daisy saw him pick up the doll and hand it to Flora, then take her by the arm and lead her off the stage, while Kate played a grand-sounding piece of music and Eddie slid the bed back behind the calico.

'Why did you just stand there not saying anything?' Lucy hissed at Flora when they were all crowded behind the hangings. She had obviously been taking more notice of what was going on in this scene; probably because she was to come on stage next. 'Everyone must have thought you were silly!'

Poor Flora had already looked as though she was about to cry; at Lucy's words, two large tears spilled from her brimming eyes and made a trail down each cheek. Benjy broke in while Lucy was gathering her breath to say more.

'Keep your voice down, Lucy, or they'll all hear you. Don't worry, Flora, you did all right,' he said, putting a hand on her arm. 'You looked good in your dress and crown and all, and you walked really nicely.'

Flora sniffed, and rubbed her sleeve over her eyes. Daisy passed her a handkerchief, which she blew into noisily.

'You'll be able to turn the pages for Kate now you've finished your bit,' Benjy said. 'That'll be a big help, I know she's been worried about managing with the music.'

Kate appeared to have managed perfectly well up till now, but Flora brightened at the suggestion. She placed the doll in its bed and returned the damp handkerchief to Daisy, then slipped out the far side of the hangings and crept around the parlour, keeping close to the walls as she went. Daisy saw Kate smile at her, and slide along the piano stool to make room.

Even with Flora gone, it was a squash behind the hangings. There was a hurried shuffling in the small space as Benjy and Lucy got ready to make their entrance. They made bulges in the hangings as they squeezed past Daisy and Eddie in a muddle of sharp elbows and trodden toes. It was much more comfortable when they had gone, leaving Daisy and Eddie to peer out at the stage from their shared footstool.

Enough time was supposed to have passed for the baby of the previous scene to have grown up into Lucy. There had been talk of a false beard made out of grey wool for Benjy, so that people could tell he was older, but Benjy had decided that would get in his way. He would just act older, he said.

He really was very good at acting, Daisy thought as she watched him walking along at Lucy's side; perhaps even better than Eddie, though of course he was nothing like as tall or impressive-looking. He did somehow manage to look older; Daisy studied him, and saw that it was to do with how he held himself, shoulders slightly bowed, and the way he walked as if just moving was an effort. It made her think of how Great-grandma had looked before she got so very old that she just sat in her chair all the time.

Benjy faced the audience and explained that his wife, the Queen, had sadly died. Now it was just him and his lovely daughter to keep each other company in their small, cosy castle, where they even opened the door themselves rather than have a servant to do it.

'Now I must give my daughter wise advice all on my own, without my poor wife to help.' He turned to Lucy. 'Remember, dear Marigold, you must always be kind to people.'

Lucy pretended not to hear him, instead twirling on the spot to show off her pretty skirt. Daisy suspected she was not having to act very hard.

'Ah, she's so beautiful, but alas, she doesn't take any notice of her old father,' Benjy said, sighing heavily.

He carefully lowered himself onto a rather wobbly stool, which did not at all look like something a king might sit on, but was the best they had room for on their small stage. 'I'll just have a little nap, I think. I do get tired of an afternoon these days.' He closed his eyes, and his head drooped to rest on one shoulder.

It was time for Daisy to appear again. She hurriedly put the mask back on, Eddie helping with the fiddly bit over her ears, and pulled the cloak around herself. She stood just behind the hangings while Eddie knocked on the parlour wall as if it was a door.

'Who's there?' Lucy called out.

'Just a poor old lady,' Daisy called back, trying to make her voice sound frail.

Lucy walked over and opened an imaginary door, then moved to make room for Daisy to take a few steps forward. 'What do you want, then?' Lucy asked.

'A cup of tea, dear, and perhaps a biscuit or two. Ones with icing would be nice. And then a little sit down to rest my weary old bones.'

'As if I've got time to fuss around over a raggy old lady,' Lucy said, screwing up her face.

Daisy took a step closer. 'I just want a bit of company, dearie. Just a friendly chat.'

'No, I'm much too busy. Go away before you drop mud on my nice, clean carpet.'

'Ooh, you're a haughty Miss, aren't you? Too busy to talk, eh? I know how to fix *that*.' Daisy remembered to laugh in the way Benjy had told her to, though she thought it sounded more like a hen that had just laid an egg than a wicked fairy.

She threw back the hood of her cloak to reveal the mask, just as Kate, who must have been paying careful attention, again played some clashing notes. At the same time, from behind the hangings came a *boom, boom* that was Eddie banging a hammer against a sheet of metal. She heard a startled squeak from one of the smaller children, and amused murmurs from the grown-ups.

The old King woke with a start. He half-rose from the stool, then sank down again, as if he was too shocked at the sight of the bad fairy to be able to use his legs.

'Why, Fairy Griselda, what a surprise to see you,' he said in a shaky voice. 'I hope my daughter has been making you welcome?' Lucy was supposed to be looking frightened, but instead she was fiddling with the fringe on her sash, making sure each small tassel was properly lined up.

'Your doom has come,' Daisy said, raising her voice in an attempt to capture Lucy's wandering attention. 'Because you were proud and haughty instead of kind, never again will you speak. Your voice is *gone!*'

The last word came out close to a shout. Lucy let the fringe drop from her fingers, then grasped her throat with both hands and turned her head from side to side, making a noise like a cat trying to bring up a hairball. Although this was meant to be quite a serious part of the play, Daisy heard people laughing. She couldn't really blame them; it was hard not to laugh herself.

Benjy struggled to his feet and went over to Lucy. He put an arm around her, as if the King was comforting his daughter with a hug, but Daisy noticed him give her a small shake, and possibly a pinch to go with it. Lucy stopped making the hairball noise, and the laughing finally stopped, helped along by a stern look from Grandma.

While the King was busy fussing over his daughter, Daisy took a step closer to the audience. 'That interfering goody-goody Mirabelle tried to spoil my spell,' Daisy said, pressing one hand just beside her mouth to make it clear she was telling a secret. 'So if Marigold was ever to do something kind for a stranger, her voice would come back.' Benjy had said it was worth having this explained by both fairies, because people mightn't pay attention and would get confused later.

She glanced over her shoulder at Benjy and Lucy, then faced the audience again. 'But there's no chance of that—not from a proud, willful girl like her.' Daisy let out another cackling laugh, and stalked off behind the hangings to join Eddie again. The mask had twisted, and was digging into the side of her nose; it was a relief to tug it off. She pushed it and the cloak against the wall, where they would not be trodden on.

Benjy was patting Lucy on the hand now. 'Oh, my poor daughter! Oh, woe, to think that I'll never hear your lovely voice again. What a very wicked fairy Griselda is, to do such a thing.'

'I think she's a *good* fairy if she can make it so Lucy doesn't talk.' That was Lucy's seven-year-old brother, Nicky. His high-pitched giggles were soon joined by four-year-old Timmy's even shriller ones. Benjy took Lucy by the wrist and held on firmly, so that she could do no more than glare at her little brothers. It took several moments for Uncle Richard and Aunt Maudie to settle the boys down; Daisy could see they were both struggling to look stern instead of laughing.

Still holding her by the wrist, Benjy led Lucy off the stage while Kate played some sad music. They were to be offstage just long enough, Benjy had said, for everyone to understand that it wasn't the same day any more. Lucy had had ideas of changing her costume at this point, but Benjy had pointed out that there was neither time nor room for this. So they just stood behind the hangings while Kate finished the short piece, then the two of them walked back out.

'Alas, a year has passed without my daughter's sweet voice returning,'

Benjy said. 'She bears it with great patience, but now that I'm old, I worry about who'll look after her when I'm gone.' He gave a heavy sigh, then went and sat on the stool and pretended to be asleep again.

This was the part Daisy knew would be the best of all: Eddie was to make his entrance at last. He pulled on a smart velvet jacket that she thought looked familiar. Over that went an old coat borrowed from Daisy's father, long enough to hide Eddie's good clothes. He finished his outfit with an ancient felt hat of Grandpa's.

Eddie rapped his knuckles against the wall, and Lucy pretended to open a door.

'I'm just a poor chap who hasn't got a home or anything,' he said, stepping out from the hangings. 'Could I come in and sit down for a bit?'

Of course the Princess could not talk to the mysterious stranger. Eddie looked puzzled when she didn't answer him, but she smiled and nodded, and waved him over to a footstool.

Lucy appeared to have forgotten that she was supposed to mime offering the stranger something to drink, so Eddie asked for a glass of water. She smiled even more brightly, and carried a small table over to him, with a glass of milk and a plate of biscuits.

'The weather's bad out there,' Eddie said. 'Do you think I could stay the night in an old shed? I only need a pile of sacks to sleep on.'

Lucy shook her head at the mention of sacks. Instead she snatched up a cushion and handed it to Eddie, and pointed to the floor as if to say he was welcome to sleep in the castle.

Daisy could just see Eddie's face. He looked at the milk and biscuits, then at the cushion, and broke into a wide smile. In spite of the battered old coat, she thought no real-life prince could look more handsome.

'You're a very kind person,' Eddie said to the Princess. 'And you don't take any notice of whether people are well-off, or important, or any of that sort of thing. Thanks very much.'

This was the part where Benjy had said the Prince should kiss the Princess. Even though Eddie had so steadfastly refused, Daisy's throat tightened as she watched him take a few steps towards Lucy.

When Eddie reached out and took Lucy's hand to shake it, Daisy let out a chestful of air and realised she had been holding her breath.

Kate played a snatch of melody full of twirls and trills, and the old King woke. 'Papa, I can talk again!' Lucy cried.

'My dear daughter!' Benjy struggled up from the stool and walked over to her. 'You must have broken the spell somehow,' he said to Eddie.

Eddie looked suitably confused. 'I don't think I did anything. I just shook her hand.'

'Well, whatever you did, you've cured her. You must be properly rewarded with my daughter's hand in marriage.' He looked Eddie up and down, his expression making it quite clear that the King would much rather not have this scruffy stranger marry his daughter.

Eddie pulled off his hat and shoved it into a pocket, then unbuttoned the old coat and let it slide to the floor, revealing his neatly ironed trousers and the smart velvet jacket. Daisy glanced at the audience to check that everyone was paying proper attention, and noticed that Uncle Richard looked startled. *That* was why the jacket seemed so familiar: she had seen Uncle Richard wearing it in the evenings when she was visiting. Lucy had obviously not bothered to ask permission before borrowing it for the play.

'I'm really a prince, with my own castle,' Eddie said. He went on to give quite a long speech about getting sick of being introduced to girls who were only interested in him because he was rich, and a prince, and wanting to meet a girl who'd like him for himself, even if he looked as if he had no money.

'Well, I got here, and your daughter was nice to me. I shook her hand, and she seems to have come right,' Eddie finished.

Kate played the music for the good fairy, and Daisy made her final appearance. 'The spell could only last until the Princess learned to be kind and unselfish,' she explained. 'When she did a good deed for a stranger, that undid the wicked spell.' She took hold of Eddie and Lucy by a hand each, while Benjy held Lucy's other hand. 'And now you'll all live happily ever after.'

'The end!' Benjy said, his voice ringing. The grown-ups all clapped, and after a nudge from their parents Nicky and Timmy joined in. Benjy beckoned Flora over; when she hung her head and looked shy, he went to the piano, took her by the hand, and tugged her back to stand with the other actors. Kate, too, was persuaded to stand and be applauded. The boys bowed, the girls curtseyed, and the clapping went on until Nicky loudly asked when they were going to have their afternoon tea.

While people were milling about saying how good the play had been, Daisy darted off to get changed in Grandma's room, noticing as she went that Uncle Richard was reclaiming his jacket from Eddie. She slipped out of her good clothes and back into a plainer dress, then left the room to Lucy and Flora, who had more complicated costumes to get out of.

Grandma and the other ladies were setting up afternoon tea on the verandah, while Benjy and Eddie hovered about looking hopeful. Daisy joined them, and the three of them trooped down the steps into the front garden.

'Everyone seemed to like it all right,' Benjy said. 'Even with Flora getting scared like that, and Lucy forgetting what she was supposed to be doing half the time. So was it much like plays in Auckland are?'

'Quite a bit,' Eddie said loyally. 'Not as long, that's the main difference.'

'I'd like to put on a real one like that. We'd never get everyone to sit through it if it was any longer, though.'

Now that she no longer had to worry about forgetting a line, or coming on at the wrong time, or getting the two fairies' costumes mixed up, Daisy felt almost light-headed with the relief. 'I don't know if I could remember all the words in a long play,' she said. 'It'd be a lot to get off by heart.'

'Maybe you wouldn't have to learn any words,' Eddie said. He sounded quite serious, but Daisy knew that expression well: one corner of his mouth turned up just a little, and a telltale glint in his eyes. 'As long as you didn't have to be someone *good,* anyway. You made it look easy as anything being the wicked fairy—I think you could just be yourself and no one would know any better.'

Daisy darted a hand to take her revenge in tickling Eddie, and got a satisfyingly loud yelp out of him. A moment later he had hold of her around the waist and was spinning her round and round, even tipping her upside-down for a moment, while Daisy giggled and batted at him with her fists.

'Eddie! Put Daisy down at once.' When Grandma Kelly spoke in that tone, only a very silly person would ignore her. Daisy was not surprised to find herself lowered carefully to the ground.

Grandma murmured something to Daisy's mother. Daisy felt a blush mounting her face; perhaps they had all seen her drawers when Eddie turned her upside-down.

Her mother came down the steps to them. 'Eddie, I think you'd better stop carting Daisy around like that. She's too big for it now.'

'But I can still carry her no trouble. And I had a good hold, I wouldn't have dropped her.'

'I know you wouldn't, but... well, you're both getting a bit too old for playing like that. Anyway, come and have your afternoon tea before the savouries get cold.'

Her mother did not look annoyed, but she did seem a little sad. Daisy's cheeks burned; they *must* have seen her drawers.

Grandma called them up to the verandah. Daisy wondered if she might be in for a scolding, but Grandma patted her arm and told her the play had been very good, and she cut a huge slice of cake for Eddie that was only a very little smaller than the one she handed Benjy.

Even though no one seemed to be grumpy after all, Daisy felt oddly shy, and in need of a quiet corner. She took her own plate of food and went over to sit by Granny, who had saved a place for her. 'Did you like the play, Granny?' she asked.

'Yes, I did. You all did very well.' Her grandmother gave a wistful sort of smile. 'It's nice to think that sometimes things have a happy ending.'

Chapter Fifteen

The play was soon no more than a small, bright memory in the greyness of the world. Eddie went back to Auckland; school started again, with Benjy absent much of the time; and one day early in October Benjy rode over to Daisy's to tell them that Grandpa had had a telegram.

Telegrams meant bad news these days. A shiver ran down Daisy's spine, and she saw her mother's hand fly to her mouth.

'It's about Danny—no, it's all right, he's only been injured,' Benjy said. 'He's in a hospital or something, so he's out of the fighting.'

'Injured' did not sound so bad; not until an official letter arrived with more details. Benjy brought the news to school one day.

'Danny's lost his foot,' he murmured to Daisy as they stood lined up outside the schoolroom, waiting for Miss Cameron to call them in.

'What do you mean, he's lost it?'

'There was a shell, or a mine, or something. His foot got mashed up that badly they had to cut it off.'

Daisy got home that afternoon to find that her parents had already heard the news.

'At least he won't have to be in the fighting any more,' her mother said. 'That's something, I suppose.'

'Yes, he'll be well out of it,' Papa said.

It was odd, the way they talked about Uncle Danny almost as if he was lucky. Of course it was much better than what had happened to poor Uncle Doug, but to have had his foot cut off!

'How will he manage with only one foot?' she asked. All day it had been on her mind: when she slid her feet back and forth along the rail under her school desk; while running around the playground; after school when she mounted her horse and then at home slipped easily from its back.

'They'll give him a wooden one,' her father said. 'He'll stay on in England till he's healed up a bit, then they might send him back here on one of the troopships.'

A foot made out of wood. It couldn't possibly work as well as a real one. And however would it be fastened onto his leg? Surely they wouldn't sew it to the skin. Daisy shuddered at the idea, but she said nothing aloud. It would only upset her mother.

Everyone seemed to want to act as if everything was all right, though Daisy knew quite well that they were worried about all the uncles. She noticed how carefully her mother studied the casualty lists in the newspaper, just in case they had somehow missed getting a telegram. When Papa came home from the factory, the first thing her mother always asked was, 'Any news?'

Miss Cameron pinned tiny flags onto the schoolroom map to mark the site of battles as they were reported in the newspapers. Every day Daisy checked the map to see how much more of it was covered by those scraps of coloured paper. Such strange names all those places in Belgium seemed to have. How on earth were you supposed to say a word like Ypres?

The strangest name of all caught her eye one day, a little to the north-east of Ypres. It looked close to where Uncle Danny had been injured; perhaps the rest of the uncles were near that town. She tried to sound it out under her breath: *Passchendaele.*

Bill Leith stared at the flimsy piece of paper in his hands, only vaguely aware of the telegraph boy still standing there.

Regret to inform Ernest Roderick Leith killed in action 12th October 1917.

'Ernest Roderick Leith' sounded like a stranger; perhaps a distant relative sometimes spoken of but never met. Ernie was his baby brother. How could Ernie be dead?

The telegraph boy was shifting from one foot to the other as he clutched the reins of his horse. In spite of his uniform he looked barely twelve years old, like a boy wagging school. The freckles across his nose and the way his ears stuck out reminded Bill of Ernie at that age.

He needed to say something. The boy could not leave till he did. But his tongue felt too thick in his mouth for any words to be forced past it.

Somehow Lily was at his elbow, though he had not heard her footsteps. He felt her hand on his arm, and heard the sharp intake of breath as she leaned forward to read the telegram.

She was saying whatever needed to be said, and a moment later the boy was mounting his horse. Her hand slipped into Bill's, her long fingers cool against his, and her eyes bright with tears.

He could hear Arfie and Will, laughing and calling back and forth to each other. Emma was dozing in her room, curled up with baby Dougie.

Bill gripped Lily's hand more tightly. 'Better go and tell them, then,' he said.

First Uncle Doug, now Uncle Ernie. The war was like a monster from a frightening story; an ogre that ate people, and would go on and on till it had swallowed up all the men. Most of Daisy's uncles were still trapped in France or Belgium, where the monster was raging and snarling.

Her mother had an even more anxious note in her voice now when she asked Daisy's father if he had heard any news at the factory. Sometimes she would come back from one of her visits to a sickly animal with news of her own, of a farmer's son injured or missing.

But her father was safe, and the older men like Grandpa were safe, because they wouldn't make married men go. That was something to cling to; something to take comfort from when bad dreams woke her.

It was late October, barely two weeks since they had heard the news about Uncle Ernie. The newspaper lay on a chair when Daisy came into the kitchen, its pages crumpled as if someone had been angry with it. Her mother made to snatch it away, but her father reached out a hand to stop her.

'Tell her,' he said. 'She'll hear about it soon enough, anyway.'

Daisy's mother poured her a glass of milk from the jug. 'Now, Daisy, you're not to worry about this,' she said, though her hand shook, and there was a tightness around her mouth. 'But it's in the paper that they're going to start taking the Second Division men.'

A hand seemed to snatch at Daisy's heart. 'But that's the men like Papa!'

'Yes, it's the married men,' her father said. 'Not the ones with kids, though. Just married men with no children, so they won't be taking any notice of me.'

Daisy nodded, and took a gulp of milk as an excuse not to answer. Her voice, she was sure, would come out squeaky and frightened if she said anything just now, and she could tell her parents were worried enough without her making it worse.

It was no use trying to believe that men who had children would be left alone; that was what everyone had said about married men. No one was safe now. The monster that was the war would see to that. Perhaps it would keep going until Eddie was old enough, and then he would be taken, too.

She longed to throw herself into her father's arms and press her face against his chest. Instead she sat quietly at the table, and did her best not to picture him being dragged away from them.

Learning the names of old kings and queens did not seem very important now, and Daisy sometimes found it hard to concentrate at school. She earned an occasional sharp word from Miss Cameron, and more than once went home with her hand red from the strap.

She usually had the back bench of the schoolroom to herself these days. Benjy was busy helping Grandpa, and whole weeks went by without seeing him at school. Miss Cameron even gave up reading out his name when she called the roll each day.

Late in November, not long before the Inspector was due to arrive for the annual examinations, Benjy surprised Daisy by hurrying into the schoolroom one morning and sliding onto the bench beside her.

'Kate said she'd do my milking for a couple of weeks, just till the Inspector's been,' he explained at playtime. 'Pa says Danny should be coming home before long, and he can milk cows even if he's only got one foot. So I might be able to do Standard Six next year, as long as I pass the exam.'

Daisy worked hard in the weeks leading up to the Inspector's visit, doing her best to make up for all the lessons where her mind had wandered, and when the examination results were given out she found that she had passed her Standard Four test quite comfortably. Benjy, too, had somehow managed to scrape through his examination.

It was good to know that she would be in Standard Five next year, and even better to have Miss Cameron tell her she was well on the way to getting into high school. But try as she might to focus on such cheerful thoughts, Daisy's mind kept wandering to the one matter that could not be avoided. These days it was hard to think about anything except the war.

Uncle Alf was coming home. That small piece of good news was chewed over till it had lost any freshness, and when Eddie, Granny and Aunt Sarah arrived for Christmas it was repeated all over again. No one seemed to have any real idea just why he was being sent home ahead of the other uncles. He had been injured at Passchendaele, Uncle Bill said, and sent to a hospital in England, but he was well again now.

Uncle Joe was in a hospital there, too; he was poorly from breathing the gas they used in the fighting, Grandpa said. But he would be sent back to France as soon as he was better. Poor Uncle Danny, who had hoped to be on his way home by now, had to wait until he got a wooden foot, and that was taking much longer than anyone had expected. It sounded as though Benjy would not be coming back to school after all.

Christmas had always been the brightest time of the year, with all the family together and long days of sunshine ahead. Eddie was there, and the usual trove of gifts had arrived, but the war cast a dark cloud over everything.

Three more of the men from Uncle John and Uncle Harry's farm had now been conscripted. Haymaking began just after Christmas, with far too few hands for the task; Daisy looked around at the workers and wondered who would be called up next. Every evening the men were out in the paddocks till barely a trace of daylight remained. Even Eddie looked tired by the time they finally came up to the house, and Daisy's father was often so worn out that he would fall asleep on the sofa as soon as he had had his dinner.

Eddie and Granny went back to Auckland at the end of January 1918, and in February Daisy went back to school. With all his brothers still away Benjy had to stay home, and Daisy was now the oldest pupil there. She missed seeing Benjy next to her in the back row, and missed his company at playtime.

At least the Standard Five work was quite interesting, and she often lost herself in it. The history text had a chapter on African explorers that reminded Daisy of books she had read with Eddie, while geography described how tides were caused, and how they were affected by the position of the Moon. Daisy sometimes told her parents of an evening about whatever new discovery she had made at school, but she was always ready to change the subject when she saw eyes glazing over.

And every day someone would say how good it was that Uncle Alf would soon be coming home.

Bill watched the *Ngatiawa* grow from a distant blob as the boat drew near Ruatane's wharf. A cluster of passengers stood on the deck by some bundled freight, and on the other side of the bundles was a solitary figure. An image showed clear in Bill's memory: his two brothers sailing off together, Ernie laughing at some forgotten joke as they dwindled into the distance.

The boat tied up. Alf hoisted his canvas pack over one shoulder, shuffled along the gangplank and stepped onto the wharf. He looked thinner than Bill remembered, and his once leathery face had an unhealthy pallor. His eyes seemed to be staring at a point somewhere past Bill's shoulder.

Words tumbled about in Bill's head; words of shared sadness, words of concern. As he stared at the old man his brother had become, words had never seemed so useless. 'Good to see you,' he said.

He took the heavy pack and tossed it onto the spring cart, then wondered if he should offer Alf a hand up. But Alf clambered up by his own efforts, and sat hunched on the hard plank seat.

The ride home had never felt longer. Alf responded with a grunt, or occasionally a one-word answer, to Bill's cautious attempts at conversation. About halfway home he looked to have nodded off, and Bill took care to avoid the roughest parts of the track so as not to disturb him.

He had left the boys to do the afternoon milking on their own. He saw Arfie and Will outside the cowshed, leading the last few animals into the bails, as the cart rattled its way up to the house and Alf shook himself awake.

Lily and Emma stood by the back door to meet them, Emma holding Dougie by the hand.

'We're so glad to have you home again, Alf,' Lily said.

Emma hoisted Dougie onto her hip. 'Look, here's your uncle—say hello to Uncle Alf.'

The little boy stared awed at Alf, then squeezed his eyes tightly closed and pressed his face against his mother's arm. Emma jiggled and coaxed, but Dougie would not move. 'He's not used to seeing strangers,' Emma said, then bit at her lower lip. 'I'm sorry, Uncle Alf, I didn't mean...'

'He'll soon get to know you,' Lily said. 'Now, do come inside—you must be worn out from the trip.'

Bill led Alf along the passage to his old bedroom, and dropped the pack by one wall. The room had been aired and the bed made up with fresh linen. A fine mist of steam rose from the jug on the washstand; Lily must have filled it with hot water when she saw them coming up the track.

'Do you want to come for a walk, give your legs a stretch?' Bill asked.

Alf sank onto the bed. 'No. I'll sit here for a bit.'

Bill hovered in the doorway, wondering if he should offer to sit with Alf. Perhaps he should give his brother some time to himself; or perhaps he was just a coward who wanted to escape. 'I'll leave you to it, then,' he said. 'I'll sing out when dinner's on.'

Dinner was a much quieter meal than normal, the scraping of cutlery against plates the loudest sound in the room. Even Bill's sons, who were inclined to talk over each other in their rush to be the first with some piece of news, were subdued by the silent figure of their uncle. Alf ate keenly enough, but made no move to join in the others' attempts at conversation.

After the evening meal the men usually went straight through to the front room, leaving Lily and Emma to clear up in the kitchen before joining them. Alf headed up the passage with Bill and his sons, but stopped at the door to his bedroom and went in.

'Come on to the parlour,' Bill said. 'I thought I might hunt out some whisky if you fancy a drink.'

'I'll be along in a while.' Alf pushed at the door that stood between him and Bill. It was a heavy door, and needed a firm shove to close. The door moved a few inches, then swung open again to show Alf sitting on the edge of the bed.

Alf had still not left his room by the time Lily and Emma joined the men. Dusk was drawing on; Lily lit the parlour lamps and pulled the drapes across. Bill touched a candle to one of the lamps and used it to show his way down the passage.

The candle cast wavering shadows against the walls of Alf's room. Bill lit a lamp and placed the candlestick by it, the smaller flame pale against the lamp's sudden brightness.

'You all right?' he asked. 'You don't want to come out to the parlour?'

Alf shook his head. 'I like it in the quiet.'

'I don't mind a bit of quiet myself, sometimes.' Bill lowered himself onto the bed beside Alf, and shifted his weight till he had found a more comfortable place for his buttocks. He knew the mattress, with all its lumps and hollows, only too well. This had been his own bed, shared with Alf, years ago, when Ernie was still in a cradle.

'It's good they sent you home pretty smartly,' Bill said. Sent him home on his own. It was impossible to find anything to say that did not call their brother to mind. 'You didn't break a bone, anything like that?'

'I woke up in a dressing station after...' Alf cleared his throat. 'They said I'd got a knock on the head. Carted me off to England a couple of days later. Nothing wrong with me, but the quack talked it up, made out I was in a bad way. It came out about me being over the age for signing up, too.'

'Well, that's good,' Bill said, giving silent thanks to this unknown doctor.

Footsteps sounded in the passage, along with Emma's murmured voice; she must be putting Dougie to bed. A fretful wailing told Bill that the little boy was tired, but in no mood to settle. The floorboards of her bedroom creaked as Emma walked the floor with Dougie, singing quietly to him.

Bill glanced back at Alf, and was surprised to see him flinching at the sound. The baby's cries were not particularly loud, especially considering the full-blown roar he was capable of when wide-awake.

'Does he make that noise all the time?'

'Dougie? No, he's a pretty good kid. Lily says he's got a tooth coming, that's why he's a bit grizzly. They do bawl sometimes, though, even the good ones.' His own children certainly had. And so had Ernie. Bill left the memory unspoken.

Alf's hands twitched in his lap; he lifted them as if to cover his ears, then let them drop to his sides. 'It's like… the blokes who'd got shot up would make a noise like that sometimes. When the banging and shooting and all stopped for a bit, you'd hear them wailing on and on like that. Then they'd stop.'

Bill's throat was too tight for words. He swallowed, and the noise seemed loud in the room.

'How about your young fellows sleep in here?' Alf said. 'I'd sooner have that room outside.'

The outside room was a lean-to that Bill had built on to the house, with Alf's and Ernie's help and their father's interference, when his sons were little boys and the bedrooms full to overflowing. It was small, unlined, and a good deal less comfortable than this one, with furniture that showed the marks of years of rough use.

'Well, if that's what you want, we'll sort it out tomorrow,' Bill said.

Alf joined the family for meals, went out on the farm with the other men, and occasionally disappeared on solitary walks. Every evening Bill tried to persuade him to join the rest of them in the parlour, and every evening Alf chose instead to go off to his stark little room. Usually Bill sat out there with him for a while; sometimes he left his brother to the solitude he seemed to prefer. He would make more of an effort to get Alf out to the parlour of an evening when the weather grew colder, Bill told himself.

His brother refused to set foot outside the farm. If Bill pushed the matter beyond a gentle suggestion, Alf had a way of turning in on himself, as if a curtain had dropped between them. Bill would have welcomed a show of irritation, or even outright anger, but not the unsettling feeling that Alf had disappeared behind his own eyes.

The only time Alf showed a flicker of animation was in the milking shed. Bill even imagined he saw the ghost of a smile as Alf worked away at the familiar task. Little needed to be said in the cowshed, where everyone knew what was to be done, including the cows. Once or twice, Bill had to bite back an unthinking remark about how good it was to have another man's help with the milking. That would have been an uncomfortable reminder of Ernie. Everything was a reminder of Ernie.

Daisy had always liked going up to the head of the valley to visit the family at Uncle Bill's. Now it depended whether or not Uncle Alf happened to be in the house when they called.

Sometimes Daisy would see him leaving the house as she and her parents drew up in the gig. Or he might sit in the parlour with the others, looking down at the floor or gazing towards the window, a cup of tea resting forgotten by his elbow. The very air in the room felt heavier when Uncle Alf was there. Everyone was quieter, but if the conversation rose above a murmur he was inclined to stand up and leave without saying a word to anyone. Uncle Alf liked to go for walks by himself, Uncle Bill said. Daisy was always guiltily relieved when he left.

She was careful to say hello to him if he was there when she arrived. She had always been told that it was polite to meet someone's eyes when talking to him, so she did her best not to look away, but it made her uncomfortable. There was an oddness about Uncle Alf's eyes, as if he was seeing something horrible, not Aunt Lily's comfortable parlour.

He had something called shell shock, Uncle Bill told them, from all the shooting and explosions shaking the inside of his head. They had asked Uncle Richard about it, and he said Uncle Alf's nervous system was damaged by the shock.

Daisy had once spent a whole afternoon helping her father burn a heap of rubbish, and for the rest of that day whenever she closed her eyes she saw flames against the darkness. It might be a little like that for Uncle Alf. Perhaps he kept hearing those noises over and over, and perhaps he kept seeing terrible things.

He was sad about Uncle Ernie, of course; they all were. But it didn't seem like ordinary sadness. He might come right, given a bit more time, Uncle Bill said. Some peace and quiet, and Aunt Lily's good cooking, might do the job. But Daisy was fairly sure he didn't really think so. Some things never did come right. Uncle Danny's foot wouldn't grow back.

People talked about broken hearts, and it was as if something was broken inside Uncle Alf, where it couldn't be seen. There were other things than being killed or having bits shot off that could go wrong in a war.

Bill's sons had the cows penned up for milking, the first two animals already in their wooden bails, but Alf had still not appeared. He had gone on one of his walks after lunch, then retreated to his room; Bill had not seen him since.

'Run up to the house and give your uncle a hurry-up,' he told his younger son. Will pulled a face, and exchanged glances with Arfie. Bill thought he heard one of them mutter 'loony'. 'Go on, get on with it.' He bit back the rebuke that sprang to his lips. It was hardly fair to lecture the boys on the sacrifice their uncles had made, or to berate them for wanting to avoid Alf, when he had to force himself to sit with his brother of an evening in uncomfortable silence or one-sided conversation.

Will loped off towards the house, and was back so quickly that he must have barely had time to call out to Alf before returning. 'He said he'll be down in a minute.'

It was more like ten minutes before Alf made his own much slower way down to the cowshed and took his place in the bail next to Bill's, with a grunt that might have been an acknowledgement of his lateness.

By the clock, milking took less time now that Alf was home, but somehow the task seemed longer. The boys talked to each other, but kept their voices low. Bill was reluctant to say anything that might disrupt Alf's calm.

The sun's angle told Bill the afternoon was wearing on. Only a few cows were still to be milked when Arfie called out, 'Hey, look at that rat!'

'It's a whopper,' Will said.

Bill looked up to see where the boys were pointing. He caught a glimpse of a grey shape crawling over grain sacks against the far wall, then struggled to keep his balance as a figure pushed past him.

Alf snatched up a wooden paling that had fallen off one of the bails, and lurched his way over. The rat scrabbled at the sack for a moment too long before darting towards the open side of the shed. Will moved to block its exit; the rat veered away, pressed itself against the wall and bared its teeth.

If the creature made any sound, Bill could not hear it over Alf's roar. His first blow broke the rat's back; his next smashed its skull. But Alf did not stop. Again and again he slammed the wood against the rat, his snarls subsiding into a grunt in rhythm with the blows.

The rat was little more than a dirty red smear around lumps of gristle, and still Alf kept up his attack. Shock had pinned Bill to the spot; with an effort, he pushed himself upright and crossed the few steps to Alf.

He hauled on Alf's arm and wrenched the wood from his grasp. Alf fought back for a moment before his arm abruptly went limp. He stood breathing heavily, his eyes glassy.

Still with a firm grip on Alf's arm, Bill turned towards the house. 'You fellows finish up here,' he said over his shoulder to his sons, who were staring open-mouthed at their uncle.

Bill marched Alf up the hill. He opened the bedroom door and pushed him inside, but rather than following him into the room he went around the house to the back door.

Lily was in the kitchen with Emma. She looked up, concern on her face, when Bill came in and strode across the room without stopping to take his boots off.

He flicked a glance at Emma, then caught Lily's eye and shook his head, sending a silent message that this was something best left unspoken. Bill reached the whisky bottle down from its high shelf, where it was rarely disturbed, picked up two glasses and went out again.

His brother sat hunched on the bed, his brief burst of vigour evaporated. Bill poured a generous measure of whisky and nudged the glass against Alf's hand till his fingers closed around it. 'What the hell was all that about?' he demanded.

Alf cradled the glass in both hands and looked up at Bill standing over him. 'Rats,' he muttered. 'Thousands of them running around in the trenches. They'd come up bold as brass and pinch your food if you put it down for a minute. Crawl over your face when you were asleep. Great brutes of things—big as cats, some of them.'

He stared down into the glass as if seeing something else. Cold fingers trailed down Bill's spine as the realisation struck him: Alf was going to speak of Ernie at last. Bill propped himself against the far wall and gripped his glass more tightly.

'It was supposed to be the last push, Passchendaele was,' Alf said, his voice so low that Bill had to crane forward to hear him. 'There'd been a good session the week before, got us halfway up the ridge.'

Bill recalled the news reports after that battle. 'Thrilling Dispatches From Flanders', the headlines had announced. It was the turning point of the war, the newspapers claimed; the New Zealanders' 'greatest and most glorious day'; 'Germany's biggest defeat'. It had felt as if the end was in sight, and he had allowed himself to believe that his brothers would come home unscathed. And a week later Ernie was dead.

'They made a big fuss about what a good job we'd done of it,' Alf went on. 'The New Zealanders were the best of the lot, they reckoned. But halfway up the ridge was no use, not with the Germans sitting up the top just waiting to pick us off. One more push, they said. Just to the top of that ridge.'

He slid his glass onto the chest of drawers and made to reach his pipe out of a jacket pocket, then let his hand drop.

'They'd messed it up, the generals had, for all their jawing. The artillery wasn't ready—half of it wasn't even there yet, they hadn't had enough time to haul it up. And the rest they couldn't set up properly, with a solid base to it, the ground was too soft. So when the big guns went off, they landed short—right in the middle of our own front line. Our men cut to bits by our own artillery.'

'Our own?' Bill echoed hoarsely. He had heard nothing of this. When the newspapers had praised New Zealand's 'Honoured Place' in the battle, they had spoken of the heavy rain, calling that bad luck. Never had there been any suggestion of blunders.

Alf nodded, a quick jerk of the head. 'We were further back, Ernie and I. Couldn't hear a thing over the noise of the guns, it was no use trying to talk, but I made sure I stuck close so I could keep an eye on him. Not only the guns to look out for, either—it was just about all you could do to keep your head above the mud. You've never seen anything like it, the mud in that place. Not a blade of grass left standing, let alone a tree. Like black porridge, it was. So you had to pick your way along the firmer bits, and all the while be ready to hop into a shell hole when the machine guns and snipers were having a go. Fellows shot down left and right of us, dropping in the mud. And then we got a good look at the wire.'

Some roughness in the wall was digging into Bill's back. He shifted a little, to free himself from what a glance revealed as an old nail head. Alf showed no sign of having noticed the movement. He took a gulp from his glass, and Bill saw a shudder run through him.

'The Germans put out these great snarls of barbed wire to stop us getting through. I'd seen it before, but the artillery chewed it up pretty well. But this time, with the artillery turning out a dead loss, it'd hardly touched the stuff. So there we were with thirty yards of wire in front of us, and Germans the other side of it in these bunkers—pillboxes, they called them—made of concrete six foot thick. That's what we were supposed to get through.

'I saw blokes up the front trying to get through that wire—some of them got a fair way into it, too. Then you'd see the machine guns picking them off, and they'd be jerking and flapping with the bullets. It was like watching a bit of washing that'd blown off the line and got caught up in the blackberries.

'Ernie and I got down in a shell hole and just lay there—not much else we could do. No use trying to go back, and I sure as hell wasn't getting into that wire. Then Ernie stuck his head up like an idiot, trying to get a better look at what was going on. A sniper took a shot at him— must've just about parted his hair for him, it was that close. He looked over at me and… well, I reckon he gave me a bit of a grin. You know that look of his when he'd got away with something he shouldn't have.'

Bill felt the corners of his mouth tug up into something like a smile.

He knew that look well. As the baby of the family, Ernie had often got away with mischief that would have seen their father take his belt to the older boys.

'So I'm shouting at him, "Get down, you great fool"—not that he could hear me. I'm crawling over to pull him back down, and next thing...' Alf cleared his throat. 'Next thing a machine gun gets him, and there's a great big hole where his chest was.'

The silence went on for so long that the room had grown darker by the time Bill regained the power of movement. He slid to his haunches, steadying himself against the wall, and stared at the dim shape that was Alf.

'A shell went off right next to me around then, that's when I got a knock on the head. I was stuck in that hole till the stretcher bearers could get out there—that wasn't till the next day. I don't remember that bit too well, after the shell went off. Woke up at a dressing station somewhere.'

Bill croaked out the word through a mouth gone dry: 'Ernie?'

Alf shook his head. 'They never found him. I couldn't get back there myself to look—they carted me off to a field hospital after the dressing station, see if they could patch me up. Then the trench foot wouldn't come right. Your feet go rotten after a while, from being wet all the time. They reckoned it was bad enough that they'd better send me off to England, to the big hospital there.

'The stretcher bearers had a jolly good look for all the missing ones like Ernie, they wouldn't leave any of our fellows behind. But there was no finding a lot of them. With all that shelling, blokes just sank into the mud. Must be thousands of them buried in the stuff.'

A treacherous memory reared itself before Bill: Ernie, no more than two or three years old, trying to keep up with Bill and Alf as they played some long-forgotten game on the creek bank. Ernie sliding face-first into the soft ground, coming up giggling and filthy and caked in mud. Now he lay in some God-forsaken place on the other side of the world. No proper grave for their little brother. Just trodden into a sea of black mud.

But there was more. Alf raised his head, and Bill saw in his eyes that there was more.

'Those fellows going out after a battle—it took six of them to a stretcher. Mud up to their armpits, they reckoned. They couldn't get out straight away after a set-to, had to wait till things quietened down a bit. Might be a day or more before they could pick up the wounded, let alone whatever was left of the dead ones. I'd seen what they brought in.'

Some trick of the twilight had set a smouldering in Alf's eyes. He stared past Bill, past the farm, past the valley. 'The rats got there before them. They go for the soft bits first. On the face, mostly.'

Silence blanketed the room. For weeks Bill had hoped that Alf might speak of what had happened to Ernie; now he would have given good money to be able to have the words unheard. His brother was dead, and the best to be hoped for was that he had been trodden into mud before the rats got at him.

He raised the glass to his mouth, his hand shaking so much that a trail of whisky spilled down his chin when he took a gulp.

'Bloody hell, Alf,' he said.

Chapter Sixteen

Daisy stared at the letter lying where it had been dropped on the table. Just a few dull-looking typed lines under an official header. The mere sight of it set a burning in her throat as if she might be sick, and yet it was not a shock. It was not even a surprise.

Ever since the newspapers had said back in February that the government would soon be conscripting married men who only had one child, she had been quite certain that her father would be among the very first called up. The knowledge had sat inside her, heavy as a stone, since then. Now it was April, and all this horrible letter did was confirm what she had known for weeks.

'But they won't really take Papa,' her mother was saying. 'Not when he explains it all to them. It's men with big grown sons they're thinking of.'

'That's right,' her father said. 'I just have to send a letter and ask to be let off, then in a couple of weeks they'll send some army fellows to Ruatane to have a talk with all the men wanting exemptions.'

'And Grandpa's going to help—he'll come along with us and tell the men why Papa can't go, with just having a young daughter still at school. So it'll be all right.' Daisy saw her mother place a hand over her father's much larger one. 'Of course they won't take you away.'

Her mother sounded so certain, as if the very thought was impossible. Daisy watched them, and said nothing.

Another official letter arrived. The Military Service Board was to spend a few days in Ruatane, and Daisy's father was told to report the following week to apply for an exemption from service.

On the day her father was to go before the Board, Daisy saw his Sunday best suit laid out on the bed, her mother's good dress beside it. She wished she could go into town with them. Instead she had to spend all day at school, willing the hands of the clock to go faster. In the afternoon she caught a glimpse of Grandpa's buggy going up the track past the school, and knew he must be taking her parents home. After that the clock seemed to go so slowly that she wondered if it was broken.

The day dragged itself to three o'clock at last. Daisy cantered all the way home, taking no notice of the horsey snorts that sounded like grumbling. Old Brownie's ears flicked as she kicked at his sides. He was not used to keeping up a canter, but today Daisy had no patience for his usual plodding pace. She had to know what the Military Board had said, and she was not going to wait a moment longer than she had to.

Her parents were sitting at the kitchen table, chairs pulled close together. They both looked up when Daisy burst into the room. One look at her mother's face, eyes red and puffy, told Daisy the answer.

'Daisy, they said Papa—'

'I'll be going off to—'

They stopped, looked at each other, and her mother tried again. 'They won't let us have an exemption. They said Papa has to go—' Her voice disappeared into what sounded like a choked-off sob.

Daisy plumped down in the chair opposite them. Her father took one of her mother's hands between both of his.

'Looks like they want me to go after all, Daisy. They said they need all the men who've only got one kid—it doesn't matter if it's a boy or girl, or whether you're on a farm or just working in town.'

'They're letting men with half a dozen great big boys of sixteen or seventeen stay at home, but they're making you go. It's just not fair!' Tears brimmed in Mama's eyes; she dashed them away with the back of her hand. 'And that Major, or whatever he was—the one with the silly little moustache—he went on about "the Empire has a need for large families", and "it's troubling to see so many couples with only the one child". As if it's our fault! As if we wanted—' She bit back whatever she had been about to say.

Worry had carved an unfamiliar crease between her father's brows. 'I don't like the idea of leaving you to manage on your own.'

'I'll help,' Daisy said at once, desperate to say something, anything, to ease the strain in their faces.

'Yes, you'll have to, Daisy,' her mother said. 'You won't be able to go to school any more.'

Daisy sat very still, absorbing this new realisation. 'Oh. I didn't think... no, I won't.'

'I suppose there might be a bit of trouble over that,' her father said. 'She's not even twelve yet, we're meant to send her to school.'

Her mother swung on him, eyes wide and staring. 'They can't go taking you and then turn around and say we have to send Daisy to school. What are they going to do, take me away too and put me in jail?'

The shrillness of her words seemed to hang in the air even after she fell silent. She slumped in the chair, and gave a quick shake of her head. 'No, there's no use making a fuss,' she said, her voice settling into its usual softness. 'We'll manage somehow, Davie. We'll have to.'

'Sorry about the school business, Daisy,' her father said. 'I know you're keen on it.'

'Well, she'll be able to go back when you're home again. You never know, you mightn't be away all that long.'

'It's all right,' Daisy said. 'I don't mind about school.' It was almost true. Losing her dream of going to high school seemed a small thing in the face of having her father taken away.

There was a scrap of comfort in knowing that he would not have to leave right away. He was allowed twelve weeks from the date of his medical examination to put his affairs in order, and he told Daisy and her mother that he intended to take every one of those weeks. Of course he had been passed as fit for service, so big and strong as he was. Daisy kept to herself the guilty thought that perhaps Uncle Richard might lie about it.

Daisy said she would rather not go to Lucy's for the May school holidays; with only a few more weeks of having her father at home, she did not want to waste a single day.

When the cows were dried off for winter, and he had more hours to spare, Papa set about doing whatever he could to make things easier for when they would be left on their own. He walked the whole farm, checking every stretch of fence and repairing any that showed the slightest need of it. He chopped an enormous pile of wood, stacking as much as would fit under the eaves by the back porch, and filling the nearest shed with the rest.

Calving time saw July's usual grim skies and downpours. Daisy's father suggested selling all the heifer calves that year as well as the bulls, but her mother insisted that they keep the best of them.

'We don't want to go running down the herd after building it up all these years. We'll manage looking after them, Daisy and me. It's just till you get back.'

Time had a way of going most quickly when you most wanted it to slow down. Daisy had never known days to rush by the way these ones did. She was still going to school; her father said she might as well for as long as she could. After school and at the weekends she helped with the farm work; feeding out hay to the cows, teaching the new calves to drink from a bucket, and milking the house-cow.

They killed a pig in July. Grandpa came over to help Daisy's father with the slaughtering. Most years Daisy hovered nearby at pig-killing, but this time she kept as far away as she could. Even with a shed and the house between the men and her, the pig's high-pitched squeals felt as if they were drilling a hole though her skull.

Curing the pig to turn it into ham and bacon meant hauling heavy slabs of meat in and out of the brining trough before smoking much of it for bacon. Daisy's father wanted the job done while he was still there for the heaviest of the work. Before the joints were dried and hung for storage there was always a special treat of brawn made from the pig's head. Somehow this year it did not seem to taste as good as it always had before.

Every evening there was sewing to help her mother with, getting her father's things ready. They made sure all his clothes were neatly mended, and stitched new shirts and handkerchiefs. Daisy knitted two pairs of warm socks to add to the ones her mother had darned.

August came, and his leaving could not be put off any longer.

'I should give you a haircut,' her mother said the day before he was to sail from Ruatane. 'Then you won't have to bother about it for a while.'

For the first time Daisy could remember, her father did not make a fuss about having his hair cut. Usually he would say he didn't need it done just yet, and her mother would remind him that he had been saying the same thing for weeks.

When Daisy was smaller they had sometimes made a game of it. She would climb onto her father's lap, and he would pretend she was so heavy he could not move. 'Now we've got you!' her mother would say, pulling the scissors out from behind her back. Sometimes the three of them ended up laughing so hard that her mother had to sit down and wait till her hands were steady enough to be trusted with the sharp scissors.

No one laughed today. Her father sat very still, an old towel draped across his shoulders, while her mother snipped carefully, locks of dark hair making an arc around the chair as she worked. Daisy saw her wind a curl around her finger, trim it off close to the scalp, then slip the lock into her apron pocket.

The three of them took the gig into town next morning, and after waving till the boat was out of sight the two of them turned for home.

They rode in silence much of the way, only exchanging a few words about the weather and the state of the track. Daisy found it easier not to cry if she did not speak, and her mother's set expression suggested she felt much the same.

'You'd better run down and see Miss Cameron tomorrow,' her mother said as they passed the school. 'I'll give you a note to say I need you at home for a while.'

'Just till Papa's back,' Daisy said.

191

'That's right. Just till Papa gets home.' She flicked the reins, and the horse picked up its pace. 'I think we could do with a nice cup of tea.'

They put the gig in its shed, and Daisy let the horse out into a paddock. She caught up with her mother in the porch, in time to see her stroking the sleeve of her father's old coat that hung from a peg.

While her mother filled the kettle and put it on the range, Daisy set out their cups and saucers. She paused with her hand outstretched towards the shelf, realising that there was no need to take down a third cup. Daisy gazed around the kitchen, struck by how much bigger the room seemed without her father in it.

They kept themselves busy for what was left of the day, and cooked a dinner that turned out to have far more potatoes and carrots than either of them felt like eating.

'It's a good thing we didn't bother making a pudding,' her mother said. 'Bread and jam will do us.' The knife stopped halfway through a slice, and Daisy saw her staring at the loaf. 'I need to make bread tonight,' she murmured.

Some of Daisy's earliest memories were of sitting at the table, propped up on cushions, watching her parents make the bread together. She closed her eyes for a moment, seeing the picture in her mind's eye, then asked, 'Can I have a go at kneading it?'

For the first time all day, her mother smiled. 'That'd be a big help. And it's high time I taught you—your Grandma would go crook at me if she knew I've never shown you how to knead bread.'

It had always been her father's job. Daisy could picture his big, strong hands covered in flour, working away at the dough. Her mother often said their bread was especially good because it was kneaded so well.

Daisy watched her mother mix the flour and yeast, then under her instructions she punched at the dough, turned it and folded it, and thumped it again. She could not get it to the silkiness her father always managed, but Mama said it was good enough. Daisy shook her hands to get the feeling back in her fingers while her mother shaped the loaves and set them to rise.

Making the bread had taken much longer than usual. 'It's about time you went to bed,' Mama said, glancing at the clock on the wall.

'I'm not very tired. I'd rather sit up with you.'

'You've got... no, that's right, you don't need to worry about school. All right, let's sit up a bit longer.'

It seemed too much bother to light a fire in the parlour so late in the evening, so they stayed in the kitchen. They tidied up after the breadmaking, made themselves another cup of tea, and washed the last few dishes.

Her mother got the broom out and started sweeping the floor, surprising Daisy; this was not a job usually done at night, and did not seem worth the effort for a few crumbs.

Daisy took the dustpan out to the porch and threw its contents over the edge of the steps, a chill gust of wind whipping at her hair. She hurried inside to close the door against the draught.

'That could do with a wipe,' her mother said, eyeing the shelf over the bench. 'I think I'll get all those dishes down and make a proper job of it.'

'But you won't be able to see what you're doing.' The small lamp on the kitchen table barely cast enough light for Daisy to make out the shapes of the dishes on the high shelf.

'You hold a candle up for me, I can manage well enough with that.'

Daisy lit a candle from the lamp and held the candlestick above her head. The flame wavered, making odd-shaped shadows that loomed then shriveled with each small movement of her hands. There was no way to tilt the candle that did not throw the shelf into deeper shadow as her mother reached for each dish. She heard the chink of one piece of china sliding into another. 'I think I might've chipped that,' her mother murmured. But she made no move to stop what she was doing.

Daisy had never seen her behaving so strangely. There could only be one reason for the way she kept finding excuses to put off going to bed: she was missing Daisy's father.

But staying up all night would not bring him back. Daisy lowered the candle to the bench.

'We should go to bed, Mama. It's late, and it's cold, and we can't see to do anything properly.'

Her mother turned to face Daisy, a protest showing on her face. Then her head dipped, and she abruptly looked smaller in the candle's wavering light. 'All right, I suppose we'd better.' She pushed a dish safely back from the edge of the shelf, lit another candle, and put out the lamp.

Daisy kissed her mother good night and went off to her room. It was chilly after the warmth of the kitchen; she undressed and got into her nightdress as quickly as she could.

She turned down the bedcovers, then stood listening, wondering why the sounds of the night seemed wrong. The creak of floorboards from her mother's room had stopped, and the house was in silence. Yes, that was it: the silence. No murmur of voices from her parents' room, her father's a low rumble, her mother's higher and softer. Mama was alone in there.

Daisy cupped a hand around the candle to keep its flame steady as she padded through the house, grateful for the thickness of her socks against the bare floor. A sliver of light marked the door to her parents' room. She pushed it open and stepped inside.

Mama was sitting on the bed in her nightdress, fiddling with something curled in her palm. Her fingers closed, and she slipped it under her pillow, but not before Daisy had recognised the lock of Papa's hair, tied with a scrap of blue ribbon.

'Can I sleep in here with you?' Daisy asked.

A smile softened her mother's face. 'That'd be nice. It feels funny, being in here all by myself—I've never slept on my own, not even when I was little. Not with having all those sisters.'

Daisy helped fold back the bedspread, its crocheted lace thin and spidery with age. 'Shall we do prayers first?' her mother said, just as Daisy was about to slide under the covers. 'Let's do it properly, like in church.'

They knelt either side of the bed. Daisy clasped her hands together, candlelight showing red through her closed eyelids. Her father was to spend a night at Aunt Sarah's before catching the train to Wellington; by this time tomorrow he would be in the big house, perhaps thinking about them back on the farm.

'Dear Lord, please watch over Davie and keep him safe,' her mother prayed.

'Please keep Papa safe, and bring him home soon.'

Nothing more needed to be said. The whole of the war was encompassed in that plea.

Eddie was the first to make out the tall figure of his uncle among the passengers pressing towards the gangplank.

'There he is! There's Uncle Dave,' he said.

'I can't see him yet.' Even on tiptoe his grandmother was overwhelmed by the people milling about. Eddie took her arm and guided her over to where the boat had tied up, just in time to see his uncle step onto the wharf.

Uncle Dave lowered a canvas bag from one shoulder and wrapped an arm around Granny. With his free arm he shook Eddie by the hand. 'I saw that hair of yours from out in the harbour, Eddie. You make a good landmark.' He smiled, but it was a thin, tired sort of smile.

'Let's get you back to the house,' Granny said. 'You'll be tired after that long trip.'

Eddie picked up Uncle Dave's bag, led the way to the carriage, and helped Granny up to her seat.

'Gee, Auckland's a big place,' Uncle Dave said, staring around as they drove past two-storeyed buildings of shops and offices, their carriage sharing the road with carts and buggies as well as motor cars. 'I'd be worried about getting lost if I was here on my own.'

'You get used to it,' Granny said. 'How's everyone at home? How are Beth and Daisy?'

'They're a bit upset about this business. I don't like leaving them on their own, but there's not much we can do about it.'

Uncle Dave looked older than Eddie remembered. He asked how Eddie was going at school, and Eddie launched into a description of his favourite classes and his latest rugby match, but he soon realised that Uncle Dave was not really listening. Eddie trailed off, embarrassed to be talking about such ordinary things when his uncle was going off to the war.

The drive home from the wharf only took a few minutes. When Eddie and the others had climbed down from the carriage, Mr Jenson clicked his tongue and set the horses plodding along the path that led behind the house.

On an ordinary day Eddie might have gone with him, to help unharness the horses and put the carriage away. He was doing what he could to help Mr Jenson with the heavy work these days, ever since the Jensons' son Walter had been called up. Eddie liked working with the horses; cleaning the carriage and digging the gardens took more of an effort. He felt a brief stab of conscience at the sight of Mr Jenson's bent old figure pulling away. But he did not want to miss a moment of Uncle Dave's visit. He would make it up to Mr Jenson on the weekend, he told himself. He would dig over a whole flower bed.

Aunt Sarah was on the verandah waiting for them. 'Do come inside out of the cold,' she said. Uncle Dave, who was staring up at the house, let Granny tug him towards the verandah steps.

'Nice place you've got,' he said when they were in the entrance hall. 'Thanks for having me to stay, it's a big help.'

'You're very welcome. I only wish your visit were under happier circumstances.' Aunt Sarah placed a hand on his arm and gave it a quick pat. 'I expect you'd like to freshen up after the journey,' she said, her voice brisker. 'I'll order tea and biscuits for when you're ready.'

'I'll show you where you'll be sleeping,' Granny said, guiding him towards the staircase.

'It's next to my room.' Eddie darted ahead to lead the way up the stairs. He saw Uncle Dave into the guest bedroom, then dashed into his own room, shrugging off his jacket as he went. It had been such a rush to get home from school in time to go down to the wharves with Granny that he had not had time to change out of his uniform. Now he flung the blue jacket and trousers onto the bed, snatched after-school clothes from his chest of drawers, and pulled them on as quickly as he could. He was still doing up the last few buttons when he went back out to the corridor, just in time to see his uncle emerge from the other room, hair damp around the edges of a face pink from scrubbing.

Granny and Aunt Sarah, as well as several varieties of cakes and biscuits, were in the drawing room waiting for them. Eddie was too busy with the food to add much to the conversation, which was mainly Granny and Uncle Dave talking about all the aunts and uncles and cousins.

'And how is Daisy doing at school?' Aunt Sarah asked, catching Eddie's attention. 'Still getting good results, I expect.'

Uncle Dave's mouth twisted. 'She's good at the work, all right. I felt a bit mean telling her she had to stop going.'

'Why can't Daisy go to school any more?' Eddie asked, startled.

'Because of me going off to the war. Her ma can't manage by herself, so we've got to take Daisy out of school.'

'Oh, that's a shame,' Granny said. 'But she'll be able to go back as soon as you're home again, won't she? It probably won't be long at all.'

'That's what we've been telling her,' Uncle Dave said.

'Yes, she'll have plenty of time to catch up before she starts high school,' Aunt Sarah said.

The talk shifted to other, less interesting, matters. Eddie took a slice of chocolate cake and chewed absently on it as he absorbed the news about Daisy. She had said nothing in her letters about having to give up school, while Eddie was guiltily aware that he had often mentioned sports and favourite lessons at his own school. Daisy's letters had been shorter ever since Uncle Dave's conscription had come through; she must have a lot on her mind, but they weren't things she wanted to write about.

Daisy and Aunt Beth had to run the farm by themselves with Uncle Dave away, and Daisy had to leave school. The most Eddie had done was help Mr Jenson, and even that might not go on for much longer. Aunt Sarah was talking of getting a boy in a few days a week so that Eddie would not be distracted from his schoolwork.

'Would you like to have a little walk and stretch your legs?' he heard his grandmother ask. 'We could go out to the garden for a bit.'

'Is it far to that place with the statue—Albert Park, is it? I wouldn't mind seeing that.'

'Oh, that's a nice idea, Davie. And it's just down the road, we'll easily be there and back before it starts getting late.'

Eddie invited himself to go with his uncle and grandmother. A gate at the back of the house opened onto a path that led to the park. They walked along the narrow lane with Granny in the middle, Eddie and his uncle shortening their paces to match hers.

It was quiet, the mossy path swallowing their footsteps, and any noise from the road coming muffled through the fences and gardens around them. Granny had Uncle Dave's arm looped through hers; from time to time she leaned her head against him. Neither of them seemed to want to talk, and Eddie caught their silence. He had been bursting with questions for his uncle, wanting to know when he would be sailing for Europe, what battalion he was likely to join, and to just which part of France or Belgium he might be sent. Now it all felt too solemn, and his questions seemed childish.

Gravel crunched under their feet as they entered the park. Granny led the way over to the statue that Eddie had visited almost every week since he first came to live in Auckland.

Uncle Dave stared at the carved figure dressed in an old-fashioned army uniform. 'It doesn't really look much like Mal, does it?'

'No, not really,' Granny said. 'But it's the same sort of uniform he would've had, and we never got to see Mal in his. It's nice to have something to remember him by.' She patted the marble hand, then turned to Eddie and smiled. 'Except I've got you to remember him by, haven't I? That's better than a statue.'

She slipped her free arm through Eddie's, and with arms linked the three of them set out for home.

After a dinner of roast beef and vegetables, with apple pie and custard for dessert, they all went through to the drawing room. Granny sat with Uncle Dave on one of the sofas, and Eddie took a chair facing them. Aunt Sarah seated herself at the piano and played one piece after another, but quietly enough to allow the others to talk.

When Granny had got Uncle Dave to tell them everything about what had been happening on the farm, from the new calves right down to the state of the fences, she turned the conversation to the old days, back when Uncle Dave and Eddie's father were boys. They talked of swimming in the creek; of climbing haystacks; of Uncle Dave's old dog Biff. Eddie's favourite story was the one he must have heard a hundred times before: the day his father won a race riding his pony against a dozen boys all older than he was. Eddie still had the silver cup his father had won that day, set on his chest of drawers where it was one of the first things he saw each morning.

Some of the stories were so familiar that Eddie almost felt as if he had been there himself. The tales of his father and Uncle Dave got mixed up with his own memories of roaming the farm with Daisy, until he was not sure which parts he remembered and which parts he was imagining. But whether they were his own stories or his father's, they were warm, comfortable ones. Occasionally Granny stopped in what seemed to be the middle of a sentence and changed the subject; after this had happened a few times Eddie began to wonder if it was because the rest of that particular story was not such a happy one.

He realised that he had not heard the piano for some time. Aunt Sarah was now settled in an armchair on the other side of the fireplace. She seemed to be paying more attention to Granny and Uncle Dave than to the book in her lap.

Granny rose from the sofa, and murmured an excuse. Aunt Sarah watched until she had gone through the door, no doubt on her way to the lavatory, then turned to Uncle Dave. 'I fully expect to see you back here in due course,' she said. 'But I do want you to know that if anything were to happen… if the unthinkable…' She paused for a moment. 'Let me just say that you've no need to worry about what might happen to Beth and Daisy. Beth's father would see to that, of course, but I'd insist on doing my part, too. I'd always see that they were well looked after.'

A thread of chill ran through Eddie, like gulping icy water. Did she really think Uncle Dave might be killed?

His uncle slumped lower on the sofa. 'Thanks, Sarah. Yes, Uncle Frank would see they were all right, and there'd be some sort of army pension for Beth, but it's good to know you'd be looking out for them, too.'

'And there are no pressing debts that it might be of use for me to help clear?'

'No, nothing like that. I've never been keen on owing a lot of money to anyone—just as well, too. That'd only be something else for Beth to worry about.'

Granny came back into the room soon afterwards, and not long after that Aunt Sarah closed her book and stood up. 'I think I'll retire early tonight,' she said. 'I'll do my best to be up in time to see you off in the morning, Dave.' She paused in the doorway, and beckoned Eddie. 'Come here a moment, would you?'

She must be going to tell him to go to bed. Eddie followed her out of the room ready to argue the point. Why should he miss any part of

Uncle Dave's only evening with them? There was no school tomorrow, and it wasn't even nine o'clock yet!

'Don't sit up too much longer.' Aunt Sarah kept her voice low so that the others would not hear. 'No, just listen,' she said before Eddie had the chance to say a word. 'I'm quite sure your grandmother would like some time with your uncle, just the two of them with no audience. She has no idea how long it might be before she sees him again, or even if… well, never mind that. But for this one evening, leave them in peace.'

The protest died on Eddie's lips. 'I thought I might go down to the station with Granny to see Uncle Dave off. Maybe I'd better not.'

'Actually I think that's a fine idea,' Aunt Sarah said. 'Your grandmother will want someone with her afterwards, and goodness knows I'm no use to anyone at that hour of the morning. Yes, it's well thought of, Eddie.'

Eddie went back into the drawing room, but soon afterwards he made a great show of yawning, stood up, and said he was going to bed.

'I shouldn't keep you up, either, Davie, not when you've got to be away so early tomorrow,' his grandmother said, but neither she nor his uncle showed any sign of moving. Eddie said his goodnights, and left them to their conversation.

It was still dark outside his window when Eddie woke next morning. He pulled the cord that turned on the electric light, and saw by the clock on his chest of drawers that it was just after five o'clock.

He dressed hurriedly and clattered down the stairs, to find that his grandmother and uncle had got up well before him and were in the kitchen. Mrs Jenson must have got up even earlier, for the kitchen was already full of delicious smells. Uncle Dave was saying she shouldn't have bothered; Granny said she would have done it herself rather than have Mrs Jenson come in so early. Meanwhile Mrs Jenson piled sausages, bacon, eggs and mushrooms onto a large plate and placed it before Uncle Dave. It looked very good.

'You can't be going all that long way without a proper breakfast, and I wouldn't trust those railway stations for a decent meal.' As she spoke, she sawed off several slices of bread, two of which she spread with butter. She added some cold meat, and handed the thick sandwich to Eddie.

His uncle finished his breakfast, Eddie demolished a second sandwich, and they were about to leave the kitchen when Mrs Jenson passed Uncle Dave a tin box with a lid on it, the sort that she kept biscuits in.

'In case you get hungry on the train,' she said. 'Just sandwiches, and a slice or two of veal pie—a few little cakes, too.' She nodded at Uncle Dave's thanks, then stood there awkwardly, hands working at her apron. 'Mr Stewart, I wonder if... when you get to France, or wherever it turns out to be, would you mind keeping an eye out for Walter Jenson? He's my boy, you see. You might bump into him over there, you never know.'

'I'll be on the look-out for him,' Uncle Dave said. 'And I'll tell him what a good cook his ma is.' That got a smile from Mrs Jenson.

They were milling about in the entrance hall, retrieving coats and hats from the hall stand, when Aunt Sarah appeared, clutching her dressing-gown closed with one hand as she made her way down the stairs.

'I thought I'd better make the effort in your honour, Dave.' She smothered a yawn, and pushed her loose plait of hair over one shoulder.

Eddie had never seen his aunt in quite such a dishevelled state, but he did not have long to study the unusual sight.

'It's nearly half-past,' Granny said, glancing at the big clock that stood against one wall. 'We'd better get a move on.'

Aunt Sarah made to shake Uncle Dave's hand, then somehow it turned into a hug. She let him go, and a few moments later they were out the front door, down the verandah steps, and climbing into the waiting carriage. Aunt Sarah held the front door open a fraction, just far enough for her to peer around it and wave them off.

It was still more than an hour till sunrise. Pale streetlights showed their way through the gloom as they hurried into the railway station. Uncle Dave's train was waiting at the platform, steam hissing around its wheels. Eddie shook his uncle's hand. 'I'll give Daisy and Aunt Beth a hand with things when Granny and I go down there for the holidays,' he said, though it seemed a small thing to offer a week or two's worth of his time.

'That's good to know, Eddie. That'll be a help to them.' He engulfed Granny in a hug, and only let her go when the conductor blew a long blast on his whistle. 'Better not let the train go without me, eh?'

He climbed into the nearest carriage, and shortly afterwards they saw him open a window and lean out. He called something that was probably a goodbye, but the words were lost in a screech of engine whistle. The train pulled away, and they waved until the smoke billowing from its stack hid Uncle Dave from sight.

Granny let her hand drop. 'I wish the war didn't keep taking them,' she murmured. Eddie had sometimes seen her looking at the statue in the park with that same wistful expression.

'Let's go home, Granny.' He tucked her arm through his, and led her out of the station.

Chapter Seventeen

Sometimes Daisy thought she caught a glimpse of her father, just on the edge of sight. But when she turned her head there was no one, and the world felt a little emptier.

The nights were the worst. Dusk drove them indoors, where the house felt full of echoes and the lamps did not seem to burn as brightly as they used to. When they were in bed, pressed back-to-back for warmth and for comfort, Daisy heard muffled weeping from her mother's side. Her own pillow was often damp with tears by morning.

Her father would have been missed just as badly in the daytime if it had not taken all their energy to manage the farm work. Everything was so hard now. Tasks that would hardly have made Daisy's father breathe more rapidly sometimes left the two of them exhausted. Before he left, he had done whatever he could to make things easier for them: lifting down farm equipment that was stowed out of reach; oiling the hinges of the heavy shed doors; moving the chaff sacks closer to where the horses were fed. But he could not predict that the gate to the cowshed would choose now to sag on its post, making it twice as hard to open; or that a particularly stupid sheep would tumble into a drain one morning. It struggled against Daisy and her mother when they dragged it out by a mix of shoving and hauling on a rope, leaving them both coated with mud and her mother with a hoof-shaped red mark on her arm that ripened into a livid bruise.

'I should've cut its throat instead,' her mother muttered as Daisy rubbed salve onto her arm.

Daisy's father had been gone nearly two weeks. She and her mother were having a cup of tea and some disappointingly stale scones one afternoon when they heard the rattle of wheels coming up to the house, soon followed by a knocking at the kitchen door.

Her mother smoothed her apron before opening the door to their visitor. With a jolt of surprise, Daisy recognised her teacher.

'Miss Cameron. How nice of you to call.' The tightness in her mother's voice told Daisy she was finding it hard to be polite. A little too hard, it seemed. 'Look, I know I should be sending Daisy to school, but I just can't, that's all there is to it. The Army people said we were expected to manage on our own, Daisy and me—well, that means I have to keep Daisy at home, whatever the law says.'

She paused for breath, and Miss Cameron took the opportunity to get a word in. 'Mrs Stewart, please don't distress yourself. I've no intention of making things any more difficult for you, and I very much doubt that the school's attendance register will be receiving close scrutiny in the near future. I didn't come here to talk about the law.'

Mama looked less stiff and awkward, and more like her usual self. 'Well, if that's... you'd better come in, then. Have a cup of tea with us— Daisy, make a fresh pot, love.'

Daisy hurried over to the bench, glad of an excuse to hide the blush that was burning its way up her face. She had never expected to hear a teacher being scolded like that; least of all by her mother.

'Oh, please don't go to any trouble on my account, Mrs Stewart.'

'It's no trouble at all.' Her mother had set out another cup and saucer; now Daisy saw her slathering an extra layer of butter on the scones to hide their staleness. 'We'll go through to the parlour, shall we?'

Daisy caught her eye and pointed at the range that warmed the kitchen. Mama nodded her understanding. 'We haven't lit the fire in the parlour just yet—perhaps you'd rather stay out here in the warm?'

The parlour fire had not been lit since the day Daisy's father had left. Every day they talked of lighting it; every day they decided it was too much bother, and a waste of the firewood he had chopped for them.

Miss Cameron said she would be perfectly comfortable in the kitchen. While Daisy and her mother got the tea things ready, she sat down at the table and placed a large leather bag by her chair.

'Several of the children have older brothers away at the war now, so they're only able to come to school on the days they're not needed for farm work,' she said. 'But Daisy's the only one with a father called up and no men left at home. And I rather think it's more of a loss for her to miss school than it is for most of the others.' She smiled at Daisy. 'I must say I miss having you in class, dear.'

Daisy hesitated, torn between the truth and her reluctance to say anything that might upset her mother. 'I miss it too,' she admitted. 'But it's just till Papa gets back.'

'Of course it is, Daisy.' Miss Cameron turned to Daisy's mother. 'Mrs Stewart, quite frankly I sometimes find it difficult to believe this war will ever be over, after it's dragged on so long. But it seems to me that we should carry on with our lives as if there *will* be an end to such times— we should go on fitting ourselves as well as we possibly can for the future, whatever it might hold. If we don't, it's as if we're forging our own defeat even in the face of victory.'

Daisy's mother was staring at the teacher. 'That's just how I feel about it.' She gave a quick, shy smile. 'Except I wouldn't be able to think out how to say it like that. I really do want Daisy to be able to carry on at school, and go to high school and all, but...' She spread her hands wide in a gesture of helplessness. 'I just don't see how I can do it. Not with her father away.'

'Well, I suggest we plan for the time when Daisy's able to return to school. I do think she'll be able to catch up—it helps that she was doing so well before—but the longer she's away from her schoolwork, the harder it will be.'

Miss Cameron lifted the leather satchel onto her lap, pulled some familiar-looking books from it, and passed them across the table to Daisy. 'I wondered if it might be possible for her to carry on with her study at home for now. I've brought the most useful of her textbooks, and I've made a list of what sections she should concentrate on—vocabulary lists and grammar exercises, sums to work on, that sort of thing.' She handed Daisy a sheet of lined notepaper covered in Miss Cameron's neat, rounded handwriting. 'That should see you through into next term, Daisy.'

The topmost book on the small pile was a history text. Daisy opened it to the account of Alexander the Great that she had been studying just a few weeks before. She closed her eyes and mentally ran through the list of his conquests; yes, she could still remember most of them.

She hardly seemed to have used her brain at all since she had stopped going to school, with the farm work taking up so much of the daylight hours and of her energy. She opened her eyes again, flicked through the rest of the book, then moved it to one side and opened the next on the pile, her latest reader.

After that came an arithmetic book, and then a geography text. Daisy turned page after page, only vaguely aware of the conversation and chinking of teacups going on around her.

A scraping of chairs told Daisy that Miss Cameron was about to leave. She went to the door with her mother, and they waved the teacher off down the track.

'That's good you'll be able to keep up with your schoolwork after all, Daisy.'

Daisy hated to take the new brightness out of her mother's voice. 'I don't know if I can, though, not when we're so busy. I don't think I'll have the time.'

'We'll *make* the time.' Her mother turned to Daisy and took her by the hand. 'It's like Miss Cameron said—we've got to keep up the important things as if everything's going to come right again. Otherwise it's as if we're saying they'll never come right. As if your father...'

She trailed off into silence, and Daisy knew why. Those were not words to say aloud. Daisy felt her hand squeezed, and pressed her mother's in return.

After the dinner dishes were done that evening, Daisy pulled out her books. 'But don't you want me to help with the bread first?' she asked.

'No, I'll do it. You get on with your schoolwork.'

It soon became their regular pattern of an evening: Daisy with her schoolbooks, memorising passages, working out sums, or parsing sentences, while Mama made the bread or did some mending. Sometimes the two of them would both be writing; Daisy filling in her exercise books while her mother answered the latest letter from Papa.

He wrote home several times a week from the camp near Wellington, where it sounded as if he was having a dull time of it. There seemed to be a lot of lining up and marching about and being inspected, and even more waiting around. The food wasn't nearly as good as at home, though he was careful to tell them he was getting plenty to eat, and was quite well. But boring though it must be in the camp, it was good to know that for the moment he was in no danger from anything worse than bad cooking.

In one of his letters he enclosed a photograph of himself in uniform, taken at a studio in Wellington. He stood with hands behind his back, staring solemnly at the viewer, an odd-looking hat shaped like a lemon squeezer hiding his close-cropped hair. Daisy's mother kept the photograph on her bedside table.

The letters were usually dropped off at their house by Daisy's grandfather or one of her uncles, depending on who had gone into town that day. Daisy and her mother rarely left the house on weekdays now. After the morning milking Benjy came over to pick up their milk and take it to the factory; they could lift a milk can between them to carry up one at a time from the cowshed, but Grandpa had said that loading the cans onto a cart would be too hard for them.

Going to the general store in town every week was too much bother. Instead, Daisy's mother gave Benjy a list of what they needed, and Grandpa picked up their supplies when he next went in.

The one regular outing that still seemed worth the effort was to church every Sunday, if only for the feeling that prayers said in church might work better than those said at home.

There were barely enough hours in the day to get through the essential tasks, and no time at all for many things that had been part of their usual work. 'It doesn't matter,' was a phrase Daisy became used to hearing from her mother. Dusting the parlour and scrubbing the floor were among the things that didn't matter. Keeping up with her schoolwork, her mother insisted, did matter.

Looking after the farm animals was the most important of the outdoor work. When they fed the new calves, Daisy had to make an effort not to speak aloud the nagging awareness that it would have made things easier if they had done as Papa suggested and sold the lot of them that year. Her mother was right: they needed to carry on as if he would be home by the time the next calves were born, let alone before these heifers were in milk.

But for now it was only the two of them, and when the morning milking was done and the calves were fed it would be time to carry chaff to the horses, or move the cows to another paddock, or cook a meal that neither of them would have much energy for eating. And in the evenings there was the schoolwork that Daisy was finding difficult to do on her own.

She had tasks to work on, but no way of knowing how well she was doing them, and no one to ask when she got stuck. It was easy enough to learn lists off by heart, but with grammar and composition and arithmetic she could only hope her answers were good enough. Sometimes she skipped sections that were just too hard, and would then be confronted accusingly by them the next time she opened that book. But she did not mention any of this to her mother.

They were feeding the calves one morning, so intent on getting the animals to take notice of the buckets instead of sucking at the nearest dress that Daisy did not realise they had a visitor until a voice called, 'Hey Missus.'

Daisy looked up, startled. Just beyond the fence was a roan horse carrying a boy of perhaps nine or ten, with ears that looked too large for his head. He seemed vaguely familiar, though he was not someone she knew from school.

'Yes? What do you want?' Her mother pressed one hand against her back as she straightened from her awkward crouch.

'My dad says will you come and look at our cow. It's got a big sore on its leg, and it won't heal up.'

'Will I come and—' Mama let out a sound somewhere between a snort and a laugh, and shook her head. 'No, I'm sorry, tell your father I'm not doing that sort of thing just now. I'm too busy here, with Mr Stewart away.'

'What about our cow, then? We've only got the one.' The boy

probably lived right in Ruatane itself; some people in the town kept house cows.

Her mother sighed. 'You need to clean it with carbolic, then make a poultice. What you do is...' She studied the boy doubtfully. 'No, you'll never remember it all straight. You wait here a minute, I'll run up to the house and write it on a bit of paper for you.'

She hurried off, and Daisy realised that the boy was now staring at her. She followed his gaze to the yellow-green streak down the front of her pinafore, where a calf had slapped its tail.

A small boy with a none-too-clean face was not someone whose opinion should be taken much note of, but Daisy felt her cheeks grow warm. She picked up one of the buckets and made a show of busyness until her mother returned with the poultice recipe and sent the boy on his way.

'I hope that cow'll be all right,' she said when the boy was out of hearing.

'It's sure to be—that poultice you make always heals animals up.' It had been known to heal people, too. Once when Daisy's father had given himself a nasty gash on the shin while chopping wood, her mother had slathered the wound with her remedy before bandaging it. It made his eyes water, but the leg had healed with barely a scar.

'As long as they do it properly.' She watched the retreating figure, her brows knitted into a frown, then shook her head. 'Well, I can't go worrying about other people's animals, we've got enough on our plate without that. It'll be different when your father's back.'

Weeks slipped by in a shapeless muddle, without school to give them a pattern. Sometimes Daisy would realise she had forgotten to mark off the date on her calendar, and then struggle to remember what day of the week it was.

But the September day marked with a carefully drawn circle drew near at last, the brightest spot in that bleak season. School holidays were about to begin, and that meant Eddie and Granny would soon be there.

The house had been let go, Daisy and her mother agreed. The two of them set about a whirlwind of cleaning and tidying, dusting every surface, washing all the sheets and airing the bedding.

They had let themselves go, too, when hauling and heating enough water for a proper bath was such an effort. The tin bath was only lifted down from its hook once a fortnight, and even then filled just a few inches, while the rest of the time they made do with jug and basin. But the day before Eddie and Granny were to arrive, Daisy and her mother scrubbed themselves pink and washed their hair till it squeaked with cleanness.

The last time they had been at the wharf was to see Daisy's father off. It was not a memory to give her any fondness for the place. But when she saw Eddie waving from the boat's rail, Granny a small figure at his side, the sun abruptly seemed to give more warmth.

Granny sat beside Daisy's mother on the driving board at the front of the cart, while Daisy and Eddie squeezed into the back between the suitcases and a sack of flour, a worn old rug protecting their clothes from the splintery wood. They made their way through town, then they were onto the beach, its packed sand muffling the rattle of the wheels and making it easier to talk.

Daisy hugged her knees to her chest, content to do more listening than speaking. Eddie's voice had grown deeper since she had last seen him, way back in January. It made her think of her father's voice.

Eddie told her about his horse riding and his latest rugby matches; the more interesting of his lessons and the doings of the household. He passed on greetings from the maids and Mrs Jenson, and produced a tin of fudge (much of which had survived the trip) the cook had sent for Daisy.

Whenever he paused to help with the fudge, Daisy heard Granny and her mother talking quietly. They spoke of the most recent letters from Daisy's father; the weather and the animals; the family. Her mother told Granny the latest news of Uncle Danny, who was still waiting for a wooden foot and to be sent home on a special boat for 'limbies'.

'Is your Uncle Alf any better?' Granny asked. Daisy did not catch her mother's answer, but she knew it could not have been a cheerful one. The two of them were quiet for a few moments, then Granny changed the subject, saying how pretty the view down the coast was. 'I always think the sea's a special colour here,' she said. 'It never seems quite as blue in Auckland.'

Granny and Daisy's mother went straight inside when they got to the farm, while Daisy and Eddie saw to the horse and cart. Eddie carried the remaining luggage into the house, where they found Granny already had tea made and scones buttered, and had persuaded Daisy's mother to sit down and rest.

'I'll need to get on with the milking as soon as I've had my cup of tea, though,' her mother said. 'It takes us a lot longer without Davie.'

'I'll do it,' Eddie said at once. 'Well, Daisy and I will,' he added, catching Daisy's eye and grinning. 'I'd probably end up losing half the cows if I tried getting them in on my own.'

'And I'll get dinner on tonight,' Granny said. 'No, I can manage it on my own, Beth, I always used to. You can just keep me company.'

Daisy's mother smiled. 'You two are going to make me lazy, doing all my work for me.'

'Well it doesn't hurt anyone to take things a bit easier once in a while, and you've had a lot on your plate just lately—you and Daisy both.'

'Thanks, Aunt Amy. Thank you, Eddie.' She clutched her tea cup with both hands, and it trembled a little. The thought stuck Daisy that perhaps, with Granny and Eddie there to help, her mother felt able to let herself show just how weary she was.

Daisy got changed out of her town clothes and met Eddie at the back door, where he was pulling on a pair of her father's boots. They went through the gate and headed down the hill towards the cowshed.

She expected Eddie to go on telling her about his Auckland life, but for the first minute or so he seemed content to walk along in a shared silence so comfortable that Daisy felt no urge to break it. And when he did speak again, it was not about Auckland or sport or his horse. Instead it was to ask Daisy question after question, about giving up school and managing the farm work, and about her father; and Daisy found herself admitting how hard it all was, and how much she missed her father; and when she could not find her handkerchief, Eddie produced one that was almost clean.

They were near the shed now, and the cows were milling around them. Cows were not interested in school or fathers or wars; all they wanted was to be relieved of their milk and put out on fresh pasture. Daisy opened the gate and led the first two into their bails.

The four of them spent that evening in the parlour, a roaring fire on the hearth for the first time in weeks. Daisy did not want to give up any of Eddie's first day by sitting alone in the kitchen doing her schoolwork. But the following evening when they were clearing the table her mother said, 'Are you going to get your schoolbooks out, Daisy?'

So of course Granny and Eddie both wanted to hear about her schoolwork. Her mother, who was looking a good deal brighter after having a restful day of it, told them about Miss Cameron bringing the books for Daisy.

'And Daisy's being very good about keeping it up—she does the work just about every day. So she won't be behind hardly at all when Davie comes home and she can go back to school again.'

It made her mother happy to believe that muddling along at home was almost as good as being at school, and Daisy had no intention of spoiling it for her. She nodded and smiled, and did her best to look as if she agreed with every word, then went off to fetch the books.

She returned with pencil and paper on top of her piled textbooks to find that her mother and grandmother had gone through to the parlour, but Eddie was still at the table, finishing off a slab of bread and jam.

'Thought I'd stay out here for a bit, in case Granny and Aunt Beth want to talk about their insides,' he said around a mouthful. 'Do you want me to give you a hand with any of that? It's probably near enough the same as what I did in Standard Five.'

In a moment, the schoolwork was transformed from duty to a companionable task. Daisy spread out the books, Eddie pulled his chair close to hers, and they set about tackling the parts she had been struggling with. Eddie helped her pick her way through a particularly nasty piece of arithmetic involving decimal fractions and long division, and checked her working before declaring the answer correct. He watched as she parsed a section of writing, nudging her with hints towards the more obscure parts of speech.

'At least it's not Latin,' he remarked, which led them down a sidetrack, as Daisy could not resist asking questions about Latin grammar that Eddie was happy to answer. They spent some time discussing strange words like declension and conjugation before returning to the work at hand.

Daisy read aloud her essay on the Duke of Wellington, and Eddie declared it very good. He wouldn't bother checking her spelling, he said, as it was at least as good as his.

It was Daisy's best evening's work since Miss Cameron had first suggested she should keep up her study at home. When she closed her books for the evening, it was with the feeling that perhaps she just might be able to manage.

The household settled into a comfortable pattern while Eddie and Granny were there. Granny and Daisy's mother generally stayed close to the house, while Eddie and Daisy spent their days out on the farm. In the evenings the two of them spent a half-hour or so on Daisy's schoolwork, then went through to sit in the parlour with the two women.

They had a fire in there every evening now. There was certainly no shortage of wood, for Eddie had spent hours chopping logs into fireplace-sized chunks, making up in energy what he lacked in skill, until the firewood was once again piled as high as Daisy's father had left it.

'I might give those roses along the back fence a trim tomorrow if the weather keeps nice,' Granny said one evening, not looking up from her stitching. She was embroidering Papa's initials on a handkerchief to be tucked into the next letter they sent him; Granny felt you could never have too many handkerchiefs. 'Just a little tidy-up before they get too straggly. They must've got quite tall—usually you can see the potatoes from out there this time of year.'

'There aren't any to see,' Daisy's mother said. 'We didn't plant any this year.'

'Didn't you, dear? Well, I suppose you had enough to think about without bothering with potatoes.'

'Davie said best not to, just in case... in case he wasn't back in time for the harvest. It'd be too hard for Daisy and me.' Her needle wavered as she said the words. It was rare for Mama to speak aloud even the faintest chance that Daisy's father would not be home soon. 'We've still got the seed potatoes, if they haven't gone rotten by now—I thought I might try and sell them, but no one'd be interested. Everyone's short-handed these days.'

Granny murmured an agreement; Mama unpicked a stitch and re-threaded her needle. Daisy glanced over at Eddie, and saw his book lying neglected in his lap.

'I'll do it,' he said. 'I'll plant the potatoes. And I'll be here for the summer holidays by the time they need digging up, so I'll be able to do that even if Uncle Dave's still away.'

The edges of her mother's mouth twitched. 'It's hard work, Eddie. It takes ploughing and harrowing before you even start planting. It's very good of you to offer, but I think it'd be a bit much for you.'

'No, I could do it,' Eddie insisted. 'I've helped Uncle Dave lots of times with ploughing.'

'Well, yes, I suppose you have. It's not the same as doing it on your own, though. And you've never done the potatoes.'

'But I could do it with Eddie,' Daisy said, catching his enthusiasm. 'I know what to do—I always help with the potatoes.'

That was definitely a smile trying to form on her mother's lips. 'Well, if the two of you are as keen as that, you might as well have a go.'

If Daisy's father had been there to do the job properly, she explained to Eddie, he would have given the ground a deep ploughing and then run a harrow over it to break up the clods before getting out the ridging plough. Daisy had some idea of just how much effort ploughing took, and she was not surprised when Eddie looked daunted at the thought of making three separate passes over the paddock.

'We'd never get it done before I go back to Auckland,' he said, staring at the heavy plough that took two horses to pull it.

Between the two of them, they came up with the idea of doing a single pass, just using the lighter ridging plough to throw soil over the potatoes. It would mean a much smaller crop, but even a small crop must be better than none at all.

When they sorted through the sacks they found that a fair portion of the seed potatoes were still sound enough to be worth planting. They piled the good potatoes onto a wooden sled and dragged them down to the paddock, where they set them out in rows.

Hercules, the largest of the farm's workhorses, was harnessed to the ridging plough. Daisy had named the Clydesdale herself, and she considered him quite strong enough to deserve a hero's name. She held the bridle and guided Hercules along each row, while Eddie walked behind pushing down on the plough. She looked over her shoulder to see the plough's blade biting into the earth, throwing a ridge of rich brown soil over the potatoes on either side.

At first they chatted away, calling back and forth to point out a bird flying overhead, admire the straightness of the furrow, or joke that Hercules was helping by adding manure to the paddock as he went. But as the morning drew on Eddie's responses became shorter and scarcer, until he was trudging along in silence, face red with exertion as he gripped the plough and leaned all his weight to keep it in the furrow.

'Eddie, you've got a face like a beetroot,' Daisy's mother said when she and Granny arrived with morning tea.

'And your poor hands.' Granny took one of Eddie's big, knuckly hands in her own and turned it over to reveal the red, raised blisters. 'I'll need to put some calamine lotion on that later.'

'It's all right, it'll callous up in a couple of days,' Eddie said, retrieving his hand and helping himself to a scone.

'Don't go wearing yourselves out, you two,' Mama said. 'It's not worth it, not for a few spuds.'

'You're not worn out are you, Daisy?' Eddie asked.

She took a scone, still warm from the oven and oozing strawberry jam. 'No, but I'm not doing the hard part.'

'It's not as hard as all that. I bet Uncle Dave doesn't think it is.'

'He's used to this sort of work, though,' her mother said.

'I'll get used to it too, then.' The remaining scone disappeared in two bites.

After they had finished their morning tea Eddie was almost back to

211

his usual self. Lunch and afternoon tea briefly revived him, too. But by the time they had unharnessed the horse at the end of the day, Eddie looked barely able to drag one foot after the other back up to the house. Daisy did not suggest getting out her schoolbooks that evening.

The second day was much the same, except that they made slower progress. When twilight came, they had sown perhaps half of the potatoes. Within a few minutes of going into the parlour after dinner, Eddie's eyes drooped and his book slid from his lap. Granny sent him to bed, and Daisy readily went off to her mother's room for an early night.

When her mother came down on her own to bring their morning tea the next day, she studied Eddie and frowned. Daisy followed her gaze to the blood seeping through the strips of cloth wrapped around Eddie's palms. Several times that day she had offered to take a turn on the plough so he could rest his hands, but Eddie had insisted he could manage, and even claimed that the blisters did not hurt.

'That's enough,' Mama said. 'You've done very well, both of you, but you're to stop now. No, Eddie, no arguing. I'm not having you do yourself an injury on my account.'

Eddie did argue, but not very hard, and not for very long. Daisy's mother extracted a promise that no more planting would be done, then left them to their morning tea.

They lingered over the lemonade and biscuits, both glad of the excuse to rest sore limbs. Granny was keeping the cake tins well-filled, and there was a satisfying assortment of Eddie's and Daisy's particular favourites. When the food was finished down to the last crumb and the lemonade bottle thoroughly drained, they set about getting the plough back to its shed and Hercules back to his paddock, then threw the leftover potatoes to the pigs before heading up to the house.

'I worked up one heck of a sweat,' Eddie said, flapping his damp shirt over his chest. 'Don't suppose there's any chance of a bath?'

'Not on a Wednesday,' Daisy said. 'We only ever have baths on Saturdays.'

'I thought I might ask Aunt Beth if it'd be all right—I'd haul the water and all that.'

Daisy shook her head. 'You'd only make her feel bad if you said that. She's worried about your hands.'

'Ah, well, I can make do with a wash. Is it really Wednesday already? I'll be back in Auckland by Sunday.' He scratched at his scalp, leaving the hair in tufts. 'Don't tell Aunt Beth, but I'll be glad to be able to stretch my legs right out in a bath again.'

Just a few more days and Eddie would be gone. The way up to the house seemed a little steeper as Daisy trudged along at his side.

She was aware of Eddie studying her, chewing at his lower lip. 'I suppose you and Aunt Beth have to haul the water yourselves when you have baths.'

'We don't always bother. Not every week, anyway. There just seems to be enough to do without getting all that extra water.'

'And here's me going on about baths and all that rot, as if I had anything to whinge about. Sorry, Daisy.'

'That's all right. It's not your fault Papa's away.'

'No, but...' Eddie trailed off. His frown cleared as a fresh thought struck him. 'Hey, we haven't been doing your schoolwork the last couple of nights. We'd better get on and do some tonight.'

Eddie would soon be gone, and no one knew how long her father would be away, or even if... 'I don't think I can be bothered with schoolwork.' She kicked at the nearest clod of earth.

'Of course you can! You don't want to get too far behind for when you go back to school.'

If I ever do go back. That was not a thought to speak aloud, even to Eddie.

'And it won't be all that long before you're in high school, you know—only another year or so. Granny thinks it's great that you're going to be a teacher.'

She had to be so careful before saying anything these days. Every word had to be turned over and checked for any harm it might do before she let it out into the world. Don't say how tired she got; how she sometimes feared that the war would go on forever, taking more and more of the people she loved. Let people think she wanted the right things, not things she could never have. Keep the fears and wishes and hopes to herself. Don't go worrying people.

But Eddie was not easily made anxious, and keeping silent was suddenly too hard.

'Everyone thinks just because I want to go to high school that must mean I want to be a teacher. I don't think I do, though.'

'Don't you? I just thought you must, with everyone saying it. I thought that was why girls went to high school. What would you like to do, then?'

'I want to be a doctor.'

The thought seemed to take proper shape along with the words. Until spoken aloud, it had been no more than a dim awareness of something wished for.

No wonder Eddie looked startled. 'You've never let on about that before.'

'Well, I do. I want to learn about why people get sick, and how to make them come right again. I think that must be the best job there is.'

She heard the animation in her voice; a moment later the brief burst of energy had slipped away. 'I probably can't do it, though. I don't know if girls can even be doctors.'

'I bet Aunt Sarah'd say they could. She read out a bit from the paper about a lady doctor a while ago, come to think of it. I don't see why you couldn't be one.'

Eddie had a way of making it sound as if anything was possible. And Daisy had grown up in complete faith that if Eddie said a thing, it must be so. The war had shaken everything, even that rock-solid confidence.

'There's a lot of study and exams. They have to know Latin, and different sorts of medicines, and the proper names for all the organs and bones and everything. I'd have to be in Standard Six and do the Proficiency Certificate so I could get into high school, and I'm not even going to get my Standard Five Certificate this year, with missing all this school.'

'Well, we'll get you back to school as soon as we can, and in the meantime we just need to make sure you keep up with your work. We'll do a good lot after dinner.'

'Don't tell anyone—about me wanting to be a doctor, I mean. I don't want Mama worrying about school and everything.'

'I won't say a word.'

They were carrying the basket from morning tea between them. A sudden warmth made Daisy glance down to see that Eddie's hand had slid along the handle to rest against hers. She pressed his in return, then frowned, noticing the filthy cloth around his palms.

'As soon as we get inside I'll give those hands of yours a good wash with carbolic and put fresh rags on them,' she said. 'You have to keep things like that clean, or you can get infections. I saw a bit in one of Uncle Richard's books about wounds and germs, it said carbolic's good for that.'

'Yes, Doctor Daisy,' Eddie said, his voice small and meek and quite unlike himself. He grinned, and Daisy felt her own answering smile.

It was getting close to bedtime that evening when Daisy packed away her schoolbooks and she and Eddie joined the others in the parlour, settling themselves on a rug by the fire. Eddie was soon engrossed in a book about mountain climbers. Daisy could not give her full attention to the book in her lap, as she had to look up from the pages every few minutes to slap Eddie's hand away from picking at the carefully tied bandages.

'Leave it alone, or they'll never heal up,' she scolded.

'I don't even know I'm doing it till you go hitting me. Anyway, it's itchy. I think you must've got them too clean.'

She fixed him with a hard stare, and Eddie made a show of placing his hands as far apart as possible, gripping his book by the outer edges.

'Only a couple of days till you have to go back to Auckland,' Mama said. 'Daisy and I are going to miss you, Aunt Amy—you too, Eddie. It's been such a help having you here.'

Granny put down her stitching and seemed about to speak, but Eddie cut in first.

'I want to stay here.' He glanced around at the three startled faces, and pressed on quickly. 'There's too much work for you and Daisy, and she shouldn't be missing all this school. I want to stay and help.'

Daisy was too taken aback for speech. Hope flared within her, but withered even before Granny spoke. It could not be that easy.

'You can't, Eddie. No, I'm sorry, you just can't. You've got that big exam coming up—he's got to sit his Matriculation exam,' she said, turning to Daisy's mother. 'He needs to get that so he can go to the university.'

Granny spoke as gently as always, but something in her voice told Daisy she would not be changing her mind. That did not stop Eddie from trying: he would catch up before the examination, or leave Matriculation till next year; 'Maybe I won't even go to university at all,' he said in a particularly wild moment.

Through it all, Granny sat listening; hands clasped in her lap, and giving an occasional shake of her head. When Eddie ran out of words and energy, she spoke again. 'Of course you're going to university, Eddie. And no, you're not going to leave your Matriculation till next year. It's no good putting things like that off, not when you don't know what's going to happen from one year to the next.'

Eddie scowled at the floor and picked viciously at his bandages. Daisy could not bring herself to slap his hands; she made do with patting the nearer one.

'I'm sure you're right, Aunt Amy,' her mother said. 'I don't know about university and all that.'

She was disappointed, Daisy could tell, and the disappointment had turned into something close to hurt. Her mother must have had her own small burst of hope at Eddie's offer.

'I don't want you to miss school, Eddie.' Daisy kept her voice low, but it was impossible to speak in their tiny parlour without everyone in the room hearing. 'I don't want to spoil things for you.' Eddie gave a twisted smile, and left his hands in peace.

'I think perhaps I should stay on,' Granny said into the silence. 'If I did the milking with you, Beth, Daisy could go back to school.'

It was just like Granny to offer such a thing, but Daisy was not in the least surprised when her mother shook her head.

'No, I can't have that. Thank you, Aunt Amy, but I can't have a woman your age milking cows for me. It wouldn't be right.'

'Fifty's not so very old,' Granny said, but Mama shook her head more firmly.

'Davie wouldn't like it—he'd be upset to think of you doing milking. Daisy and I can manage till he gets home. Whenever that is,' Mama added in a lower voice.

'All right, dear, I'm sure you know best. I'll just help you around the house, then, to make things a little bit easier for you.'

Mama looked doubtful. 'Shouldn't you be going back with Eddie? Sarah will be expecting you.'

'Eddie can take the boat on his own, can't you, Eddie?'

'Of course I can—I don't need looking after. But you can't stay here, Granny. Aunt Sarah's having that party for you, you've got to be back for that.'

'Is she?' Granny looked startled. 'She hasn't said anything to me about that.'

'It's a surprise, that's why. I suppose I shouldn't have said about it,' Eddie added, rather too late. 'But she wants to have one because it's a special birthday. She said turning fifty couldn't go unmarked.'

Granny sighed. 'It's very kind of your Aunt Sarah, but I'm not sure I really feel like a party. I hope she won't go to too much trouble.'

'She said it'd just be a quiet one, because it wouldn't be appropriate otherwise, not with the war on. Just Mr and Mrs Wells and people like that, and a supper and music and things.'

'Well, I'll need to go back in time for it. I mustn't disappoint Aunt Sarah.'

'Of course you mustn't,' Daisy's mother said. 'Don't feel you have to stay on here, Aunt Amy, not when Sarah's expecting you.'

'I'll stay another week or two, anyway. I wish it could be longer, but...' She sighed again. 'Sometimes it's hard to do the right thing by everyone.'

'Specially when you're not allowed to,' Eddie muttered.

*

On his last few days on the farm Eddie split a batch of kindling, swept out the sheds and cleaned all the harness. He and Daisy kept busy all day long, and every evening they got out her schoolbooks.

'You're going to carry on with this lot after I've gone, aren't you?' Eddie said each evening, and each evening Daisy assured him that she would. Eddie wanted her to keep up with her study; that was reason enough to promise, even as it became harder and harder to cling to the hope that she would ever go back to school.

They took Eddie in to Ruatane on a day of grey skies and wind gusts.

'There's a good swell out past the bar,' a man on the wharf remarked. 'You'll have a lively trip of it.'

'It's lucky you don't get seasick, Eddie,' Granny said.

There were hugs all round, with a particularly warm one for Daisy; then Eddie was on the boat, the gangplank was slid aboard, and the *Ngatiawa* pulled away from the wharf. Daisy waved Eddie out of sight.

Chapter Eighteen

Mr Jenson was at the Auckland wharf to meet Eddie when the boat arrived. Eddie flung his bag into the carriage and stepped up to share the driver's seat.

He asked after Walter; 'Well enough, going by his letters,' Mr Jenson said. The horses, too, were in good health, he reported, as was Mrs Jenson. They spent the rest of the short journey to the house in silence. Mr Jenson was generally a man of few words, and for the moment this suited Eddie's mood.

'The garden looks good,' Eddie said as they pulled up to the front steps.

'Yes, not too bad. That new boy they sent along from the orphanage is keen as mustard. No need for you to be bothering yourself with the digging and such now.'

No need for him to do anything useful here. If he could only have stayed in Ruatane and helped Daisy...

Aunt Sarah emerged from her study as Eddie was hanging up his coat in the hall.

'Eddie, how nice to have you home again, it's been far too quiet lately,' she said. 'How is everyone on the farm?'

'They're all right.'

'I'll write to your grandmother at once, to let her know you're home safely. I'm also going to impress upon her that I expect her back herself in the very near future, though I won't say anything to spoil the surprise of her birthday celebrations, of course.'

Eddie grunted something vaguely like a 'Yes', picked up his bag and headed for the staircase. It seemed too much trouble to answer properly, even when his aunt mentioned that Mrs Jenson planned an especially nice dinner that evening to welcome him home.

'I expect you'll want a bath tonight,' Aunt Sarah said. 'And I believe the maids have your school uniform all ready for tomorrow, it should be laid out in your room.'

Back to school, and lessons, and assemblies, and playing at cadets. Eddie usually bounded up the stairs two at a time; today it was all he could do to drag a foot from each tread to the next.

Granny returned two weeks later. She seemed quieter than usual on the first evening, and Aunt Sarah fussed over her, saying she must have overtired herself.

'No, I'm quite all right,' Granny said. 'A little bit of work around the house didn't do me any harm, and Beth wouldn't let me help with the milking.'

'I should think not! I don't know what you were thinking of, Amy, suggesting such a thing. Though I must say it's a shame Daisy's education has had to be interrupted like that.'

'Well, she wouldn't hear of it, so it came to nothing. It's a struggle for them, though—Beth's father helps when he can, but it's all he can do to manage on his own farm with the boys away. And we're all worried about Dave,' she said, so quietly that Eddie barely caught the words.

Aunt Sarah patted Granny's hand. 'Of course you are. But he's safe enough for the moment—I imagine the worst danger in that training camp is boredom.'

'Yes, but he could be sent off any time now. I saw Beth taking note of bits in the paper about troops sailing.'

'Things do seem to be going a little better with the war these days, though, we're not hearing so much of those dreadful battles.'

'I'm not sure we do hear the worst of it. I think they keep a lot of it quiet.'

Aunt Sarah was silent for a few moments. 'I'm afraid you're probably right,' she said.

Letters from Daisy still arrived most weeks for Eddie. As he read them, he pictured her sitting at the worn old kitchen table, tired out at the end of a long day, and with nothing to look forward to but more days just the same.

He found it hard to know just what to write back. It would not be fair to say much about school, not when Daisy had to work on the farm instead of going to her own school, and she would not want to hear a lot of talk about the war. So he cobbled together bits and pieces about his horse, what birds and insects he had seen lately; told her when Mrs Jenson and the maids asked to be remembered to her. When Granny had her birthday party he told Daisy all about that, though he had found it rather a dull affair himself. Granny had seemed to enjoy the evening, and she had said nothing to Aunt Sarah about Eddie's spoiling the surprise.

She said she only wished you and Uncle Dave and Aunt Beth could've been there as well, he wrote. *I wish you could have, too. The supper was really good.*

At school barely a lesson passed without talk of the war. Often during morning assembly the headmaster would read out the name of some former pupil who had been killed at the Front. School prayers always made special mention of the brave men away fighting, and Eddie would add his own silent one for Uncle Dave, who would soon be there with them.

In cadet lessons the boys practised marching up and down until their timing was slick when they turned in response to the orders barked at them. Sometimes a man who was a retired officer came along to give them a talk about the army and the war. Major Parnham had grey hair and a bristling moustache, and he walked with a limp that they were all sure he must have got on active service. He always made much of what fine soldiers the New Zealanders were.

'Which of you boys have family at the Front?' the Major asked one day.

Every hand shot up, though when the Major asked each boy it emerged that some of them were stretching 'family' to include quite distant connections; 'The chap who delivers the bread, but I think he's a sort of cousin,' was the best one boy could manage. But many had older brothers or even fathers away at the war.

'What about you, Stewart?' Major Parnham asked.

'My uncle, Sir.' At least half a dozen of the men Eddie called his uncles had been called up: Aunt Beth's brothers, and a few of Uncle John's and Uncle Harry's sons; but it was his Uncle Dave who sprang to mind first. 'He's in camp waiting to be sent off.'

'Yes, no doubt he's looking forward to doing his duty for the Empire. I expect your father has responsibilities here that prevent him from signing up.'

'My father was killed in South Africa fighting the Boers, Sir.'

'You hear that, boys? Stewart's father was a hero.' Major Parnham fixed the group with his piercing stare before returning his attention to Eddie. 'That must make your mother proud—and you should be proud of him, too. There's no finer thing a man can do than to die for his country.'

'Thank you, Sir. I am proud of him, Sir.'

No need to tell the Major that his mother was also dead. It was true enough that she had been proud of Eddie's father. Among the clearest memories he had of her were the stories she had told of his father riding over the plains of Africa, wearing a smart red coat and shooting at bad men. He was strong and brave and the best rider in the world, she had always said.

He had Latin that afternoon, a subject he enjoyed, along with mathematics, which he did not. Mathematics lessons always seemed particularly long, and the chairs grew increasingly uncomfortable.

The bell to mark the end of lessons sounded at last. Eddie packed away his books and made his way out of the building, calling goodbyes to the classmates heading off in a different direction.

A group of younger boys had gathered near the gates; Eddie glanced over, and saw that they were swapping cigarette cards. He had been just as keen on those cards himself a year or two before, and at something of a disadvantage with no smokers in the house. That was before Walter had gone off to the war; fortunately for Eddie, Walter had taken up cigarettes rather than smoking a pipe like Mr Jenson, and had been happy to hand over the cards that came with each pack. Twenty empty packets were enough to send off for a War Zone map that Eddie had pinned to his wall, and by swapping cards with his schoolmates he had eventually built up the entire set of twenty-five Victoria Cross Heroes.

Collecting cigarette cards; marching up and down with the other cadets playing at soldiers. Treating war like a game. Eddie looked up at the motto over the school gates: *Per Angusta ad Augusta.* 'Through rough ravines to hallowed heights,' was how the headmaster sometimes translated it; 'Through difficulties to greatness,' his Latin master preferred. Eddie had always thought it sounded grand; now he felt dishonest claiming the motto as his own. What difficulties did he ever have? His life could hardly be more comfortable. Making a fuss about lessons and sports and exams, when men like Uncle Dave were taken away from home to fight in the war.

He rode his usual tram to Queen Street, so caught up in his thoughts that he almost missed his stop. There were few people about as he trudged along the footpath past shops and offices.

Two men in uniform, one leaning against a brick wall while the other lit a cigarette, caught Eddie's eye. He looked at the building behind them, and at the sign on its door. *RECRUITING OFFICE,* it read. He had passed the building a hundred times without giving it a second glance. Today he went inside.

The last part of his walk home, up a steep path into Albert Park and then a brisk few strides to the house, always left Eddie with a sharp appetite. He thought he smelled fresh baking when he opened the front door.

Alice, the older of the maids, emerged from the door that led to the drawing room.

'Good afternoon, Master Eddie. Your grandmother's out, but she's expected back any minute. Miss Sarah's around the house somewhere. And I do believe Mrs Jenson's just taken a chocolate cake out of the oven,' she added, smiling.

Eddie dropped his satchel against the wall, then shrugged off his jacket and slung it in the direction of the coat stand as he headed towards the kitchen. The jacket just missed catching on one of the stand's hooks, instead sliding to the floor.

'That's all right, I'll see to it,' Alice said, crossing the floor to the coat stand before Eddie could turn back. 'We don't want that cake to get stale waiting for you.'

She gathered the jacket up from the floor and shook out the creases. Something more or less white fell from a pocket; probably a handkerchief. Eddie hoped it was a fairly clean one as he saw Alice bend to pick it up, but for the moment fresh chocolate cake seemed more important.

Mrs Jenson had heard him coming. 'Let's see if this manages to last you more than two bites, Master Eddie,' she said, handing him a plate with a tall slice of cake wobbling on it.

The cake was rich and dark and delicious, and it took at least half a dozen bites to demolish the slice. Eddie had just finished mopping up the crumbs, and was debating whether or not he could fit in another piece, when he heard the door open. He glanced around to see Aunt Sarah in the doorway.

'Eddie, I wish to speak with you in my study. At once, if you please,' she added when Eddie did not immediately shift his attention from Mrs Jenson's cake.

He followed her from the kitchen, wondering what was suddenly so important. A notice from school? Another soirée? Not bad news from the farm, surely?

He had barely taken a step into the study when his aunt rounded on him, holding out a sheet of paper he had not noticed her carrying. Eddie recognised it at once, crumpled as it was from being shoved into his pocket earlier: the enlistment form from the recruitment office. *That* was what had fallen out of his jacket in the hall.

'What's the meaning of this?' Aunt Sarah's voice sounded like the hissing of a cat. 'What do you think you're doing, bringing such a thing into the house? I won't allow it, do you hear me?'

Eddie made a grab at the paper, but Aunt Sarah snatched it back out of his reach. He felt heat rising up his neck and flooding his face.

'That's nothing to do with you! Why are you going through my pockets, anyway?'

'There's no need to go through your pockets when you leave things lying about on the floor for the maids to pick up after you. I noticed

Alice putting this on the hall stand, and I could hardly believe the evidence of my own senses when I saw what it was.'

She crushed the paper in her hand. 'I don't want to hear this spoken of again. A boy your age has no business even thinking about enlisting. I absolutely forbid it.'

'Don't tell me what to do! I'm not a little kid, you know.'

'You're behaving like a child—a particularly stupid one at that. Don't you dare raise your voice to me. I've a good mind to—'

Aunt Sarah stopped in mid-sentence and looked past Eddie's shoulder. He turned to follow her gaze and saw Granny standing in the doorway.

'I could hear you two from the front door, you're making so much noise. Whatever's going on?'

'Eddie came home with *this*, if you please.' Aunt Sarah straightened out the enlistment form just enough to make the heading readable, and held it out.

A moment before Granny had looked puzzled, and just a little worried. Now she looked as if she might be sick.

'Oh, Eddie, *no!*' Her voice made it sound as if the words were being squeezed out through a narrow space.

'There, you see?' Aunt Sarah turned on him again. 'You've upset your grandmother. Are you happy now?'

'Sarah, please.' Granny placed a hand on Aunt Sarah's sleeve. 'I'm not upset, and there's no need for you to be. I just got a bit of a shock, that's all. I expect you did, too.' She let go of Aunt Sarah, and slipped her arm through Eddie's. 'Come outside with me, Eddie. Let's have a little sit in the garden.'

Eddie let her lead him from the room. As they left, he saw Aunt Sarah rip the form into several pieces and fling them into her wastepaper basket.

Granny chose a wooden bench under a large puriri tree in a quiet corner of the garden. Eddie used his hand to sweep the bench clean of twigs and leaves for her before they sat down.

'Eddie, I'm not going to let you sign up, you're much too young for that,' Granny said. 'But I just want—no, before you start arguing—I want to ask you something. You're not unhappy, are you? There's nothing upsetting you at home, or at school maybe, that's making you want to go away to the war?'

'No,' Eddie said, puzzled by the question. 'Nothing like that.'

'Then there's no need for you to. I know you'll have to go when you're older if the war's still on by then, but they don't expect us to send

223

boys of sixteen.'

'They don't always ask how old chaps are, though—or they just believe what you tell them.'

His grandmother sighed. 'No, I'm sure you're right. They didn't in the last war, I know that. But why would you want to go signing up now?'

Explaining would be far easier if he understood it properly himself, so that it would fit neatly into words instead of being a jumble of nagging thoughts all tangled up together.

'I just... I mean... I'm just hanging around here, no use to anyone. It doesn't seem right.'

'Of course you're useful, Eddie—you are to me. I wouldn't like to have to do without you.'

'But I don't do anything that *matters*. I thought... I don't know, maybe if I was to go away to the war then some other chap wouldn't have to. Someone who's useful to people. Like Uncle Dave.'

Granny's mouth twisted. 'I don't think it works like that, darling. I think perhaps they'd take you both.' Eddie was picking at the fabric of his trousers; she put her hand over his and stilled it. 'You want to do your duty, I know you do—you're a good boy. And so you will, when you're old enough.'

She squeezed as much of his hand as she could get her own around. 'I don't want to have both my boys away at once, Eddie. Wait until Uncle Dave's home, and you're older.'

'But Uncle Dave's doing his duty now. So did my father in the last war. He went off and fought for his country—and they didn't make him go, did they? He just went because he thought he should.'

'Your father.' Granny's voice sounded as if it was coming from somewhere far away. 'He was just about the same age you are now, he'd not long turned sixteen. Much too young, but he was so keen to be off, and after all the trouble between him and your grandfather—'

She bit the words off. Granny only rarely mentioned Eddie's grandfather, and no one else ever seemed to at all. 'I helped him, Eddie,' she said quietly. 'I helped your father go off to South Africa, even though he was under age. So when he died, it felt as if it was my fault. I sent my boy off to war, and he never came home.'

Tears were trailing down his grandmother's cheeks, though she did not seem aware of them. Eddie considered offering his handkerchief, but thought better of it and offered words instead. 'He was really brave, though, and I bet he was really good at the fighting.'

'He was a brave boy, yes.' Granny did have a handkerchief of her own after all; she released Eddie's hand, drew a small piece of lace-edged cotton from one sleeve and dabbed at her eyes. 'But I don't think he can have seen much fighting over there. The war was nearly over by the time he got to it.'

Eddie frowned in confusion. 'But he was killed in one of the big battles, wasn't he? They were fighting thousands of those Boer fellows, all outnumbered, and he was on his horse in the middle of it. He killed dozens of them before they got him, and even after he was shot he...'

He trailed off, realising just how much it sounded like a tale from one of his adventure books, or one of the battles he had staged with his toy soldiers when he was a little younger. In his mind's eye, his father was on raised ground at the centre of the battlefield, dressed in a general's uniform and swinging a great sword that somehow turned into a rifle. That couldn't be right.

Granny was staring at him, her eyebrows raised. 'Is that what your mother told you?'

'I think so—some of it is, anyway. I know she said about him riding his horse and being in a big battle. She used to talk about that a lot.'

'Well, I expect that's what she thought had happened—it's not as if there was anyone to tell her different except me, and we never did talk about how your father died. Poor Milly, there was no need to upset her with that.' The handkerchief was in her lap; she twisted it between her fingers. 'But I think perhaps I should tell you, Eddie.

'Your father got sick—a lot of the soldiers did in South Africa, I found out later. He caught something called enteric fever.'

'What's that?'

'It's... well, it's a bad thing. Do you remember that time you got sick from eating a sausage that had gone off? Back when you were still at primary school.'

Eddie shuddered at the memory, which was not one he was likely to forget. One lunchtime he had swapped a perfectly good roast beef sandwich for a cold sausage from a paper bag full of them that a boy had brought to school; probably food the boy's mother had thrown out for being too old, Granny had said afterwards. 'That was awful,' he said. 'I kept throwing up and having to run to the lavatory. I didn't even feel like eating anything.' And it had been months before he could face a sausage without retching.

'You were only little, I felt so sorry for you. But at least I could sit up with you at night and look after you.' She stroked his cheek, and Eddie recalled the coolness of her hand on his forehead whenever he was feverish. 'Well, the enteric fever's a bit like that, except it's much worse. And when it's bad enough to kill someone, they just go on and on with the vomiting and dysentery until they die of it. That's what happened to your father, Eddie. That's how he died.' Granny was crying again, wiping her eyes with a handkerchief that must have been too wet to be much use.

It was as if all the air had been knocked out of him by a blow to the chest. Eddie found himself quite unable to speak, but that did not stop his mind from racing. Images that had always been bright in his imagination were suddenly like wet paint rain-smeared into the mud. His father's death had nothing glorious about it.

He took a deep, steadying breath, and felt the pressure in his chest ease. A thought had been pricking at him for some time, ever since Granny first spoke of helping his father go off to fight the Boers. Now it managed to get his full attention, and presented him with an unexpected calculation.

'Was my father sixteen when he got married?'

He heard his grandmother's sharp intake of breath; in the silence that followed, an even more unexpected realisation broke upon him. 'Weren't they… didn't they get married?'

'They would have, Eddie, I'm sure they would. But it all happened in such a rush, him going away like that. He didn't have the chance to tell us he wanted to get married, and he didn't know there was going to be a baby. All by himself, all that long way from home, and he died without ever knowing he was going to be a father.'

She placed her hand over Eddie's again. 'It doesn't really make any difference, you know, about them not being married. You're my grandson just the same, and the rest of it's no one else's business.'

Eddie made no response other than a nod, but Granny did not seem to mind. There was no one better to sit with and just be still than Granny. She had her own special kind of quietness that seemed to spread out from her and wrap you in it.

When his thoughts were back in some sort of order, he stirred himself to speak. 'I won't try and join up, then. I suppose it was a bit stupid thinking I could get away with it.'

'Of course it wasn't stupid. You just want to do the right thing, and sometimes it's not easy to know what that is. If you still think you want to when you're eighteen or nineteen, I won't stand in your way.' She patted his hand and smiled. 'Anyway, you can't go off now. You promised Aunt Beth you'd dig the potatoes.'

'I'd forgotten about that. So I did.' It felt like something that had happened months ago, not a mere few weeks.

'And don't go saying you're no use. You can help on the farm again as soon as the Christmas holidays start—they need you for that.'

'I was going to write to Daisy tonight. I could mention about going down there for Christmas.'

'Yes, you should. But don't say anything about signing up, that would only upset her when she's worrying about her father. They're being very brave about it all, but Daisy needs help keeping her spirits up. And I think you're the best one for that.'

Chapter Nineteen

Daisy marked her calendar with the date the holidays were to begin. Eddie would be there just a day or two after that.

It was good to have something bright to look forward to, but in the here and now the best that could be hoped of each working day was that she would still be able to stand on her feet by its end. There was more sunshine, and the days were a little longer, but the warmer weather meant the grass grew more lush than ever, the cows gave more milk, and milking took more of the daylight hours.

Grandpa generally left a newspaper for them when he brought their weekly supplies from the store. Daisy knew her mother read the war news as carefully as she did herself, though neither of them commented on anything more important than the weather forecast or farm produce prices.

As the school term wore on, the newspaper sometimes mentioned visits from school inspectors and when the examinations might be held. She should have been looking forward to the Standard Five examination that would allow her into the final class of primary school the next year; instead she was still plodding away over her textbooks every evening at the kitchen table. Schoolwork had once again become a chore without Eddie's company, especially when she struck particularly difficult exercises and had no idea if she was doing them properly. She thought of running down to ask Miss Cameron for help, but soon decided against it. She did not want to upset her mother by seeming to complain about missing school. Her mother had enough to worry about without that.

School and exams, and even the secret hope of learning to be a doctor, were small things compared with whatever might happen to her father. Daisy pored over the newspapers, looking for some hint of just when he might be sailing from New Zealand, but there was never more than the usual vague talk of the Colony's fine troops and valiant efforts. In his letters her father could only say he thought it might be 'any time now', or 'before too long'.

With no real news, it was hard not to expect the worst. The newspapers might be coy about shipping, but every issue had a long list of the latest deaths from the Front. The writers talked of imminent victory, but Daisy found those rows of names far easier to believe. What chance would her father have once he was bundled onto a ship and sent over to France?

The constant fear brought a weariness quite separate from the tiredness left by each day's work on the farm. Physical tiredness had always helped her into a sound sleep; now the dragging fear kept her awake long into the night, resisting the urge to toss and turn because that would disturb her mother.

Not that her mother slept any more soundly than Daisy did herself. Her face had a pinched, anxious look about it, and she had lost so much weight that her clothes hung loose. That was yet another thing to worry about: her mother's health. Could all the strain be too much for her heart?

Once or twice Daisy managed to snatch a look at her mother's pharmacopoeia if she had the kitchen to herself for a few minutes, but if there was anything about hearts in the pages of treatments for everything from thinning hair to chilblains she was unable to discover it.

The thought nagged at her that if she could somehow get to Uncle Richard's, perhaps she could find out more about hearts and how to look after them. Her uncle was very busy, Grandpa mentioned one day when he brought their stores; it seemed there was a lot of flu around this year. If he was not at home, even looking at some of his books might tell her something useful, but there was no chance of that. They never went out visiting now.

One gusty November morning, Daisy and her mother were out in the paddocks moving the cows to fresh pasture. The animals had churned the ground around the gateway, and mud dragged at her boots as Daisy swung the gate closed.

'Who's that coming up the track?'

Daisy followed her mother's pointing finger and saw a rider approaching. 'I think it's Benjy,' she said. And then she realised that Benjy could not be coming to deliver an ordinary message about the milk or the stores; not cantering at that speed.

A cold shudder ran through Daisy, as if someone had tossed ice down the back of her dress. A voice seemed to be whispering inside her head, telling her that she had been right to be frightened through all those long, wearying months. Something had happened, the voice said. Something terrible.

Benjy had seen them; he called out, but the wind whipped away his words. He slithered down from the horse before it had quite stopped moving, and clambered over the fence.

Daisy stood rigid as she watched Benjy running towards them. Moving seemed as impossible as if her feet had taken root in the mud.

Her mother was at her side, murmuring the same words over and over.

'Not Davie. Please don't let it be Davie.' She clutched at her chest as if it was hurting, and Daisy felt her own heart pounding.

Her father was supposed to be safe in the training camp, while so many of the uncles were already at the Front. Perhaps it wasn't sensible, Daisy realised later, for the two of them to think of him first. But being sensible and being frightened didn't have much to do with each other. *Not Papa. Please, not Papa.*

Benjy reached them, so out of breath with running that he crouched for a moment, hands on his thighs. He stood upright, and what Daisy saw in his eyes lit a tiny spark of hope inside her.

'It's the war,' Benjy gasped out. 'Pa heard about it at the factory. There's an armistice—the Germans are surrendering. The men are all coming home. It's over. The war's over.'

Daisy stood beside her mother on Ruatane's wharf. The place was busy with men stacking cargo ready for the next sailing, and with boys hanging about hoping for messages to run, but the two of them had found a quiet spot by one of the sheds where they were shaded by piled-up bales of wool.

The days since Benjy brought news of the Armistice had seen a flurry of telegrams from Papa, and one from Granny just yesterday to say he was on his way. Now it was only a matter of waiting.

'There's the *Ngatiawa*,' one of the boys called out.

It seemed an age until the small blob on the horizon grew into a boat, and then all at once a figure at the rail stood out from the vague shapes on the deck, waving and smiling and wonderfully familiar. Her father.

A moment after the boat tied up, Papa was striding down the gangplank and onto the wharf. He dropped his bag, wrapped an arm each around Daisy and her mother as they flung themselves at him, and lifted them right off the ground.

On the way in to meet him, they had agreed that they must be careful not to make a spectacle of themselves and embarrass Daisy's father in front of the whole town. But there on the wharf, encircled by those strong arms, it didn't matter how many people might see that she and her mother were crying. Nothing mattered except having him home again. The war had not killed him, and it had not sent him back broken and empty inside like poor old Uncle Alf. He was home, and he was still Papa.

He lowered them carefully. Together they made their way off the wharf and over to where the horse was tethered.

It felt good to have the three of them comfortably squashed on the seat of the gig; it felt *right*. Her father sat in the middle holding the reins, Daisy and her mother either side of him with arms linked through his. People nodded and smiled at them as they drove through Ruatane.

They left the town and its houses behind, and now they had the road to themselves. Her mother rested her head against Papa's sleeve, and Daisy did the same on her side.

She felt the warmth of him through the thick cloth of his jacket. The heavy wool was prickly against her cheek, but that was not what made her nose wrinkle. Daisy straightened up, and saw her mother do the same.

'Davie, you smell a bit.'

'I know. I haven't been out of these clothes the last couple of days, and it's been pretty warm.' He shifted the reins in his hands; the horse flicked its ears but kept its plodding pace.

'What, you've slept in them and all?'

'Well, I haven't done much sleeping since I left the camp, and that was the day before yesterday. As soon as the news came through about the Armistice, I more or less lined up outside the boss fellow's office asking when I could leave. They had to wait for orders and the right forms, that sort of thing. I think he was glad to see the back of me in the end.

'The minute they said I could go, I headed off for the train. I had my bag packed ready, I wasn't going to waste time getting fresh clothes on—I didn't want to give them the chance to change their minds about me going.'

Daisy gripped his arm more tightly, exulting in the knowledge that he was now well beyond the reach of any changing of minds.

'The train was pretty full, blokes from the camps as well as all the people who'd got on in Wellington. Then it seemed to stop at every station along the way and pick up a few more. I think we all must have smelled as bad as each other by the time we got to Auckland.'

'I thought you might've had to stay the night in Auckland,' Daisy's mother said.

'I was cutting it a bit fine. I got Ma to book the boat for me, and I just trusted to luck that the train would get there in time to catch it. She met me at the station, and we went straight over to the wharves—I didn't even go up to Sarah's. I just had time for a cup of tea with Ma at a hotel by the waterfront, then I was on my way again.' He slid his hand down to scratch at his lower leg. 'You think I smell bad up the top—wait till my boots are off and you get a whiff of these socks!'

Mama gave a little snort that turned into proper laughter; long and rippling, and high-pitched at the top of each breath. Papa joined in with his own lovely deep laugh, and Daisy felt her shoulders shake as a bubble of happiness burst from her in something between giggles and sobs. She could not remember the last time she had heard anyone laugh.

Tears were streaming down their faces, and they were a good deal further along the road, by the time everyone calmed down. White Island was clear today; Papa smiled at the sight. 'Feels a long while since I saw the island.'

They turned away from the beach and up the road to the valley. The hills either side seemed to pool the sunlight, warming the air.

'Do you want to go and see your ma and pa?' Papa asked.

Mama shook her head. 'Tomorrow, maybe. Let's just have it the three of us today.'

As they drove past the school Daisy saw faces at the window. A moment later Miss Cameron herself came out to the steps and waved to them. 'Welcome back, Mr Stewart!' she called.

Her father nodded to the teacher and tilted his hat. 'You'll be able to go back to school now, Daisy, if you're still keen on it.'

It was only a few weeks till the end of the school year, and she had missed so much of the term that she was sure she would have to do Standard Five all over again the next year, but it didn't seem to matter. Daisy looked over her shoulder and waved to Miss Cameron as the school and the teacher shrank into the distance.

Now they had reached the boundary of their own farm, and there was the track that led to their own house. Daisy's father gazed around him, staring at the paddocks and the bush and the tall hills.

'Gee, I've missed this place,' he said.

He asked about the animals and the farm work; how much milk they were producing, how all the cousins on the other farms were doing. They were things that had been discussed in letters back and forth over the months he had been away, but now they all seemed to need saying again, and not just as pen marks on paper.

The gig was put away, the horse turned out to graze, and still the talking had not slowed. Daisy put in an occasional word, but mostly she was content to listen to her parents, the two voices twining around each other and making a sort of music.

The three of them went into the kitchen, and with her father there the room looked its own proper size again. Her mother took her apron down from its hook on the door. 'I'll put the kettle on,' she said. 'I expect you haven't had a decent cup of tea in months.'

'I'll do it,' Daisy said. 'You have a sit down, Mama, you look tired. You too, Papa, you need a rest after that long trip.'

The two of them sat down next to each other, and her father grinned at Daisy. 'You reminded me of Grandma Kelly for a minute there, love. Sounds like you're in charge of things these days.'

'I'd never have managed without her,' Daisy's mother said. 'Not being here all by myself.'

Papa took hold of her hands, stopping them from trembling. 'I'm back now, and I won't be going anywhere in a hurry.'

Daisy stood at the bench watching them. When the water had heated, she placed the teapot on the table along with two cups. Her own empty cup she replaced on the shelf.

She stepped quietly across the room and slipped out of the house, careful not to make any noise as she closed the kitchen door behind her. At the bottom of the steps she turned to the left, where her bedroom was, and glanced up at its window as she walked past. That morning she had taken her nightdress from her parents' room and put it under her pillow. She would be back in her own room tonight, sleeping in her own bed again.

A lilac bush grew in front of the house, in full flower at this time of year. Daisy settled into a hollow between two low branches from where she had a view down the valley and out to sea.

The sky was like blue glass, bright and clear and flawless, and the sea was the colour of the sapphires in Granny's necklace. Daisy tilted her face to the sun and felt its warmth on her skin, but with a light kiss of breeze from the sea. She took a great breath of lilac-scented air. Tears of pure happiness welled up and spilled down her cheeks.

Her father was home. The war was over. In that place, at that moment, it was impossible to believe that anything bad could ever happen again.

CPSIA information can be obtained at www.ICGtesting.com
Printed in the USA
LVOW13s1610180614

390646LV00003B/615/P